Other titles by the author

Mirror Image
Faith
A Knight's Challenge

The Girl Who Wanted a Broken Heart

Erika Crosse

For Mum and Dad

Chapter One

September 1800

'Rebekah?'

A voice drifts into my hearing and it comes from the darkened corner. The familiar sensation of my stomach twisting tightly inside of me begins – it happens every time I hear him call my name. A faint ray of sunlight runs down his face, but other than this, my pa lives in the shadows.

'Yes, Pa?' I leave the warm glow of the open fire, and although I can still see the flicker of the flames on the rough uneven wall, the heat hasn't followed me and I give a little shiver.

'Can you spare a little time to sit with your dear old pa?' A brief smile crosses his face as he turns his head to focus on me, the pleasure of seeing his daughter dampened by the heavy burden he is carrying.

It's a simple request, one I never reject, but I can't help allowing my eyes to trail to the door. Our poor tiny cottage only has one room, there's nowhere to hide if she comes back early.

'Don't worry.' Pa sees my hesitation and clasps a hand around mine. 'I'll take the blame.' He winces suddenly. 'This blasted straw!'

Leaping to plump the spiky straw-filled mattress underneath him and ease his discomfort, I forget about my concern. 'Is that better?' I don't know why I've asked: how could anything be better lying on a thing like that? But it's the best bed we have – correction, it's the only bed we have and we are fortunate to have it.

'I'm as comfy as I can be.' He smiles weakly, deep creases forming around his eyes as they half close in pain. My stomach stabs and twists again – this is a waste of a good life and it pains me that I can do nothing to change it.

'Please, will you talk to me?' Pa's chestnut brown eyes rest on mine, they are large and desperate. It's nearly been four months since he set foot outside of our low-beamed, thatch-roofed cottage.

A lump forms in my throat and I immediately swallow it down - this is not the time to get emotional, it will help no one. With a deep breath, I steady myself. Speaking in the soothing tones that have become so natural in recent months, I begin. It sounds almost as if I'm telling Pa a bedtime story, like he did for me when I was a little girl. I don't talk about anything in particular and I simply recall news from the out-side world – the price of bread, the quality of the harvest and insights about our acquaintances.

The rendition ends as the front door swings open with a bang, causing the words in my mouth to dry up.

'What are you doing sat there?' Ma slings a crying baby down from her hip and onto the floor. 'Buttons don't make themselves. Mary makes more than you and you're nearly twice her age.' She nods towards my sister who has been dili-gently working away as I've been sitting with Pa. At the men-tion of her name Mary lowers her head and does not look up, continuing to smooth the rough round circle of wood in her hands.

'Pa asked me to...' I don't finish my sentence because, well – what's the point? Caring for her husband is not a priority anymore.

A loud huff travels across the room and Ma stomps across to lift a cast-iron pan off a hook on the wall, banging it down with considerable force onto the solid oak table before her. 'At least let her sit by the light of the fire, Tom,' Ma says, directing the words towards Pa, loud enough so she can be heard over the baby who's still whimpering. 'The girl can't make buttons if she comes to you over there, it's too dim for her to see.'

Pa closes his eyes and leans back, his breathing even and smooth. 'I wanted to see her face. Is that too much to ask?'

'Yes, it is.'

I close my eyes and sigh, shaking my head. Ma is always un-reasonably blunt when she wants to be. I know she's tired, cold and hungry, but we all are - it shouldn't be an excuse to speak so abruptly to a crushed and broken man. However, clearly right now, she isn't in the mood to pander to other people's emotions.

'We are drowning in poverty if you haven't noticed,' she continues jerking her head and allowing her straw-like hair to flick around her face in frustration. 'You can't take the girl away from her work – it's the only livelihood we've got.'

'What about Daniel?' says Pa.

'A seven-year old's income doesn't count.' Her fists are clenched and an angry red hue appears in her cheeks as the tension in her body rises. My little brother collects the fallen wheat left behind after harvesting the crop - Ma is right, he gets a pittance.

Pa sighs. 'Don't be so dramatic, Margaret. I'll be back to work soon.'

'If that's what you think, then the accident has damaged your head too.' Ma opens her mouth to speak again, but the chance is taken away from her as a mucky faced little boy barges into the room. He stops suddenly, the sight of Ma's reddened face causing the five-old-year to take immediate caution and he lowers his head before holding out a blackened object in front of her.

'Sorry Ma - it was the best he had.'

Ma wrinkles her nose. 'This is the best he had?'

I wince upon hearing the accusing question fly out of her mouth - it wasn't Tommy's fault. If anyone is going to get something worth having from Mr Allen it is my overly determined brother who thinks he can take on the world single-handily. He would have got something better if he could.

Another child, a girl this time, comes running in and stands beside Tommy. 'It's all he'd give us, Ma… for the little we had.'

'Maggie's right, Ma,' says Tommy supporting his twin sister's announcement.

'I don't care how much you had… this is fit only for animal feed.' She waves the blackened loaf in the air. 'And not even that!'

'You should make it yourself like everyone else,' Pa's gruff voice floats across from the darkened corner. 'You'd be certain of getting the best then, no more blackened undersides.'

Ma recognises the humorous tone in her husband's voice. I did too, despite being unable to see his features clearly. 'Do you think this is funny, Tom?' She randomly picks up a rolling pin lying on the table and whirls it about in the air.

'Bread is bread,' Pa adds with a shrug of his shoulders. 'It looks edible from here.'

Ma replaces the rolling pin with the burnt loaf and cracks it hard on the solid oak table. 'It's at least four days old, maybe even five!'

Pa chuckles. 'I wouldn't put it past Allen to have given you a chalk one as well.'

From the corner of my eye I see Mary has stopped carving the half-smoothed button in her hands. Her body is still and her eyes are focused directly upon her lap and I can tell she's intently listening to the argument brewing around her. Distressed, I look from Pa, to Mary, to Ma...

'I can make bread.'

As soon as the words leave my mouth I lift my chin in readiness for a scolding, because I know that's what I'll get – but the tension needed to be diverted somehow and, in the circumstances, it was the only way I could think of... however, Ma and I, we've had this conversation before and it's never gone well.

Ma scowls at me from across the room, but I'm committed now and I must continue. 'Pa is right, everyone makes their own bread and it would save the high prices of the bakers. The miller isn't far, just across the stream, it would be cheaper to buy grain directly from him and grind our own flour.' I pause and wait for the reaction.

'You certainly will not make bread!' Ma exclaims as if I've suggested performing some kind of immoral act. 'I need you to make buttons - buttons, buttons, buttons... until they're coming out of your nose.'

At this point the shouting gets too much and the baby's whimpers turn into a yell. Ma's voice rises over the noise. 'You can't waste time baking bread, Rebekah. I want to hear no more about it, do you understand... oh, please can someone shut that baby up?'

Being the closest, I bend down and scoop up Henry. Jiggling him up and down, I pat his bulging bottom. 'I think he needs a change, Ma.'

Ma waves her hands frantically in the air. 'Do I have to do everything around here?' She makes no movement to relieve her youngest son's discomfort and Henry continues his earth-shattering cries.

'I'll do it.' The soft angelic voice of Mary floats over from the fireside and she tips a lap full of finished buttons into the neatly woven basket by her feet, keeping her eyes low and out of Ma's direct gaze. 'Someone needs to watch Georgie though.' She nods to my chubby-legged three-year-old brother who is playing amongst a large pile of logs we use for the fire. Changing Henry has provided an escape for her. Mary's nature has always been sensitive to excessive noise and tension, which is not exactly a good trait to have in our tiny one-roomed cottage. Discontent surrounds us daily and there are very few places to escape from it, especially in the winter months when we are trapped inside for longer periods of time. Frustrations, bitterness and disappointments all too often take away the peace and rarely is there a calm and comforting environment for any of us to dwell in.

As Henry is soothed and Ma stops screaming, I take a glance around our crowded room. Everything we own is enclosed within these four thin walls – which really doesn't add up to much. Firstly, there are more children than chairs – two mismatched plain and tattered chairs sit by the fire for Mary and me to work on, but apart from these, all that remains to sit on is the crooked three-legged stool. Pa has the only bed - the rest of us sleep on the cold stone floor. The only table we own is specifically reserved for preparing meals, nobody eats there because, as I've said, we only have two chairs and a wonky stool. No knickknacks sit on the shelves and a few cast iron pans on hooks decorate the walls. There are no wardrobes containing beautifully handcrafted clothes, because the clothes we are wearing are the only ones we own. But at least we have a roof over our heads, which I remind myself is better than a lot of people have.

We haven't always lived in such desperate times. I actually think things might not have escalated so quickly if the accident had happened ten years ago, when there were fewer mouths to feed. For a long time it was only the three of us – Pa, Ma and me. Every so often I remember flashes of what it was like and I get the faint remembrance that we were happy, even Ma at times. She hasn't always been so bitter and disillusioned with life, but it's not a secret that the addition of every new baby has taken its toll.

Of course, my parents wanted more children when there was only me. But every time Ma was hopeful another miscarriage occurred. I heard Ma say once that she was grateful, that many poor women brought their babies to full term only to have them stolen away in childhood – she was one of the lucky ones.

I was seven years old when Mary came along and this, for some unknown reason, ushered in a series of successful pregnancies every two years, until nature kindly gave Ma a very brief break before Henry arrived in April to join our overcrowded room – and, I have to admit under the current circumstances, his entrance into the world now makes nine mouths too many to feed.

Standing between Georgie and the open fire, I tug a piece of wood out of his chubby hands. It's wet and has splinters of wood sticking out from where he has been soothing his aching gums. Unfortunately, having his makeshift teether taken away immediately sees his bottom lip begin to wobble.

'Don't start, Georgie.' Ma is watching the child from where she is leaning over the table and her head falls into her hands.

Watching Ma wearily I try to soothe the boy. 'You'll get a splinter, Georgie.' Crouching down beside him, I rub his little shoulder in an attempt to give comfort and I mimic putting the wood inside my own mouth. 'Ouch, bad wood – hurt Georgie.'

'H-ert?' says the little boy whose eye lids well with unshed tears.

'Yes, hurt.' He seems to understand.

'Come on, Georgie,' says Maggie, skipping over to us. 'Play with me and Tommy.' She reaches the boy and picks him up, squashing him against her chest, but Georgie doesn't seem to mind, even when he almost slips out of his sister's grasp and Maggie heaves him back up, squashing his face all over again. The trio go to sit quietly side by side on the floor where a slither of sunlight sneaks in through the ivy-covered lattice window.

Mary casts a cautious glance over her shoulder as she's changing Henry and catches my eye. Silence is often worse than all the shouting – especially when no one knows how to end the oppressive tension which has built up in the room. Suddenly

Ma gives a frustrated cry, causing Mary to flinch and focus her attention back onto Henry.

The exclamation is left to echo around the walls.

'Are you all right, Ma?' I ask.

She presses her lips together and runs a hand through her thin hair. 'It's no good.' She chokes back a sob. 'All of this...' Her hands gesture around the sparsely furnished room and her eyes fix upon each of her starving children. 'It's no good.'

Chapter Two

My offerings have been pitiful recently, but at least I have always brought something… today, I have nothing. I carry my basket with me, empty though it may be, in case a miracle happens on the way – it doesn't.

'Good morning, Mr Baker.' I smile down on a pile of old rags and see a worn rough face twist round in my direction, followed by a grin which is wide and gummy. 'I'm afraid I've come empty handed.' I call the gentleman Mr Baker, but it's not his real name. I found him last year hiding behind Mr Allen's bakery and since he couldn't tell me his real name, I christened him Baker.

The man utters a soft groan in greeting and a pair of welcoming eyes meet mine as I crouch down by his side.

'How are you today?' I mouth slowly.

He taps his back.

'The pain is still bothering you?' He hasn't understood my words, but he nods anyway.

'You sit down too much,' I say pointing to the hard ground. 'Try and take a walk today.' I gesture with my fingers through the air like two legs running away.

He nods again.

I sigh and lean back against the wall causing Mr Baker to point a gentle finger towards me and spread out a pair of questioning hands.

'Pa?' I ask to confirm my understanding.

He nods for the third time.

'The same,' I say sadly and he shakes his head compassionately understanding from my face that things are still not good.

After a while I stand to leave the small alcove behind the haberdasher's store. 'Have a good day, Mr Baker.'

He smiles and waves me away to continue the rest of my round, but frustratingly I can only offer a warming smile and polite conversation - their stomachs will all remain empty.

'Thank you, Rebekah.' The old woman places a shrivelled hand on top of mine.

'I don't know what you are thanking me for, Mrs Harris. I've brought you nothing.'

A gush of chilly air rushes through the draft-riddled window of the widow's rented room in the high street.

'I'll manage, my dear.' She smiles comfortingly before leaning over to the basket by her feet. She takes the last remaining lump of coal and throws it onto the fire. 'What I'm more bothered about is this sad face.' With a struggle she heaves herself upright and takes a shaking hand, lifting it up to my lowered chin. 'It is not good for a beautiful young woman like yourself to be filled with such sorrow.'

'Don't worry about me.' I sigh. 'I only have a grudge, Mrs Harris.'

The widow's eyes open in surprise. 'Oh, with whom?'

'Poverty.' My face crinkles in a pathetic laugh because the only alternative is for me to cry.

'Ah...' The old woman nods knowingly. 'I've borne that grudge for many years. Would you like to hear the wisdom I've gathered since the death of my dear John?'

'Of course, I would be happy to listen to any advice you've got, our current situation is not an easy one.' I shuffle to the edge of my seat and lean forward eagerly waiting to hear what she has to say.

Mrs Harris squints her eyes to focus her poor vision upon me and clears her throat. 'Don't bother fighting it, poverty always wins.'

'Oh...' This wasn't what I expected the old woman to say. I was waiting to hear a flow of kind and comforting words, telling me that everything would be fine... not the truth.

'Learn to accept it.' She taps my knee lightly before sitting slowly back in her chair. 'Then the long hungry days and endless cold nights will become more bearable.'

'Thank you, Mrs Harris.' I force a smile. A sudden desire to leave the widow's damp-smelling room overcomes me and I stand to make my excuses. 'I'm afraid I must be getting home to Pa.'

'You are such a good girl, send him my love.' Her thin bony arms tremble under her weight as she grips the armrests on both sides of the chair to push herself up.

'Don't get up, Mrs Harris,' I say stopping her. 'I'll see myself out.'

'I know where you've been.'

Pa's voice floats towards me from the shadowy corner of the cottage and instantly I feel guilty. It's not that I've done anything wrong, but without Pa by my side I'm playing a dangerous game.

'So, what have you given them?'

'Nothing, Pa.'

'You're telling me you took an empty basket all the way to town and back?' When he sees my embarrassed face, he chuckles softly. 'Your dedication is going to make this a lot harder for me. Come over here, I want to talk to you.'

As I perch on the edge of the bed, his laughter comes to a stop and his face becomes serious. 'I'm sorry, Becks.' He presses his lips together and inhales loudly. 'You need to stop.'

'It's all right, Pa,' I say seeing the worry in his face. 'I know there's nothing to give them, we've only crumbs and I'll not make the babies starve.' I glance over at Georgie who's learned to tickle his baby brother without pushing him over.

'Tickle, tickle!' Georgie says wriggling his fingers and making Henry squeal with pleasure.

I smile before turning my attention back to Pa. 'My empty basket didn't seem to bother anyone this morning, they all appear to value a little conversation - Mr Baker's back is still bothering him, you know. I told him to go for a walk—' Pa places a hand on top of mine putting a stop to my report.

'No,' he says sternly enough so I realise he's serious. 'I mean, you need to stop everything – I don't want you having contact with them anymore.'

'Pa!' Pushing his hand away I stand to my feet, my hurt expression meeting his own.

'Please, don't look at me like that, you know I've turned a blind eye since the accident.'

'But you were the one who told me to do it in the first place.'

'It's different now, surely you can see that?' I drop back down on the bed and let my hands to fall to my sides. 'I don't feel right letting you go, Becks - it needs to end.'

'I can't stop seeing them.' My head shakes in disbelief at what he's asking me to do.

Pa's hand reaches up and softly rests on my shoulder. 'Becks, it's not safe.'

I twist my body to face his again. 'You know these people are harmless.'

'It's not about them, it's the others I worry about. If you had an older brother it would be different. I know you want to help, but I can't protect you anymore. Every time I see you leave I worry it's the last time I'll see you.'

'They'll think I've stopped because we've hit hard times. I wasn't going to let it affect anything... what does that say about me?'

'It says you're a sixteen-year-old girl who can't go out to feed beggars alone.' Pa's eyebrows rise together and he tilts his forehead forward, he means what he says and the decision isn't going to change. I want to say more, but out of respect for the man who has safely guided me through life so far, I hold my tongue.

Another finished button flicks into the basket. I've made thirty today, but it won't be enough. As the flames from the fire flicker shadows across the wall our failure to meet our daily quota is the least of my worries. I'm still brooding over what Pa said - he's right and I know he is... nevertheless, it's still hard to let it go.

'I'm going out to stretch my legs,' I say to Mary who's been working away silently next to me. We've both been sitting in the same position for several hours and I don't know about Mary, but my back is aching and my eyes are sore.

Outside, I lean against the cold wattle and daub wall and gaze up at the stars beginning to creep out into the night sky - I won't be making any more buttons today. Our final candle fizzled away last night and we can't afford any more, not even the tallow ones that stink of animal fat when they burn. From tonight our only source of light will be from the fireplace, and with the dull ache that is slowly spreading across my forehead, it will be impossible for me to produce any more buttons worth selling until the morning.

To my side lies an old plank of wood, standing up against the wall. It's only ever been used for one purpose and since then it's been abandoned. I shudder, as the horror of the day it arrived comes flooding back into my mind.

Nothing can prepare you for the day your pa is brought home to you lying on a dirty old plank of wood. There was no prior warning of his arrival - no opportunity to prepare ourselves. The door was simply flung open and there he was.

At one time my dear pa rose and slept with the sun, labouring away in the fields as the seasons rotated, year after year. Without fail he would be out there, leaving his muddy boots on the mat when the day was done and he returned home for his supper. But, in an instant the changing seasons no longer mattered and his body's inability to move dictated the end of his labour, his mud-stained boots left abandoned by the door waiting patiently to be worn again.

It could have happened to any family, but for whatever reason it happened to ours. Even now town folk who know our family pass us by, hardly daring to catch our eye for fear that our misfortune might be contagious – God forbid it should happen to them, that their provider should fall and be crushed under the same horrid sentence.

'Your pa's a hero, Becks - he saved a child's life.'

A hero? This is what Uncle Will had told me. He was one of four men who carried Pa home from the fields that day. How can a hero be rewarded in this way? Even now my head spins trying to solve a question that can never be answered. I close my eyes at the memory. All I see before me is Ma standing in shock, unable to move and frozen in time with her mouth wedged open. 'Pa-pa!' Georgie's excited squeals mix into the chaos, seeing only his pa returning home and not understanding the circumstances he's returned home in.

'Mary, take the children outside,' I say instinctively doing all I can to shield them from the shocking reality before me. Mary nods in obedience and herds up the twins, the baby and chubby little Georgie. I look to Ma hoping she'll take the lead, but she's still standing speechless besides me.

The men begin to exit the cottage now their job is complete and Pa has been brought home to us. Each takes off his cap and bobs his head respectfully to Ma and myself as they pass us on the way to the door. Will is the last to leave.

'Uncle Will.' I grab our unrelated neighbour by the arm. 'What do we do?'

He can hardly bear to look me in the face. 'Make him comfortable.'

'What do you mean?' My voice wobbles - that's the kind of thing people say when there is no hope of life left.

'Make up a bed, manage the pain best you can.' He glances at Ma who is continuing to stand trance-like looking at Pa who has been abandoned in the shadows. Shaking his head in disbelief Will follows the rest of the men out of the door.

Tentatively I move toward Pa. His upper body is writhing around, his face grimacing in agony. He's clamping his upper teeth down onto a badly split lip, fighting desperately against the urge to let out a tortured cry of pain - I don't know what to do. This is my pa; he's not supposed to be lying helpless before me.

Something bothers me the closer I get and when I reach the bedside it's obvious - his legs aren't moving. His upper body, arms, head and neck all move like a man in utter agony, but his legs, they are completely still.

'Pa?' I'm scared beyond anything I've ever experienced before. When Ma gave birth to Mary I was seven. I'd never heard such terrifying cries before, but Pa held my hand and told me everything was going to be all right – and it was. But, this time no one is holding my hand. In fact, the person who should be gripping hold of me is the very person causing my fear to rise.

'Rebekah.' He grimaces. 'I can't feel my legs.' He is panicking, I can hear it in his voice - my pa is panicking and this isn't like him. Thomas Barnes is the calmest, most optimistic man I know, he shouldn't sound anxious. This isn't good – it can't be.

He's trying to reach out a hand to me and I watch him, letting his arm linger in the air. I can't make myself hold it, as if touching him confirms all this is real.

'Rebekah?' His eyes clench shut and I take a step closer. Swallowing, I try to moisten my dry throat and slowly take his cold, yet clammy hand in mine.

Now I'm in the shadows, I see his legs aren't the only problem. Blood is trickling down from his split lip, a deep gash crosses his forehead and a bright purple bruise is forming around his eye. When I manage to prise my eyes away from his disfigured face, I notice there's a strange lump on his arm which I'm certain wasn't there before.

There's nothing I can do for the pain, but I call Mary to fetch a bowl of water and the cleanest cloth she can find. She brings it immediately, casting a worried glance towards Pa before hurrying back out again.

'Ma, will you help me bathe Pa's injuries?' I ask, thinking she should be over the initial shock by now.

I get no reply.

When I look over my shoulder she's gone - I press my lips together in determination, this is all up to me.

'I'm going to clean your lip first, Pa.' I dip the old, but clean rag into the water and after wringing it out, dab it onto his face.

He winces.

'Sorry.' I instinctively pull away not wanting to cause him any more pain.

'No, no...' he says hoarsely. 'Do it.' I repeat the action and this time Pa holds his breath, keeping the pain inside for my sake.

Finally, his lip is clean, although the cut hasn't clotted yet and fresh blood is threatening to trickle out at any second. I go on to wipe the dirt from the rest of his face before starting on his forehead.

'Your arm, Pa. Does it hurt?' He tries to move it, but this time he can't hold back a scream. It's broken, that lump is probably the bone. A wave of nausea comes over me and I step backward, sucking in a deep breath - I need to hold myself together.

Attempting to focus my mind I scan the room for a possible splint. The basket of logs catches my attention and I rush over to the fireplace. Hurling to the side all those which won't help me, I find the flattest, longest log possible. Next, I untie the rope from around my waist, taking away the makeshift belt and allowing my baggy dress to flap wildly around as I run back to the bed.

'I'm going to make a splint,' I explain to Pa. 'To ease the pain in your arm, but...' I pause, not wanting to cause him more suffering. 'It's going to hurt whilst I'm fixing it in place.'

'Do it,' he speaks almost in a whisper and beads of sweat start rolling down his face.

Lightly, I take his arm, seeing the dark hair matted with blood and I slowly begin to straighten it out.

'Do it quick!' he yells.

'No... I can't.' I hesitate. 'It will cause you more pain.'

'Do it!'

I do it. Half closing my eyes and looking away, not believing any of this is happening to me and my pa. I snap his arm back into position.

Once the arm is straight, I place the flattened log underneath and fasten them together with the rope. I see the pain ease slightly in my pa's face, but something's still wrong.

'Where else is the pain, Pa?'

'My back – it's burning.'

'Burning?' I move away to observe him, but there's not much to see, considering he is lying flat on his back. I need to lift him up, it's possible there is a deep wound I cannot see.

'Pa...' I whisper.

'Do what you need to do,' he mutters through clenched teeth.

I stand back and wonder how on earth I'm going to lift him onto his side. Pa has been a farm labourer his whole life and so naturally his muscles have developed over time. Unfortunately for me, muscle equals weight and I'm a slight sixteen-year-old girl.

I glance towards the front door in contemplation... Uncle Will won't come back to help, the fear in his eyes told me that, Mary couldn't lift a stone, never mind Pa, and Ma, she's gone, goodness knows how long for - I'm on my own.

'I'm going to lift you... I'll count to three.' I rub my hands together nervously. I don't know if I can do this, or if it's even the right thing to do, but I need to try and so I place my hands directly underneath his back.

'One...' I plant my feet firmly on the stone floor ready to lift. 'Two...' My body tenses ready for the strain. 'Three!'

I yell in determination.

Pa yells in pain.

I think I lifted him an inch off the mattress, but I didn't see a thing. It all happened too quickly and my strength gave way.

'Do it again,' says Pa with his eyes closed tightly. I chew my lip and observe him for a second time - I need to get this right. I can't lift him for a third time, for Pa's sake.

I scrunch his tattered blooded shirt half-way up his chest so his flesh is visible - I only need a quick glance to estimate the damage. Resuming my position, I count down again, heave and push. My arms shake as I try to hold him on his side long enough to see the whole of his back. I want to slam his body straight down, my arms immediately overwhelmed by his tremendous weight, but somehow, I manage to bring him gently down onto the bed.

'What's wrong?' he asks weakly.

I stand back, rubbing feeling back into my aching arms, not certain what to say.

'Rebekah?'

'Nothing – nothing's wrong.'

'Nothing?' He tries to lift his head, but he can't, and clutches a hand to his forehead.

'There is no wound,' I say. 'No marks - nothing.'

He doesn't speak.

He doesn't move.

All I see is his chest heaving up and down as his body begins to deal with the pain.

Chapter Three

'Do you want more, Pa?'

I'm ladling Ma's thin potato soup into chipped bowls.

'More!' screeches Ma. 'Why should *he* get more? He does no work and hasn't earned the right for a second helping.'

'He's sick, Ma,' I say gently, not wanting to rouse her any more than necessary. 'He needs to build his strength.'

'His strength is good for nothing,' she speaks in bitterness and turns her face away.

Poor Ma. She's got every right to feel this way. Pa's wages used to feed us all and put a roof over our head. Even in between seasons his good character and strong work ethic meant he was never out of work for long and, though there was rarely money left over after the necessities had been bought, we were never living in poverty. But Pa's inability to work has left us battling against destitution and Ma isn't handling it well. Mary and I continue to make our buttons, but we can't physically make enough income to support a house full of people. We try to work faster, at Ma's bidding, but the results are not desirable, and the quality is often sacrificed… and so is our profit.

The problem is Ma's always had a bad habit of relieving her tension by aiming bitter remarks at whoever is irritating her the most. I've learned to grow a thick skin over the years, letting her words float over my head. I know she doesn't mean it, that at one time her family gave her more joy than it does now. You see, I have this memory I can't shake. A vague remembrance of someone singing over me when I was a small child. The voice was beautiful, high and sweet and I'm almost certain this was Ma, though to this day I can't put a face to the blurred image of my memory. Someone who can sing such sweet lullabies to her baby had once known how to love, I'm sure of it, and I don't think it's an impossibility that she can love us again…

October arrives and we're all getting thinner. There's been a chill in the air this last week and I've got a sinking feeling winter is going to come early this year. The thought sends my mind drifting to poor Mr Baker and I wonder if he'll survive another year?

The haberdasher's door closes behind me - it wasn't a good deal, especially after Mary and I had deliberately made sure those buttons were our best work. I shake my head. I'm afraid to admit now Pa isn't here to defend us people are starting to take advantage of our situation. My eye glances to the side of the store, the last place I saw Mr Baker. No one is there today and my heart sinks.

A noise from behind my shoulder causes me to look back after I've walked a little way down the high street. There's a brawl going on. Three young men, shirt sleeves rolled up and caps on their heads are dragging a body out from the alley next to Mr Allen's. There's an awful noise and a crowd is quickly gathering, cheering on the men at the centre.

I pull my thin shawl closer round me as a bitter gust of wind causes an involuntary shiver. Hastily, I begin to walk away, trying to put as much distance between the fight and myself as possible... that is, until I hear the groan. It's instantly recognisable and without thinking I turn and run straight towards the commotion.

'Stop that!' I yell. 'He's done nothing to hurt you.' I push my way passed Mrs Allen and her daughter standing on the perimeter of the crowd, who look at me strangely, but don't stop my perilous actions. 'Hey... leave him alone!'

By now I've pushed my way to the centre of the crowd. I don't pause to think about what I'm doing. Without hesitation, I leap onto the back of one of the men and grab hold of his shirt, trying to pull him away before he gets a turn to kick the hunched-up figure on the floor.

'Stop it!' I cry. The broad-shouldered man, whose shirt I'm tugging, swipes an arm and pushes me away. Although I momentarily lose my stepping, I spring back, this time aiming for another of the men, one with a thin wispy beard, and begin to thump him with a clenched fist repeatedly on the back.

At first, he ignores me as if I'm an insignificant little bug, but my persistence provokes his attention and he eventually swings round. 'Get out of the way,' he snarls flashing pointed teeth at me, one of which is missing.

'I'll get out of your way when you leave that man alone.'

The other two men stop their attack and wait for the bearded man, who seems to be the leader of the pack, to get rid of me. 'He deserves it, so get out of my way.' His face draws dangerously close to mine.

I lift my chin, trying to disguise the shaking feeling in my legs. 'Why does he deserve it?' I ask boldly. In answer to this my feet suddenly leave the floor as the man grabs hold of my shoulders and begins to lift me of the ground.

'Becks!'

It's Daniel. He must be on his way home from the fields and I see him crawl his way through the crowd underneath several pairs of legs. 'Get off my sister!'

The bearded man laughs, the scent of his stinking breath spreading up my nose. He throws me down to the ground against my little brother. We both topple to the floor. Daniel twists his face in anger, but he knows better than to get involved with these thugs.

'Come on, Becks,' he says dusting himself down, he doesn't see I've gone marching straight back into the fight.

'Let go of him!' I demand again.

This time the leader stands for no nonsense and smacks me straight across the face. The crowd gasp as they see me crash straight to the ground again, but no one intervenes.

Momentarily the faces around me become a blur and I touch the side of my smarting cheek. The sound of Daniel's running feet drum into my ears and I know he's gone for help.

'Clear off,' shouts the broad-shoulder man with a rising anger as I shakily stand to my feet.

'Hey!'

Now someone new is pushing their way through the crowd and I see Daniel following closely behind. I take note of the newcomer's height – he's tall, so tall it's almost like his body forgot to stop growing, and he's using to it his advantage, towering over the man with the thin wispy beard.

'Is there a problem?' the newcomer asks.

The bearded man glowers and spits at the figure heaped up on the floor. 'Nah,' he says whilst considering the height of his new opponent. 'I'm fine.' He moves arrogantly away as the crowd parts and his two cronies follow after. Now there is no entertainment it doesn't take long for the throng of people to disappear.

I kneel on the floor besides the wounded man. 'Mr Baker?' I gently pull back his trembling hands covering his face, the rough crinkled skin is swelling quickly.

A single tear trickles down his face.

'Can you tell me what hurts, sir?' asks the young man who broke up the fight.

'Mr Baker can't speak,' I say on the man's behalf. 'He's deaf, that's the only reason why those horrid men did this.'

The young man doesn't seem shocked by the information, but his eyes soften, and his mouth presses together in thought.

'Becks.' Daniel tugs at my dress. 'We need to go home – Pa will be worried.'

'I can't,' I say looking anxiously at Mr Baker. 'Not until I know he's all right.'

The tall young man glances at the injured man on the floor and then steps forward looking at me. 'I'll take care of him; you go home with your brother.'

I hesitate.

'It all right.' He smiles kindly. 'You can trust me.' My eyes become transfixed and I'm drawn into his soft stare urging me to place Mr Baker into his care.

'Becks?' Daniel's anxious voice pulls my attention away from the young man.

'All right,' I say still feeling uncertain and glance one last time at Mr Baker. 'Let's go home.' Slowly we walk away leaving the poor helpless man alone with the stranger.

I didn't sleep well last night. The events of the day were racing continuously through my mind, causing me to dissect them over and over again and look at them from every possible angle. Even now, I can't decide if I did the right thing. He was a stranger – I left Mr Baker with a stranger.

As the first rays of sunshine try to break their way into our poorly lit cottage, I finally give up trying to sleep. My brothers and sisters lie next to me, breathing heavily and huddled together for warmth. Since it appears no one else is stirring, I tiptoe barefoot over to the door.

'Going somewhere?'

I should have known Pa would be awake, it's been drilled into him to rise with the sun since his days labouring in the fields began.

'Thought I'd get some milk, the children haven't had any for weeks, it will do them good.'

'Don't blame yourself, Becks. It wasn't your fault.'

I don't reply. How can he say it's not my fault? If I hadn't stopped contact with Mr Baker then maybe I could have protected him in some way, the outcome could have been different. Quietly, I lift the lock and let myself out.

It's only half a mile to the farmhouse, but I take a detour... a long detour. Another half-mile on top and I've made it to the deserted high street where a few tradesmen have already begun their day and I bob my head to the miller who is offloading a bulky load of flour to Mr Allen.

I look in all the places Mr Baker used to find shelter, all the alcoves and alleyways, but he's nowhere to be seen. He was badly injured and I reckon he suffered a few cracked ribs from the way that notorious gang of thugs had kicked him. I retrace my steps and walk despondently back down the high street. It was foolish of me to think the overly tall young man would have brought Mr Baker back... that's if he ever returns home.

I call to buy milk on the way home, careful not to spill any of the precious liquid we really can't afford. A gust of wind blows through my thin cotton dress and I tug my grey shawl closer to my shoulders. It's bitterly cold for October and the chill instantly reminds me of the other thing weighing on my mind, another worry that deprived me of sleep last night. Pa was directly in my line of vision. It's always bothered me that his bed is on the other side of the room, far away from the warmth of the fireplace where the rest of his family sleep. But Ma won't hear of moving him, she's convinced there's not enough space and the bed would block too much heat. Through the darkness it was impossible to discern what was wrong and eventually, when I couldn't stand watching any longer, I had to patter across the room to touch his forehead. 'I'm not hot,' he had mumbled, tugging his thin frayed blanket closer over his shoulders. He was right, there was no fever. The trembling I had seen across the room had begun because Pa was ice-cold, and his body was shaking violently to keep warm.

Arriving at the front door, without having spilt a single drop of milk on the way, I make a decision. I know Pa hasn't asked, but he will need it if he's going to survive the winter.

Ma is peeling potatoes at the table as I walk in.

'Do you need a hand?' I ask placing the milk on the tabletop.

She stops peeling and looks at the jug. 'Did you take a penny from the jar?'

'Yes, but only to buy a quart of milk.'

'You shouldn't have done that,' she says and begins peeling again.

'I didn't pay for the best, Ma,' I say trying to defend my action. 'It will be watered down; I didn't see the cow being milked. Look, I'll put the half-penny back.' I purposely show her the coin I'm holding in between my fingers, walk to the windowsill and drop it inside the crazed and chipped porcelain jar, hearing it clink as it reaches the bottom. 'I'm sorry if you didn't want me to take it, but the children need something nourishing once in a while.'

Ma grunts and doesn't look up. It's important I smooth the feathers I've ruffled if I'm going to ask her to buy a new blanket for Pa. 'Can I help?' I ask again.

Ma raises a careworn face. 'I'd say yes, but this is all we've got, not much you can help with.' She nods towards two peeled potatoes lying on the table. This doesn't look good for what I'm about to ask, it's no wonder she didn't want me buying milk.

'Ma…' I shuffle my feet as I build up the courage to speak. 'H-how much money do we have to spare, just roughly, it doesn't need to be exact.'

Ma stops peeling again. 'What for?'

I take a glance at Pa across the room and lower my voice. 'I'd like to buy a woollen blanket for Pa – he's going to need one.'

'He has a blanket,' she says in a gruff voice. I wouldn't use the word *blanket* for what Pa has on his bed. The material is thin and flimsy with more holes in it than can be counted.

'The draughts will give him a chill lying there all day.'

'He's no longer sick and he doesn't need it.'

I open my mouth, but find it hard to form any words - she has a point. Pa's arm had healed weeks ago, the scars gone from his face, the initial fever hadn't reared its head again and, apart from his continuous inability to move the lower half of his body, his strength had returned.

'Tell him if he's cold he can sleep on the floor with the rest of us by the fire.'

'Ma, you know he can't sleep on the floor.' My eyes flicker towards the bed, hoping Pa can't hear our conversation, but it's so dark today I can hardly see if he's moving. 'If there's something to spare I'd like to buy one, despite your reluctance.' It's a bold speech on my part, not knowing how Ma might respond.

She tuts, shakes her head and peels away another slice of potato skin before looking up at me. Naturally I step back, not wanting to be near the knife in her hand - not that she would do anything to hurt me, but I'd rather be safe than sorry. Her eyes hold mine and to my surprise they aren't glaring at me in hostility, but are quietly subdued, though her chin lifts lightly to maintain her defiance. 'We have nothing.'

'Nothing? What, nothing at all?'

'Let me put it like this, we are no longer welcome at Mr Allen's establishment until we've paid off our credit and it won't be long until the grocers and the haberdashers follow suit."

'But the money for the last bundle of buttons?'

'Gone.'

'The pennies Daniel earns in the fields?'

'Gone.'

'What on?' My voice becomes louder and I check myself, glancing over to Pa again. 'What on?' I say again in a quieter tone.

'Potatoes,' she states simply still holding my gaze. 'I can't believe you are shocked, child, just look at that empty jar.'

'This can't be, Ma. I know our last batch of buttons didn't bring in much, but it should have bought us more than potatoes.'

'Do you really think making a few buttons is going to feed and clothe us all?' Ma's tone is patronising and she views me like a small child who has no understanding of the world.

'No, Ma, I don't think that, but what are we to do?' I frown crossly, it's not like she is contributing anything. Ma claims she can't work because of the babies, but I think it's an excuse... especially since Mary and myself provide them with more care and love than she does.

'Go back to town,' she says in answer to my question.

'What for?'

'To enquire for work.'

I've spent the afternoon walking up and down the affluent upper end of Belmont high street, calling at each grand house belonging to the gentry of our town. Four or five extremely prosperous families live here, all of whom keep servants and might possibly take on a local girl like me to wash or iron on a daily basis.

Another housekeeper closes the door, denying me any opportunity to work.

'I heard they're hiring up at Belmont Park…'

From the top step of the classically inspired house, I look down towards the voice calling up behind me. 'I beg your pardon?'

A woman stands directly below me with chocolate brown hair hidden underneath a bonnet and lilac chin straps fluttering lightly in the breeze. 'Belmont Park – I heard they're hiring.' She claps a hand over her mouth. 'I'm sorry, I didn't mean to eavesdrop, but I heard you say to the housekeeper you were looking for work.'

'Belmont Park is three miles away,' I say coming down the steps. 'I'm not looking for live-in, I need to stay at home if possible. Do you know what they are looking for?'

'I'm afraid I don't, only heard they're hiring.' She smiles. 'I'm Mrs Parsons, I live down the lane.' She nods in the direction of a small pathway leading out of town. 'If you don't mind me asking…' She hesitates momentarily. 'Your pa…Thomas Barnes?'

'Yes?' I wait to hear what she has to say. It's not unusual for people to ask about Pa, the accident is still fresh in people's memories, but it is strange for someone from the gentry to ask after him and from what I can see of this woman's outfit, she isn't poor.

'Horrid thing that happened.' She shakes her head.

'Yes, it was.'

'Are you coping well?'

'As well as can be expected.'

'That's good,' she says and I wait for her to move on, but it looks like she wants to say more. When she doesn't speak, I decide to end the conversation.

'Well, good afternoon, Mrs Parsons.' I nod and try to pass by, but her hand reaches out and stops me. I feel slightly alarmed but am reassured by the hustle and bustle of shopkeepers going about their business further down the street. If this woman is a danger, she surely won't try anything in broad daylight.

'How's your ma?' she asks.

I narrow my eyes. 'She's holding up under the circumstances.'

'Good… good.' The woman directs her gaze to the left of my shoulder as if contemplating something. 'It will be difficult for her to bring up sons, I suppose.'

'Why will it? My pa is still here, he can give guidance.' I lift my chin a little, fed up with people assuming Pa was dead to us simply because he's an invalid.

'Oh yes, yes, absolutely.' She removes her hand from my waist and smiles. 'I'd better let you get on.' I watch her walk away down the lane before turning round myself and heading home.

The tension in the room is obvious the moment I come in through the front door. 'I'm so glad you're home,' whispers Mary sidling up beside me.

'What's going on?' I ask in the same hushed tone.

'Pa knows you've been looking for work – he isn't happy.' She looks up at me, her crystal blue eyes round and anxious. 'You're not going to leave us, are you Rebekah?'

My heart tugs inside me as my nine-year-old sister waits for an answer. If I leave, I know running the home will land on Mary's young shoulders, Pa can't help her and Ma crumbles under pressure when the children become too demanding.

I don't know what to say – my words fail me.

'Ah, Rebekah!' shouts Ma sitting by the fireside when she sees I have returned home. Henry is sitting dribbling by her feet and Georgie is asleep in front of the warm flames. 'Come and put a stop to your pa's complaining. What news do you have?'

'Not much… Belmont Park is hiring.'

Ma claps her hands together. 'Ah, yes,' she remembers. 'I did hear that myself, a kind woman in the grocer's told me… it's for a maid of all work, I think.'

'You can't send her to be a skivvy!' cries Pa jolting his head too quickly in his agitation, making himself wince. 'Send Tommy up the chimneys instead, that will give us a few extra pennies.'

'I'll have no boy of mine going up into those death traps, I'd rather starve myself.'

'I don't fancy chimney's, but I'll go to work in the fields.' Tommy's eyes widen eagerly, he's sitting in the chair opposite Ma, fiddling with a stone he must have found outside. Every day he grumbles that he can't go with his brother to labour in the fields, but Daniel is only seven and there's no way he can be responsible for his five-year-old brother. 'I'll add to the coffers like Danny... and like Pa did.'

'Like Pa *does*,' corrects Pa. 'I'll be back soon and I'll take you with me, I'm sure there'll be a job for a little 'un like you.'

Tommy grins with delight at the idea, but his broad smile doesn't last long and fades away immediately when Ma snorts and stands to her feet. 'You'll be back to work when pigs fly. Rebekah will go to work, she's the eldest. No one will take Mary, she's all skin and bone and the slightest gust of wind will blow her over, no one will hire her.' I see Mary tugging self-consciously at her baggy dress at the mention of her name. 'Rebekah needs to go to work,' continues Ma. 'Since she has such a desire to help others, she can jolly well help her family for once.'

Ma's speech angers me – how dare she say that? I have never abandoned our family... not once. Before I went out to care for anyone else, I always made sure my quota of buttons was completed, made Pa comfortable, cleaned the house and fed the babies. What does Ma do? Not half as much as me.

'Margaret!' Pa's eyes flash angrily and with difficultly he pushes himself up onto his elbows. 'Enough, if you can't speak truth then don't speak at all. Rebekah has not once neglected us, so hush and be quiet.'

Ma is momentarily chastised as silence envelops the room and my own anger begins to subside. It would not do to test Ma's patience; it wouldn't help the situation in any way.

'The Belmont's are a well thought of family, you will do well there, Rebekah,' says Ma sitting down and folding her dress straight across her knees.

'But Ma, surely you need me here. Belmont Park will be a live-in position, there's no way I can walk eight miles every day. There must be another way.'

'Are you saying I can't cope without you?' I see Ma's fists clench tightly as she raises an eyebrow high and stares at me wildly.

'No, not at all!' It's the correct response, even if I am lying. But I can't help remembering Ma's face the day Pa was brought home to us after the accident. She was completely and utterly incapable of looking after anyone - she couldn't cope. On that day, without a word, Ma left us – her own children – to survive the worst day of our lives alone. I will never forget when she did finally return home, there was no apology or tenderness, her eyes wouldn't meet mine, nor would she acknowledge Pa's existence. All of his care was left to me. Pa wouldn't be alive today if he had to rely on his wife for help. That's how I know she won't cope if I leave, why the burden will fall onto Mary's much-too-young shoulders.

'You're going to work Rebekah - I need one less mouth to feed.'

Maggie gasps, she's been sitting on the floor this whole time beneath her twin brother's chair, keeping as silent as possible.

Tommy sees his sister's distress. 'Ma!' he exclaims sitting up. 'Does that mean you'd get rid of us too?' He lifts his eyes up in all innocence.

No one speaks.

I cast a disbelieving look across at Ma's refusal to give any reassurance. 'She won't get rid of you,' I say. 'I'm old enough to work away from home, that's what Ma means.'

'Of course, you have no references,' says Ma ignoring the distress she has caused. 'But they'll probably take you, the Barnes' have a good reputation in town. I'm sure Lord Belmont has heard of us, your pa's been a labourer on his farmland for years.' I didn't want to disillusion her, but the chances of Lord Belmont having heard of us was highly unlikely.

'I won't let you send her, Margaret,' Pa speaks out again. 'She does most of the work around here and keeps everything in order.'

'What is this? Two of you who think I'm useless. Mary, do you agree with your sister and pa, that I can't cope with the simple task of maintaining our household without Rebekah?'

Mary's cheeks heighten in colour as the eyes of the room fall on her.

'Ma, don't...' I plead.

'No, Rebekah – I want to know what she thinks. Do you agree Mary?'

Mary shuffles and looks down at her bare feet. 'Of course

not, Ma,' she mumbles.

'Thank you, Mary.' Ma nods her head in triumph and looks between Pa and me. 'I'd like you both to offer suggestions on how we can stay alive without money... come on, Tom, any suggestion will do?' She folds her arms and waits impatiently for Pa to answer. But he, very wisely, keeps his mouth shut. His silence infuriates Ma and she races over to the table, grabs an object lying on it and charges across to his bed. 'This is all we can afford!' She waves the object in his face, it's another black-ened loaf from Mr Allen's bakery. 'The girls' buttons bring in a pittance and I can't exactly work in the fields with two un-breeched little ones swinging from my hips. I don't choose not to work, Tom, no matter what you think - I can't work. So, if you've got a solution then tell me.'

Pa's jaw tenses, but he still doesn't speak.

Ma has won and she knows it. 'Go now, Rebekah – apply for the position now.'

'What... right now?' I glance out the window, not that I can see much through the ivy, though I can see the afternoon is nearly over and I know it's a long trek to Belmont Park.

'We can't have someone else stealing the post from under-neath our noses. Hurry up and you'll be home before supper.'

I feel the touch of her hand pushing against my back as she leads me out of the cottage, shutting the door behind me so I can't come back inside.

Chapter Four

The town of Belmont has been home to the Barnes family since my grandparents moved here from Market Ashton when Pa was a small boy. We are well established and known by many of the working families in the neighbourhood, but our connections to Belmont Park are few and far between. The house is situated three miles on the other side of town and, although Pa has worked on the farmland for many years, the current Lord Belmont leaves all dealings with his seasonal labourers to Mr Curtis, the land steward, and Mr Greaves, the tenant farmer.

As I walk at a brisk pace, I'm hoping I don't lose my way. I rarely travel this side of the town and, I must admit, I'm concerned about finding my way home – especially if I'm delayed and darkness falls.

Slowing down, I reach the top of a hill and look across to where a house the colour of sandstone, symmetrical in all its classical glory, can be seen behind a clump of trees in the distance. It's imposing and dominates the landscape - I am left in no doubt that this is Belmont Park.

It's a shame the back entrance has clearly been forgotten in Lord Belmont's remodelling of his Elizabethan mansion five years ago. The paint on the door is peeling and numerous drips falling from the roof have left a trail of moss slivering down the brickwork. I wrinkle my nose at the strong earthy odour and knock loudly. No one answers, so I knock again. If I hadn't been watching I would have easily missed the two cautious eyes staring out at me through a slit in the barely open door.

'Can I help you, miss?' squeaks the voice belonging to the eyes.

'Oh, my ma has sent me to apply for a position.'

The half-face blinks.

'You are still hiring for a maid of all work?'

'You need to see Mrs Langley,' squeaks the voice again before the eyes promptly disappear and the door closes.

I look around the yard feeling a little bemused. What am I expected to do now since I haven't been asked to wait, or leave... and who is Mrs Langley?

'You look lost.' A scruffy young man carrying a pitchfork comes round the corner and smiles at me.

'I'm waiting for... oh, it's you - how is Mr Baker?' I ask without any further preamble, amazed at how fortunate I am to come across the same tall young man who had come to my rescue yesterday. 'Please tell me he is well?'

'Don't worry, he's well.' This is all the information he gives, but the slight nod he gave when speaking and the reassuring half-smile, settle my anxieties. 'You said you are waiting?'

'Um, yes...' I look uncertainly back towards the paint-peeled door. 'I'm waiting for... or, maybe I'm not, a girl came and went - I don't know...' my voice trails away pathetically unable to explain.

'Little girl, as tiny as a mouse?' questions the young man.

'Erm, yes, quite possibly, but I only saw half a face.'

'That's Lucy, she's scared of her own shadow - bless her. Can I help?' He puts the fork down, balancing it against the crumbling brickwork.

'I'm enquiring about work.'

'You'll need to see Mrs Langley.'

'That much I was told. Who is—' I'm about to ask about the woman's identity, but as I do the door creaks open, a little wider this time, and the girl who really does have remarkably mouse-like features, steps out with her shoulders hunched together and her eyes staring fixedly at the ground. 'Come in miss,' she squeaks avoiding eye contact. 'Mrs Langley will see you now.'

'I only want to apply – you know, put my name down for the position, I don't need to see anyone.' Aware that dusk is drawing in quickly, I don't want to be delayed much longer and would happily return for an interview at a more convenient hour.

Lucy, the mouse-like girl, glances anxiously at the lanky young man, as if I'm a threatening figure.

'It's alright Luce,' he says softy, bending slightly towards the young girl before looking across at me. 'You won't get the position if Mrs Langley doesn't see you, she's the housekeeper and interviews all prospective staff in person. If she wants to do that now, well – you do it now. You won't be asked back if you leave.'

'Ah...' I ponder for a second, but it's obvious I don't really have a choice and I hope my sense of direction is just as good in the dark. 'I suppose I'd better see her now.'

The mouse-like girl leads me wordlessly down a narrow ill-lit corridor, scurrying along in front of me without looking back, trusting that I'm following her. Eventually, she stops before one of several doors and taps nervously. An authoritative voice calls from inside and we enter the small room together. The girl dips a knee and hastily retreats, leaving me to face a stern looking woman with a long triangular nose, observing me in silence from behind a desk.

'Name?'

The suddenness of her sharp tone breaking the silence makes me flinch and I watch the woman lick a finger and take a single sheet of paper from a neat pile sitting in front of her.

'Rebekah... Rebekah Barnes,' I answer and swallow nervously.

'Mm...' The woman, who I presume is Mrs Langley, writes something down on the paper. Without looking up, she holds out a hand as if expecting to receive something in it. Apprehensively, I cast a glance over my shoulder wondering if someone else has walked in behind me, but we are alone. When her hand remains empty two beady eyes shoot up and she looks down her pointed nose at me.

I swallow again, my mouth suddenly becoming dry. The presence of this woman is terrifying... I don't need this job that badly, do I? Visions of Ma parade through my mind and I can almost hear her exclaim, in a tone of great agitation, how beggars can't be choosers and to take whatever I can get. I know deep inside if this position if offered to me, I cannot refuse.

'Don't tell me you've come without a character reference?' Mrs Langley snarls.

'I haven't worked before, miss.'

In disbelief the woman shakes her head and I notice the once auburn hair is streaked with strands of white. 'How old are you?' she asks.

'Sixteen.'

'And you're telling me, that a girl of your age and status has never worked a day in her life?' She wrinkles her nose, casting judgement upon my tatty appearance. I don't blame her for doing this. My dress hasn't been washed for over a month, far too long ago, even by my mother's standards. I want to explain myself to this woman, tell her how I have a younger brother who simply couldn't fit into his breeches anymore, and how my spare dress became an item of attire for his rapidly growing legs. But I can't utter any explanation, her formidable presence allows my tongue only to speak what is necessary.

'What I mean is… yes, I have worked, but at home, I make buttons.' I smile weakly seeing she is not impressed.

'Mm…' She observes me again without speaking. 'How am I to know you are honest? The last girl took half the silver spoons.'

'I have no proof of my integrity, miss, apart from my own witness.'

The beady eyes fall on me again, making me squirm uneasily. Why can't she simply say no and dismiss me now – I am clearly not the person for the job.

'If you make buttons, why do you need to work?'

'My pa cannot work and my family has fallen on desperate times. I'm needed to provide a better income.'

'What about your mother?'

I pause before answering. 'She runs the house; my sister and I make the buttons.' It's not a complete lie, Ma does complete household chores, just not all the time.

Mrs Langley goes back to the paper in front of her, picks up the quill and writes.

'Your father,' she asks looking up at me. 'Is he looking for work?'

'No, miss. He's paralysed.' A deathly silence descends on the room and I swear from the look on her face that Mrs Langley is fighting her emotions. A faint slither of a thin half-smile appears only to suddenly contort into a strange combination of pursed lips and a set straight line.

'You will do,' she speaks without emotion. I stare at the woman wondering if I have misheard her words. 'One month's trial,' she continues ignoring my surprise. 'If you fail to give satisfaction, you leave without a reference – is that understood?'

'Y-yes, Mrs Langley.' I nod.

'You will be here with your belongings tomorrow morning at nine o' clock – prompt. If you're late I will dismiss you on the spot.'

'Yes, miss.' I wait in front of the desk as she writes, uncertain if I am to leave. But nothing else is spoken, and so after a half-curtsy, where I nearly fall over my own feet, I exit the room as quickly as possible.

Chapter Five

I don't have many belongings and the little wooden box I have packed remains almost empty. I own nothing of value and what I do own has been so well used it's hardly worth taking with me. There's one thing, however, sitting inside the box that makes my heart swell in hopeful anticipation every time I touch its soft cotton and worn-out stitches.

Never will I forget the day it was placed into my hands when Pa was walking with me into town ten years ago with a warm hand enfolded over mine. It wasn't often Pa had time off from working in the fields, so I'm not sure why on this particular day he was with me, neither does my memory recall the purpose of the trip, I simply know it happened. With eyes closed, I lift the doll out of the box, put it to my nose and take a deep sniff, allowing its ageing scent to rouse my childhood memories as if they happened yesterday... There is a commotion in full swing outside the haberdashers and Pa grips my little six-year-old hand, scanning the rowdy crowd for signs of danger. However, he needn't have worried because the throng is mainly made up of children, many of whom I know, lifting up their hands in eagerness and shouting out cries of, 'Me, miss me!'

'Children!' A loud but kindly voice floats from the middle of the crowd. 'I've only one left.'

A shout of 'Me, miss, me,' starts again.

Pa begins to pull away and I drag behind whilst still holding onto his hand. I'm watching the children with great interest, wondering what it is they want so desperately. Suddenly a break in the crowd allows me to see who is standing in the middle. Holding an empty basket is the most beautiful lady

I have ever seen. Her eyes are a dazzling green and her smile is delightfully enticing, beaming widely underneath two rosy cheeks. Her golden hair parts in symmetrical curls on either side of her face and on top sits a pretty pale blue bonnet matching perfectly her blue-speckled, high-pleated gown.

The lady's soft green eyes meet mine over the heads of the children surrounding her feet. Pa tries tugging me along, but my feet have stopped moving and he mutters my name crossly under his breath. But when he sees the beautiful lady coming our way, he gives up trying to make me move and waits politely for her to speak.

Bending low, the lady, whose golden hair sparkles in the sunlight, dips a knee to my height as the crowd of envious children stand silently behind, watching her every movement. 'This is for you.' She smiles and holds something out to me. I hesitate and look up at Pa. He doesn't say I can't have it, in fact he doesn't say anything at all, so I slowly move my hand out and take it.

It is the most beautiful thing I've ever seen. The face is made out of the softest cloth imaginable and stitched into it are two black eyes and a little pink nose. Strands of yellow cotton have been made into hair and a tiny white bonnet sits on top. The dress is blue, just like the lady's, and stitched onto its feet are dainty beige shoes.

The rosy-cheeked lady stands up straight and the children encircle her again. 'That's all children, I have no more. I wish you all a good day.'

Running lightly away she steps into a carriage waiting close by and we watch her leave, my hand wrapped tightly round the only gift I have ever been given.

This was the beginning. Something ignited within me that day, awakening my heart to what can happen when humanity dares to love. The tiny hand-stitched doll sitting inside my box represents hope. Hope that there is more to life than simply caring about self, and hope to believe that maybe even I, who have so little, can give the same joy I felt on that day to someone else.

From the moment the doll was placed into my hands it was as if my eyes had been opened. The poor, the homeless and the sick seemed to be lurking around every corner and I remember a distinct feeling of agitation, questioning constantly why these people had nothing, who was going to help them and if the kind lady would bring them a doll too.

'Pa... Pa?' I sit up, rubbing my eyes. 'Pa?' I kick my foot lightly against his leg.

'What is it, Rebekah?' Pa groans sleepily.

'I can't sleep.'

'Again?'

It's not the first night I've been restless and he props himself up onto his elbow. Ma is snoring next to him with a leg wrapped round the cotton blanket – this is how it used to be, the three of us sharing the bed - Ma and Pa at one end, me at the other.

Pa sighs. 'Come here.' I wriggle under the blanket and snuggle down beside him. He wraps his large muscular arm around my tiny frame. 'I see I'm going to have a problem with you.' He smiles in amusement with half-closed eyes.

I poke him. 'Don't fall back to sleep, Pa.'

'You know what we need to do?' he whispers into my ear leaning his sleepy head lightly against my dishevelled hair.

'What, Pa?' I whisper back, my wide but tired eyes glued to his face.

'I think we need to fill a basket of whatever delicious things we have leftover, take it into town for whoever we see is less fortunate than ourselves, and then let them take their pick... what do you say to that?'

'I say it's a wonderful idea.' A great smile spreads over my face showing the gap in my gum from the tooth I lost the day before. 'But...' I bring my voice back down to a whisper. 'What about Ma?'

'I'll deal with your ma, don't worry about that... we'll start tomorrow.'

If it wasn't for Pa discerning my need to reach out to others when I was six years old, I don't think our acts of charity would ever have taken place. We never had much in the basket, but as a young girl I thought we were changing the world. As I grew up, I began to realise our contributions to the poor were like a tiny pin prick, invisible to the rest of the world, though highly valued by the few who began to rely on our acts of compassion... But now, all this has come to an end - we gave what we had until there was nothing left to give.

My stomach churns with nerves as I knock on the back door of Belmont Park. I didn't sleep much last night with the figure of Mrs Langley terrifying my dreams. How am I to work with such a fearsome woman? Ma is harsh, but I know how she works and she's not unkind. However, this housekeeper, how am I to know if her stern frontage has compassion underneath? My life might be on the verge of becoming unbearable and I'll be wishing myself back to making buttons and living on the edge of poverty within a week.

The door opens. It's Lucy, the tiny mouse-like girl.

'Good morning.' I smile despite my trepidation. 'My name is Rebekah. I'm the new maid of all work.' The girl doesn't smile back, her lips are set straight and I'm drawn into her red-rimmed eyes which are gazing up at me like a startled rabbit. 'Mrs Langley is expecting me. I'm on time... I think.'

The girl blinks once and then opens the door wide. 'Come in,' she squeaks quietly.

Lucy guides me down the long narrow corridor again, but this time we stop at the first door on our right where she leads me into a large high-ceilinged kitchen.

'Please sit,' says Lucy timidly. 'I'll fetch Mrs Langley.' I do as I'm told and take a seat at the longest solid oak table I've ever seen, situated in the middle of the room. In front of me is a large imposing range where a rounded woman with frizzy dark brown hair is working busily away, clanging pots and sharpening knives. Her back is turned to me and, as far as I can tell, she hasn't even noticed I have entered the room. Another two girls stand at the opposite side of the kitchen peeling potatoes and carrots. They are facing away from me too, but one of the girls repeatedly turns her head and eyes me with caution. I smile nervously at her, but she turns back to her work without any acknowledgement of my friendly gesture.

Eventually Lucy returns with Mrs Langley following closely behind. I stand and dip a knee as the housekeeper stares at me down her triangular nose and I quickly decide not to speak unless I'm spoken to first.

'Kitty,' the housekeeper summons and the girl who has been watching me comes forward. 'Show Barnes to her room.'

The girl beckons me to follow, which I do with my wooden box tucked underneath my arm. She takes me further down the long dark corridor, it feels like we've hit a dead end when suddenly a set of stairs comes into view round the corner and we climb up, going round and round for what feels like forever.

'What is it like working for Mrs Langley?' I ask trying to make conversation with the silent girl, who looks about my own age and is walking up the stairs in front of me.

She doesn't answer and we continue climbing the stairs in silence.

'Have you worked here long?' I try again, this time slightly out of breath.

Kitty stops abruptly with her foot perched on the final step. 'Listen, you need to know I don't make friends with the lower staff.'

'Oh, I'm sorry.' I apologise, but I can't help thinking I couldn't possibly be much lower than this girl. There can't be much difference between a kitchen maid and a maid of all work.

'They don't often stick around for long,' she explains haughtily. 'I find it best to not get too attached.' I want to ask her why, fearful of what I might encounter, but she moves on and opens the second door along the attic corridor. 'This is your room.'

'Thank you.' I attempt a smile. 'I'm Rebekah, by the way.' Kitty wrinkles her nose and heads back down the stairs, the sound of her footsteps is heard pattering quickly away.

My room feels like luxury. I have a bed and a little side table which fits snuggly next to it. I suppose anyone else might say the space felt bare, but for me, it's absolutely perfect.

I follow the stairs back down to the basement where I find the kitchen again at the end of the long corridor. Kitty and the other girl have gone, but the cook is still there with her back to the room, mixing something with a wooden spoon in the biggest pot I've ever seen. Her upper arm muscle bulges as she grasps the utensil firmly in her hand and I can tell she's repeated this action many times before.

I cough to make my presence known. 'Excuse me, do you know where Mrs Langley is?'

The cook doesn't turn and continues rotating her arm, stirring whatever sauce or stew is in the pot before her. I loiter by the table when she doesn't answer, my stomach knotting with uneasiness - maybe I should find Mrs Langley myself?

Looking up and down the corridor I try to remember which way Lucy took me yesterday. I walk part way down the corridor, passing five or six doors to my left and right. Standing before one I think looks familiar, I knock twice, but no one answers. Hovering my hand over the handle I turn it and peek inside - I'm wrong, this room is not the housekeeper's chamber and I'm met by two petrified eyes gazing back at me. 'Oh, I'm sorry,' I say slightly startled myself.

Lucy has her sleeves rolled up as high as possible and her arms are deep in soapy water scrubbing away at what I assume are the breakfast pots. She's frozen dead-still as if she really were a mouse and is deciding whether it is best to scurry away or keep still in the hope she hadn't been seen.

I smile kindly, trying to put the girl at ease. 'It's Lucy, isn't it?' The girl nods slowly and I notice she's standing on a little wooden step to reach the oblong shaped sink.

'Can you show me where Mrs Langley's room is, I'm trying to

find her?' I've naturally lowered my voice, aware of her timidity and afraid I might scare her away if I speak too loudly.

Lucy pulls both arms out of the water and dries them on her clean white apron. Her eyes dart away from mine as she walks past me, pausing by the doorway for me to follow her.

We stop on the other side of the corridor two doors down and Lucy fleetingly lifts her face to mine. 'It's here,' she whispers, casting her eyes to the ground and scurrying away before I can thank her.

Tentatively, I knock on the door. No one calls or responds so I knock a little louder. After the third attempt I realise no one is there, however this time I'm too scared to open the door to discover who is on the other side and I decide to head back to the kitchen.

Kitty has reappeared and is kneading bread at the long table. She glances briefly at me before focusing on the dough again.

'Is there anything I can help with?' My voice echoes around the high-ceilinged room and my cheeks redden a little in my nervousness.

The girl frowns. 'How would I know?'

'I don't want to sit idle while I'm waiting for Mrs Langley. If there's anything I can do, I'm happy to help.'

'I'm a kitchen maid, I don't dish out orders.' Kitty scoops up the stringy dough in her hands and removes herself to the other end of the table. After her conceited attitude up in the attic, I'm a little surprised the girl doesn't take advantage of the situation and flaunt her own, very limited, authority.

I'm also concerned Mrs Langley hasn't appeared. She knows it's my first day, surely she would want to give me instructions? I don't know where anything is, or what routines the house has... I don't even know what a maid of all work is supposed to do. I mean, obviously the name suggests I do *all* things, but what do I do first and when should it be done? Dragging a chair out from behind the table I sit down feeling incredibly out of my depth.

'Why are you sitting down, child!'

My backside has barely touched the base of the wooden seat when I hear Mrs Langley call out, appearing as if from nowhere. The shrill voice brings me standing quickly to attention.

'I am paying you to work, not sit.' Mrs Langley's forehead contracts immediately into a deep frown.

'I-I'm sorry,' I stutter. 'I was looking for you...' I trail away knowing this woman isn't likely to accept any excuses - how had I got it wrong all ready?

Kitty scoops up the dough with one hand and tosses it into a bowl. Carrying it in her arms she brushes past the housekeeper, giving me a sideways glare and mutters quietly under her breath. 'Looks like we might have a lazy one, Mrs Langley.'

My mouths drops – I can't believe she just said that. What have I done to offend her?

The kitchen maid smirks and exits the room, her slender figure swaying arrogantly at the hips.

'Go and help Lucy in the scullery,' demands the housekeeper who lifts a bony, long finger in my direction. 'If I find you sitting idle again, you'll be sorry.'

This place is unbearable - is there a kind soul anywhere?

I scurry out of the room with my head hung low and work my way hurriedly back along the narrow corridor, trying to remember which room I found Lucy in before.

I come across the door again.

Heaving a sigh, I twist the handle and enter...

Chapter Six

To my surprise Lucy has vanished when I enter the scullery. However, the room isn't empty because this time, elbow deep in water, is the tall young man I met yesterday. I'm a little taken aback by his presence and momentarily hesitate with my hand holding onto the handle.

'Good morning.' He smiles kindly, it's the first warm welcome I've had in this place. 'I heard you got the position.'

'Erm, yes... I've been told to help Lucy.' I take a sideways glance over my shoulder in case she's standing behind me, the girl's small enough to fit behind the door.

'She's gone to fetch more soap.' He pulls a large copper pan from the sink. 'Lucy struggles with the heavy pots and I like to help her out when I can.'

I smile, but don't respond. Kindness? This feels strange in such a hostile environment and I wonder if he's mocking me in some way. He looks to his side and down over his shoulder at me, his lean long body arching over the sink. 'I'm Emmanuel, Emmanuel Smith.'

'I'm Rebekah Barnes.'

'It nice to meet you, Rebekah... do you go by anything else?'

'My pa and brothers call me Becks.'

'Suits you... Becks.' He looks out of the window before him in contemplation. 'You can call me Manny; all my friends do.'

'How do you know we're going to be friends?'

'Just got a feeling. Ah...' He looks straight across the yard. 'Here comes Lucy.' He dries his arms and hands with a nearby cloth and rolls down his sleeves.

'All right, Luce?' Manny asks the tiny maid when she enters the room.

'Yes thanks, Manny.' Lucy almost smiles, but stops when she sees me, a look of nervousness spreading across her face.

'I think you'll be fine with this one,' Manny says as he reaches up to a hook on the back of the door holding a faded jade green jacket. Taking it down he flings it over his shoulder and gives Lucy a soft kindly wink before leaving the room.

'Does he often help you?' I ask as Lucy closes the door.

'Yes, but don't tell Mrs Langley.' It's the most I've heard the girl speak and her high little cheeks turn pink.

'Doesn't she know?'

'Manny's a groom,' she whispers with a squeak. 'He shouldn't even be in the house, never mind helping me.'

'I see.' Through the window I catch sight of the young man striding across the yard and my mind wanders to Mr Baker. It looks like Manny really did help him and my anxiety eases even more as I hold onto the hope that the poor man is convalescing somewhere in safety. Bringing my attention back into the room I bend lower so I'm level with Lucy's face. 'I promise, I won't say a word.'

Lucy's mouth flicks into a cautious half-smile.

'So...' I stand up tall and rub my hands together. 'You're in charge, what do I do first?'

To my surprise the other half of Lucy's mouth curls up, completing the half-smile she had started. 'I'm not above you – you're older,' she says softly with a small laugh.

'You've got more experience than I have - how long have you worked here?'

'Two years.'

'Then, you're in charge.' I smile encouragingly and wait for my instructions.

Lucy studies my face. 'Well...' She hesitates. 'After washing the breakfast pots, I normally make the beds.'

'Do we need fresh linen?'

'Not today, they only need airing.' Her cheeks turn a rosy pink, very conscious of my interest in what she's saying. 'Tomorrow we'll strip them for washing.'

The following morning, I wake with a jolt. Thinking I'm at home I almost fall out of the bed and it takes a few seconds to shake off my sleepy disorientation. Sitting up, I stretch and move my stiff aching joints - I don't think I've worked so hard in my life. Button making is laborious, however it's not tough on the body. I'm used to getting an aching back and sore eyes from working long after dusk, but that's all: after one day at Belmont Park, I'm aching all over. As I step over to the wash basin sitting on top of the bedside table, a short sharp pain jabs through my shins and my legs almost buckle underneath me. Recovering, I splash my face with cold water and use the fresh white towel laid beside it to dab myself dry.

Breakfast is a quiet affair even though the kitchen is full with every maid and manservant Belmont Park employs. The butler, whose name oddly enough is Mr Butler, sits at the top end of the table, with Mrs Langley to his right. Two footmen dressed in full livery are next and beside them are Kitty and the other kitchen maid whose name I still do not know. Manny sits opposite the footmen, leaving Lucy, a stable boy and myself at the bottom end. No one speaks. The sound of tea being sipped is heard and knives clink against the butter dish, but there is no conversation. Lucy perches on the edge of her seat, looking ready to scurry away at any second.

It's not long before everyone leaves to continue their various jobs and Lucy leads me out into the yard and round the corner to a small outhouse. 'This is the wash-room,' she says stopping beside a red brick building and entering through the door. A strong smell of soap greets me as I enter the dim room. 'I normally start with the linen,' she adds with a squeak before making her way over to the bed sheets we had removed earlier in the morning whilst the family were breakfasting.

'Shall I put them in the pot?' I ask lifting up half the pile and bringing it over to a large cauldron bubbling with boiling water. Lucy nods and goes to collect a long thin wooden stick which is leaning against the wall in the corner. Carefully, I place the linen into the water making sure I don't cause any of it to splash out at us. Lucy stands on a step, identical to the one in the scullery, and begins to stir as if she's making a stew.

'Your wooden steps are useful,' I comment nodding towards Lucy's feet raised above the ground.

'Manny made them.' A pink hue rises in her cheeks. 'I can't reach things, you see.'

I smile and watch her stir the contents of the cauldron. 'How old are you Lucy?'

'I'm nine.' Suddenly the similarity hits me between the eyes. This quiet, timid little girl reminds me so much of Mary. An unexpected surge of emotion almost overwhelms me, and I have to press my lips together in order to fight it down. Fortunately, Lucy's back is turned and doesn't notice my distress.

'My sister is nine,' I say when I can trust myself to speak without losing my composure. 'I cannot imagine her having to work like you do.'

'It was either here, or the workhouse.'

She looks so sad watching the bubbling water boil violently over the heat of the flames, that I can't help but ask, 'What happened, Lucy?'

Her wide red-rimmed eyes gaze at me. 'I wouldn't want to burden you with it, Rebekah.' I expect the timid little girl to dart her eyes away, but she holds them firmly onto my own, desperate, almost pleading me to ask her more.

'I know I'm a stranger to you, Lucy, but you don't have to carry it alone... you can trust me.'

Her lower lip momentarily wobbles until she lightly presses her teeth down to stop it.

'Sometimes,' Lucy begins, her voice barely audible. 'I think the workhouse would have been better.'

My lips part slightly at the revelation and I draw in a slow steady breath. 'Is it really that bad for you here?'

'Mrs Langley didn't want me – she beats me if I get things wrong.' She bites her bottom lip. Something tells me this story isn't going to end well.

'What happened to your family?' I ask in a hushed voice.

'House-fire,' she states simply. 'No one else survived, the parish sent me here.'

My heart breaks. It's no wonder the poor girl looks so scared, she is all alone, without a single soul to protect her, and Mrs Langley is her guardian - I wouldn't wish that on my worst enemy. 'I'm so sorry.' There's no need for me to apologise, but I feel life has not dealt Lucy a good hand and now she's suffering for it.

'Don't be sorry for me, Rebekah.' She hops down from her wooden stool and unexpectedly takes my hand. The warm touch brings a tingle to my nose as Lucy's moving tale blends with my own fears and anxieties for my family. 'I cried every night when I first arrived at Belmont Park,' continues the little girl. I look down at the tiny hand holding mine, then up into her face, and immediately I know, the touch isn't for Lucy's comfort, but for my own, because spreading slowly across her lips is a slight hint of a smile. 'When I thought all was lost, I prayed for a miracle.'

I'm drawn in by her soft tones. 'Did God give you a miracle?' I'm the one who squeaks this time, wishing more than any-thing that this little girl might give me some hope, that not everything in Belmont Park is going to be as insufferable as I've found it so far.

Lucy's smile widens and a twinkle forms in her eye. 'Yes...' she says confidently lifting up her face. 'God gave me Manny.'

The little girl's confession reverberates around my mind all morning. By my definition a miracle is when the impossible happens. Manny seems like a nice young man, but he can't be the answer to every problem. He can't perform the impos-sible. I think of Pa, my constant source of strength, my pro-vider and confidant, but even he can't perform the impossible. He couldn't fix his legs or prevent us spiralling into poverty - the impossible remains impossible and not even Manny can change this.

'Mrs Langley wants you to wash the floor in the entrance hall,' says Kitty after lunch.

'Is that such a good idea?' I query, even I know there are certain chores that shouldn't be done in broad daylight.

'Are you questioning me?' The girl puts a hand on a hip.

'No, of course not. I'm concerned I will be seen, you know, since it's in such a well-used part of the house anyone coming or going could trip over me.'

Kitty rolls her eyes. 'Don't you think I know that, the Belmonts are to be out of the house all afternoon.'

'I-I didn't know that.'

'Maybe next time you'll listen to instructions without questioning them.' She picks up four empty tea cups left on the table and loops her fingers round the handles. 'I'd hurry up and take the opportunity to get the task completed before their return.'

I don't hesitate. If Mrs Langley wants the floor washing now, I'd better get started. The thought of the family returning home early and being greeted by a maid on her hands and knees is a prospect I don't fancy facing.

So here I am, scrubbing furiously on the cold hall floor, allowing my frustrations and anxieties to be thrust into my work. I'm on my knees, with my arms vigorously pushing the bristle-filled brush from side to side. Sweat is running down my face, curls of hair have loosened and are peeking out from underneath my lace cap. My thoughts dwell on home and Pa's shadowed face, alone in the corner of the cottage. What if Mary can't cope, looking after the children and Pa...

Out of nowhere a shadow falls over me and I freeze.

The tips of two pointed shoes come into my eye-line and I sit up, using my arm to wipe the perspiration away from my forehead, my hot cheeks are flushed and slowly, I lift my face to meet the figure before me.

My eyes widen in horror, conscious that the mistake I've made might jeopardise my entire future at Belmont Park.

Chapter Seven

I've not seen Lady Belmont before. Occasionally I've seen her carriage ride through town, but I've never actually seen her face to face. Rumour has it that she used to be a pretty girl in her younger years, though time has now started to work against her, nevertheless, it's said she remains at the height of fashion and doesn't miss a season, strolling along the streets of London looking for the latest styles and trends to bring back to Belmont.

I don't think I can be wrong then, to presume the lady standing before me is Lady Belmont. Her white high-waisted Empire dress, cut in a low square line around the neck, flutters lightly down her slim figure almost as if she's a Greek goddess. She's meticulously turned out, everything from her hair to the tips of her toes reflects a grandeur and opulence I've never seen before - nothing is out of place...

Unlike me.

I stand self-consciously and tug down my grey pleated dress which is damp from my vigorous scrubbing. My hand nervously finds a stray piece of hair and I tuck it behind my ear, even though several other wild locks continue to wisp around my head. Clumsily, I perform a curtsy before keeping my focus resolutely on the wet soapy floor.

Kitty had distinctly told me the family were not at home. Am I being overly suspicious to think she instigated this unfortunate meeting from the beginning?

'Who are you?' asks Lady Belmont in tones that reflect puzzlement rather than displeasure.

'Rebekah, ma'am.' I continue to keep my eyes down, the only thing in my eye-line being her ladyship's dainty embroidered shoes.

'Are you new?'

'Yes, ma'am.'

Lady Belmont utters a distinct tut under her breath. 'What's your position?' The question confuses me, shouldn't she know who she's employing?

'M-maid of all work, ma'am.' When the hall remains quiet, I slowly lift my eyes to see her ladyship observing me with great interest.

'Tell me, Rebekah,' she asks upon seeing my face. 'Does this hat match my gloves?'

It's not what I expect her to ask and I'm temporarily taken aback. Why would I know anything about fashion? I know that rags go with rags – that's about my limit. Lady Belmont, either ignorant of my confusion or choosing not to notice, shows me both her arms covered by two long cream-coloured gloves, joined together by a row of exquisitely made buttons. The hat is of a similar colour with a lilac trim.

'It's all right,' she says suddenly noting my hesitation. 'I don't bite.' Her grey eyes, almost the colour of silver, are sharp and expectant of an answer. The rumours of her beauty certainly match up with her appearance in the flesh, though the beginnings of deeper lines etched into the corners of her eyes indicate that her ladyship is well beyond her prime.

'They look very well together, ma'am,' I reply timidly, uncertain what else I should say.

'Explain further, if you could.' Her long thin face is serious as she waits for me to speak.

'Well...' I hesitate and try to swallow. 'The buttons particularly make them a good match, ma'am.' Perhaps it's because I've made buttons for so long that my eye is naturally attracted to them, but whatever the reason for my observation, all I know is that I'm thankful for their appearance on her ladyship's attire. Now I'm praying she doesn't ask me to elaborate further.

'Why do you say that?'

The heat prickles in my cheeks to an even greater degree. 'Well, ma'am, they are covered in a lilac cloth, it matches your trim.'

Lady Belmont turns both her hands palm up and considers the gloves again, allowing her eyes to run down the row of buttons on each side. 'So they do. Thank you, Rebekah.'

'Y-you're welcome, ma'am.' My hands clasp tightly together in front of me as I wait for further questions. But she says nothing more and side steps around the bucket of soapy water before exiting the house and climbing into a carriage waiting for her on the drive.

Remaining just long enough to confirm her ladyship isn't returning, I pick up the bucket by the thin metal handle and splash soapy bubbles on the floor as I retreat to the nearest servant's exit. Leaving a trail of puddles behind me is the least of my worries as I hurry along to the outhouse as quickly as my legs will carry me without tumbling over.

Bursting open the door I find Lucy continuing with the wash we started yesterday. She's standing on one of her specially made wooden steps and ironing the creases out of the bed linen. The little girl looks a bit startled by my sudden entrance, but manages to give me a nervous smile, curling her mouth slightly up in at the corners and trying to overcome the wariness created by my unexpected ambush.

'I've seen Lady Belmont!' I cry out in horror. '... Oh, I'm sorry, Lucy. Did I scare you?'

'Only a little.' She looks down at the iron and smooths out a crease. 'Her ladyship is very pretty, isn't she?' Timidly, she casts her eyes back up. 'Rebekah...' Her cheeks turn pink and she glances away self-consciously. '...Your appearance,' she whispers in alarm.

'Oh!' I try to tuck the wild curls under my white cap, but immediately they flick out again and I flap them away. 'I can't worry about that right now; I need to know if the mistake I've made is as bad as I think.' Lucy doesn't speak, but I know she's listening, because her large tired eyes lock onto mine - I have her whole-hearted attention. 'You see, I was scrubbing the floor in the entrance hall when Lady Belmont appeared out of nowhere—' I pause in my recollections as Lucy's mouth suddenly hangs open and she looks utterly aghast.

'Did she speak to you?' the little girl asks switching the iron in her hand for the one heating up on the fire.

'Yes, she asked me about her outfit...do you think she'll tell Mrs Langley?' I grimace and screw up my face, waiting for an answer that will almost certainly be in the negative. Lucy's red-rimmed eyes blink several times in my direction, and I can see they are full of fear on my behalf.

I sigh and my shoulders droop. 'What am I to do, Lucy?' I'm almost trembling at the thought of being sent home on my second day - what would Ma say? She'd never forgive me.

The sound of the iron is heard steaming on the linen. 'Her ladyship might not say anything,' Lucy's voice wobbles as she speaks, and I can tell she's dubious about the words she's spoken coming to pass. 'Try not to worry, Rebekah,' she adds gently. 'You can't change it now.'

She's right.

I take a breath...

'What can I do to help?' Distraction is essential if I'm to stop anxiety taking over.

'The petticoats need boiling,' suggests Lucy and so silently, I empty a basket of petticoats into the cauldron of bubbling water, take the long wooden stick and begin to stir.

Not long after the petticoats are boiling away, we head across the yard towards the kitchen for a much-needed break. A warm comforting drink will do my jangled nerves some good.

Cook is arching over the large range mixing something in a copper pan. I glance across at her rounded figure and wonder if she ever leaves the kitchen, or if in fact, she stands there cooking in her sleep. As I'm contemplating this, a body moves away from the stone fireplace - it's Manny and he smiles on our entrance.

'Just warming my hands, it's chilly out there today.' He blows into his hands and rubs them together.

'Here you go, Rebekah.' Lucy passes me a steaming cup of hot milk and I cradle it in my hands.

Manny opens his mouth to speak, but whatever he is going to say is quickly forgotten when Mrs Langley bursts into the room with dark bulging eyes.

My stomach flips – this must be about Lady Belmont.

'What is this?' The housekeeper holds up a dripping petticoat.

My mouth falls open and all thoughts of her ladyship vanish from my mind. I stand looking quizzically at the item being held high in the air and I can't work out why it's not boiling away in the cauldron with the others.

'I found this on the ground - look at the grass stains!' Mrs Langley rants as Kitty nonchalantly walks in from the yard.

'I wasn't on wash duty today,' the kitchen maid pipes up immediately upon seeing the dripping item of attire. 'Not now we have the new girl.' She abruptly glowers at me through narrowed eyes.

'Mm... I thought as much.' The housekeeper ogles her beady eyes at me. 'Barnes, petticoats are not dried on the ground and stains should be removed before drying takes place, I thought that was obvious, but I warrant your knowledge is limited since you are only a button maker.'

I hear a snigger coming from Kitty's direction, however a glare from Mrs Langley soon shuts her up. Lucy stifles a gasp at the insult, although she stays close to my side and doesn't side-step away in fear as I thought she might.

'It wasn't me,' I begin in my defence. 'I put them in the pot to boil not ten minutes ago.'

'So, are you telling me it was Lucy?' Mrs Langley crosses her arms tightly over her chest and lightly creases her forehead in a scowl directed at the tiny maid, who in response, shuffles closer to me.

'No!' I exclaim - I can't get Lucy involved, there's an instinct inside of me urging me to protect her as if she were my own sister.

Mrs Langley's head jolts and her eyebrows rise, affronted and displeased in equal measure by my excessively abrupt tone.

'It wasn't Lucy, Mrs Langley.' I lower my voice and look away.

'Then let me ask again,' says Mrs Langley pointing her nose at me. 'Was it you who left the petticoat on the floor?'

I glance towards Manny; I don't know why. But he's watching me, tilting his head to the side with curiosity, waiting for my answer.

'Y-yes.' My head lowers with a shame that doesn't even belong to me. 'It was me.'

'If such a thing happens again, Barnes, I will see to it that your position is filled by somebody more capable than yourself. I have many girls with more experience waiting for such an opportunity. Am I understood?'

'Yes, Mrs Langley.' The offending wet object is flung directly to me through the air, drenching me as I catch it. Kitty sniggers again, but this time she isn't warned to stop.

I'm left wondering why Mrs Langley even hired me – a girl who came with no experience and no reference. If the other girls she speaks of are better than myself, why am I here at all?

Silence fills the room and the housekeeper exits, satisfied she has given an exemplary scolding. Kitty follows behind picking up an empty basket on her way out, only stopping to send a triumphant smirk in my direction. Cook continues to stir, like she had done through the whole commotion as if no one else was in the room.

'Wood ash, an olive oil-based soap and a lot of elbow grease.'

I turn to see Manny has left the fireplace. 'Pardon?'

He takes the petticoat from my hands which has made a puddle on the floor by my feet and he walks over to the sink, twisting the material and wringing out as much excess water as possible. 'Wood ash, an olive oil-based soap and a lot of elbow grease – to get the grass stains out.'

'Oh, thank you.'

'You can come to me for the elbow grease, but everything else you'll find in the scullery – Lucy will show you, won't you Luce?'

I look down at the girl who still looks a little dazed from the incident.

'It's all right, Luce.' He places a comforting hand on the girl's shoulder. 'Mrs Langley won't hurt you; Rebekah took the blame.' Lucy nods slowly and presses her mouth together. 'Why don't you go and find the soap Rebekah needs from the scullery?' She nods again and puts her cup down on the table.

'Poor mite,' Manny comments watching the little maid leave the room. 'Mrs Langley treats her rotten. Lucy doesn't deserve it, especially after losing her family the way she did.' He shakes his head compassionately. 'So,' he says bringing his focus back onto me. 'How are you finding things?'

I'm not certain how to answer this – can I really say this place is horrendous, that every limb in my body is aching and that my mind is overloaded with anxieties about how my family are coping without me? Every second I picture Pa alone in his darkened corner of our cottage and imagine Mary on her knees, being suffocated by the demands of all the children. Manny seems nice, but can I be so truthful with someone I do not know?

'You can be honest with me,' he says as if reading my thoughts. 'I won't tell.'

'It's...' I'm going to edge on the side of caution. '... a very difference experience from what I'm used to.'

He chuckles. 'It is, isn't it?'

'Does anyone...' I pause to think of the words.

'Have the ability to give a warm welcome?' he asks as if reading my mind... again.

'Erm... yes, actually. The only people who have uttered a kind word to me have been Lucy and, well... and yourself.' My cheeks blush as I say the words, hating that they've betrayed my embarrassment at being so open with a relative stranger.

He turns away bashfully hiding it well by looking across to the large woman who is still faithfully stirring the pot. 'Well...' he says folding his arms and leaning against a pine cupboard with three doors. 'You won't get a welcome from cook, no one ever does – she's deaf. Her days are spent facing the wall and rarely sees anyone come in or out. But I tell you, when she does turn round, she'll give you the biggest broadest smile you've ever seen... and Lucy...' Manny's face lights up in animation. 'You will find she is as loyal and faithful as they come – but put the child into a room with a stranger and she'll shrivel into a shell - seems to like you though.'

'Actually, Lucy reminds me of my sister, they don't realise how strong they really are.'

'That's exactly right.' He nods slowly, clearly impressed by my intuition of his small friend's true character. 'Now Kitty,' he continues. 'She's a different story altogether.'

'She's told me already we won't be friends.'

'Don't worry, you're not missing out.' He wrinkles his nose indicating his dislike. 'And Mrs Langley, she...' Manny looks over his shoulder, presumably checking we're still alone. 'Hates my guts,' he whispers.

The revelation shocks me. Manny's the kindest person in this place, I find it hard to believe someone can hate him.

'It's true,' he says upon seeing my stunned reaction. 'Ever since my very first day she's eyed me suspiciously, I've no idea why... and those beady little eyes of hers are enough to give anyone a nervous disposition.' He shudders.

'I've experienced the feeling already.'

Suddenly cook lifts the large pot from the range and turns, her muscles bulging as she carries the heavy load. 'Ma-nn-y!' the woman mouths - it's difficult to distinguish the sounds, but you can tell she is saying his name - and Manny was right, the biggest smile spreads across her face from cheek to cheek. She nods in my direction before lifting her two little fingers on each hand, locking them together and reversing the action.

'Yes.' Nods Manny and smiles warmly at the cook. 'She's a friend.' He taps his index and middle finger to his head. Cook watches him, waiting for more. 'RE-BECK-AH.' He mouths slowly and then turns to me. 'I don't know all the signs yet, so I have to mouth the words more slowly, shout and hope for the best...my alphabet is particularly shocking, always getting T and U mixed up.'

'How do you know what she's saying?' I ask fascinated by how the two of them are communicating.

'Hetty comes from London and went to Braidwood's deaf school for a while, one of the lucky few. He taught her to speak using hand gestures – now she's teaching me.'

I'm speechless. I had no idea such a language existed.

'Ma-nn-y.' Hetty moves her mouth slowly and directs her signs to me. She points at the tall young man and sticks a thumb up in the air before lifting a finger horizontally, rubbing it against her chin.

Self-consciously I look to Manny for an explanation and I notice he's got a bashful smile on his face. 'What's she say?' I ask.

'She says I'm a good boy.' He's clearly embarrassed by the praise and deflects the attention by sitting on top of the long wooden table and turning to me animatedly. 'I'll teach you, if you'd like, different hand signals mean different things - it makes Hetty's day when we talk. She'd love it if two of us could talk to her, Lucy knows a few too—'

A cough interrupts his excitement.

'Mr Smith, I think your break is over.' Mr Butler's deep thick eyebrows are set in a frown and I get the impression this isn't the first time Manny has been caught talking in the kitchen when he should be working.

'Yes, Mr Butler.' Manny jumps down from the table, hiding his face from the butler so that his humorously raised eyebrows are only seen by myself and leaves the kitchen as Lucy returns with the items needed to clean the petticoat.

When we return to the outhouse, I help Lucy with the ironing, the bed linen being so large it almost drowns her as she attempts to fold it. Once it's all neatly packed into a basket Lucy takes it back into the house, leaving me to begin work on the grass-stained petticoat.

I can't help but chuckle to myself as I'm sitting scrubbing the petticoat outside in the yard. *Come to me for the elbow grease* that's what Manny had said. From the look of his grubby breeches and the faint smell of horse manure which seems to linger around him, I doubt if he knows a single thing about getting grass stains out of lady's undergarments – and I certainly don't expect him to show up and offer assistance.

The sound of footsteps stops my thoughtful musings. I look up to see Manny standing in front of me, as if he had heard my thoughts... again, for the third time today.

'Squeeze along,' he says shimmying me down the wooden bench fixed onto the wall of the wash-room.

I stare at him in wonder.

'What?' He laughs. 'I told you I'd come.'

I'm beginning to see why Lucy referred to Emmanuel Smith as a miracle. Taking the garment from my hands he rubs and scrubs with all his might for the next hour until the smudged green stain disappears.

Chapter Eight

December 1800

I wake in a sudden panic and sit bolt upright in bed. The room is spinning and my heart races. I know it's not real, but it takes a while to convince myself what is reality and what is not.

I can't hear the birds singing, but that doesn't mean it's not time to start the day. My room has a high sloped ceiling with a tiny little window far out of reach. I look up. The sky is dark and spots of rain bounce off the glass. It could be three o'clock in the morning, then again it could be six - there's no knowing once the winter months have arrived.

It's been a long two months at Belmont Park. Not a day goes by that I don't allow my thoughts to dwell upon Mary and Pa struggling to survive in our tiny dilapidated cottage. I've had no word from them, and I don't know if my wages have helped in any way to lift the shadow of poverty. But my contribution won't rescue them, I know that much to be true.

If concerns over my family's welfare were the only issue I had to face, then life might be more bearable. But, as it turns out, I have to deal with Mrs Langley too. Every day I follow the housekeeper's instructions, obey every rule and go beyond the call of duty, yet she is not satisfied. I'm threatened with dismissal on a daily basis and have cruel words spat in my face. She lurches around corners and creeps in the dark waiting to jump out and lay blame upon me for any conceivable thing she can imagine.

It's in times of greatest suffering that I have to force myself to count my blessings – though they are few and hard to find. In particular, I call to remembrance how my arrival has at least taken the housekeeper's focus away from Lucy, who now silently fades into the background. Mrs Langley's frustrations are vented only on me and with determination I take the burden of her insults and battering, continuing to develop a hardened skin like I had done with Ma. But I'll sacrifice anything for Lucy, my dear sweet and loyal companion, and the thought that she is protected because of me brings a strange comfort amidst the trials.

Shaking away the final torments of the nightmare, I promptly wash, change and head down to the kitchen. It's empty and cold and a sigh of relief escapes my mouth - I haven't overslept. Neither have I heard the chime of the grandfather clock standing on the first-floor landing, so I assume it's in between the hour... but which one? As I'm considering if I should start my working day or head back to bed, a silhouette moves across the back door in the yard outside.

Who else is up and awake?

Slowly, I creep towards the door. It would be foolish of me to examine the yard for intruders alone, for this is who I think is skulking in the yard – what law-abiding person would be up at this hour... whatever hour it may be?

My hand hovers over the handle as I decide whether I should open it or stay in the sanctuary of the kitchen. However, my deliberations are interrupted, and I'm caught by surprise as the door swings open from the outside. I can't do anything now but hold my breath and hide in the shadows, believing it best not to reveal my presence until the intruder has been identified.

It's dark, made even more so by the persistent rain outside, so I have to squint in order to see who has entered. It's definitely a man, the figure being too tall to be a woman, very tall in fact... I let out a relieved breath and step out of hiding from behind the door.

'Manny?'

He visibly jumps and lifts a hand to his chest. 'My goodness, Becks. I thought I saw someone in here - what are you doing up so early?'

'How early is early?'

'Two o'clock!'

'Oh, I had no idea it was that time. I was thinking about starting the fires.'

Manny chuckles and shakes his head. 'Trying to impress a certain housekeeper?'

'I don't think I could do anything to impress that woman, I actually thought I'd overslept.'

'What are you doing awake, sleep doesn't normally evade you doing the job you do?'

'You're right, it doesn't... normally.' I'm hoping the darkness will covers the anxious chewing of my bottom lip... It doesn't.

Manny bends closer and inspects my face. 'What's the problem?'

'Oh, it doesn't matter,' I say lightly waving his question away with a hand and heading towards the door leading into the dark corridor.

Manny's prediction on that first day, that we'd be friends, hadn't failed. In fact, he, Hetty and Lucy have become my closest allies. But while my friendship with Lucy and Hetty remains limited in many ways, I find my relationship with Manny has grown into something very different.

Lucy has become almost like a sister, whose sensitive nature has become an incredible comfort to me. But her quietness, whilst being a great strength, is also her biggest weakness and a lack of confidence in herself often renders a conversation with the girl useless, particularly when she loses all ability to communicate and is left only with the capability to nod along in agreement.

Where Lucy is often void of conversation, Hetty is the opposite. You'd think her inability to hear sound would have created a reluctance in her to communicate with others. However, when the cook finds a willing person, you can't shut her up. Hetty is a large and high-spirited woman and her hands, when not cooking, are in constant use, particularly whenever myself or Manny are present, signing shapes and gestures that often leave me baffled. Keen to learn, Hetty teaches me new signs daily, but until I've mastered the art of this new language our conversations will always be limited.

But Manny... I can't even describe the friendship we have. He has this amazing ability to put me at ease no matter how troubled my spirit becomes - whatever the time, he'll listen, nothing is too difficult for him - if you ask, he'll always come. I've found there's a desire within him that matches my own, an inner need to be compassionate and shower kindness into the deepest, darkest places of people's lives. Of course, Manny has his flaws just like the rest of us, but all I know is that it feels like I've known him my whole life.

'Sit.' He pulls a chair out scraping it loudly across the floor in the empty kitchen. 'Talk to me.'

'Manny, we shouldn't be here together.' I glance cautiously towards the door and then back to his face hidden in the darkness.

'Who's going to know, it's two in the morning?'

'Mrs Langley sleeps down the corridor, she might hear.'

'She doesn't have a bed *in* the corridor, she's not on patrol... come and sit.' He gestures to the chair again and I see through the darkness his oval face staring at me in earnest, willing me to sit down - which I grudgingly do.

This I've learned about Manny, as compassionate as he is, he's strong-willed and won't give up until he gets his own way. I know this sounds like a criticism of the character I've only just praised, but it isn't a completely negative aspect of his nature since his obstinacy always contains a great deal of sensitivity. But it is the reason why I haven't revealed every detail of my life to Manny. This sounds like a contradiction too, after what I've said about him and the way he makes me feel. However, at the smallest hint of anxiety within me he'll have the entire thing dragged out and analysed until he's satisfied a solution has been found for the problem. This I can't deal with, for there are many things in my life where a solution is simply not possible.

I hadn't intended to share the cause of my disturbed sleep with him. Not that there's anything to hide, but it's a haunting recollection of the day of Pa's accident and I don't really want to relive every little detail because... well, Manny doesn't know about that awful day and he'll want to know everything from beginning to end, inside and out.

The rain has stopped and a fleeting break in the cloud casts moonlight across his face – the determined glint in his eyes tells me I might as well give up now.

'It's nothing really, just a nightmare.'

He watches me silently. This is how he gets his information out of me so easily; he knows there's no need for speech when his soft sympathetic eyes produce the best results possible.

'Really Manny, it's nothing, an irksome nightmare that keeps recurring.' He continues to stare whilst my own eyes dart around for anything else to focus on but his face.

'Manny... please.'

My shoulders lower in defeat.

'It's bothered me, that's all,' I finally admit and sit back in the chair.

His presses his lips together and kneels before me, his focus soft and aimed toward the bridge of my nose.

'My heart beats in my ears...' I begin to explain looking down at my hands locked together on my lap and twiddling my thumbs round and round. 'It gets louder and louder until the noise is unbearable – that's when I wake up.'

Manny blinks - he knows intuitively I've missed out half of the nightmare, but it's important I conceal it if I can.

I move my face away from him so I don't catch his eye. 'There's no way I can sleep after that.'

'And...' he finally says, shuffling his feet round until he finds my eyes again.

'And what?'

'Before the beating heart?'

'Manny, do we have to do this?'

'I'm only trying to help, Becks.' He sits back - I've offended him now. Manny hates it when I shut him out, it's as if I'm throwing his kindness back in his face.

I give a deep sigh.

The secret's over now, I guess I've done well keeping it from him for this long. 'It's about Pa.'

Manny pulls up a chair for himself opposite me and resumes his sympathetic posture. He won't say anything else until I've told him everything.

'Every nightmare begins with Pa being carried into our cottage screaming in agony followed by a confusion of voices.' I pause as the sounds from the dream echo around my mind, but I quickly continue in order to cover my fear, although I know Manny's already become aware of it. 'A crowd of faceless bodies block my view so I can't see Pa, or reach him... that's when the panic starts and the heart-beat begins in my ears.'

Manny blinks twice and watches me thoughtfully.

'That's it.' I shrug my shoulders.

'Have you been home yet?' he asks.

'I didn't know I was allowed.'

'Beck's, half-days are given once a month – you're owed at least two.'

'No one told me.'

'Go home,' he says leaning forward and resting his elbows on his knees. 'Visit your family and you'll see your pa is fine – singing and dancing probably.' He smiles light-heartedly which normally would have eased my mind immediately. But his cheery face soon disappears when he sees I'm not smiling in return. 'What... what's the matter?'

The problem is Lucy's comment about Manny being her miracle still bothers me. You see, Manny's a man of many talents and as I've already said, if there's a problem he'll find the solution or die trying. My issue is that there's absolutely nothing he can do to change Pa's condition – nothing - but Manny wouldn't accept this. He'd go on and on making the reality even more heart breaking than it already is. Maybe I'm an awful friend for keeping such a huge part of my life secret, but I did it for the best.

I twist my face even further away from his, trying not to catch a glimpse of those soft, dark emerald eyes.

'What is it?'

'Nothing.' I swallow and look right at Manny in an attempt to convince him nothing is wrong. 'You're right, I'm sure Pa's fine.'

Manny leans back in his chair, silently folding his arms.

'I think I'll go back to bed.' I try to ignore his eyes trailing me across the kitchen and when my hand twists the handle and the latch clicks, I think I've gotten away with it.

'What's wrong with your pa, Becks?'

The question floats through the air as I hover in the doorway, my back turned towards him – he's not going to let this go.

Slowly I spin round in the darkness. 'Manny,' I whisper. 'You don't need to know.'

He stands and comes towards me. 'But I want to know... please, let me help.'

'Manny, you can't change it.'

'What's wrong with your pa?' he asks again his voice so low and calming I can feel tears threatening to surface as my thoughts clash together. Everything within me is screaming to answer him and I'm longing for the comfort that I know he brings, to hear words flow from his mouth that tell me it's all going to be all right. But how can I tell him, when I know what the results will be? Manny cannot perform the impossible and the slightest hint of Pa's suffering will send him off on a lifelong journey that will only result in failure.

I close my eyes and allow a tear to roll down my cheek. 'He's paralysed – my pa cannot walk.'

The news has upset Manny and he's temporarily stunned into silence.

'For how long?' he eventually asks coming back to reality.

'A few months, there was an accident in the fields and he's

never recovered.'

'I'm sorry.' He shakes his mop of curly hair. 'Your ma, is she working?'

'No, that's why I'm here.'

'They're surviving on your income?'

'Not entirely, my sister makes buttons, my brother works on the farm.'

He eyes me suspiciously knowing I've left out some crucial details. 'How old are they?'

I breathe out in frustration. He's doing exactly what I predicated, draining me of every possible detail in order to find a solution. 'Nine and seven.' I look away as his face drops.

'They're earning a pittance.' He shakes his head furiously. 'That's not fair.'

'Life's not fair, Manny, have you not worked that one out yet?' The colour has heightened in his cheeks and I can tell what I've revealed about Pa has troubled him.

'Tell me about the accident?'

'Manny, it's late.'

'But we won't get to speak in the morning, you know what it's like, I'll be preparing the horses and you'll be on your hands and knees scrubbing something or other.'

'We'll find the time.'

'You must tell me now, Becks.' He begins pacing up and down in agitation. 'I won't settle all day if you don't.'

It's true, he wouldn't.

This is the other side to Manny, as much as his presence brings a calmness and he teases the truth out of me with his silence, when something really hits a nerve, he becomes increasingly restless.

'It happened in one of the barns,' I say watching him stride the length of the table and back again. 'A small child, who had been hired along with Daniel to pick up the leftover wheat, had climbed the ladder leaning against the first floor of the barn, but he lost his balance and found himself dangling over the side.' Manny pauses his pacing and sits down in the chair with his head in his hands, he doesn't tell me to stop so I continue. 'Pa saw what was happening and he saved the child, but for some unknown reason Pa lost his footing and fell over the ledge to the ground.' I close my eyes as I remember. 'He was brought home to us in agony lying on a plank of wood—' I can't say anymore, the screams of the nightmare returning to my ears.

Manny lifts his head out of his hands and looks up. 'You're worried about how your family are coping without you at home, you need to visit them and put your mind at rest, otherwise I'm afraid to say the nightmare is here to stay.'

'You know Mrs Langley won't let me go, if she can deny me a half-day off, she will.'

'Try.'

I tilt my head and wrinkle up my nose, dubious anything I could say will persuade the housekeeper to agree. If she wanted me to have a half-day off, she would have told me I was eligible to have one in the first place. 'Manny, she hates me – she won't let me.'

'Please, try.' His earnest gaze is back, and I'm trapped in his dark green eyes.

'Oh... on your head be it, Emmanuel Smith.'

His eyes soften and he smiles. 'All right, on my head be it.'

'So,' I say swiftly changing the conversation. 'You've squeezed the truth out of me, what are you doing up at two in the morning?'

'Me?' He sits back in the chair and stretches out his arms, yawning as he does so. 'I heard the horses stir and went to check they were all right.'

'You heard the horses all the way up from the attic?'

'It's possible when the wind blows, and my hearing is tuned into them.'

'Were they alright?'

'They were fine, must have been a noise that startled one of them, it is particularly windy out there. Well...' He stands up rubbing his hands together. 'I don't know about you, but I'm heading off to catch a bit more sleep, are you coming?'

I didn't think I'd get anymore sleep, but suddenly I'm awake again. This time there is no rain and the clouds have gone, allowing the moon to shine across the wooden floor. I groan and rub my eyes as the dim sound of the grandfather clock on the first-floor finishes chiming five. The extra two hours of sleep haven't benefitted me at all, and I've woken with a heavy head, feeling drained.

When all my morning chores have been completed, I join the rest of the staff for breakfast.

'You asked yet?' whispers Manny in my ear as he rounds the table to sit opposite.

I don't have chance to answer before Hetty grins widely at me and passes along a bowl full of steaming hot gruel. She taps her hands together twice and I look to Manny for a translation.

'She hopes you enjoy your meal,' he says interpreting.

I smile at Hetty and take my fingers, extending them and tapping my chin once. 'Thank you.' I haven't learned many signs yet but interacting with Hetty brings me an unexplainable joy and my weariness begins to lift a little. I'm reminded of Mr Baker every time I see her. Manny never told me what happened to the man, but I have no need to worry because Manny is the most caring person I've ever met and leaving the poor deaf and dumb man in his hands was the best place he could have been left.

'Raining again?' I ask Manny seeing his mid-length curls are wet and he smells of a mixture of damp and horses. You'd think the smell would be off-putting, but it's becoming strangely comforting.

'Started as I came across the yard, so...' He leans across the table and lowers his voice. 'Have you asked yet?'

My face twists with uncertainty. 'I don't know if it's a good idea.'

'Why not? You're owed two half-days.'

'I feel like I'm taking liberties.'

'How?' He frowns as Kitty sits down silently next to me with her own bowl of gruel. 'You need to ask.'

'What are you whispering about Manny?' asks Kitty fluttering her eyes coyly.

Manny pulls his attention away from me and onto the cup in front of him. 'Nothing of importance.' He sips his hot milk.

'You look worn out, Rebekah,' comments the kitchen maid, though she isn't bothered about my welfare. I can't prove she set me up for a fall when I came face to face with Lady Belmont, but I've never trusted her since, and she's given me no reason to think differently. True to her word we've never been friends and I don't think we ever will be.

'I didn't sleep well,' I mumble into my bowl.

'Don't think you can get away with being idle today.'

'Why would I think that?' I scoop up a spoonful of creamy oats.

'I know what folk like you are like.'

'Folk like me?'

Kitty casts her eyes down the table to see Mrs Langley looking our way and she lowers her tone, leaning towards my ear. 'Well, you were caught sitting down from your very first day.'

'If I recall correctly,' I say in an equally hushed voice and staring straight ahead. 'That's because you wouldn't give me any work to do.'

I sense the fixed gaze of the housekeeper's eyes upon us and Kitty laughs suddenly as if I've told an amusing joke. 'Come now, Rebekah. Let us put the past behind us... Oh Manny.' She refocuses her attention across the table to where he is sitting. 'Will you give me a helping hand?'

'What with?' he asks frowning.

'There's a sack of potatoes waiting to come into the kitchen and a girl like me can't lift them.' She pouts her lower lip towards him.

'I'll be in the stables all morning – ask Matthew.'

'Oh no, those footmen aren't as strong as you.'

Lifting my eyes up from my bowl I see Manny squirming in

his chair – he's going to give in to her. It's funny, Manny is one of the most helpful people I know, but he's always kept his distance from Kitty, although to be honest, I don't blame him.

'I'd much prefer your help,' Kitty continues with her pout. 'I'll meet you in the yard, you can do it on your way back to the stables.' Passing her bowl down the table to Hetty she leaves the kitchen, knowing Manny is too good natured not to follow.

She's not mistaken in her judgment.

'Make sure you ask,' Manny whispers in my ear before following the kitchen maid out of the room.

Chapter Nine

'Ask about what?' whispers Lucy who has been sitting silently next to me and is scraping up the last traces of oats in her bowl.

'Manny wants me to ask Mrs Langley for a half-day off.'

'I wouldn't recommend it,' squeaks Lucy, her eyes wide and full of warning. 'Mrs Langley won't allow it.'

'I won't allow what?'

Immediately our chairs scrape backwards, and we stand to attention. Lucy's leg is trembling because of the sudden brusque words of the housekeeper, even though thanks to my presence, she hasn't been beaten for over a month.

We remain silent and Lucy stares intently down at her feet.

'What won't I allow?' asks Mrs Langley again and neither of us speaks. 'Spit it out, I haven't got all day.'

'Well, I... I've been told staff get half a day off every month.'

Mrs Langley looks appalled. 'I hope I am misunderstanding your meaning, Barnes. Are you requesting time off?'

'I haven't seen or heard from my family for over two months, I'd like to visit them and see they're all right,' I speak boldly, trying to maintain eye contact, but fail at the final word and cast my eyes away to the range where Hetty is working.

'How dare you ask for such thing?' Mrs Langley says pronouncing each word slowly and clearly. 'You are a lazy, insolent girl.' She lunges forward and for a moment I think she's going to slap me across the face, but she composes herself at the final second and speaks from the corners of her closed mouth instead. 'Get back to work.'

I don't dare ask again.

With great speed and urgency, I push Lucy out of the kitchen for her own protection. We're half-way out of the door when I hear the sound of my name being called, 'Rebekah, where's Rebekah?' Lucy hesitates and turns her head to look back into the room, but with a final push she's in the yard, safe from the housekeeper's anger. I close the door behind her.

'Your ladyship,' coos Mrs Langley with a curtsy.

'I need Rebekah...' Her ladyship scans the room and spies me at the door. 'Ah, Rebekah—'

'If you please, ma'am,' inserts the housekeeper. 'I can get Kitty to—'

'No,' her ladyship says bluntly and walks straight past Mrs Langley without a second glance. 'Diamonds or pearls?'

Two sparkling necklaces dangle in front of my face.

'Oh...' My eyes dart fleetingly towards Mrs Langley, who I see is observing me closely, and my cheeks slowly begin to burn - it's the first time I've seen Lady Belmont since my unfortunate encounter in the entrance hall almost two months ago.

'If I can suggest Kitty, your ladyship, she has a very good eye.'

'Mrs Langley,' snaps Lady Belmont turning her tall and commanding figure towards the housekeeper. 'If I wanted Kitty, I would have asked for her.'

'I do apologise,' says Mrs Langley slightly bent over. 'But Rebekah is only the maid of all work.'

Lady Belmont raises her nose high with indignation. 'Mrs Langley, have you provided me with a lady's maid who can give me advice?'

'No, your ladyship, though I'm sure you are aware we haven't had any interest in the post - I know you have had to suffer many weeks of waiting, but Kitty—'

'I want to hear no more about that useless girl. Let me make this clear to you, until you provide me with someone suitable, I will ask who I like for advice on my attire.' She pauses as Mrs Langley's mouth falls slightly open. 'You may go now, Mrs Langley.'

'Yes, your ladyship.' The housekeeper cowers into a low curtsy and backs out of the kitchen.

'Meddling woman,' her ladyship mutters under her breath before turning her attention back to me. 'So…' Lady Belmont smiles. 'This is my outfit.' She runs a hand down a beautifully stitched, long-sleeved gown, the colour of buttercups and the sleeves of which are covered in a delicate cream lace. 'I'd appreciate your opinion since my daughter is away and the gentlemen are of no help whatsoever in fashionable matters. Kitty is useless, though Mrs Langley keeps thrusting her upon me.' She then completes her speech by turning in an elegant circle. 'I'd like to know what you think.'

'I-I don't know, ma'am.'

'But I think you do… don't make me ask Kitty, not after the whip-lashing I've given Mrs Langley - how humiliating would that be.' She fiddles with the pearls in her hands. 'I haven't forgotten your very favourable advice about the gloves with the lilac buttons… and to think I nearly wore a different pair and would have missed out on so many compliments from my acquaintances.' She looks at me enquiringly, but I keep silent, not wanting to step above my station. 'I value your opinion, Rebekah.'

'Well, ma'am…' I chew my lip in thought. 'If you really desire that I give a judgement…'

'Yes, I do.'

'I'd say… the pearls.'

'Interesting,' says Lady Belmont studying the jewels in her hand. 'Why is that?'

'The cream colour matches the yellow of the dress.'

'Yes…' She considers my assessment and holds the pearls against her dress. 'I think you're right. Thank you, Rebekah.'

'My pleasure, ma'am.' She looks at me thoughtfully, pauses and then smiles before leaving the kitchen.

'I can't believe she said no.'

'I don't know why you're so shocked, I told you she wouldn't agree.' The sun is setting behind me as I unpin a bed sheet from the hedges surrounding the stables.

'Don't...' Manny says watching me with his arms folded, leaning back against the wooden doorframe.

'What?'

'I can see you giving me that look.'

'I don't know what you're referring to,' I try to say in all innocence, but can't hide the glint in my eye.

'You know perfectly well which look I mean, the one that gleefully basks in being right.'

I laugh at him – he doesn't like being wrong.

The linen in my hands is still damp as I fold it into the basket. Now it's December I know it will never fully dry outside, and there are probably loads of better places I could hang it, but why would I want to seek them out? Out here, far enough away from watchful eyes, I can see Manny.

'Anyway, I've been thinking about that...' He pushes himself away from the stable door...

This is it. I'm actually surprised it's taken him most of the day to present me with the solution to the problem I laid before him with in the early hours of the morning. I throw a peg into the basket, waiting to hear what far-fetched unrealistic suggestion he has to get Pa walking again.

'You said you haven't heard from your family since you arrived...'

'I did.'

'Then why don't you write to them - I'll pay?'

'Thanks, but I'm sure if something's wrong they'll let me know.' I fold another sheet and place it in the basket with the others.

'I'm serious, at least let them know *you* are well, they're probably worrying about you as much as you're worrying about them.'

'Manny, it's fine.' I move along the hedge and remove the final damp bed sheet.

'I said I'd pay, Becks. Don't worry about writing more than

one sheet, I'll pay the double fee.'

'It's not about the money, Manny.'

'Then what is it?'

I heave a frustrated sigh - he really needs to learn to let things go when he's not getting his own way.

'What was that?' he asks recoiling.

'What?'

'This…' He mimics by frustrated puff of breath. 'I've irritated you, haven't I?'

'Oh Manny, please drop it.'

'Why won't you write a letter?'

'You're really infuriating when you don't get your way, did you know that?' I pick up the woven basket full of wet linen and start moving away.

'Where are you going?'

'Back to the house before I'm caught talking to you out here.'

He follows alongside me. 'That's never bothered you before. Please, tell me why you won't send a letter?'

His voice sounds so pathetic that I have to walk a little faster so I'm not tempted to stop and look into his equally pathetic face, otherwise I'll be trapped and will reveal too much… I know I will.

'Becks!' he shouts as I hurry ahead. 'Rebekah!'

I walk a little further.

He calls again. 'Becks!'

Not being able to withstand any more of his plaintive cries, I swivel on my heels and allow him to catch up. 'Because, Manny, I can't do it.'

'I don't understand, did you have a disagreement with them before leaving home?'

'No, Manny, please listen, I'm telling you, I am not able to do it.'

His forehead wrinkles in confusion as the golden glow of the setting sun reflects on top of his curly mop of hair – I know he still hasn't understood.

'Manny, I don't know how to write.'

'You can't write?' he says scrunching up his face as he tries to comprehend my disclosure.

'Ma's the only one who can read and write in our family.'

He lets out a single bewildered exclamation, shaking his head slightly from side to side. 'You're full of revelations today, first your pa's accident and now this... is there anything else you're not telling me?' He folds his arms lightly across his chest, but I know he's not cross because of the humorous twinkle in his eye.

'It's not really a revelation, many people of our class don't read or write, it's not unusual.'

'I know that, but...' He's processing something and pauses as he deliberates. 'What are your prospects?'

'I have none.' I stare at him unblinkingly - it's a simple fact I've known for a long time.

'You don't seem too disappointed.'

'Where has being able to read and write taken you?' I asked turning the attention away from myself. 'You've really gone far - the groom at Belmont Park.'

'I'm happy with my position, besides I'm talking about you... you're clever, Becks.'

'Whether I have the intelligence of a genius or not, the ability to read and write won't change anything for me. The reality is, as well you know, there's a limit to how far someone from our class can reach. I've risen as high as I am able. This is all life has for me.'

'I don't believe it,' Manny says arching his head closer to make his point.

'Those poor beggars I used to help with Pa, the ones I told you about, that's all I'll amount to,' I say before adding sadly, 'Though even now that's gone.'

'You can't truly believe that?'

'I do.'

'There's more to life than this, Becks.'

'All right.' I place my free hand on my hip leaving the other one free to hold onto the basket. 'Tell me, if there's more, how do I get it?'

The top of his mouth curls up into a smile. 'It starts with a broken heart.'

'What?' I've heard many of Manny's problem-solving solutions, most of which perform the desired effect, but this...?

'A broken heart,' he repeats looking proud with himself for having an answer - even though the answer is complete nonsense.

'Erm, I would have thought a broken heart is something to avoid.'

'Ah, that's where you're wrong,' he says wagging an excited finger in my direction before grinning in self-satisfaction.

'So, are you going to tell me your secret to life, or are you going to stand there looking all smug?'

He laughs. 'The key to living a life of "more" is to discover what breaks your heart, and then you allow that brokenness to transform you, to guide you and direct your innermost desires.'

'Manny, you're really not making any sense.'

'It will make sense in time; all you need to know is that there is a greater purpose for Rebekah Barnes than being a maid of all work.'

'And how do you know that?'

'I just know,' he says slowly and with great emphasis bringing his face even closer to mine.

'You can't say something like that when you've no evidence to support it... Manny?' I've lost him. He's looking away over my shoulder and is not listening. 'Manny...?'

'I know!' He snaps his fingers suddenly. 'I'll teach you how to read and write – that's your first step.'

'No, thanks.' I answer without any consideration for the suggestion and immediately start walking back towards the house.

'Why not?' he whines like a spoilt child who isn't getting what he wants. I shush him, conscious our raised voices might be heard in the kitchen.

'Nobody will hear us, Becks.' He rolls his eyes. 'You haven't even considered it.'

'I don't need to.'

'Imagine where it could take you... there's still an opening for a lady's maid, you know?'

'I can't go from being maid of all work to lady's maid, you know it doesn't work like that. Learning to read and write isn't magically going to make a difference and overturn society's rules.'

'I agree, but it would help.'

'You forget what comes in between - I'm not even a kitchen maid, let alone a house maid, and I have no experience in the area. Anyway,' I turn again to face him resting the basket on my hip. 'You don't know I want a better position, like you, I might be happy with what I have. If I ever wanted to better myself it would be for the benefit of others, and this I know for sure, being a lady's maid isn't going to alleviate the utter devastation of poverty sitting right on our doorstep.'

Manny's eyes soften and for a moment he doesn't speak. 'I understand, you know I do, but I really think you are limiting yourself if you don't try.'

The sound of a shrieking owl awakens me to the darkness that is forming now the sun has disappeared from sight. I shouldn't be here with Manny, not out in the open yard. But I can tell he's got more to say... and I need to hear it. 'How am I limiting myself?' I ask tilting my head with interest.

'You'd give anything to feed the poor again, wouldn't you?'

'Yes, you know I would. I know it didn't transform lives, but it made a difference, even if it was only a small one.'

'I'm sure it did brighten the day of the lives you touched, but...' He looks over my shoulder as if trying to decide upon his next words. '...what you did was too safe.'

'What do you mean?' I ask my skin slightly prickling getting ready to leap to my defence.

'You gave what you had and nothing more, you didn't strive

to offer something greater.'

'I couldn't.'

'Why not?'

I turn away, glancing at the candlelight flicking through the high kitchen windows. 'Poverty doesn't really allow you to strive for greater things.'

'Don't be offended, Becks. All I'm trying to do is make you understand. Someone with a broken heart holds nothing back, they can't be stopped and will do whatever it takes to make a difference for whatever passion has become their driving force. I think you're limiting yourself and making poverty an excuse. Learning to read and write might seem like a pointless exercise to you, and you may think it will achieve nothing, but I can assure you it won't be a waste of time and it will open doors you never thought would be available for you to walk through.'

I open my mouth to speak.

'Wait.' Manny takes a step towards me bending his long neck low to see my eyes. 'Before you yell and tell me how wrong I am, listen.' My hand drops to the side and I reluctantly close my mouth, pressing my lips firmly together and forming a scowl with my eyebrows. 'When I said you need to start with a broken heart, I mean, that sometimes the best things in life come from what weighs us down the most. When we give all we have to help others the burden we carry for them can sometimes hurt, almost as if we are being broken, but out of that brokenness...' He lowers his tone and takes another step closer. '...come things of great beauty. I'm not saying how you used to help those poor beggars was wrong – it was admirable, but I'm saying what if there's more, and by sitting safely in the world you know so well, you'll never impact more than one or two of the people your heart aches for the most.'

I stand silently, not certain if I should scold him for belittling me or admit he might be right. 'I'm sorry, Manny, but I still don't see how I can have anything more than I have now.'

'Don't be so quick to dismiss things, Becks.' His eyes plead with me to consider his words and I have to look away, not being able to withstand their determined gaze.

'You don't need to fix everything,' I whisper.

'I'm only trying to help; I know you're not happy with your life.'

'Many people aren't happy, if I aim for more what is there for me apart from disappointment?'

'Lots of things.'

'All right, name them,' I say darting my face back to his.

'Well, let's start with being lady's maid at Belmont Park.'

'Alright, what else?'

'The very first things that come to mind are... nursery maid, governess, lady's companion.'

I laugh. 'You must be dreaming Manny, that isn't going to happen.'

'I believe it could. These titles will give you a higher position in society and then you can help those you really want to help, there's a lot you can do with wealth and position.'

'Rarely is there an example of someone from our class rising to such heights.' I shake my head, laughing at his delusions - he lives in the land of make-believe sometimes.

A second owl shrieks and I know it's time for me to head back to the safety of the kitchen. With one final plea for me to consider what he's said I leave Manny behind and head across the yard to the back entrance.

A broken heart?

I wouldn't admit it to his face, but what Manny said did make some sort of sense. Ever since I was a child, my spirit has always become restless when I come across someone who is starving and hopeless and I feel... miserable, I really do, because I know deep down there's nothing I can do to stop it. Is this the brokenness Manny is referring too?

Wait a minute...

It suddenly dawns on me. The real reason why Manny has created this ridiculous idea of *wanting* a broken heart. He's trying to fix my life and the poverty my family has fallen into.

It has nothing to do with the people my own heart longs to help. It's a selfish notion to satisfy himself. To prove he can find a solution. Money and position might buy us a better home, but it won't enable Pa to walk and it certainly won't comfort the marginalised.

Emmanuel Smith cannot change the impossible – he never will.

Chapter Ten

'You may go.'

I'm polishing the smooth oak handrails of the grand staircase when Mrs Langley's breath tickles my ear and causes me to flinch.

'I beg your pardon, Mrs Langley, I did not see you there?' The housekeeper purses her lips and glares at me as if I've done something wrong. 'And if I may ask... where am I to go?'

'Your half-day.'

'I don't understand... my half-day, you declined me yesterday?'

'Well, now you may go.' She speaks through clenched teeth as if letting me go for a mere five hours is the most torturous thing she's ever done in her life. 'Am I correct in thinking your parents live on the other side of town?'

'Yes, Mrs Langley.'

'Good - we need bread, lace for Miss Sophia's bonnet and ducks from the butcher, you also need to post this...' Mrs Langley thrusts a sealed wad of paper into my hands. 'and don't forget the tea leaves.' She stalks away without further explanation.

A few moments later Lucy peeps her head around the corner. 'Is she gone?' she whispers to me.

'Yes, she's gone.' I say slightly bewildered by Mrs Langley's sudden about turn.

The tiny maid gives a small sigh of relief and comes fully out of hiding. 'I saw her coming up behind you...' She looks down to her hands and picks at a fingernail. 'I'm sorry, I ran away.'

'Don't worry about that, Lucy.' I wave away the comment. 'Listen to this, I've been granted my half-day off this morning.'

'That's good to hear...' Her ears prick up at the chime of the grandfather clock. 'Seven already - you'd better get going, otherwise you won't have much time left. Leave the polishing to me.' She takes the cloth out my hand.

'I don't understand why Mrs Langley's changed her mind, she was so set against it, it doesn't make sense?'

'Can't you guess?' Lucy squeaks.

'No, should I be able to?'

'You really can't guess?' A pink hue colours her cheeks from her obvious pleasure of the knowledge she holds.

'No, I told you, it really doesn't make sense.'

'It makes sense to *me*.' She gives a knowing little smile.

'What do you mean?'

'Looks like I have to share my miracle.' Lucy says no more and begins polishing the handrail, smiling happily into the shining wax-covered wood.

'Manny?' An icy wind blows straight through my shawl as I pop my head round the stable door.

'What are you doing here?' Manny's head appears from behind a horse smiling in obvious pleasure at seeing me.

'It's nice to see you working for a change,' I observe with a mischievous grin.

'What a cheek!' he exclaims standing up with a brush strapped to his hand.

'You do spend an awful lot of time warming your hands by the fire.'

'I'll have you know it's cold in the stables.' His mock offended posture melts away into a gentle laugh. 'What are you doing here?' His hand rests on the horse's neck and he pats the animal gently.

'I wanted to say thank you.'

'Thank you?' He scratches his head pretending not to understand.

'I know it was you, Manny.'

'I don't know what you are talking about?' he says with a

half-smile spreading slowly across his face - he's a bad liar.

'How did you do it?'

Manny rounds the horse and strokes its long stripy white nose. 'I have my ways.'

'No, really, how did you do it?'

His attention is fixed on the horse and I can tell he's deciding whether he should reveal his secret to me or keep it hidden away. 'I sacrificed my own half-day... my ma won't be happy.'

'Why would Mrs Langley accept that, you don't work in the house, it's not an equal exchange?'

'I don't know why, but it worked.' The horse nods its head in agitation and Manny starts to brush down its short, soft coat, muttering something into its ear to calm it down. As I watch him, I know there's something else he's not telling me.

'Anyway... I want to say I appreciate it.'

'No problem.' He turns and smiles. 'I wouldn't waste it all in the stables.'

It takes me a moment to realise what he's talking about. 'Oh, yes... you're right.' I step backwards, nearly bumping into the door frame.

'And don't be late,' he calls after me.

'I'll leave in plenty of time, of course Mrs Langley couldn't let you claim a total victory.'

'What do you mean?'

'I've a few errands to run on the way back.'

Manny's face instantly distorts in anger and furrows appear across his forehead. However, I'm not going to hang around to hear his complaints about the housekeeper, he can tell me later. Lifting a hand, I wave and hurry away.

It's a long walk from Belmont Park and I've walked at quite a pace, so much so that by the time I reach the brow of the hill where our little cottage sits, I have to pause to catch my breath. But there it is, one of three farm labourers' cottages – I'm home.

The lock turns in the door as I apprehensively twist the

brass knob, hoping and praying things haven't become worse since I've been away. I haven't heard anything from Mary, so it is possible my wages have helped significantly, a lack of communication doesn't necessarily mean anything disastrous has happened.

I'm greeted by an onslaught of chaos.

Henry is wailing in Mary's arms. Tommy is piggybacking Georgie around in circles. Maggie is chasing wildly from behind screaming in anger. Georgie squeals in glee. Daniel is sitting in a chair by the fire with a protruding bottom lip. His leg is propped up on the wobbly stool. I look around the sparsely furnished room – Ma is nowhere to be seen... And Pa? Presumably he's lying prostrate somewhere in the shadows.

'Mary!' I shout above the noise in order to be noticed. My nine-year-old sister spins and her eyes brim with tears the moment she sees my face. No words form on her lips and she simply casts wide overwrought eyes upon my own. Even though the noise continues around us, I can't take my focus off her and further speech escapes me. Living in the relative comfort of Belmont Park, I've completely forgotten how bad things really are. Suddenly Tommy barges into me and breaks my trance. 'Tommy!' I yell taking charge. 'Put Georgie down.' He does so immediately.

'Beck-beck!' Georgie grins in delight clapping his hands together.

'Tell Tommy it was *my* turn to carry Georgie on *my* back,' demands Maggie stomping her feet.

'Don't bring me into the argument,' I say sternly and Maggie forlornly stares at the ground.

I take a glance at the table - it's empty. From the chaos I entered into I don't suppose breakfast has even been made, let alone eaten. 'Tommy, have you eaten breakfast?'

'No, Becks, nobody has.'

I look to Mary who is still trying to comfort the baby.

'Right, Tommy, I want you to take Georgie.'

'That's not fair!' starts Maggie again, but I glare at her and she becomes quiet, lowering her bottom lip.

I remove a crying Henry from Mary and pass him to Maggie. 'Here, take the baby. It's a mild day, though slightly chilly, grab a piece of sacking to sit on and a blanket to wrap around you and get some fresh air... don't go far mind.'

'Yes, Rebekah,' the twins both say demurely as I walk across to the forgotten fireplace and throw a few logs onto the fire which is slowly burning down to cinders. After they've left, I turn back to Mary.

'Oh Rebekah.' Her lip wobbles. 'It's all so awful.'

'What's awful?' I speak softly, coming across to take her hand. 'Tell me.'

'I don't even know where to start.'

'How about telling me when you all last ate?'

She doesn't speak and looks to the floor.

'Mary?'

'Last night,' she whispers.

'And what was it?'

'Potato stew.'

'How thin?'

She lifts her face and chews her lip. 'You'd be lucky to find a potato in it.'

'What else did you eat yesterday?' I feel like Manny, trying to prise out every detail possible so I can properly evaluate the situation.

She looks to the floor again. 'Nothing.'

'Oh, Mary.' I squeeze both her hands in mine. 'What's happened... aren't my wages enough?'

'Not always, there's still a big shortfall between what you earn and what Pa brought in from the fields.'

'But it should stretch if you're careful.'

'Danny and Tommy are always hungry, whatever we eat is not enough. Without Pa's wage it's a struggle, we still have eight mouths to feed and the price of bread is not cheap.' She sounds so grown-up, as if she's speaking about her own children and not her brothers and sister.

I close my eyes feeling distressed. 'What about Daniel's contribution, that must help make up some of the shortfall?'

'Daniel sprained his ankle, he can't work.'

I look to Daniel and move across to him. 'Is it definitely a sprain?' I ask Mary sitting on the floor and taking hold of the boy's leg.

'Doesn't matter, Becks,' says Daniel moodily. 'Whatever's the matter with it I can't work.'

'Stick your bottom lip back in Daniel Barnes,' I scold and he obeys immediately, though the scowl stays on his face. I carefully take his foot and try to turn it in a slow circle, he winces slightly, but doesn't stop me. I'm under the impression not much discipline has gone on in my absence - Pa would never have allowed such sulking or rowdy behaviour to happen under his roof when he was fit and well.

'I think it's a sprain too,' I say in assessment. 'Did Ma look at it?'

Mary doesn't answer.

'Mary, did Ma look at it?' Again, there's no answer and I twist round on my knee to face her. 'Did Ma look at Daniel's ankle?'

'No.' Mary looks to the ground.

'Why not?' My forehead furrows in a light frown. 'Ma knows more than anybody.'

'She's not home much at the moment.'

'What do you mean?'

'We got in this row not long after you left.' She circles the floor with her foot.

'You got into a row?' I don't believe this of my quiet softly spoken little sister.

'Well… Ma and Pa did, I got caught in the middle. The problem is I can't make buttons anymore.'

My forehead furrows even deeper. 'Why not?'

'Ma doesn't…' Her eyes dart to the door.

'She's not here, Mary. Ma can't hear you.'

She looks one more time to the door, just to make sure we're alone, before focusing her tired eyes back on me. 'After you left she started getting these headaches, so I had to look after the children all the time and do the cooking... the buttons had to be left.'

'Is she ill?'

'I – I don't think so. When Daniel came home hobbling along on one foot, she blew a fuse and started spending most of her time out of the house, it got worse when Tommy—' Mary falters.

'When Tommy what?'

'Don't blame him Rebekah, it wasn't his fault.'

'What wasn't his fault?'

'He got caught stealing food from Mr Allen's.'

I close my eyes and I tip my head back slightly – could anything else go wrong?

'We had no money for bread,' continues Mary. 'Henry and Georgie were crying with hunger and we had nothing to give them... when are your next wages?' she asks anxiously chewing her lip.

Guilt hits the pit of my stomach. Here I am living the life of luxury up at Belmont Park with food to feed an army, a bed I don't have to share and candles to light the way when darkness falls. Four miles away, however, is my own family teetering on the edge of starvation, sleeping on a cold hard floor, with nothing to burn on the fire but a few skimpy twigs they find in the woods. I look away, not wanting to see my sister's hallow cheeks. 'Tomorrow - I'll send them straight away... How's Pa?' I ask fearing the answer.

'He has good days and bad days.'

After all these weeks I would have thought the burning sensation wouldn't be as prevalent. 'Is the pain still bothering him?'

'No, it's not the pain.'

I immediately turn my focus back to Mary and become locked in her desperate eyes again. I can't bring myself to ask how much Pa is really suffering. I used to sit for hours by his side, trying to distract his troubled mind from his fate. Who has sat with him since my absence? I fear the answer is - nobody.

'Why don't you start on breakfast whilst the children are occupied,' I suggest with the cheeriest tone I can muster. 'Have you got anything to give them?' Mary nods slowly in a way that reminds me so much of Lucy. How can I help her bear the burden upon her shoulders, like I would protect the tiny maid from Mrs Langley's sharp words and cruel blows? If there was a way I could carry the weight resting upon her, I would. But I know I can't, because if I was here then we would have no money at all and we'd all starve together.

I leave Mary and enter into the shadows. 'Pa...' I whisper.

'Rebekah?'

'Yes, it's me.' Sitting down on his bed I take his hand in mine. 'How are you?'

'Maybe it's best we don't answer that one in too much detail.' He tries to sit up and winces and I plump the pillow behind his back as if I've never been away.

'Are there any changes?' I ask in hope that some feeling has returned to his legs.

'Do you think I'd still be lying here if there were?' My lips press together not knowing what to say and he squeezes my hand. 'How's Belmont Park?'

'It's... different.' I stand up and walk round the bed, tucking in the edges of the blanket, sensing his eyes watching me as I do so.

'Helped anybody in the gutter recently?' he asks with a slight chuckle.

I tuck in the final corner and straighten my bent figure. 'You told me to stop.'

'Why would you listen to an old man like me?'

'That part of my life is over now, you were right to tell me to end it.'

'No, Becks, I was wrong to ask you to stop.'

I don't answer him. What is there to say? It's over.

'I remember when you were little.' He smiles warmly at a

returning memory and I notice the wrinkles in the corner of his eyes are deeper than they used to be. 'You used to chase butterflies; do you remember?'

'You said I could catch them...I never did.'

'But it kept you busy and out of mischief.'

'You should tell Tommy to go catch a few, sounds like he needs keeping out of mischief.'

Pa chuckles. 'You weren't much better, always wandering off and finding someone who needed help.' He grabs my hand again and looks at me seriously. 'You shouldn't ever stop chasing, Becks.'

'What, after the butterflies?' I shake my head in amusement, ignoring the plea in his voice. 'I grew out of that a long time ago, Pa... probably when I realised it wasn't possible to catch one without a net.' I poke him lightly in the arm and hope he changes the conversation.

'That's not what I meant.' He looks at me with his soft chestnut eyes searching my face to see if I'm listening. 'Your heart is full of compassion, it's part of who you are. Please, don't ever stop chasing after who you are, Becks. I know if you don't help others you'll soon fade away into nothing, being a maid of all work is not enough for you, not when you have a God-given gift burning away inside of you waiting to be used. There are people who will remain untouched by human kindness if you don't go to them. Just look at Mr Baker, no one else came to his rescue, his only ray of light was you. Now, I know your ma has sent you off to Belmont Park, but if you put your mind to it, you'll find a new way of helping the people who cross your path. I stand by my words when I told you not to go out alone to feed those poor people, it wasn't safe for you. But please, find some way to overcome the circumstances blocking your way, otherwise I'm afraid you'll always feel unsatisfied with your lot in life and your desire to serve will be lost.'

You're limiting yourself and making poverty an excuse.

Pa's words are so reminiscent of Manny's that I don't realise my mouth is hanging half open. I always thought poverty was something that wrapped its thin bony arms around you and that when it had you in its grasp you could never get away. Had I spent too much time with poor Mrs Harris on my charitable rounds, whose wisdom for fighting poverty was – don't bother, it always wins? Now even Pa is urging me to push aside the barriers I face and search for a new way to serve others.

'How's Ma?' I ask feeling uncomfortable discussing something I'm yet to understand myself.

'Not well.'

'Mary said she's had headaches, is she ill?'

'No.' Pa's mouth is set straight and he says no more.

'Mary's doing the best she can, but she's nine years old and can't possibly raise five children alone – she needs Ma.'

'I know.'

'You've got to talk to her.'

'She wouldn't listen to me.'

'You've got to try.'

'I've not seen your ma this bad before, Becks. Talking won't work.'

'You can't give up and watch your family suffer,' I say suddenly frustrated. 'If Ma's not going to help Mary in the home, she could at least get a job and help out financially. If she's going to absent herself from the house anyway, she might as well make it count.'

'Your Ma won't work, she's too proud.'

'She's no more important than the rest of us... besides she used to make buttons.'

'Yes, but she could make them out of sight.'

'What does it matter if people see her working?' I stand and pace to the end of the bed.

'It doesn't matter, the main thing is our buttons won't bring us out of poverty and your ma knows it, the only thing that will help is to get a position out in the open and her sense of propriety won't allow it.'

'I've never understood Ma's need to hide herself away, who does she think is watching?'

'It's not for you to understand.'

'It is when our family is suffering because of it.'

There are things about Ma's past that Pa keeps under lock and key. Maybe he worries I'll think less of her, but truth be told I couldn't think any less of her than I do right now.

'Forget about your ma, she'll come round and start pulling her weight again.'

'Fine.' I come back and sit on the edge of the bed. 'I'll forget about Ma, but I won't forget about you. I know you can't physically help, but you could support us in other ways... Mary needs it.'

He doesn't reply.

'Where does Ma go anyway?' I ask knowing I won't get a response to my previous comment.

'I don't know, Becks.' He rubs a hand over his tired eyes.

'Don't you care?'

He sighs. 'It's not that I don't care, Becks. But your ma gave up on us a long time before the accident.'

'Gave up on *us*?'

'Well, to be more correct, she gave up on me.' He closes his eyes and moves his hand to rub his forehead.

'Pa?'

'I'm getting tired, Rebekah.'

I want to push him further, but I can see he's not looking too well. 'Promise me you will help Mary, otherwise I won't be able to leave you like this.'

'You're going to have to.'

'Pa...' I study his face and notice how much thinner he has become.

'You will go back,' he orders in a low, gentle tone. 'We need your money, otherwise we will all die of starvation.'

The front door swings open and Maggie comes in with Georgie crying by her side.

'He's scraped his knee,' explains Maggie. 'Tommy was swinging him around.'

I clean George's cut and find an old rag to wrap around the

boy's chubby knee. Then, after helping Mary feed the children and scolding Daniel several times for sulking, I know the time has come for me to leave because the sun is full in the sky and I probably should have been back at Belmont Park an hour ago. With an aching heart I lean to kiss Pa on the cheek and bid farewell to Mary at the door. I've still to run the errands for Mrs Langley on the way back and if the housekeeper discovers my lateness, I'll never be allowed a half-day again.

Walking at a brisk pace, I begin the trek back up the hill, and reaching the bend that will hide our cottage from view, I almost bump into a woman as I hurriedly walk round the corner. 'Beg your pardon, ma'am,' I say dipping my knees lightly in apology.

'Oh, it's you again,' exclaims the woman in all friendliness. 'Did you get the position at Belmont Park?'

I look up for the first time and I'm surprised to see Mrs Parsons, the woman who had originally advised me about the position at Belmont Park. 'Erm, yes, thank you… I did.'

'I am pleased to hear; I have been thinking about you.'

It strikes me as strange that Mrs Parsons would be thinking about me and the comment makes me feel uneasy, but I've no time to waste and so I wish her good day, bob politely and turn away.

'Have a pleasant day.' I hear her call back and apprehension creeps into my stomach as the voice is replaced by the sound of her footsteps moving away down the hill. It's not often strangers are seen down our little lane, mainly because it leads to nowhere other than farmland.

Before I round the bend completely, I cautiously glance over my shoulder to see Mrs Parsons hovering directly outside of our cottage. Then, as if she sensed I was watching, the woman looks up and waves at me with a bright jolly smile. I don't return the gesture, but head quickly down the lane, so that after two more strides, she is hidden out of sight.

Chapter Eleven

The town is busy when I finally reach it with carriages carrying people from the surrounding areas for Belmont's weekly market. As I push my way through the crowds, I begin the checklist in my head.

Bread – lace for Miss Sophia's bonnet – ducks from the butcher – a letter to post – tea leaves.

Hurriedly, I call at the haberdashers and then at the butchers, working my way through the different items on the list.

'Excuse me, miss.' A small child slips out from amongst the crowds.

'Yes?'

The little boy's face is dirty and one of his cheeks hosts a crescent-shaped scratch running from underneath his eye to the bridge of his nose. 'Can you spare a penny?'

'Where's your ma?' I ask looking around the bustling shoppers.

'Gone.' This could mean any number of things without further explanation.

'Gone where?'

'Dunno, miss.'

I look sadly at the boy. 'Where do you live?'

'Wherever there's dry ground, miss.' He stands with a pair of icy grey eyes staring hopefully up at me and my heart stabs with distress, seeing that this little boy is defenceless and alone.

'What about your pa?'

'Died when I was a baby.' He squints with one eye as the

midday sun shines into his face. 'My brother's gone to ask Mr Greaves for work.'

'He's a good man is Mr Greaves; he'll give you work if he has any. How old is your brother?'

'Ten, miss.' My heart sinks, even if the tenant farmer employed his brother for some odd out of season job, the pay would be terrible and certainly wouldn't be enough to feed them both.

The sound of a loud rumbling in the boy's stomach meets my ears. 'So… can you spare a penny?'

'I am sorry, but I have nothing a spare.' The boy looks crestfallen… have I really got nothing to give him? I mustn't let my own poverty be an excuse. 'However,' Instantly the boy's face brightens. 'I work at Belmont Park, if you and your brother can find your way there, I will see what I can find for you… it won't be money though.'

'Oh, thank you, miss.' The boy hops on one leg. 'Did you say Belmont Park?'

'Yes, don't come until late and make sure you knock on the back door… quietly.'

'Who am I to ask for, miss?'

'Ask for myself – I'm Rebekah.'

The little boy disappears behind a market stalls and I watch him weave in and out of the crowd, hoping I've done the right thing. When I can't see him any longer, I push my anxieties to the side and try to refocus my thoughts: *Bread – lace for Miss Sophia's bonnet – ducks from the butcher – a letter to post – tea leaves.* Mr Allen's doesn't have much of a queue and so, after sending the letter, I wait in line to collect the bread.

'Becks!' Coming out of the bakers, a call from across the high street turns my attention as I'm stuffing a large loaf of bread into the basket. Manny bounds towards me in a pair of grubby breeches and stockings that have seen better days.

'What are you doing here?' I'm surprised to see him, knowing he had sacrificed his own half-day off for me and therefore he should be busy in the stables.

'Blacksmiths.' He waves a handful of horseshoes in the air and crosses the road, waiting first for a carriage to pull away. 'And also to meet you, where have you been, it's gone twelve?'

'I know, I should have been back at Belmont Park at least an hour ago, but things aren't good at home and I needed to help Mary.'

'You need to get a move on,' he says cupping an arm round my back and escorting me further down the high street in the direction of the lane that leads back to Belmont Park. 'Have you finished shopping?' he adds as an afterthought and pauses his long strides. 'I'll walk you home and cover for you with Mrs Langley if need be?'

'Let me check...' My tongue sticks out slightly as I recall the list. 'Bread – lace for Miss Sophia's bonnet – ducks from the butcher – a letter to post and...' I look at Manny. 'And...'

'Don't look at me, I have a memory like a sieve.'

I look at the grocer's behind me, searching my memory. Manny is right, I must get back to Belmont Park and it would be useful to have a strong pair of arms to carry the dead weight ducks sitting in the basket.

'Come on, Becks. Lucy can't hide your absence from Mrs Langley forever.'

The thought of the little maid having to lie on my behalf speeds up my decision. Passing the ducks to Manny I ignore the niggling voice in the back of my mind. I'm certain something's been forgotten, however, between Manny's distraction, the chaos at home and the starving boy, my memory has been rendered useless.

Lord Belmont's carriage is rolling to a halt on the drive as we enter through the gates.

'Goodness, he's home from town early.' Manny pushes the ducks into my hands and starts running ahead, until he realises he's abandoned me. 'Sorry, Becks!' he shouts apologetically and turns around clearly caught between protecting me from Mrs Langley and performing his duties as his lordship's groom.

'I'll be fine, don't worry.' I wave him away and watch as he hurries away to take charge of the horses.

Silently, I lift the lock on the back door and through a tiny crack I see the narrow corridor is empty. Making a dash for it, I push the remainder of the door open and tiptoe quickly into kitchen.

Hetty is cooking at the range when I enter with her back turned towards the room and so I tap her on the shoulder, she smiles and greets me with a warm embrace. Closing my hand and extending my index finger, I brush down my cheek twice. It's our name for Mrs Langley, we simply call her Woman. Hetty shrugs – she doesn't know where the housekeeper is and hope starts to rise within that I might have got away with my tardiness.

I reach up the wall to where my apron is hanging on a hook and lift it down. Whilst tying it round my waist I move quickly towards the door which will lead me out into the yard - but my exit is abruptly halted, when suddenly I come face to face with a freckled-face boy, who brushes straight past me into the kitchen.

'Who are you?' the boy asks, frowning as if I'm the one who's misplaced and doesn't belong. I look to Hetty for an explanation but she already has her back turned and is cooking again at the range.

I watch him suspiciously. 'I'm Rebekah - can I ask who *you* are?'

The boy crunches confidently into an apple he's holding and sits himself on top of the long wooden table in a single jump. 'Gus Langley – I've been looking for you.'

'What for?' I ask noticing a smaller version of the house-keeper's pointed nose on the boy's face.

'Nan said you'd done a runner and I was to go and find you.'

'She gave me a half-day off, I had permission to leave the grounds.'

'That's what they all say.' He crunches into his apple again.

'May I ask why you're here... apart from to look for a person who isn't missing?'

'Ma had a message for Nan... hey, how's Danny?'

'My brother?' I frown – how does Gus Langley know Daniel when I've never set eyes on the boy before?

'That's the one, we all miss him down in the fields.'

'Oh...' I suddenly realise the connection. 'You work for Mr Greaves.'

'Occasionally, when we need money. Is Danny coming back?'

'His ankle's almost healed, I expect him to return next week.'

'Good, good.' The boy jumps down. 'I'll tell Nan you're back.' He walks out of the room chomping on his apple and nearly bumping into Kitty as she enters with a handful of potatoes.

'Watch your step, Kits,' complains the boy before disappearing into the dark corridor.

'You know him?' I ask.

'He's an old neighbour... got them ducks?' Kitty tosses the potatoes into the sink before coming across to rummage through the basket I had left on the table when I returned.

'They're not in there.' I go to the side and pick up the two limp and lifeless ducks.

Kitty pauses over the basket before snatching the birds from my hands. 'I'll start plucking.'

The rest of the day runs smoothly and it looks as if the housekeeper hasn't heard about my lateness, despite what her grandson might have told her. When our chores are finally completed and the family have retired to their beds, we find ourselves sat around the long wooden table. Lucy is sat silently by my side, her little head nodding lightly as sleep tries to overcome her.

'Na-ah.' Hetty shakes her head. She signs to me, lifting both hands together, curling all her fingers and the thumbs round to make two circles.

'Oh yes.' I laugh at my mistake and copy the cook again.

'Yah.' Hetty nods enthusiastically and sticks her thumb in the air - she's teaching me to spell my name.

'Let me try one more time,' I say lifting a single finger to indicate my intention of ending the lesson after this attempt.

Hetty grins and watches my hands as I work my way slowly through the letters. 'R-E...B-E-K...A-H – is that right?' I raise a questioning eyebrow.

Hetty brings one hand into a fist and lowers it at the wrist before quickly lifting it again. ''Yah!' She gives me a great embrace, her large rounded arms squeezing me tightly to her.

Lucy yawns and lays her head flat on the table with her arms supporting it underneath.

'You need to go to bed, Lucy,' I say as the cook releases me.

'I do,' the girl agrees rubbing her eyes. 'Are you coming?'

'I'll be up in a minute.'

Hetty hangs her apron up for the day and follows Lucy out of the room. I'm left behind in the empty kitchen and once their footsteps have faded away the only sound I can hear is the drip of a leak in the roof. Tentatively, I take the candle from the table and make my way down the silent corridor towards the pantry.

The small cupboard-like room is laden with shelves full of cold pies, preserves, loaves of all sizes and butter...everything a man could ever want. I stand frozen to the spot for a second, trying to convince myself that the Belmont's have more food than they could ever desire - they are not going to go hungry from what I'm about to do.

Come on Rebekah, it's now or never.

Wrapping the oldest, smelliest piece of cheese I can see, I begin to load a small basket full of items that won't be missed in the light of day. To this I add a stale chunk of bread, so dry that even Hetty wouldn't consider it fit for the servants, and a couple of battered apples – my shaking hand dare not take anything else.

Coming back into the kitchen I sit at the table with the basket in front of me, my left leg tapping nervously up and down. This is not what Pa meant when he told me to find a different way to help, this isn't overcoming the constraints of poverty and giving all *I* have, this is giving all the Belmont's have, and not much at that. I'm not surrounded by a brokenness of heart that will spur me onto greater things, instead I'm trapped by a guilt that makes me want to cower away in shame, fearing the consequences of losing my position if I'm caught.

A light tap startles me out of my anxious thoughts and I stare wide eyed towards the door leading out into the dark corridor. Calming my nerves, I take the basket and head to the back entrance carrying the candle in my free hand. The creak of the door, as it echoes in the quietness makes me glance warily back over my shoulder.

'Are you Miss Rebekah?' whispers the boy with the crescent-shaped scratch on his cheek, straining his eyes to see through the darkness. 'This is my brother.' He points to a taller boy standing by his side.

'Yes, it's Rebekah.' I hold the basket out towards them, and the little boy takes it. 'I'm sorry I can't help you again.'

'Thank you, miss.' The older boy takes the food from his brother. 'We are very much obliged to you.'

I watch them walk quietly away before locking and bolting the door behind me. My heart is beating rapidly as I swiftly pass the kitchen door and head towards the stairs that will take me safely up to bed.

'I saw you.' The voice catches me off guard and if possible, my heart begins hammering even faster in my chest.

Full of alarm I retrace my steps back into the kitchen. Manny is sitting at the table with his long legs stretched out in front of him and his hands resting gently behind his neck. 'Are those boys your brothers?'

'No, he's a little boy I met in town today, I don't even know his name.' In the flickering candle-light I see Manny arching an accusing eyebrow. 'Don't look at me like that, they were starving.'

'You could lose your job, what were you thinking?' He sits up abruptly in the chair, his relaxed posed quickly forgotten.

'You would have done the same, Manny.'

'You can't feed the poor like you used to, Becks, not unless you want to remain poor yourself.'

'It's late, Manny, I don't need a lecture from you right now.' I turn with the candle in my hand, its flame still burning its way down the wick, and hurry along the corridor with Manny following me.

'What are you doing?' I ask as he follows me up the stairs. All the servants sleep in the attic at Belmont Park, but a permanently locked door divides the male and female quarters in half, the stairs Manny should be taking are on the other side of the house.

'I need you to promise me you'll never do anything so foolish again.'

'Don't worry, I won't.'

'Make sure you don't, otherwise you'll throw everything away.'

'If you're talking about the lady's maid position, I've told you already I don't want it.' We continue up the stairs and I lower my tone as we come closer to the bedrooms.

'Becks, it's the only way you can help the people you care for the most, did you not listen to what I said before?'

'Yes, Manny, I listened.'

'Then what's the problem?'

We've made it to the top of the stairs and I swivel round on him. 'You know what my problem is, you go on about having a broken heart and the evils of living life too safely and yet, I don't see you doing much other than providing his lordship with well-groomed horses.'

'This isn't about me.'

'It's never about you, is it Manny?'

'Why are you getting cross with me?'

'You're putting pressure on me to do something you're not even doing yourself.'

'You don't know what I'm doing, Becks, so don't try to speak of it.'

We've reached the bedroom door and I want to run inside and hide away, but Manny is standing resolutely in front of me and isn't moving anywhere. 'All I know is, if you continue in your current position, you'll never be able to offer the people you care about any more than what they already have. You can always find food to give, but never enough to take away their hunger. If you really wanted to make a difference, you'd want to offer them more.'

The words hit me deep inside – and I know he's right. I couldn't face seeing those poor boys starve, but my tiny offering will be gone by the morning and their stomachs will be empty again before the sun rises – what lasting good have I done for anyone?

I run a hand over my eyes, sleep suddenly taking over my urge to fight. 'Manny, it's late. You need to go otherwise we'll be seen together and both be let go with our reputations in ruins.' I twist the handle of the door to my room and go inside.

'What's that?' Manny pushes out an arm and stops the door closing on him, his eyes are fixed on my bed.

Following his focus, I see he's staring at my little hand stitched doll. My cheeks redden with embarrassment. 'It was a gift.'

'Where'd you get it?' He swallows as if his mouth is becoming dry.

'Oh, it was a long time ago, some lady came into town with a basket full of them for the children... please don't laugh, it's very special to me.'

'Laugh?' He looks shocked by my suggestion. 'Becks, I would never laugh at you.' His eyes soften, but his focus remains on the toy.

I walk over and pick the doll up, stroking the golden hair and smooth cotton dress. 'She's the reason why Pa suggested we start feeding those who were poorer than ourselves.'

'She? You mean the lady, not the doll.' He gives a light laugh, causing one of his cheeks to dimple.

'Yes, the lady - apparently my six-year-old self was extremely distressed to discover no one else was helping these people... when I think about it that lady taught me what it really means to love beyond your own means, not that she was poor, but she didn't have to concern herself with us, yet she chose to do so anyway.'

Manny smiles warmly taking his gaze from the doll and onto me. 'Don't lose it, Becks,' he whispers in a barely audible voice.

'Oh, I keep her hidden under the pillow normally, no one knows the doll's there.'

'That's not what I meant.' He takes a step towards me and takes my hand in his. 'You don't realise your heart is already broken, but only you can decide if you allow it to shatter into a million tiny pieces or bind it back together before the cracks become too heavy to bear the weight.' His mouth curls up into a smile and his eyes meet mine. 'On the other side of heart break great blessings await, not only for you, but for everyone you meet... it's worth the pain, Becks, you'll see.'

Chapter Twelve

'Here she is Mrs Langley.'

I'm greeted by an accusing finger from Kitty as I enter the kitchen the following day. The housekeeper spins round holding an empty tea caddy in her hands.

'What's the meaning of this?' she shouts stepping close enough so I can see the dilated pupils in both of her unblinking eyes. 'I sent you to get the tea yesterday.'

The blood drains out of my face – I knew I'd forgotten something.

'I-I am sorry, Mrs Langley,' is all I can mutter.

'Sorry isn't good enough!' Without warning she stomps down a foot, the heel of her shoe landing with a great thud upon my toe. The pain causes my eyes to water, but I don't cry out because I don't want to encourage her to repeat the action. 'Be gone with you,' she spits. 'And woe betide you if you're not back before his lordship and ladyship request breakfast.'

It feels like my lungs are about to burst open and I puff breathlessly, trying to ease the pain running down my side. It is a huge relief when I reach the lane which will bring me out onto the high street.

Standing outside the grocer's shop the heat generated from the run quickly disappears and I begin to shiver, pulling my thin cotton shawl tighter around my shoulders. It's so bitterly cold I cannot feel my toes, although perhaps numbness is a good thing since it appears to be masking the pain in my throbbing foot. I'm sure the bone isn't broken, but one can never tell, especially since I haven't had time to examine the damage. I clench my toes and wince, transferring my weight onto the opposite leg.

My face presses up against the pane of glass inserted into the front door of the grocers and I begin to tap my pain-free foot impatiently on the cobbles - nobody is inside and I wonder if the shop will ever open. I lean back with a deep sigh... Bread – lace for Miss Sophia's bonnet – ducks from the butcher – a letter to post – tea leaves... the list is still tucked away in the depths of my mind and I feel a stab of frustration at having forgotten what was probably the most important item on the list.

The faint sound of footsteps comes into my ears and through the window I see the grocer has finally come to open the door. He rubs his hands together as white puffs of warm breath leave his mouth and hit the icy morning air.

'It's another bitter one, Miss Barnes,' says Mr Gale standing in the doorway.

'Yes, it is a particularly bad frost,' I acknowledge in agreement thinking about the frozen well I'd had to crack open in the early hours of the morning.

Mr Gale, whose long black beard is flecked with strands of white, looks at me for further comment, but I keep my mouth tightly closed knowing how long and drawn-out conversations with this man can be. It's the reason why the grocer's store always has a queue of people waiting outside the shop, it's not that the produce is better, it's simply because Mr Gale has no shutter for his mouth. This is why I hurried into town, hobbling on what I hope isn't a broken toe, to be his first customer of the day and avoid delay.

I clear my throat and try to be blunt. 'I need tea, Mr Gale - the one his lordship buys.'

'Ah...' He blows into his cold hands, however, remains standing in the doorway. 'The finest leaves in my shop – I only stock them for the Belmonts.'

I smile and keep my mouth closed, refusing to comment further and praying he doesn't start off on a tangent about all the different types of tea leaves, their subtle flavours and the best ways to serve them.

'Erm, if you don't mind Mr Gale, I am in a hurry,' I say trying to encourage him along. 'His lordship has no tea for breakfast – they could wake at any hour.'

If anything was going to shift the grocer, this would. Every shopkeeper in town treats the Belmonts like royalty, if the family want a new exotic tea or an unknown spice, it's provided for them no matter what the cost. Without fail, the comment about his lordship waking up to no tea has the desired effect. Mr Gale sweeps into action and hurries behind his mahogany counter, he wastes no time in scooping up a selection of little black leaves and places them into the container I provide for him. Once the tea is tucked safely inside my basket, I thank the grocer and proceed quickly out of the shop – I will never forget the tea leaves again.

I'm still two miles away from Belmont Park. The limp I've developed is becoming more and more pronounced with every step and the pain is slowing me down at a tremendous rate. I can only hope the Belmonts will eat breakfast late today.

A carriage slows beside me and I courteously step aside to let it pass by, taking the opportunity to catch my breath as I do so. However, to my surprise, the coachman sitting on top calls the horses to halt and a young lady's head pokes out of the window.

'Are you all right there?' she asks.

'Oh, yes...thank you, I am,' I reply a little bewildered by her sudden appearance.

'Have you injured your leg?'

'Only a toe, ma'am.'

'Where are you heading?'

'Belmont Park.'

'We are passing there; can I offer you a lift?'

'I wouldn't want to impose; I will be quite all right.'

The young lady swings open the small door showing the soft red velvet covering on the inside. 'I am not leaving you here... please, I insist.'

I look up and down the lane caught in two minds. I've never desired to travel in a carriage before, but a ride in such transportation would see me arriving back at Belmont Park within half the time it would take me on foot, and under the circumstances it would be foolish of me to decline the offer. I climb inside and offer my thanks.

The young lady, who looks no more than my own age, signals to the coachman to continue and sits back in her seat. Observing me she asks, 'Do you have a name?'

'Rebekah, miss,' I answer politely whilst stifling a rising indignation - what does she think, that I'm nameless because I am poor?

The girl smiles and takes her gloves off one finger at a time. 'My father will not be pleased I have done this.' She laughs childishly, her eyes shining as if she's experiencing some kind of wild adventure.

I feel my eyebrows knit together as the carriage jolts us from side to side and the girl continues, seeing that her statement was lacking in specific details. 'What I mean is, to have one of *you* in our carriage, it's simply not done – Papa will have a fit.' She cups a hand round her mouth and whispers. 'You see, my friend dared me to do it – what a lark!' The girl lets out a high exclamation. 'She said, "Eliza, you simply cannot do anything to defy your father," and I said, "yes, I can, Caroline" - that's the name of my friend - and then Caroline said she'd buy me a new bonnet if I proved her wrong... so here I am, proving her wrong.' She giggles again and nearly falls forward onto me as the wheels rock over a pothole. 'You don't tell a Montague they can't do something, it's not in our nature to fail, and *mon nom signifie la victoire.*' She pauses and looks at me strangely. 'You don't talk much... Oh, I am sorry, it's because you don't understand, not having had an elite education like myself. My name is Eliza *Colletta* Montague - Colletta means one who is victorious... it's French.'

I feel my cheeks burn with rising indignation and set my lips tightly together - I might not have an education, but I'm not a fool. Casting a look out of the little window I see we are nearing the entrance gates of Belmont Park. 'I will walk from here, miss,' I calmly announce. 'Thank you for the lift, I hope it hasn't taken you out of your way.'

'Not at all... I suppose I can set you down here, after all, I have won, Caroline's not to know I didn't drop you directly outside the front doors.' She tilts her head towards the partly opened window. 'Stop please!' she orders the coachman, and the carriage pulls to a halt.

Without a word, I watch the carriage move away, splashing through the puddle-filled lane.

'You made it back, I was getting worried,' calls Manny jogging through the gates. 'Who was that?' he asks seeing the carriage fade away behind the hedgerows.

'Miss Eliza *Colletta* Montague,' I say slowly pronouncing all my letters correctly and precisely as the girl had done and accenting the foreign name. 'Did you know *Colletta* is French? Apparently, I wouldn't know these things because my poverty leaves me with the inability to form a single thought.' I snort with the offence still bubbling through me and march through the gate.

Manny laughs and takes a final look down the lane before chasing after me. 'Becks, you're limping.'

My eyebrows sink deeply into a furrow. 'It's not a surprise, that woman's boots are made out of metal.'

'Let me take a look.'

'No, there isn't time.' I flap his hand away and attempt to shake off my irritation so I can focus on the problem at hand. 'Here...' I shove the basket into Manny's arms. 'Run ahead and pass this to Hetty... are Lord and Lady Belmont awake yet?'

'No, but it won't be long before they are...' He pauses and glances down at my shoe. 'I can examine it quickly.'

I push him away with a light laugh. 'It won't fall off... now go.'

'You're certain you'll be all right?'

'I won't be if that tea doesn't get to the kitchen on time.'

He takes the hint and runs ahead, leaving me to follow slowly behind.

'Do you need a hand?' I look behind to see the heir to the Belmont estate striding confidently in my direction down the drive.

'No, thank you, sir.' I've never spoken to John Belmont before and my cheeks blush rapidly, focusing my attention onto his shiny black boots.

'But you're limping… did you have an accident?'

'No, I…' I stop to reconsider my answer, I can't exactly tell him the truth because if word got back to Mrs Langley there'd be much to pay. 'Erm, yes… I did.'

He laughs softly. 'No, erm, yes?' He raises an eyebrow humorously.

'I'm sorry, I can't tell you how it happened, sir,' I say as my cheeks turn a deeper shade of red.

'You work in the kitchens?'

'I am the maid of all work.'

'Give me your arm,' he says pushing out an elbow towards me. 'I will help you back, you seem to be struggling.'

'Oh no, sir, I cannot do that.' Horrified at the thought of dangling from John Belmont's arm I step back with a wobble and almost topple over in my haste to make the gap between us bigger.

'You are employed by my father and as his son it is my duty to look after your welfare.' He speaks with a superior air, but he isn't being unkind and I believe he genuinely wants to help. He bows slightly and offers me his arm again, holding it straight out in front of me as if I'm a lady he's asking to dance. 'Now I'm afraid it will be rude for you to decline my offer.' His brilliant blue eyes watch me from underneath his top hat - he has a point. With no other option I lean my arm on his and within a few minutes he has led me into the yard and round to the back entrance.

'Thank you, sir,' I say as he releases my arm.

'My pleasure.' He brings his feet lightly together and gives a long, slow bow with his head, before disappearing from sight.

The encounter fills me with a strange mixture of unease and delight. Being physically so close to the family I serve is not an act I would like to repeat, but John Belmont's gallantry stirs up memories of the beautiful lady who placed the most incredible gift into my hands all those years ago and, for some reason, the joy I experienced on that day reignites inside of me. Pa is right, I will never be satisfied with life if I cannot pass on even a small part of this happiness to someone else.

Mrs Langley glares at me when I enter the kitchen. 'Took your time.'

'I ran as fast as I could, Mrs Langley.'

'Mm...' She eyes me suspiciously as a footman brushes pass with a tray of breakfast rolls. 'Go scrub the yard, the chickens have made a mess.'

'Yes, Mrs Langley.' I watch the housekeeper leave the kitchen before sinking straight into a chair. My foot is throbbing and I quickly prise off my shoe to see a red bruise appearing on my very swollen toe.

'Don't get ideas above your station, Rebekah,' mutters Kitty passing with a basket of eggs.

'What are you talking about?' I ask continuing to rub my foot.

'You know.'

'I'm sorry Kitty, but I don't.' I haven't got the patience for her attitude, not after the morning I've had so far.

'I saw you; you know.'

'Saw me?'

'With your arm on John Belmont.'

'My toe is badly bruised; he was helping me back to the kitchens.'

'That's what they all say.' She lifts an insinuating eyebrow.

'Excuse me!' I bang the table - I will not be taunted by this girl. 'I think you are letting your fancy run wild.' A faint whistling is heard coming closer as we stand glaring at each other defiantly. Manny enters the room and he stops his jolly tune as soon as he sees us.

'Everything all right?' He eyes the kitchen maid with suspicion. 'Have you a problem, Kitty?'

'*I* have no problem, Manny. I'm simply advising the lower staff; it's not my fault Rebekah has taken offence.'

'Rebekah isn't lower staff,' he says scowling by my side.

'Don't let your emotions block your view, Manny,' Kitty says smugly. 'I'm a kitchen maid and I have a whole room allocated to my position, but maid of all work... it's the leftovers nobody else wants.' Manny's cheeks heighten in colour, but Kitty doesn't give him a chance to respond. 'You might want to know your friend is dallying with Lord Belmont's son, she doesn't want that information getting in the wrong hands, does she now.' The girl arches her chin slyly and walks away, swaying her hips against the egg basket.

Manny turns to look at me. 'What's she talking about?'

'Oh, she's trying to invent something that didn't happen. John Belmont saw me down the drive, was concerned about my foot and gave me an arm, that's all.' Manny's scowl is still chiselled onto his face. 'I didn't ask for his help, Manny, so you can wipe away your accusing look. John Belmont insisted, I would have been reprimanded for being rude if I hadn't accepted. Kitty saw it and wanted to cause trouble – you know what she's like.'

Manny opens his mouth to speak, but the entrance of Mr Butler silences him.

'Emmanuel.'

'Sir?' Manny stands to attention.

'Is there a reason you are here when his lordship has requested his horse after breakfast?'

'To warm my hands,' he says not quite believing his own excuse.

'If I had a penny every time you came into this kitchen to warm your hands, boy, I'd be a member of the landed gentry - get back to work.'

'Yes, sir.' Manny instantly obeys, but upon hearing the butler exiting down the corridor, he swings back to grab my hand, marches me out into the yard and rounds the corner of the wash house so we are hidden out of sight behind the wall.

'What's the matter with you?' he doesn't shout, but neither does he speak calmly.

I shake my hand out of his grasp, highly displeased with his manners and concerned we might have been seen. 'You're going to have to explain, Manny, because as far as I know nothing's the matter with me.' I hold my chin high and wait for his response.

'That girl rules over you.' He points towards the house.

'Who, Kitty?'

'Yes, she's a kitchen maid, hardly a high-ranking role.'

'You know what it's like Manny. People with a higher status, even if it's a slight advantage, lord it over the ones beneath.'

'Kitty is one tiny little rung higher than you on the ladder, but as a person you are equal…in fact you are *her* superior.'

'Let us not speak of it Manny, it's not worth the fight.' I try to walk around him, but he puts his hand out to stop me.

'Let me teach you, Becks, please… you're better than this.'

I cross my arms, unimpressed with his pleading. There's a yard full of chicken droppings to clear and I'd rather get the job started before Mrs Langley reappears and adds more unpleasant chores to the list. 'Manny don't… you can't solve this, I am what I am, so leave it alone.'

'But Becks, you're a clever girl and I've noticed how quickly you are learning your signs with Hetty. I know you can better yourself and improve your family's prospects and then who knows what you could do, the better your position the greater impact you can have.'

'My family's prospects will never rise, how can they? You don't seem to understand my pa will never work again.'

'This has nothing to do with your pa. If you improve your own prospects your family's will naturally follow.' He stares intently at me. 'Come on, Becks.'

'I'm sorry, Manny,' I say turning my face purposely away

from his. 'I understand what you are saying, but I'd rather help people on my own terms. My heart is broken enough as it is and I'm not willing to experience any more suffering because of it. Look how Kitty treats me, it will only get worse if I manage to acquire a higher standing in a world where I'll never belong.'

'That's not true.'

'It is... I'll find new ways to care for the poor, and if I only ever impact one or two people, rather than the many you claim I could, then so be it.'

'You're telling me you are content with all of this, to remain a maid of all work for the rest of your life?'

'No, of course I'm not content with this,' I say calmly. 'But I'll learn to live with it... I have to.'

'Learning to live with poverty?'

'Yes, Manny, with poverty, don't say it so disgustedly it's not a disease.' I don't understand him sometimes, he spends his own life working away in the damp, smelly stables, it's not exactly a life of luxury.

'There's more to life than ensuring mouths are fed,' he says leaning closer.

'Well, if there is more, I'll never know it.' Manny's jaw is set firm - so is mine and I scowl at his tall, sulking figure blocking my way. 'Can you let me go, please? I have chicken droppings waiting for me.'

Silently he steps to the side.

Without looking back, I head back inside to collect a brush and bucket from the scullery. Seconds after I've entered Lucy swings the door wide open in obvious distress. 'Rebekah, someone's at the back door for you.' Her eyes are wide with alarm.

'Who?'

'I-I didn't ask.'

Curiously, I make my way along the dark narrow corridor, half-worried the two boys from last night might have returned to beg for more food.

I open the door with its familiar creak to reveal a girl standing before me, her eyes reddened and bloodshot from the shedding of many tears.

Chapter Thirteen

'Georgie has been taken.' Mary sniffs and chokes back a sob.

Warily I look over my shoulder, checking no one has seen my visitor, and gently I close the door behind me stepping out into the yard. 'How long has he been missing?' I ask in calming tones.

'Since yesterday afternoon.' Her shoulders visibly shake as she tries to steady her emotion. 'I didn't want to disturb you, but Pa said—'

'It's all right, Mary.' I stretch my arm comfortingly round her shoulder and feel the bone underneath her skin as I do so – she's hardly eating a thing.

'He was playing with Maggie yesterday and I called her in to help me with the washing - I didn't know Georgie was with her, I would never have asked her to leave him.'

I calm her again. 'Are you sure he was taken?'

'Yes, I saw someone leading him away by the hand... right at the top of the hill. I screamed for Uncle Will, but it was too late, they'd disappeared by the time we got up there.'

'Have you searched for him?'

'Everywhere, all over the surrounding fields and the neighbouring cottages, Uncle Will went further along the lane and to the farmlands beyond as well.'

'Did you see who took him?'

'No, the figure was outlined against the setting sun... it was a woman though, she was wearing a gown and carrying an umbrella - you must come home.' She wipes her nose on one of her long sleeves.

'Mary, I can't. I've just taken a half-day off; I'll never be allowed another.'

'But you must, when Ma came home last night and I told her the news she didn't even care, she simply shrugged her shoulders and went straight to sit in front of the fire. I'm all alone, Rebekah... I can't handle this without you.' A fresh batch of tears flowed down her face.

I take a breath, feeling incredibly distressed at seeing my quiet softly spoken little sister in such a state. Helping Mary will mean instant dismissal... but what will become of our family if I leave her to fight this alone?

'It was cold last night.' Mary chokes. 'If Georgie's been abandoned, he'll freeze to death, he's much too young to defend himself.'

The sound of a wheelbarrow with a squeaky wheel draws my attention and Manny appears from the direction of the stables pushing along a load of manure. As soon as he sees Mary and me huddling together, he changes course and pushes his wobbly contraption towards us.

'What's the matter?' His tone is soft, though his face is scowling and he doesn't look in my direction, still being too cross with me for declining his offer again.

'My little brother's been kidnapped – this is Mary, my sister.' I don't care if Manny's upset with me, I'm not going to play games – I need him. My eyes search for his as unsurfaced tears threaten to fall down my cheeks too.

'He's only three,' sniffs Mary. 'They'll have him up chimneys.'

Manny's scowl melts and he gazes directly at me. Instinctively, I know he's working out a plan. 'You need to go,' he suddenly says.

'Manny,' I lower my voice. 'I can't go home with Mary; this position is too important... they will all starve if I lose my job.'

'I'll figure it out.'

'How?' I search his face and without hesitation he gently places a hand on my shoulder.

'Do you trust me?' he whispers.

I watch his dark curls blow lightly in the breeze and his open honest face stares intently back at mine. That's when I know - I'd entrust this man with my life.

'Let's go, Mary.' I guide her out of the yard and don't look back.

We search everywhere, inside barns and along hedgerows, as we make the long walk back to our cottage. If we pass someone along the way we stop to question them, 'Have you seen a little boy - he's tall for his age - light brown hair - blue eyes?' But each time we ask the passer-by looks vacantly at us - no one has seen Georgie.

When I arrive at the cottage Pa is beside himself with grief and doesn't speak a single word to me, Henry is constantly wailing from a hunger no one can satisfy and ma is missing... again. We spend several hours searching for the boy, but not a sign of him remains.

'Poor Georgie,' sobs Mary again as I prepare to leave.

A sudden heaviness descends upon me and my heart feels completely and utterly broken. If Manny knew, if he really understood what brokenness felt like, then he wouldn't be asking me to pursue it... how can anything good come out of this suffering?

Casting a final look back into the shadowy corner I see Pa turn his face towards the rough and uneven wall - I wish I could do the same. If only I could hide away from the horrifying reality surrounding us and rid myself of the searing pain of leaving my family in such torment. But already it's time to head back to Belmont Park, Manny can't cover my absence forever, and besides, there's nothing more I can do – Georgie is gone.

I've only taken a few steps outside the cottage when I see Ma walking down the lane - it's the first time I've seen her since leaving home.

'Ma!' I call and wave in her direction.

She lifts her head but doesn't respond.

'It's good to see you, Ma,' I say when we come closer together, but she still doesn't speak, almost as if it would be too much effort to do so. 'Have you found him?' Perhaps it's wrong of me to assume she's gone looking for the boy, but Ma's got a heart, it's possible she's rediscovered her maternal instincts.

'Found who?'

'Georgie.'

She looks at a little confused and blinks several times. 'Why would I look for Georgie? He's been taken and we will not see him again.'

'He's your son, Ma.'

'Don't think less of me, Rebekah, but I can only see it as a blessing. You've heard me say it before and I'll say it again, it's one less mouth to feed.'

My jaw drops, she can't really mean this. 'Ma,' I say softly. 'I know things are tough, but you can't say that.'

'I can and I did,' she says defiantly, but as she lifts her head, I can see her eyes are filling with tears. 'Shouldn't you be at work?' I nod and she brushes past me without even saying goodbye.

By the time I arrive back at Belmont Park I'm exhausted and would give anything to retire to my room and hide away under the bedcovers – but I can't, not when there's work to do. To my relief Mrs Langley hasn't greeted me at the door, so I presume whatever Manny did to hide my absence has had its desired effect. I unhook my apron and go to find Lucy in the scullery.

'You're back.' Her shoulders instantly lower in relief and she comes away from the sink. 'Did you find your brother?'

'No, I'm afraid he's gone.' I say sadly. 'There's no trace of who took him or where he's been taken.'

'I'm so sorry, Rebekah.'

'Where's Manny, I want to thank him?'

'I haven't seen him all afternoon,' says Lucy stepping back onto her wooden step and plunging her hands into the soapy water in the sink.

'Let me…' I pick up a cloth and urge Lucy to dry her wet hands so I can replace her at the sink. 'You sit down for a few minutes, you've done my work all day, I'll find Manny later.'

She obediently steps down and takes the cloth. 'Before I forget,' she says. 'I need to tell you, you're sick.'

'I'm sick?' The door opens and Mrs Langley bursts in, looking almost as confused as I am. She takes a moment to recover herself.

'I don't know what you are doing down here, Barnes, but if you go passing things onto the other staff, there'll be trouble – I'm not having everyone struck down by influenza or some such illness.'

Passing things on – what is she talking about? For a moment I don't know how to respond until a light dawns and I realise what Manny has done. 'I'm feeling much better, Mrs Langley, I wanted to help Lucy catch up with the jobs I've missed today.'

'Can't have been much wrong with you if you're downstairs already.' She considers me suspiciously. 'Don't take liberties Barnes, or you will be out on your ear.'

'No Mrs Langley, of course not.' I look directly down to the stone floor hoping she will not pry further, which thankfully she doesn't and removes herself from the room, obviously forgetting what had brought her to the scullery in the first place.

'Becks…Becks!' I hear Manny calling me from inside the hen house the following day.

'In here!' The air is cold and fresh this morning and a white puff of breath escapes from my mouth as I shout out in answer.

'Mr Butler will be cross, you know,' I comment as the capped head of Manny pokes itself round the rickety half-open door. 'I don't think you'll be able to use the hand warming excuse in here.'

Manny laughs and a faint blush covers his cheeks. 'Mr Butler will only be cross if he finds out.' He ducks his head and enters the hay-scented low-roofed hen house. 'Besides, Lord Belmont is in a meeting with his banker and won't need me for hours.' He tries to stand to his full height, but the top of his cap brushes against the roof. 'How are you doing?'

'Bearing up under the circumstances.'

'I'm sorry you couldn't find him... is it possible the boy's been abandoned and is hiding out in a barn or something similar?'

'I think that would be harder to swallow than a simple kidnapping, he's a three-year-old boy who's not even breeched - who's cleaning him, feeding him and keeping him warm? Georgie is tall for his age and whoever took him will think he's older - the poor boy is small enough for chimney's, but too young to follow instructions, they made a mistake and Georgie will have to pay for it.'

'You think they've taken him to sweep chimneys?'

'Yes, I don't see what else they'd want him for.' Manny looks away and I know the stark reality of the truth is too much for him to bear. It's out of his control and he can do nothing to fix it. 'Make yourself useful and collect those eggs,' I say pointing to a nest of hay in the corner. 'The little dears have laid twice as many today and I've a load of jobs still to do, I can't leave them all to Lucy, not after how she covered for me yesterday.' I pick up a brown speckled egg with a feather stuck on top and blow it gently off. 'To make matters worse Mrs Langley has threatened to cancel lunch for anyone behind schedule today – she particularly had her eye on me.'

'Well, you are a trouble-maker.' He lifts his head and a twinkle of mischief appears in his eyes.

'It's not funny Manny, you don't have to work for the woman, she hasn't forgiven me for the tea incident yet.'

'I tell you; the caddy was full last week and Lady Belmont didn't have any visitors to tea.'

'How do you know that?'

'Hetty told me.'

I pause, holding an egg in my hand. 'What are you suggesting?'

'Tea is expensive, it doesn't take much for a forbidden hand to slip in and help itself.'

'Mrs Langley has the only key for the caddy, it's hardly likely she'd steal her ladyship's tea.'

'I'm not suggesting it was Mrs Langley.' He raises a knowing eyebrow.

'Kitty?' I whisper remembering the kitchen maid hovering over the basket before taking the ducks, could she have noticed the missing tea and used it to her advantage...surely even Kitty isn't that conniving?

'Possibly – it's only a theory... but she's never liked you.'

'Whether she stole it or not, it doesn't change the fact that I forgot to buy the precious commodity, does it?' I clench my toes at the memory, still feeling the impact of the housekeeper's heavy blow. 'It's all black and blue under the nail.'

'Her shoes are as hard as her heart.' He looks down at my shoe. 'Have you had someone look at it yet?'

'I'm fine, Manny.' I hold out the basket to let him place his eggs inside.

'I noticed you were still limping at breakfast.'

'What am I going to do about it? I can't rest, I'll be let go.'

'Let me have a look.'

'No.' I bend down and rummage amongst the hay for more eggs turning my back to his.

'Come on, Becks, no one will see - we're in the hen house.'

'No, Manny, it's inappropriate - I'll have to take my stocking off.'

'I've seen feet before; you're not going to make me blush.'

'What would people say?'

He gestures with his hands to the wooden planks of the hen house wall to reiterate his argument and knocks lightly on the panels. 'Last I knew mankind cannot see through wood.'

I stand my ground.

'Fine,' he huffs. 'Don't come crying to me if the doctor has to cut your toe off.'

'Can't afford a doctor, so he couldn't saw it off even if he wanted to.'

Manny laughs and leans his lanky frame against the wall.

'See, you're smart.'

I lift a warning finger. 'Don't, Manny.' I'm not starting that conversation again.

'I'm simply making a comment.' He smiles and doesn't push further. 'Hey, do you want to see something impressive?'

'Depends what it is?'

'An example of misspent youth...' In a flash he swipes three eggs out of the basket and begins juggling them through the air. 'Shall I add a fourth?' he asks with his focus trailing the eggs as he continues to fling them round in a circle.

'You will not,' I say half-scolding, half-laughing.

'Emmanuel!' A call from the garden halts his progress and he catches all three eggs without breaking a single one. He places a finger to his lips and hides behind me.

'Why are you hiding? Mr Butler can't see through walls, you just told me so yourself.' My mischievous remark is lost, however, as Manny crouches down and lowers his face to a crack in the wood.

He peeks through the tiny gap. 'He's coming straight towards us - quick pretend to be a chicken.'

'A chicken?'

'He can't find me here with you, there'll be a great row.'

'And you're telling me this?' My hands go to my hips and I give him a disapproving stare - haven't I only just said the same thing about being stocking-less in his presence? 'To be fair, Manny, even if you weren't in here with me there'd be a row – you should be in the stables.'

'Come on, Becks... cluck,' he begs. 'I'd do it for you.' He begins a low clucking, leaving me to stifle a sudden attack of giggles, made even worse when he starts doing wing movements with his arms and bobbing his head up and down in rhythm – he's forgotten yet again that Mr Butler cannot see through the hen house walls.

Minus the chicken-like actions, I join him and my worry over Georgie momentarily lifts as I help cluck Manny's way out of trouble.

'I think he's going...' Manny's eye presses up against another crack in the planks, his other eye tightly shut. 'Yes... yes... phew, he's gone.' He turns and sinks down onto the hay strewn floor, blowing a lock of his wavy dark brown hair off his face, he grins. 'Nice clucking, Becks.'

Walking back towards the house I enjoy the feel of the sun on my face, it's been a while since its low rising rays have warmed the wintry ground. A bird flits into the hedgerow which splits the hen house and vegetable gardens from the yard.

Wait a minute...

As I look closer two little dark eyes blink back at me through the leaves – it's not a bird at all.

'Good day to you,' I say kindly to the figure in hiding. 'It's all right, you can come out.'

A little girl clambers out of the hedges on her hands and knees, she looks at me uncertainly with a piece of twig stuck in her dishevelled hair.

'Can I help you?' I ask with a smile.

The girl doesn't speak.

'What's your name?' I enquire trying things from a different angle.

The girl taps her mouth and points to an ear before shaking her head – the girl is deaf.

It's unlikely she'll understand, but I might as well try, so I point to myself and then make my right hand into a fist, rest it on my left palm and push both hands away from my body, it's a sign I use all the time with Hetty and speaking loudly I clearly add, 'Can I help you?'

The girl brings her finger-tips together, lifting them to her mouth as if she's pretending to eat - I'm not certain if she's understood my sign, or has simply formed enough courage to communicate with me.

Anxiously I look over my shoulder towards the kitchen, the day is in full swing and it will be practically impossible to find food for this girl without being seen. I tap three of my fingers onto my open palm. 'Where's your ma?'

The girl blinks with her mouth set straight, whilst her eyes stare directly at me in desperation.

What am I to do? I can't explain my concerns to this girl about taking food that doesn't belong to me, nor can I ask her to return later on in the day, because I know she hasn't understood my signs.

'Wait here.' I lead her quickly back behind the hedge and hold out a hand instructing her not to move. She crouches low amongst the leaves and sits perfectly still as I walk away.

My mind is racing and Manny's warning rings in my ears – I promised I wouldn't do this again.

Hovering uncertainly in the kitchen Hetty bumps into me and pushes a large pot into my arms, she then uses her free hand to mime throwing something on the floor.

'Rubbish?' Hetty gives me a thumbs up, nodding her head in approval before heading back towards the range again.

I can't quite believe my luck - this is a Godsend. Inside the pot are pieces of stale bread, bruised vegetable scraps and a piece of half-eaten apple pie. Surely if this food is about to be thrown out, it's not going to be missed?

I head back to the girl and I smile as she comes out of hiding. Showing her the pot full of scraps she holds out her grubby apron so I can pile the food inside. A wave of sadness floods over me as I watch her scurry away. This poor child hasn't only to overcome the hurdle of poverty, but her deafness will create an obstacle that will block her way through life, never allowing her to thrive. Some might accept her as she is, but not many, and I fear one day she will share the same fate as Mr Baker – lost, alone and abandoned…

But now isn't the time to stand around musing, one final look shows me the girl has vanished and I limp back across the yard again.

'Rebekah!' Turning towards the sound of the voice calling my name I feel my stomach tighten with fear - it's Lady Belmont and she's caught me feeding that poor starving girl on her property… with her scraps.

'C-can I help you, your ladyship?'

Lady Belmont is hiding behind the kitchen wall, purposely ducking to conceal herself from the long upper window – it looks like she doesn't want to be seen. 'I'd like to ask you something,' she says, her high-waisted pristine blue gown looking highly out of place against the backdrop of the moss-covered brick wall.

'Yes, ma'am?'

'Not here, come with me.' Immediately she turns away to lead me round the front of the house, but I pause in hesitation.

'I cannot enter the house from the front entrance, your ladyship.'

Lady Belmont retraces her steps, straightening out her back. 'My dear girl, I must talk with you, but it is absolutely imperative that I do not take you through the back entrance. You need not be afraid; you will not get in trouble.'

I swallow nervously. 'Very well, ma'am.'

Reluctantly, I follow her ladyship round the side of Belmont Park, up the grand steps and into the hallway. She opens the first door on her right. 'Please, follow me, Rebekah.'

I am taken into the breakfast room and wait silently for her ladyship to speak. I cannot think what is so important that I cannot enter the main house through the back entrance and feel very uneasy as I stand shuffling my feet back and forth on a creaking floorboard.

'I'm sorry to take you away from your work.' She eyes the empty pot in my hands and my cheeks turn red.

Please don't ask me any questions, I silently plead.

She focuses back on my face. 'It's important I speak to you without a certain housekeeper poking her nose in where it's most certainly not wanted. You will be aware I have been without a lady's maid for almost three months?'

'Yes, ma'am, I had heard.'

'Mrs Langley claimed she knew the best women out there to

fill this position and I foolishly left it in her hands, however, for whatever reason, she has produced nobody.'

'I'm sorry, ma'am.'

'It is not your fault. I am now taking matters into my own hands for I cannot last much longer without an aide by my side.'

'That is very wise, ma'am.'

'Let me not waste any more of your precious time by dithering around the subject. I would like you to be my lady's maid.'

'Ma'am, I—' I am so taken by surprise that I cannot speak.

'You are shocked?'

'Yes, I am not qualified for the position, ma'am.'

'I will train you.'

'But I know nothing... I'm a maid of all work.'

'You have proved you have an eye for good fashion.'

'Only on two occasions, ma'am. I really know nothing.'

'You are reliable.'

'That I cannot disagree with, but I could not perform the duties you would require.'

'You are teachable.'

'I cannot read and write.'

'I've not asked you to be my scribe, Rebekah, simply to help me dress and pin my hair. Do you have sisters?'

'Yes, ma'am.'

'They are younger?'

'Yes.'

'Then you must have pinned their hair?'

'Well, yes, but not for the fashionable circles you frequent.'

'And you must have dressed them?'

'Yes, of course I have, ma'am.'

'Then I don't see the problem.' She looks at my troubled expression. 'Are you really reluctant to accept?'

'Yes, ma'am. It would not be right.'

'I will readily increase your wages as appropriate.'

'That would be extremely kind of you, ma'am, and would help my family dearly, however I am still disinclined to accept your offer.'

'If you are concerned about Mrs Langley, I will deal with her, she won't be a problem.'

'Thank you, ma'am.'

'I would like you to seriously consider my proposal, Rebekah. Would you do that?'

Saying no would close the door forever... what if Manny is right, that wealth and position will lead the way to greater things?

I need to decide now what I really want...

'Yes, ma'am, I will consider your offer.'

Chapter Fourteen

What have I agreed to consider?

I walk back to the kitchen in a daze, the smell of lunch greeting me as I enter from the corridor. Manny is arching over a bowl of soup and I watch him suspiciously from afar. He's been so adamant I claim the position as my own it wouldn't surprise me if he's planted the thought into Lady Belmont's mind, though I don't know how he's had the influence to do so.

'You will go into town this afternoon, Rebekah.' Mrs Langley's shrill command breaks into my suspicions and my thoughts are disrupted as I turn to watch the housekeeper lift her triangular nose up high enough to peer through the slither of a window which runs along the top of the kitchen wall. 'It looks like rain,' she adds.

'Yes, Mrs Langley.' I could have protested against the order, but it wouldn't do any good. Whenever the weather is bad and a trip into town is necessary, I am always the one chosen to suffer the elements. I dare not risk making a fuss in case Lucy, who started with a cold this morning, is sent instead of me.

'Don't forget the tea this time,' sniggers Kitty sitting at the table opposite Manny.

'The caddy should have been full,' grumbles Manny into his soup.

'But it wasn't,' she says with a smug cock of her head. 'May I offer a suggestion, Rebekah?' I don't answer, but she continues anyway. '*I* never forget anything when I shop for errands because I carry a list…oops, how rude of me.' She lifts a hand to her lips as if to cover her "mistake". 'You cannot read and write, can you?'

Manny thumps a fist on the table, preparing his body to

spring to my defence when Mr Butler, sitting at the head of the table, speaks up first. 'Have you finished your soup, Emmanuel?'

'No, sir.'

'Then you have no time for talk, Lord Belmont requires the carriage in less than an hour.'

Manny scowls into his lunch as Hetty hands me my own bowl of steaming hot potato soup. It's thick and full of not only potato, but onions and carrots too. As I take my seat along the table my thoughts are replaced by a mental picture of Mary, ladling thin, almost boiled hot water into bowls and the baby crying with hunger pains at her feet. My stomach tightens with a sudden stab of guilt, knowing that a plate of rolls will accompany my soup, followed by some form of fruit pie.

'It won't bite you,' Manny mumbles raising his head and watching me stare with a look of great concern into the creamy coloured liquid in front of me. I smile weakly and begin to eat.

The room falls silent apart from clinking spoons and tongues slurping soup. Without the distraction of conversation my mind is easily overwhelmed by an array of anxious thoughts coming at me from all angles. How could I not accept Lady Belmont's offer when my family are fighting starvation? It would be selfish of me to decline it... but it's not what I want. I don't want more money and a better position... but what do I want? For my family to be happy and to live more than a survival existence, that's the first thing. Next, I want to serve the people I care about again, to find my purpose within the joy of offering what I have to others... but only what I have and nothing more. I've no desire to achieve more than my position in society will allow. I don't want to spend my life chasing something that's impossible. Suddenly my mind changes direction from what I want, to the reality of what will be if I continue as I am and a whole host of terrifying thoughts rush into my head - the boys will need more to eat as they grow bigger and the pressure to fill their stomachs will push Ma even further away... and what if someone fell sick? My chest tightens and I struggle to swallow a lump of potato down my throat.... not one of my family is strong enough to fight any possibly fatal illness, there would be no hope, no strength to overcome it and what if something happened to Mary? I feel a panic rising... it would be the workhouse for those left behind – this can't happen. I instantly shut the idea out of my mind as quickly as possible and lift my eyes to find something else to focus on.

Manny sits opposite and I watch him innocently mopping up the final contents of his bowl with a piece of bread and my mind begins to escape down a new path...this was Manny's doing, I'm almost sure of it, why else would Lady Belmont have asked me to be her lady's maid - it doesn't make sense? I know Manny, he's trying to fix everything... again. But it's subtle, he's not attempting to mend Pa's broken body, or seeking to find a doctor who can, he's trying to improve my prospects and increase our income, that's why he's so adamant I learn to read and write, it's all part of his grand master plan to solve my problem – it's the closest he can get to making the impossible possible.

Before I can look away, he lifts his head and sees me staring at him. 'What's the matter?' he asks still bad-tempered from being reprimanded by Mr Butler.

'Nothing.' I avert my eyes and focus back on my soup - I'm not going to confront him, not here anyway.

'Did the washing dry, Rebekah?' asks Lucy as the rim of a cup of hot milk touches my lips.

My heart sinks - the master's breeches are still hanging on the hedges outside.

'Don't get them now,' Lucy continues seeing I am about to get up. 'Wait until you've drunk your milk.'

'No, I'd rather get them now, once I've sat down, I'll be good for nothing.' I heave myself out of the chair I've hardly had chance to warm. Today has been exhausting, but it's more than physical exertion that's weighing me down, after two months at Belmont Park my body has pretty much adjusted to the laborious life of a servant. The truth is, I've been battling fears and anxieties all day and I don't think my mind can take much more.

The light from the moon guides my way across to the hedges, although I know my way to the stables well enough without it. As I come closer, I see the stable doors have been swung wide open and I know I'll be seen if he's watching.

'You shouldn't let her treat you like that.' I hear Manny's voice float out into the night as I pass by.

'I guess you are talking about Kitty?' I ask, purposely not looking through the double doors and placing my basket down in front of the hedge so I can begin gathering up the damp clothes.

'She treats you like some kind of idiot.'

'I have to live and work with the girl, I'd rather live in relative peace, than make an enemy.'

'She's already your enemy, when has she ever been pleasant to you?'

I don't answer and sigh deeply. What's the matter with us? All we seem to do at the moment is disagree... it never used to be like this when I first arrived.

Finally turning round, I watch him through the open doors hanging up a saddle onto the wall in his ill-fitted baggy white shirt and a deep frown spread across his forehead.

'What's wrong?' I ask dropping a pair of damp crinkled breeches into the basket before stepping into the stables. The air is warmer in here, the heat from the horses causing the space to feel stuffy compared to the coldness outside.

'Nothing.'

'Well, try telling that to your face.' It was supposed to lighten the atmosphere and not meant as a reproach, but Manny doesn't see it this way and he continues working in silence, picking up a brush and sweeping the hay-strewn floor.

'What, are you not talking to me now?'

He stops brushing, straightens his back and looks directly at me. 'Why won't you stand up for yourself... and I'm not only talking about Kitty? You could have a better life and you're not even trying to fight for it... please, tell me why? I need to know because I'm failing to understand.'

What is there to understand? I want something different to what Manny wants for me. It's my life, shouldn't I get to be the one who decides the outcome without people questioning my motives?

'What's the point, Manny?' I should have chosen my words more wisely - this is only going to irritate him even more.

Manny glares across the open space between us. 'What's the point... did you really say what's the point?'

'I did.' This is the moment when I should back down, but out of my tiredness comes frustration and I cannot control it. 'Why are you getting so cross about it, Kitty didn't insult you? I'm sick of having the same conversation with you over and over again - why can't you leave it alone? I'm a nobody... we are nobodies. Are you trying to make me do this because *you* want greater wealth and position for yourself and you know it's something you cannot have... because that's what is bothering you, isn't it, that I don't want to better myself?'

'It's not about me.'

'No, don't skirt around the question, answer me.' His mouth is set and I can see his teeth clenching – he's not going to answer. 'The problem is, Manny, is that you are stubborn. You think your way is the best way and if someone dares to say differently then they're wrong.'

'I want to help you, Becks, I'm not saying you're wrong, but...' he falters momentarily. 'I'm only being stubborn with you because...'

'Because...?'

'I can't say.' He kicks the end of the brush with his foot.

'If you're not going to tell me then please, stop interfering with my life.'

He scrunches up his nose as if I've spoken complete nonsense. 'I'm not interfering.'

'Please, Manny... I'm asking you to stop.'

'Are you're giving up? Please don't tell me you're not even going to try and make a better life for yourself?'

'Manny, I'm not giving up because I'm not trying.'

'I think you're wrong, Becks, you could do so much better.'

'You're entitled to your opinion and I'm entitled to mine, let's leave it as that.'

He lets out an irritated groan. 'You are always like this, Becks. There is more for you than chamber pots and scrubbing clothes – why can't you see that?'

'Why can't you see my life's greatest achievement will be working myself to death trying to keep my family from starvation?'

'What about if something is offered to you that would improve your prospects, would you decline it because you're happy living in poverty?'

He did it – he needn't say any more. Manny's meddling has secured me an offer to be Lady Belmont's lady's maid, a position I told him I didn't want.

I rub a hand across my face, feeling exhausted and frustrated in equal measure. 'That is not what I said, you're twisting my words – I'm not happy living in poverty, who would be?'

'Then let me teach you to read, please... you don't know what opportunities might come your way.'

'Oh, is that right?' My arms cross my body and I meet his puzzled eyes dead on.

'Are you accusing me of something?'

'I really need you to stop fixing all my problems.'

'Becks, I don't know what you think I've done, but I swear I've done nothing.'

'So, you know nothing about the conversation I had with Lady Belmont today?'

'No. You spoke to Lady Belmont today?'

I don't reply and scan his face. 'You really don't know?'

'No, Becks.'

My lips press tightly together and I turn away, heading back to the basket outside the stables. I feel like I'm fighting against something that's desperate to lock its arms round me. Is Manny right, am I choosing to stay trapped within the bounds of poverty? Taking the position of lady's maid is a great opportunity for me. I can't be sure if obtaining a higher position and greater wealth would disconnect me from the people I want to help the most - it might be the starting point I'm looking for. Would I be a fool to turn it down simply because Manny went behind my back to secure it for me?

I snort out a short breath of frustration through my nostrils and pick up the basket before marching back towards the house.

'Where are you going... Becks?'

I hear Manny bang the brush with some force onto the stable floor and a distant sneeze follows as a result of the straw particles that have floated up into his nose. 'Becks!' He sneezes again.

I don't pay heed to his calls but walk faster so the darkness becomes a barrier between us. If I turn around now and go back, he'd catch me in those soft consoling eyes of his, and I'd tell him everything. Right now, he doesn't deserve to know everything.

The following day I try to keep a low profile which is particularly hard when Manny sits opposite me at the table, but I keep my head down and don't look up. Lucy's noticed something's wrong. I can see her flicking worried eyes between myself and Manny, trying to figure out the problem which both of us refuse to speak about. I make sure I leave the table before he does and go in search of a job that will take me deep into the centre of the house, to a place where grooms would never go... or even be allowed.

When I finally re-enter the kitchen later on in the day, desperately hoping Manny isn't warming his hands by the fire,

I find Mrs Langley on the hunt.

'Have you seen Kitty?' she demands as if I'm the one in trouble for being absent.

'No, I've been cleaning the fires in the bedrooms.'

'Go to her room.'

'I don't think I can do that, Mrs Langley.' I reel at the thought of the girl catching me in her private quarters.

'She has my darning needle and I need it now, go and get it,' the housekeeper says through gritted teeth. 'It will be in her room.'

I don't move.

'It's an order Barnes.'

'Yes, Mrs Langley.' I perform a tiny bob and leave the room in direct obedience.

I count down the doors to Kitty's room, two down from my own and open the door. The room is an exact replica of mine, except Kitty has more personal belongings to fill the space. From the doorway I stand on tiptoes to see the top of the bed-side unit, but it is empty - there is only one more place the darning needle can be. Before entering the room, I check up and down the corridor for signs of movement, then over the banister and down the stairs - I shouldn't feel guilty, but I do. A confrontation with the girl is the last thing I desire right now.

When I slide the single drawer open the darning needle looks straight up at me and I reach my hand inside. In my haste to withdraw from the room as quickly as possible I knock my hand into a brown paper packet and the contents spill out into the drawer. I know I should retreat, because if Kitty catches me here, she'll never believe Mrs Langley sent me, but the sight of the tumbling contents compels me to reach back into the drawer...

I find myself frozen to the spot, not quite believing what I'm holding in my hands. My breath comes quicker and my empty hand desperately flays around trying to find something that will hold me up. It's not the contents of the drawer making the room feel like it's walls are caving in on me, but in a flash, I've realised - this is my life. Mrs Langley forever abusing me, Kitty repeatedly insulting my character, starving children and their families asking me for help - help which I am not able to give... my own family are trapped within poverty and I cannot free them, for the rest of my life I will watch them struggling to clasp onto anything which might pull them out...

I'm trapped.

My eyes shut tightly on the spinning room. Somehow, I find the cold whitewashed wall behind me and slip down to my knees as a tingling begins in my hands. In the back of my mind a warning surfaces... *Kitty might return any second.* I should flee, but my body won't let me and my chest tightens – I can't breathe.

She'll demand what I'm doing and want an explanation...

A creaking floorboard on a lower level diverts my panic and the warning finally pushes its way to the forefront of my mind... I cannot allow Kitty to find me here.

Taking deep steadying breaths, I manage to calm myself enough so that the room comes back into focus. Lowering my head between my knees, I wait, as the dizziness eases and my strength returns. I must wait a few more seconds until I trust my legs to carry me away.

I close my eyes, tilting my head gently against the wall - Why did I not listen to him?

This overwhelming revelation is exactly what Manny has been driving into me from the very beginning. I see it now; my eyes have been opened...

I want a broken heart.

Chapter Fifteen

When I finally come to my senses, I almost fall down the stairs in my haste to withdraw as quickly as possible from the attic. I want to go straight to Manny, to explain the revelation and apologise profusely for not believing him before… but I can't. Darkness covers the open yard and I have no excuse now his lordship's damp washing has been brought inside, and so, in silence I must suffer until the morning.

I find my sleep restless, full of blurry unrecognisable faces and voices that don't make sense, so even though I've slept, I find it takes a while for my body to wake up and I perform my first duties with half-closed eyes and wide-stretching yawns. Finally, with my eyes fully awakened and the basket full of yesterday's damp washing under my arm, I head across to the stables.

'You were right!' I exclaim breathlessly through the stable doors having walked across the yard at double speed in my eagerness to get to Manny.

The stable boy looks up in alarm. 'I beg your pardon, Rebekah?'

'Oh…' The sight of the twelve-year-old boy takes me by surprise. 'Good morning, Nate… I was looking for Manny?' I say looking round for him.

'He's saddling up for Lord Belmont.' I smile my thanks and head round the back of the stables where I see Manny lifting a saddle onto a tall grey mare.

'Are you talking to me now?' Manny doesn't welcome me with his usual warmth but focuses on the saddle he's wrapping around the horse.

'I'm sorry.' I stand nervously, a little distance away.

He pulls the leather straps underneath the horse's belly, securing the buckle with a tight pull before turning in my direction and searching my face. 'So... I'm right?' A small curve of a smile appears in the corner of his mouth – he heard my cry when I mistakenly began to tell the stable boy about my revelation.

'Yes.' I look down to the ground and feel my cheeks blush under his scrutiny. 'But don't get used to it.'

Manny laughs. 'What am I right about?'

'I found the tea leaves concealed away in Kitty's drawer.'

'You found what?'

'The tea leaves.'

He comes round the side of the horse, taking hold of the noseband when the animal jerks its head up and down. 'I knew it,' he whispers. 'Where are they now?'

'Still in her room.'

'Becks! You could have got rid of her for good. Can you go back and get them?'

'I don't want to do that, Manny.'

'She's been nothing but hurtful to you since the day you arrived.'

'I'm aware of that, but we don't know how badly she might need this position, what if she's like me and has a starving family to feed. Besides, it's made me realise something else...' Manny begins to lead the horse back towards the stables and I fall in by his side. 'I'd like to take you up on your offer.'

Manny tilts his head and crinkles his forehead. 'My offer?'

'I want you to teach me to read and write... I'm beginning to think that perhaps you're right.'

'Can you repeat that?' he asks with a twinkling of mischief in his eyes. 'Did you say I'm right for the second time?'

'Yes,' I say ignoring the pleasure he's clearly taking from my surrender.

He laughs again and passes the horse into the hands of Nate who's greeted us at the double doors. 'So, tell me, what wisdom have I offered that's all of a sudden so pleasing to you?'

'I want a heart that's shattered into a million pieces.'

Manny pauses before he speaks, pressing his mouth together in thought. 'You can't hold anything back, Becks.'

'I won't.'

'Things won't change overnight.'

'I know.'

'All right then.' He nods his head seeing I am serious. 'When will lessons commence?'

'After working hours, I suppose.'

'I'll meet you here… don't tell anyone, not even Lucy, she'll worry carrying a secret like this around for such a long time.' He pauses again and casts his soft emerald eyes upon mine. 'We'll do this together.'

I take the basket over to the hedges, my heart feeling lighter even though it's supposed to be breaking. 'Oh, Manny?' I turn back to face him.

'Yes?'

'I need to ask you something, if we're going to do this together.'

'We are going to do this together.' He takes a step towards me as if he's reaffirming his commitment.

'I need to know… what does your heart break over?'

He looks over his shoulder as if he's scared someone has heard my question. 'One day, I'll tell you.'

'Why can't you tell me now?'

'Because…' he hesitates. 'My heart isn't fully broken yet.'

'Neither is mine.'

'Becks, do you trust me?'

'Yes, you know I do.'

'Manny!' It's Nate coming out of the stables. 'Lord Belmont will be waiting; shall I take the mare?'

'No, I'll do it.' Manny takes the reins from the stable boy and begins walking the horse away.

I follow by his side abandoning the washing. 'How will you know?'

'Know what?'

'When your heart's broken to its fullest extent?'

'You'll know... or at least that's what I've been told.' He clicks his tongue at the horse as he leaves me behind. 'Come on, old girl... see you later, Becks.'

I head back to the house feeling slightly dissatisfied by Manny's evasive answers. It's not a surprise then, as I step into the narrow corridor, which is as dark and gloomy as the day I arrived, and with my preoccupied mine mulling over Manny's reluctance to be open with me, that I crash into a body aiming for the exit just as I am shutting the door behind me.

'Oh,' I say breathlessly as the unexpected visitor startles me. 'I'm sorry.' My eyes adjust to the dimness and a sudden alarm replaces my lightness of heart with a great feeling of trepidation when I discover Mrs Parsons standing right before me.

'What a surprise!' the woman exclaims. 'I forgot you work here.'

'It's nice to see you again.' My face doesn't match the pleasant words and I form no smile to indicate any pleasure at meeting the woman again.

'You are arriving back from somewhere?' she asks.

The question raises a suspicion inside of me - Mrs Parsons doesn't work here, what does it matter to her where I've been?

'I've been hanging out the washing.' It's a lie, because the full wash basket has been abandoned by the hedges, but she doesn't need to know that.

'Good day to get it dry.'

'Yes.' I stand to the side, coming up against the damp brick wall. 'I'll let you be on your way.'

The woman nods and pushes pass. 'Have a pleasant day.' She smiles and then stops with her hand on the handle about to twist it open. 'Are your brothers well?'

Immediately the image of this woman loitering outside our cottage returns to my mind and I'm filled with a strange suspicion that unnerves me. 'Yes, thank you.' I'm not going to explain Georgie's fate to her, she's a stranger and doesn't need to know.

'Tough job, your ma has.'

'As I said before, Pa is still alive and he can discipline well enough.'

'I know, but poor man to have his dignity taken away, he must be broken.'

'Nothing that can't be mended.'

'Of course not and I'm sure your neighbours are good to you.'

'Yes, thank you, they are.'

'Good... good.' She repeats the words to herself as if contemplating something in her mind. 'Very well, I will leave you to your work. Good day, Miss Barnes.' She performs a slight curtsey, twists the handle and exits into the yard.

'Mrs Langley wants you to clean the fire in the parlour,' says Kitty as I enter the kitchen.

'What, now?' The request is a strange one, especially at this time of day when, if the family are home, anyone could walk in - I'm not going to fall for that one again.

'Something is wrong and it needs cleaning this instant, her ladyship will catch her death.'

'There wasn't a problem this morning, besides her ladyship can sit in the breakfast room if she's cold, I know the fire is burning in there because I lit it myself... Ah, Lucy.' I turn to the girl who has just passed us carrying a bucket of water. 'This morning when you saw to the parlour fire, did it light or was there a problem?'

'It was fine, Rebekah.'

I turn back to Kitty with a raised eyebrow.

'It's not for me to question an order, I'm simply passing on the message.'

'Fine.'

'And don't take all day about it.' Her superior attitude grates on me and it takes everything inside not to mention the tea – I could get rid of her so easily.

Caught in two minds whether to trust the girl or not I head towards the stairs that will lead me up to the parlour. As I'm climbing, I pass Mrs Langley on her way down.

'Where is that darning needle?' she demands upon seeing me. 'I sent you to fetch it yesterday.'

Instantly I reach down into my apron where I'd stored the item. 'I'm sorry, Mrs Langley, I forgot all about it.'

The housekeeper tuts before snatching it out of my hands. 'May I ask where you are heading when it's almost time to prepare lunch?'

Now I'll find out the truth... 'I'm going to see to the fire in the parlour, Mrs Langley.'

The housekeeper looks aghast. 'You will do no such thing at this time of day. Go immediately to the scullery and if I catch you near the parlour you will be gone in a blink of an eye.'

'Yes, Mrs Langley.' I scurry away, the scolding rolling off my back knowing I've gained an advantage over the kitchen maid.

'Watch Kitty,' I whisper to Lucy who's ducked down and washing the kitchen floor.

'Why?' She sits up on her knees.

'Just let me know if she's doing anything unusual.'

'Like what?'

'I don't know exactly.'

'Oh... all right.' That's what is so lovely about Lucy, she's so faithful and loyal and the details are unimportant to her.

My first lesson goes without a hitch. Working under candle-light, Manny uses dust from the straw particles to draw the first letters of the alphabet on the ground, being unable to provide me with a quill and ink with so little notice. Remembering these new sounds come easily to me, but sketching their forms is trickier. Manny is extremely patient and he feels confident I'll master this new skill quicker than initially expected. I'm not as convinced, but if I remain dedicated, I know I'll succeed with his help.

I lie down in bed, repeating the letters over and over again in my head, full of determination. Under no circumstances can I allow my position to be an excuse, what kind of person would I be if I saw a problem, but did nothing to fix it?

With a yawn and half-closed eyes, I stumble into the kitchen the following day. Lucy and Hetty are already up and preparing for the day's work. 'You look tired,' comments Lucy.

I yawn again causing my eyes to water. 'I had a late night.'

Lucy looks innocently up into my face. 'You can tell me, Rebekah' she whispers as I look at her quizzically. 'I saw the candle flickering in the stables.'

My cheeks blush hoping she hasn't misconstrued our meeting. 'Manny is teaching me to read and write.'

'Don't worry, I won't tell anyone.' She places a hand on my shoulder as Hetty comes across with a puzzled expression on her face, wanting to be part of the conversation.

'Manny is teaching me to read...' I say slowly holding one hand flat and striking two fingers against it from top to bottom. '... and write.' Keeping the same palm flat I use my finger to mimic writing with a quill.

Hetty's face beams and she claps her hands together in joy. 'Ah, Ma-nn-y,' she says slowly before sticking up her thumb and lifting a finger to rub her chin horizontally - Manny is a good boy. I can't help but smile as she proclaims this several times a day.

'I didn't have a brother,' says Lucy suddenly. 'Just sisters... I love Manny like I would a brother, he's all the family I have left.'

Hetty sees the little girl's sombre face and looks to me for a translation.

'Manny...' I say loudly and then I close my hands into fists and rub my knuckles together. '...like a brother.'

The cook nods her head in agreement and places a gentle hand on the tiny maid's shoulder.

Lucy looks up at me with round engaging eyes. 'Wouldn't you agree, Rebekah? You don't have an elder brother, do you?'

'Erm, no, I don't, just lots of younger ones.'

'Don't you think Manny would make the perfect brother?'

I want to say yes, it seems like the right thing to agree with, but the thought of referring to Manny as a brother somehow feels wrong and I can only bring myself to smile awkwardly before saying, 'I'm sure some people would see him as a brother-like figure... have you started lighting the fires?'

'No, not yet.'

'Come on, I'll help you.'

After lighting the fires I'm back in the kitchen plucking a duck in preparation for dinner. I'm feeling strangely optimistic and realise I haven't felt this way in a very long time. Maid of all work should be a job for life, but I'll make sure this is not the case, it won't limit me.

'Rebekah?' It's Matthew, one of the footmen. 'Lady Belmont would like to see you in the breakfast room.'

I look at Hetty, who hasn't even heard Matthew come in. 'Now?' I query. The young man confirms that her ladyship requests my presence immediately. I wipe the feathers stuck to my hands across my apron, signal to Hetty that I'll be back and then scurry along the corridor.

It seems strange being asked to enter the main house in broad daylight, any work I do in this part of the house is normally completed so early that the family are still asleep, but now, knowing the family have already breakfasted, causes a knot of distress to form in my stomach. I knock on the breakfast room door and wait for Lady Belmont to call me in.

'Ah, Rebekah.' Her ladyship smiles with pleasure upon seeing me and I walk softly across the patterned rug and stand before her, holding my hands behind my back and nervously twiddling my fingers together. 'I know I haven't given you much time, but I wanted to hear if you've made a decision about my offer. I am in desperate need and do not want to wait a moment longer than is necessary.'

'I have considered the matter, ma'am.'

'And what is your conclusion?'

'I still believe I am ill-qualified, but I am seeking to rectify this.'

'What precisely are you seeking to rectify?' She crosses a leg elegantly over her knee, straightens her gown and looks at me with interest.

'I'm learning to read, ma'am and hopefully not long after that the writing will follow.'

Lady Belmont laughs softly. 'I have told you I don't need a scribe, Rebekah. I do not require you to read in order to curl my hair and fasten my buttons.'

'I know, ma'am, but if I can read then I can study the fashion magazines and read the descriptions that go along with the engravings, I believe then I would be more competent to fill the position.'

'Very well, if you are adamant to learn then I will not stop you, but I do not see why your inexperience should prevent you from starting immediately, I do not intend to wait for you to master the art of reading before employing you.'

'It's a big risk, ma-am, I really know nothing.'

'Yes, I agree, but I also do not want a lady's maid chosen by Mrs Langley. Since my acquaintances do not know of anyone suitable, I must find someone myself - I'm not having a stranger I don't trust in my own home. I've been watching you, Rebekah, I saw you feed that poor little girl hidden in the hedges – no, I'm not angry...' she adds seeing my eyebrows lift up in alarm. 'You're loyal and that's what I need the most... So, will you do it?'

My answer is instant. 'Yes, I will.'

'Very good.' Lady Belmont smiles and her face relaxes now she's accomplished her aim. 'I will tell Mrs Langley, from now on you take your instructions from me.'

'Yes, ma-am.' I curtsy and retreat from the room.

My heart races faster as I make my way back downstairs. A lack of self-belief causes me to instantly regret my decision, her ladyship caught me off guard when I thought I could really do this... what will Mrs Langley say when she discovers the truth? She'll think I've gone behind her back and life will almost certainly become even more unbearable. I might no longer take orders from the housekeeper, but we still have to live together in the lower quarters - I must find Manny.

Lucy scurries across the yard carrying a pile of muddied shoes. 'I hate the winter.' She sighs. 'So much mud... on everything.'

'Cheer up, Lucy, not long until lunch and you can have a sit down... have you seen Manny?'

'In the scullery washing the large pans.'

'Of course, I didn't realise it was that time all ready. I'll help you with those once I've spoken to Manny.' I catch a shoe about to fall from the top of Lucy's pile.

'Thanks, Rebekah.' She gives a little smile and as I watch her shuffling away, I realise the mistake I've made - offering to scrub muddy shoes is no longer my duty, I'm a lady's maid now, should I be scrubbing muddy shoes? The problem is I can't tell Mrs Langley about my new position before Lady Belmont sees her, that would be a disaster. I really must find Manny; he'll know what to do.

Entering the narrow corridor, I count the doors down to the scullery, as I'm still in the habit of doing more than two months after my arrival and open the door. However, the sight I'm greeted with causes me to shut it again immediately and I lean against the cold wall, trying to calm myself. How could I have been such a fool? His hatred for her was a ruse and I've fallen for it. Tears form in the back of my eyes as the sight of them together makes me realise why I was so reluctant to call Manny my brother.

'Are you well, Rebekah?' asks Lucy passing me in the corridor still carrying the large collection of shoes. 'Looks like you've had a fright.'

'I...' The scullery door opens and Kitty stalks out with her cheeks flushed red. I walk away without answering Lucy. There's no way I can speak to Kitty right now, if she were to give me a snide comment I'll only lash back and say something

I'd regret. I could kick myself, leaving those tea leaves in the drawer has got to be one of the worst decisions of my life.

'Rebekah?' questions Lucy as she watches me patter away up the stairs before she follows me to the bottom and looks up. 'What's wrong?'

'Did you know?' I whisper looking over the banister and down the corridor to check Kitty hasn't trailed behind us. Lucy looks puzzled. 'About Manny and Kitty?' I explain, but she still doesn't respond and keeps her wide round eyes upturned to mine. 'I've just...' Her pure, innocent expression stops me and I shake my head. 'It doesn't matter... everything's fine - it's fine.' I repeat, trying to reassure myself more than anyone else.

All day I've been fretting. Firstly, because Mrs Langley hasn't mentioned anything about my new position, and so I have to presume that, until she does, Lady Belmont hasn't informed her. So, I've decided to continue my chores and routines as usual. If I'm wrong, I'll deal with the consequences later, but without consulting Manny, I don't know what else to do... which brings me to my second source of anxiety - the looming dread of seeing him again. When Mrs Langley questions me about why the wet washing hasn't been hung out on the hedges to dry, I can't find a reasonable excuse - I'm not exactly going to tell her the truth – and immediately she sends me out to complete the task.

A strong wind blows in my face as I step into the yard. To be honest, I'm not surprised Mrs Langley was so cross with me for missing such ideal drying conditions, especially when the linen has been damp for days. The double doors to the stables swing open and closed, the hinges creaking and groaning with each and every bang. As I come closer, with the basket tucked under my arm, I realise I can use the weather to my advantage. Perhaps, if I'm quick and the unpredictable wind is on my side, I can conceal my presence when a new gust strikes the doors shut again.

I stand and wait.

The wind drops and a silence fills the air... I make a run for it as a huge gust bangs both the doors closed – I'm going to make it... but, to my dismay, the wind changes direction before I'm clear and the left door flies open, revealing my presence to whoever might be inside. I scurry over to the hedge and begin to hurriedly lift out the damp clothes in the basket.

'Hey Becks.'

My hands freeze as I lift the master's breeches half-way up the hedge and my cheeks turn crimson in colour, hearing Manny's heavy footsteps saunter out of the stables followed by a horse clopping behind him.

'Not going to say hello?' he questions with a friendly smile.

'Sorry, Manny,' I say trying not catching his eye. 'I'm busy, got a lot of chores to do.'

'You've always got a lot of chores to do, it's not stopped you before.'

'Well... today I've more than normal.'

'What's that old woman got you doing now?' He laughs lightly, referring to the housekeeper.

'Oh, this and that...' I pick up the basket which is still half-full of washing. 'I'd better go.'

'You haven't finished putting it all out yet, let me help you.' He ties the horse's reins to a metal hoop in the brick stable wall and grabs hold of the basket, which I tug back. He lets go and stands back in puzzlement. 'What's wrong, why won't you look at me?'

My cheeks redden even more now I feel his eyes watching me. 'It's nothing, Manny.'

'It must be something.'

I stand awkwardly looking towards the ground.

'Have I done something to offend you?'

'No, not really.'

'Not really?'

'It's your life Manny, you can choose to do with it what you wish.'

His brow crinkles as he unties the horse. 'So, I have done something you don't approve of, that much is clear.'

'I really must be getting back to the kitchen.'

'Without hanging all the washing out?' I try to walk around him, holding the basket firmly in my arms, but he steps in front of me, the body of a large chestnut stallion also blocking my way to his side. He doesn't speak but stands observing me.

Not being able to stand the silence any longer I slowly move my eyes up and instantly meet his soft searching eyes. 'Manny, it's not any of my business.'

He raises a pair of questioning eyebrows but doesn't comment.

'Really Manny, please let me go, I haven't time for you to do this.'

'Do what?'

'Stand there wordlessly, softening my unwillingness to speak with those imploring eyes of yours.'

He steps backwards as if this is some kind of revelation of his character he didn't know before. 'I don't do that.'

'You do, all the time and normally it would work, but this is...uncomfortable for me to discuss with you.'

'You can talk to me about anything, we're friends.'

'I know, but this... I can't.'

'Tell me,' he speaks softly moving closer, the horse planting a foot forward in unison with his own.

'Manny, did you not hear what I said?'

'Yes, of course I did, but I need you to tell me, now I know something is bothering you it will bother me.'

'Manny...'

'Tell me.'

'No, I can't.'

'Please.'

'Fine, Manny...' I bang the basket down onto the ground. 'Have it your way... I saw you, all right, I saw you.'

'Saw me?' He jolts his head back.

'Yes, you and Kitty...' I wince with embarrassment hoping

he doesn't get me to describe exactly what I saw.

'You saw us!' His hands run through his hair. 'It was all *her*, Becks.'

'I didn't know you...you and Kitty were...'

'We're not!' he yells so adamantly I'm sure someone must have heard. 'You need to believe me, she kissed me and I pushed her away, immediately - it's the truth.'

'It looked like...' I trail away unable to finish the sentence.

'I don't care what it looked like. Becks, you know how much I dislike the girl, she's been after me since the day I arrived, clinging onto me like a leech. That's why she's so jealous of you, she sees you as a threat. From the moment you stepped foot inside Belmont Park you had the potential to take me away. It's why she won't make friends with you, why she sends you off on fool's errands, why she stole the tea—'

'Who stole tea?'

We both twist round – somebody had heard Manny shouting.

'Have you been sneaking into my room?' asks Kitty standing before us with her arms folded obstinately across her chest.

'Mrs Langley sent me to find a darning needle,' I explain mirroring her stance.

'So, you searched the rest of my room while you were there?'

'Of course not, the tea leaves were right next to the needle, it didn't take a genius to find them.'

'Before you go telling on me, you need to know, I didn't do it,' she says smugly arching her face.

'You can't get out of this one, Kitty,' says Manny stepping forward. 'Rebekah's seen the evidence, there only needs to be a search of your room and you'll be gone.'

'Actually Manny, this has nothing to do with me.' She lifts her chin looking him square in the face, his refusal of her obviously still hurting her deeply. 'You'll have to speak to your precious little Lucy if you want more of an explanation.'

I spring forward, how dare she bring Lucy into this - but I don't get far before Manny pulls me back and places a hand on my shoulder.

'What do you mean?' he asks calmly.

'Lucy stole them.'

'Liar!' I yell. 'You're lying.'

'Why don't you ask her yourself.' Kitty waves across to Lucy who is coming round the corner holding a bucket full of something that is too heavy for her to carry. She hobbles across and puts the bucket down, looking shyly at us.

'Tell them,' prompts Kitty.

Lucy's bottom lip trembles and instantly she fixes her eyes on Manny, looking as if she's about to burst into tears. 'I did it,' she says with a wobble in her voice. 'I stole the tea.'

Chapter Sixteen

Mrs Langley's voice breaks into Lucy's startling announcement. 'Get back to work, all of you...and you.' She points a finger at me. 'I want a word with you in particular - go straight to my room.'

Lady Belmont's seen her - she knows.

Manny looks at me, wondering what's going on, but I can't explain it to him here. I leave Lucy behind, poor girl, whatever has happened I don't believe Kitty is innocent for a second - she can't be.

The door to the housekeeper's room has hardly closed behind me before I get a verbal lashing. 'How dare you, you disloyal, ungrateful child!'

I meet her eyes dead on, though my legs are shaking and I can't say a word.

'You can't go from being maid of all work to lady's maid...' Her mouth continues to move, but she's so furious no further words form on her lips, that is until she manages to spit out, 'I'll make sure you stay under *my* authority, you are not qualified and never will be.'

'Mrs Langley,' I say quietly, bravely easing my mouth open. 'If I may speak.'

'No, you may not. You are nothing, your family are living in poverty and you will not rescue them by climbing the social ladder and missing out the stages in between. I don't know how you've done it!' She waves her hands madly in the air. 'You might have fooled Lady Belmont, but I will open her eyes, yes, just you watch me. Kitty is to be the lady's maid at Belmont Park - not you, she's the one I've trained and presented before her ladyship, even though every time she has been dismissed as unworthy... but I will succeed, and you will remain a maid of all work where you belong.' She draws herself uncomfortably close to me and I take a small step back as her long-pointed finger juts out at me like the long triangular nose on her face. 'You will not respond when Lady Belmont summons you to her side, do you hear me? Mark my words, you will never be lady's maid here, at least not whilst I'm at Belmont Park. Now leave this room, I do not want you in my presence.'

There's nothing I can do whilst her anger is so fierce and in direct obedience I retreat, almost bumping into Kitty as I shut the door behind me.

'Well, congratulations, Kitty' I snarl bitterly. 'Seems like you're taking everything I want today.'

The kitchen maid looks momentarily confused before she lifts a single sly cocked eyebrow and says 'What is it you want, Rebekah?'

I push past her. 'It doesn't matter.'

It really doesn't...*friends*, that's what Manny had called us, he sees me as a sister, someone to protect and guide. I don't suppose he'll ever think differently, and just like Lady Belmont's offer, the door remains closed - there'll never be anything more.

'Tell me what happened, Luce.' Manny is still outside the stables, kneeling down before the tiny maid, when I come storming back across the yard. Lucy is sniffing, I can tell she's been crying and her eyes are red and sore.

She stifles a large sob. 'I – can't – Manny'

Manny stands up and whispers in my ear. 'Someone's scared her into silence.'

'Do you think she did it?'

'I think she was made to do it.'

'If Kitty tells Mrs Langley, Lucy will be let go and she'll be sent back to the workhouse, she's under the guardianship of the parish.'

Manny stands in silence and presses his lips together looking anxiously at the little girl. 'They won't send her to the workhouse, the parish will move her on somewhere else, she's under-age and in their care.'

My anger seeps away and I wrap an arm around her shoulders. 'Come on Lucy, let's get you a cup of something hot.'

When we arrive in the kitchen, I sit Lucy down and glance over at Kitty who is whispering in the corner to a visitor. Both have their backs turned so I cannot see their faces. As Hetty passes me a cup full of hot milk, the visitor turns and smiles at me. 'Good day, Rebekah.' I instantly feel sick in the stomach - she's here again.

Kitty scurries away as I hand Lucy the cup and saucer and urge myself to answer politely. 'Good day, Mrs Parsons. Here, drink this Lucy,' I say focusing back on the girl. 'It will make you feel better.'

'Poor girl,' comments Mrs Parsons. 'Is she not well?'

'She's fine, miss.'

Mrs Parsons lifts her face and looks towards the range, her fancy gown looking out of place in a kitchen full of plainly clothed servants. 'I wouldn't mind a tea myself.' Wordlessly I collect another cup and saucer from the cupboard and lift a large pan off the range, topping up the teapot with more boiling water. 'How's your ma?' the woman asks watching me.

'She's well.' I lie - why is she always enquiring after my family?

'I hear she is not home often, is she working?'

'I don't mean to be rude, Mrs Parsons, but what my ma does is my family's business, not yours.'

'Of course.' She smiles. 'I'm a nosey old thing, you're right to shut me up.'

I stare at her seemingly innocent expression. 'Come on, Lucy.' I lift the girl up lightly by the shoulder. 'If you'll excuse us, we've a lot of work to do.'

We walk across to the outhouse and as we do so I see Kitty sauntering across the yard. 'I'll be back in a minute,' I say to Lucy dropping her off by the door. Without thinking, I stalk across to the kitchen maid. 'Who is that woman?'

'Who?' asks Kitty slightly shocked by the ambush.

'Mrs Parsons.'

Kitty frowns. 'She's Mrs Langley's daughter.'

The revelation comes as quite a shock for the two ladies look nothing alike at all. Mrs Langley is tall and slim, with hints of her previously curly auburn hair underneath her lace bonnet, whereas Mrs Parsons has broad shoulders, and her hair is dark and straight, not to mention the stark differences in position and wealth, which the younger woman's outfit exudes.

'What business has she with you?' I ask standing straight in front of the girl to block her from escaping.

'Wouldn't you like to know.' She smirks.

'I wouldn't get involved with the woman, if I were you.'

'Why ever not?'

'It's a feeling I have.'

'To be honest, Rebekah, I don't care what you *feel*... oh, and neither does Manny.'

The sound of his name rolling off her lips pulls me back. 'What are you talking about?'

'Don't let him fool you.' She laughs lightly seeing my discomposure. 'You poor girl,' she lowers her voice. 'He won't be yours for much longer.' She walks away continuing to laugh.

'Becks!' Manny strides round the corner and I twist to face him – there's no time to contemplate Kitty's meaning behind her comment.

'I have a very curious message,' he shouts across the yard. 'Matthew has been looking for you.'

'Oh?'

'Lady Belmont wants you to dress her for luncheon... why does Lady Belmont want you to dress her for luncheon?'

I touch a hand to my head as he reaches me.

'What's wrong?' he asks.

'Everything's in a mess... as of an hour ago, I'm her ladyship's new lady's maid.'

'What!'

'Don't look so shocked, I know you set it up.'

He looks at me in confusion. 'No, I didn't.'

'Don't worry Manny, I won't ask how you did it, I know you won't tell me.'

Manny shakes his head. 'Why is it a mess, I thought this is what you wanted?'

'Mrs Langley has forbidden me to answer any summons coming from her ladyship.'

'Ah, that is a problem... so perform two jobs, only do one in secret.'

'That's a risk.'

'You will be let go if you fail to obey your mistress, that is more of a risk.'

'But I have to live with Mrs Langley, she'll make my life a misery.'

'You have her ladyship's ear now, use it to your advantage.'

'Manny!' I'm shocked by his suggestion of dishonesty.

'It's true, that's why old Langley is so upset, she's lost her opportunity to influence the family.'

'She wanted Kitty to be lady's maid.'

'Precisely.'

'You think I should go?'

'Yes, deal with the consequences later.'

'All right.' I nod lightly to affirm my decision. 'Thanks.'

'What for?'

'For making it happen... however you did it!'

All my fears are quashed as I realise, I'm more than qualified to help her ladyship dress. Surprisingly, I actually feel quite satisfied coming back down into the kitchen.

'Where have you been?' scowls Mrs Langley.

'Doing some jobs in the house.' It's the best excuse I can utter without lying, actually, I have been working in the house, just not on anything Mrs Langley has summoned me to do.

'Mm...' She observes me, looking down her long-pointed

nose. 'I do not need you in the house, go and collect some apples from the shed.'

'Yes, Mrs Langley.' This is going to be tiring, performing two jobs for two women who mustn't know what I'm doing.

In the little storage shed not far from the hen house, I rummage around trying to find the boxes of apples which have been hidden away to survive the winter. After discarding a batch of pears, I find what I'm looking for and start piling the green apples into my arms for Hetty's apple pie.

'You're wanted in John Belmont's room,' says Kitty stepping into the darkened shed.

'Why?' It's such an odd request, we don't normally go in the bedrooms at this time of day, and she has duped me before – twice.

'The fire is broken. He sent a message to Mrs Langley and you are to go now while the room isn't in use.'

'Very well.' I pile one last apple on top of the others. 'Lock the door behind me, will you?'

Kitty rolls her eyes but turns to flick the latch anyway.

After leaving the apples with Hetty I go straight to knock on Mrs Langley's door. I won't be caught out this time, if Kitty's message is false, I want to know.

The housekeeper calls and I enter. 'You want me to fix the fire now, Mrs Langley?'

'Yes, I want you to fix the fire now,' Mrs Langley says irately. 'And be quick before Master Belmont wishes to use his room.'

I have to admit I'm shocked Kitty was telling the truth.

'Is he home, Mrs Langley?' I do not want to find myself in a compromising position... and I still don't fully trust Kitty.

'No, he is not home – go now and do as you're told.'

'Yes, Mrs Langley.' I bob and hurriedly leave the room.

Something stirs uneasily inside of me as I go up to John Belmont's room to inspect his fire. I'm not fully convinced it is even broken because I was the one who lit it last, before the household arose this morning, and it was fine then. But I can't disobey a direct order from Mrs Langley... although officially

I only take orders from Lady Belmont now - when did life become so complicated?

Knocking on the large white panelled door I wait for an answer, just in case John Belmont is lurking inside the supposedly empty room. No voice sounds and so I assume it is safe to enter. My head pokes around the door first and a sigh of relief escapes my mouth when I see the room is truly unoccupied. To the side of a large four poster bed stands the fireplace which is where I spread out a large sheet onto the floor. Kneeling down, I begin removing the coals one by one. Once the fireplace is clear, I lean my head in to where the coals had been and look closely for any build up in ashes, but there's nothing that seems to be a problem, so I lay the coals back in their places.

Stepping back, I look questioningly at the fireplace - something doesn't seem right. The fire-place is not broken, but Mrs Langley confirmed Kitty's message. What is going on? I stand for a few more minutes considering what my next move should be. Finally, I decide the best thing is probably to light the fire myself, so I can check for certain if it is broken or not. So, I turn on my heel and head out of the room to fetch the items I need from downstairs. However, the moment I turn round is the very moment the door swings open and John Belmont appears, standing before me.

I'm sure I almost stop breathing as my arms freeze stiffly to my sides. I do not move - that is, until I realise my hands are covered in sooty coal and I self-consciously wipe them on my apron leaving a dirty black streak behind. Embarrassed, I touch my cheek and immediately regret this foolish action when I realise I've probably left a black streak behind there as well.

'I beg your pardon,' John Belmont says looking almost as mortified as myself. 'I didn't know anyone was here.'

I bob a curtsy and feel my cheeks burning hotter every second. 'I was told your fire was not drawing properly and to see to it while you were away from home.'

'The fire is fine; I sent no message to say it was not drawing properly.'

I've been fooled again, but this time Mrs Langley was involved. It can only be her revenge because I claimed the position of lady's maid - is she trying to get me dismissed?

Collecting the sheet, I waste no time exiting the room. When the door closes behind me, I pause to compose myself and touch my burning cheeks with the back of my hand.

'Becks?'

I look up to see Manny standing at the end of the long corridor. What is he doing up here? A gasp escapes my mouth as I suddenly realise what he is thinking - now it's my turn to deny all falsehood. 'I was sent to see to the fire,' I explain.

'Don't lie to me, I saw John Belmont going inside.'

'It is his room... why are you even up here?' I have to ask, though I can probably guess the answer. Kitty had said he'd no longer be mine and a taint on my character would see that happen...but if this is a plot for Mrs Langley to remove my presence from Belmont Park, how can it also be a ruse to break apart my friendship with Manny, Mrs Langley couldn't care less about that?

'Kitty told me what was going on.'

'And you believed her?'

'I didn't... at first.'

John Belmont walks out of his room before Manny can say any more and he stares at us both curiously. 'Is there a problem?'

'No, sir.' I bob again and hurry along the corridor to the hidden staircase used only by the servants. Manny has already escaped and he follows me down the stairs.

'You can't blame me for suddenly questioning what the girl says, we blamed Kitty for stealing the tea leaves and it wasn't her,' Manny whispers as we climb further down towards the basement.

'Lucy didn't do it, Manny.'

'She did, Becks.' He stops me. 'Lucy doesn't lie, if she said she did it -she did it.'

'You can't mean that?' I continue to step lightly down the stairs.

'I do, Lucy hasn't told the whole truth, but she certainly did it. So, when Kitty said that you and John Belmont... anyway, I had to find out for myself.'

'Nothing happened, Manny.'

'Why are you not attending to the fire-place, Barnes?' asks Mrs Langley coming out of her room and meeting us at the bottom of the stairs, she turns to see Manny following behind me. 'Mr Smith, you won't find any horses up those stairs.'

'I think Manny has just discovered the ugly truth.' Kitty, who has conveniently appeared next to the housekeeper, smirks with pleasure. 'Rebekah has been caught with John Belmont in his room.'

'Did Lady Belmont see you?' asks Mrs Langley.

I frown as the housekeeper looks at me in expectation. 'No, she didn't... Mrs Langley, please tell Manny you sent me to fix the fire.'

Mrs Langley ignores my request. 'Kitty,' she snaps. 'A word... now!' She marches the girl into her room and bangs the door closed.

Manny and I only have to stand awkwardly for a few minutes before Kitty appears in floods of tears, brushes past us and runs up the stairs.

Mrs Langley stands in the doorway. 'What are you two still doing here... do you want a reference in your hand too?'

'You've let Kitty go?' I say in disbelief.

'That's what happens to people who don't do what they're told.'

I can't understand it, not one bit. Surely Kitty and Mrs Langley were working together, they were trying to trap me so Kitty could be the lady's maid...but clearly, I'm mistaken.

'Back to the stables immediately, Smith.' She pauses before adding as an after-thought, 'Barnes is innocent, you have my word on that.' You can tell she isn't pleased with the words she has spoken, but she's cleared my name despite her unjustified hatred of me... which is another thing that doesn't make sense, all the times I've fallen short of her high standards and I'm still here, Kitty does one thing wrong and she's gone.

I glance at Manny, but don't speak as I move past him. His eyes are beseeching me to forgive his error, but right now I need to walk away, he didn't believe me and that really hurts.

Entering the yard, I aim for the outhouse where I left Lucy, but as I'm half-way across I hear Kitty crying on the bench outside the wash-room. She stands upon seeing me.

'Oh Rebekah, what a fool I've been, my ma will disown me now.'

'You've only yourself to blame, Kitty.' I should walk straight past her, but I don't, and I wait to hear what she has to say.

'I was jealous... you might as well know now.' The former kitchen maid slumps back down on to the bench and sniffs. 'He didn't want me.'

'I take it you are talking about Manny?'

'He's the kindest man I've ever met, not that it takes much, my pa is a violent man, and my elder brother has followed suit.'

'I'm sorry.' To my regret I find my heart softening a little, as her shoulders tremble trying to prevent a sob from escaping.

'He was so caring, I thought he would do me some good. I was envious of you from the beginning - I could tell by your face he'd like you.'

'My face?'

'Yes, you've got an honest face... and pretty, despite the freckles.' I touch my cheeks self-consciously at the few freckles which remain on my face even during the winter months. 'I'm sorry I told you fibs, you know, about when the family were out when they were really home, that was wrong of me... oh, and the petticoat... and the tea leaves too.' Her cheeks redden at her disclosures.

'No harm done,' I say knowing I'm being too nice.

'Only to myself,' she admits and sniffs again before standing to leave.

'Erm, Kitty, can I ask you something, before you go?' There's something I really need the answer to before she disappears from my life forever.

Kitty looks at me expectantly and dabs her long sleeve to her wet face.

'What is Mrs Langley planning against me? I presume it was her plan to have me caught by Lady Belmont and you simply used it to your advantage to ruin my friendship with Manny.'

'I'm sorry, Rebekah, I don't understand.'

'You've been plotting with Mrs Langley?'

'That's one thing my conscience is clear on.'

'But you were whispering with Mrs Parsons, you told me that's her daughter... is she in on it too?'

'Mrs Parsons paid me to send you up to John Belmont's room, I don't know why, and I know nothing more... as you say, I saw my opportunity and it led to my downfall.'

'So, you don't want to be lady's maid to Lady Belmont?'

'No, why?'

'Mrs Langley gave me reason to believe she wanted you to take the position.'

'She never spoke anything of it to me. Well...' She attempts a smile. 'I'd better go and collect my things.'

I watch her walk across the yard; the poor girl has no reason to lie now she's lost everything. I might have one problem out of my way, but I'm left with an uneasy feeling in the pit of my stomach whenever I think about the housekeeper – she's out to get me, I'm sure of it. I remember that flicker of a smile spreading across her face the moment she found out my pa was paralysed, I'd dismissed it at the time, but now I believe there's something deeper, some reason why she's keeping me at Belmont Park.

Lucy has gone from the outhouse by the time I arrive, but it doesn't take long to find her hiding away in the scullery, shaking in a corner after hearing the commotion of Kitty's dismissal and not daring to come out.

'Kitty's gone,' I coo as if I'm trying to entice a small mouse out of hiding. She questions me with her eyes and blinks twice as I sit down beside her. 'Will you tell me what really happened now... with the tea?'

The girl stands up and shakes the dust off her dress before nervously interlocking her fingers and lowering her head. 'I did steal it, Rebekah, but only because Kitty made me. I was to take it all so the caddy was empty and then store it in Kitty's drawer for safe keeping. She told me not to tell.'

'Why did you do it? You should have come to me, or Manny, we would have helped you.'

'Kitty told me she'd do something to hurt Manny if I said anything and she would ruin his reputation. I wasn't going to let that happen, not after all he's done for me.'

'Oh Lucy.' I stand with her, taking a stray hair from behind her ear and tucking it underneath her bonnet. 'She can't hurt Manny now; she's going home and there'll be a new position for you.'

'A new position?'

'You'd be a good kitchen maid and you work well with Hetty.'

'What about you? You should have the position, you're older.'

'Lady Belmont has made me her lady's maid.' I smile with pride for the first time realising how valuable my new position will be. Lucy squeals with joy and flings both arms round my neck, I've never seen her so animated before. 'And' I say when she lets me go, 'It means I have more influence than Mrs Langley, so if you would like the position in the kitchen, I'll speak a few good words on your behalf.'

'Oh, thank you, Rebekah, thank you.' The appreciation beaming from the little girl's face wraps around me like a warm embrace and I can finally see how having a higher position might make a difference after all.

Chapter Seventeen

July 1801

One year ago the accident happened. That was the day everything changed.

It's important I'm with Mary today. She took it hard losing Georgie the way we did. If it had been a death, the grieving process would have been further along by now, but as it stands there's been no closure... anything could have happened to the boy. It wasn't Mary's fault - it wasn't anybody's fault, though Pa takes the blame upon himself. 'If I was able-bodied... if I could have searched for the boy,' he is often heard uttering, more frequently in recent weeks, in the moments of his greatest despair and knowing the anniversary of his accident was drawing near.

If... what a terribly unsatisfying word. If man had the ability to go back in time many tragedies could have been avoided. But as it stands, *if* today had never happened Pa could be in the fields where he belongs, Georgie might still be with us and I never would have set foot in Belmont Park.

I'll be forever thankful to Lady Belmont - such a kind and generous mistress. Since I informed her ladyship of my intention to learn to read and write not a week has gone by without a new book being placed in my hands from her husband's library - so keen is she that I accomplish my ambition. Of course, when Manny first started teaching me, the words on the pages made no sense and he had to read them to me, but now even the longer words hardly trouble me and I can read as fluently as the next person... I only wish the same could be said about my writing.

Without fail, Lady Belmont ensures I take my allotted half-day off every four weeks and I'm grateful to her for this because after that fateful day when I visited home, forgot the tea and lost Georgie, Mrs Langley never did let me out of her sight again. Now I can keep an eye on Pa, whose mental state is deteriorating rapidly now a whole year has passed by without him taking a step out of the cottage, and I can take the pressure off Mary, even if it's only for a few hours, and reinstate some much-needed discipline and order amongst the children.

I'm not expecting to see Ma today, she's never home anymore. Mary tells me she leaves the cottage early in the morning and returns once darkness has fallen. Nobody knows where she goes and so each day, she takes away any opportunity for her family to help lift the shadow that weighs so heavily upon her. Even when Mary told her my wages would increase, she continued to be resolutely mute. I'd harboured a faint hope this news might lessen her despondency, even though it would still never be enough to replace what Pa had earned, but sadly, she continues in her apathetic state.

So, here I am once again, mounting the crest of the hill to see the familiar farm labourers' cottages standing in a row.

As I reach the front door things are strangely quiet. I left Belmont Park as the sun was rising so I expect everyone to be home... apart from Ma. Daniel will be leaving for the fields soon and he should be taking Tommy with him on the off chance there will be work for them both. Maggie will be attempting to carve out some buttons, even though her six-year-old fingers aren't able to produce anything worthy of selling yet. Mary will be flitting from one thing to another, making sure the unsteady Henry doesn't fall into the fireplace and that Pa is comfortable. Our home is never quiet and the thin walls make sure every noise uttered on the inside can be heard on the outside. That's why when a soundless welcome greets me at the front door, I feel an uneasiness rising from within.

I twist the handle and step inside tripping over Pa's boots, which are still waiting patiently to be worn again, sending a cloud of dried mud into the air. My eyes dart around taking in the sight before me. It's too soon to panic. I must keep calm.

Without a second glance I hurry next door to Uncle Will's and bang furiously on his front door, but no one answers, probably because he's already left for the fields, Will's a regular worker like my pa used to be, he'll be out until sunset.

Feeling extremely bewildered, I turn back to the cottage and stand dazed in the middle of the lonely single room. Everything is gone. The wonky stool, the mismatched chairs, the solid oak table, the basket of firewood, Pa in his bed – gone.

In great haste I run the mile back into town, stopping at Mr Allen's, Mr Gale's and the haberdashers. Nobody had seen Mary for days, nor have they seen the boys searching for work, or ma wondering aimlessly.

'Manny, Manny!' I run breathlessly into the stables; half my hair having fallen out from its pins. After Kitty's exit, the accusations concerning John Belmont had come to nothing. The wound inflicted on my heart by Manny's doubts over my character have long since vanished and he has remained my faithful confidant and friend, as I believe he always will do, no matter what might happen in the future.

Shocked by my dishevelled appearance, Manny turns to face me. 'What's wrong... shouldn't you be at home?'

I bend over and place my hands on my knees, gasping for breath. 'They've gone...' I breathe heavily and try to rub away a stitch stabbing down my side. 'Everything's gone.'

'You mean Mary?'

'Yes, everyone, no one's seen them - they've all gone.'

'Your pa?'

'Yes!' I emphasise the word - is he not hearing me? 'The house is empty, Manny. Pa hasn't been out of that cottage for a year, something terrible must have happened.'

'Slow down Becks, there might be a simple explanation.' Manny rubs his stubbled chin in thoughtful consideration. 'Are you sure you've asked *everyone* who might know anything about their whereabouts?'

'Yes, of course I have. Mary wouldn't leave without telling me, and Pa… oh Manny, he shouldn't be moved, what if something's happened to him?'

He comes quickly too my side and gently takes my hand. 'We'll find them, Becks.' I'm so distressed, I don't even realise my hand has naturally tightened around his.

'How?'

'You've got to think… is there anybody else who might know where they are… anybody?

'There's one person I was unable to find, I called on him first – my Uncle Will, I must try again.' I try to make my way straight back out of the stables, but Manny keeps a firm hold on my hand and pulls me back.

'Hey, you'll make yourself ill dashing around like that. Tell me, where is your Uncle Will?'

'He works on the Belmont's farm; he could be anywhere in the fields.'

'Rebekah!' A call from outside the stable awakens me to the warm touch of Manny's hand holding onto mine. My cheeks flush at the touch and I let go without meeting his eye.

'Rebekah…?' Lady Belmont's head appears round the corner of the open double doors. She's initially taken aback by the strong smell of manure and damp straw, and she squints into the darkened stables, the brightness of the sun from outside temporarily limiting her vision. I have to remind myself to perform a curtsy, so shocked I am at seeing my mistress in such a place. Manny mutters a polite greeting under his breath and bobs his head so low that his face stares directly at the dirty floor.

'Is anything all right? I saw you running down the drive and you did not look well.'

I feel a drop of sweat trickle down my face and for the first time notice a pounding in my head. 'I am well, ma'am.'

'But shouldn't you be at home?' she asks cautiously side stepping a pile of horse manure.

'Yes, ma'am.'

'Then tell me, what is the matter?'

'I do not wish to burden you, ma-am.'

'Nonsense, you will do nothing of the sort.'

I search her face and realise she is genuinely concerned. 'My family are missing, ma'am. I have not been told they are moving to a new home, indeed, there is no reason for them to do so.' From the corner of my eye I see Manny picking up a hand brush and sidling behind a large grey mare to comb its long fine mane, his eyes are firmly upon the creature, but I notice his ears have pricked up and he's listening to every word spoken.

'What is being done,' asks Lady Belmont. 'Someone must be looking for them?'

'I was about to search for my Uncle Will on the farm.'

'Which farm?'

'Mr Greaves', ma-am.'

'That is on the other side of town,' she says in shock. 'You cannot walk all the way there in your condition - take the carriage.'

'Ma-am, I cannot not do that, it wouldn't be right.'

'Then send this man.' Lady Belmont glances to the tall grey mare where the top of Manny's curly locks can be seen bending behind the animal. He lifts the brush to his face and scratches an itch with the back of his palm. 'Take the horse and find Rebekah's...' She circles her hand in the air, trying to remember the name.

'Will, his name is William Godwin,' I insert.

'Yes, take the horse, find Mr Godwin and bring back a message.'

'Yes, ma-am.' Manny dips his head low and leads the horse out of the stables with the animal between himself and Lady Belmont.

'Is there a chance your father has moved on for better work? You may get knowledge of it in the coming days through a letter.'

'No one in my family can write, ma'am,' I say, not bothering to mention about Ma, the details of her condition are too complicated to explain and of no interest to her ladyship. 'And, there is not a chance of my pa finding better work, he is paralysed.'

Lady Belmont raises a hand to her mouth, clearly disturbed by the news. I can tell she's embarrassed – she has no idea about the hardships we face and what we have to suffer. I don't blame her, how could she know, having lived her whole life in luxury.

Recovering herself, but not enough to look straight at me, her ladyship finally responds, 'Please inform me when you hear any news... I assume I will see you at midday?'

'Yes, ma-am, I will be there to dress you as usual.'

I cannot settle. The needle pushes in and out of the fabric lying across my knees as if nothing is wrong, but my mind is a jumble of irrational thoughts. Every few minutes I find my eyes flitting towards the back entrance leading out into the yard, checking to see if the door is about to open and allow Manny into the kitchen with some news about my family

Lucy keeps watching me as she's peeling the vegetables at the table. My distress is upsetting her - she knows only too well the heartache of being separated from your family. She has no hope of reclaiming her own, but the possibility that I might recover mine sees her bottom lip being anxiously chewed.

Hetty brings me another cup of tea on a tray and as she draws closer, she puts a finger to her lips to share a secret. Keeping her hand low and hidden behind her hip she extends her middle and index fingers and moves them swiftly together from side to side in small movements.

The gesture makes me smile. 'Thank you, Hetty'

She spoons two mounds of sugar into my tea, completely against Mrs Langley's rules since the servants are not allowed any of this precious commodity. I'm grateful for the sweetened liquid and take a sip.

'Did you hear that?' says Lucy flicking a piece of carrot skin from her knife and lifting her head alertly.

It's Manny.

'Becks!' he cries stumbling into the kitchen. 'I f-found h-him.' He takes large gasps of air and takes a moment to regain control of his breathing. 'I'm sorry it took me so long, your Uncle Will is a hard man to find.' Hetty slips him a cup of tea. 'Thank you, Hetty.' He signs his thanks and blows a single curl off his sweaty forehead. 'They've been evicted.'

I stand at the news, placing Lady Belmont's gown onto the chair next to me. 'Mr Greaves has thrown them out?'

'They haven't been paying rent for at least six months, did you not know?'

I find myself sitting down again, mouth slightly ajar. 'No... I had no idea.' Hetty silently plops another spoonful of sugar into my tea.

'Will said Mr Greaves has been as lenient as possible, more so than for any other family, since your pa had been such a good worker, but he had to move them on, he needs the cottage for able-bodied labourers.'

'But Daniel works for him... and Tommy's just started, ever since he turned six.'

'Becks...' Manny kneels on the floor before me and softens his voice. 'They're children, Mr Greaves is not going to keep the cottage for them.'

'I suppose you're right.' Staring at my knees and trying to digest this new information I see Manny move his hand, it almost reaches mine when Lucy speaks and he snatches it away.

'Do you know where they are, Manny?' she squeaks in her small, hardly audible voice.

'Will says they've gone to claim parish relief.'

I feel my face being drawn of blood and hold tightly onto the arm of the chair.

'What's the matter?' he asks with a face full of concern.

'My pa wasn't born in Belmont; he was born twenty miles

away in the neighbouring parish. He can't be moved twenty miles, not in his condition.'

'Will said they left two weeks ago.'

I feel tears prickle behind my eyes. 'Why has no one told me?'

'He didn't say.'

'I'm sorry, Rebekah,' says Lucy apologetically. 'Lady Belmont is ringing the bell; would you like me to dress her for luncheon?'

I sniff. 'Erm, no… it's all right, Lucy, she wanted to be kept informed, I will go and tell her the news.' I turn to Manny. 'Thank you for riding all that way, I hope it won't get you into trouble with Mr Butler for neglecting your duties.'

'You know I'd do anything for you, Becks, you only need to ask. Besides, Lady Belmont sent me… and I'm not afraid of Mr Butler.' He cups a hand round his mouth and whispers. 'I actually think he rather likes me.' He smiles momentarily allowing his eyes to rest on mine before he stands up and moves away.

The day passes slowly and I find it difficult to concentrate on anything. The problem is, I know what getting relief from the parish means and my uneasiness only grows with every passing hour. The journey Pa had to undertake must have been horrendous, anything could have happened, what if…no, the thought is too much for me to contemplate and I hurry upstairs to attend to Lady Belmont before dinner.

As I pin another curl in place, I know her ladyship is discussing plans for her summer season in London, but the words don't lodge in my mind because my anxieties immediately push them away.

'What do you think, Rebekah?' She looks at me through the reflection in the mirror and the sound of my name alerts me to her voice.

'I do beg your pardon, ma'am, could you repeat the question?' I push in the final pin.

'I was discussing materials for my new gown, but I see you

are preoccupied?'

My cheeks flush with embarrassment, I had not intended my detachment from the conversation to have been so obvious. I turn to a side table so I can collect a diamond encrusted necklace from its box, but as I do so, my heart begins to pound in my ears and suddenly the room feels like it's closing in – I can't do this.

'I'm sorry, ma-am.' I twist back to the mirror and hang the necklace round her ladyship's neck and fasten the clasp. Lady Belmont rotates her figure to look at me, her arm resting on the back of the shield-backed chair.

'What are you sorry for, Rebekah? I understand you must be extremely worried about your family and here I am prattling on about trivial matters like dress designs.'

'No, ma'am, I'm sorry because I must hand in my notice.'

Lady Belmont stands and, in her astonishment, forgets to brush the creases out of her gown. 'This is shocking news; may I ask why? I do not want to lose you Rebekah, I will give you whatever support is necessary for you to stay here.'

'I thank you for your kindness, ma'am, I truly do. But I must find my family, I will not settle until I do.'

'I have my season in London, perhaps you will have found your family by the time I return, there is no reason to do anything so drastic as handing in your notice. I release you, go and find them until I return, how about that?' Her proposal makes sense, for I was not to travel with her ladyship to London anyway. It had been arranged that I would stay behind at Belmont Park to help Mrs Langley with some much-needed repairs and restoration on the house that cannot normally be attended to whilst the family are present.

'I am sorry, ma'am, but I'm afraid once I have found them, I will need to stay close by to help my sister, Mary. If you could be so kind as to inform me of any suitable positions in Market Ashton, I would be forever in your debt.'

Lady Belmont looks visibly disappointed. 'Of course, I will write and ask Lady Montague, she is a close acquaintance and has many contacts in the area... in fact, she was telling me only in her last letter how she needed a new governess for her daughter... I'll ask her.'

'Ma'am,' I begin, horrified by her thought process. 'I do not need such a high-ranking position; a simple maid's situation will do.'

'You will take on no such position, you are too good to accept a lower position.'

'I must work, ma'am, I'll take anything.'

'You are more than capable of teaching, you have read nearly half of my husband's library, have you not?'

'Yes, ma'am.'

'And you are good at retaining the knowledge you read?'

'Well...' I hesitate not wanting to sound boastful.

'I will answer for you in the positive.'

'But my writing—'

'Is not important. If I had children, I would hire you as their governess.'

'Thank you, ma'am.' I look bashfully down to the floor at the compliments hitting my ears.

'I will be sorry to lose you, Rebekah, I feel as if I have trained you with my own two hands.'

'You have ma-am, and I greatly appreciate all you have done for me.'

'I will give you a good reference.'

'Thank you, ma'am.' I dip a knee and begin to proceed out the room.

'And the book you currently have from Lord Belmont's library...' Her ladyship adds as an afterthought. 'Keep it, as a token of your time here at Belmont Park.'

Under the bed I find my wooden box, which has collected a layer of dust since I left it there over a year and a half ago. Walking into the kitchen with it tucked under my arm, Hetty and Lucy instantly take notice and gather around me. They are deeply grieved to hear of my decision to leave. Hetty steps forward to embrace me, her round figure and broad arms encircle around, causing such a comforting sensation to radiate through me that I find it hard withdraw from her hold. With overwhelming regret, I say goodbye to my loyal friends and wipe away the single tear which I have allowed to escape down my cheek. Lucy's sniffles sound as I close the door gently behind me and enter the dark narrow corridor for the final time.

As I step foot from the dimness of the corridor into the bright sun-filled yard, I hear Mrs Langley calling out behind me. 'Where are you going?' she asks chasing me out through the front door.

'I have handed in my notice, Mrs Langley.'

'I haven't been informed.'

'I beg your pardon, but I answer to Lady Belmont, I am sure she will inform you herself in due course.'

Affronted by the bluntness of my speech she stares down her long triangular nose at me. 'Why are you leaving?'

'My family have gone to claim parish relief in Market Ashton, I must go to be with them.'

'Parish relief?' Her forehead furrows. 'And your ma has gone with them?'

'They've all gone, why would my ma not go?'

'I assumed, since she is the only able-bodied adult in your household, that she would stay and earn a living.'

'You have assumed wrongly, Mrs Langley.' I'm not going to explain my family's problems to this woman, she does not need to know.

A small grunt escapes her mouth as she eyes me up and down. Without a further word she retreats back into the house and closes the door in my face.

There's now only one more person I cannot leave without saying goodbye. Butterflies begin swarming in my stomach – he's not going to like this. I purposely left no time to consider my decision, otherwise I know he'll try to persuade me to stay and spend every waking hour searching for another way for me to rescue my family. But this way, I've rendered him helpless. My notice has been given; the decision has been made.

It doesn't take me long to find him. Manny is in the stable yard carrying over two buckets of water. He smiles when he sees me. 'What are you doing here at this time?' His eyes suddenly focus on the wooden box under my arm and his face drops. 'Where are you going?'

I see it in his eyes - he knows exactly where I'm going.

'I need to find them, Manny.'

'You're coming back though, aren't you?'

'I can't be twenty miles away from them, you know it's not possible for me to come back to Belmont after I find them...' I swallow nervously. 'I handed in my notice to Lady Belmont.'

He doesn't say anything and the sound of a horse snorting loudly is heard from inside the stalls.

'How are you travelling?' he asks with his voice catching and he coughs to clear his throat.

'I haven't sent my weekly wages to Mary yet, I was going to hand them to her today, so I'll catch a stagecoach, then walk on foot until I find them.'

'What will you do for food?'

'I had a big breakfast; it will keep me going.'

He draws a line with his foot self-consciously in the dusty ground. 'Be careful, won't you.' He lifts his head and holds my gaze.

My heart pounds inside my chest - I know he doesn't want to let me go. The longer I stand face to face with Manny, the harder it's going to be to leave him behind. 'I must go now, if I've got any chance of finding them before nightfall.' He nods lightly and with great difficultly I tear my eyes away from his and begin to walk away.

'Wait!' I can hear his footsteps drumming on the ground behind me. 'I can't let you go.'

'Manny, my pa's health is worsening and Mary will need me, I cannot not stay here.'

'No, that's not what I meant... I'm not asking you to stay.' He lowers his eyes self-consciously to the ground and shuffles his feet again. 'I can't let you go without...' He takes a step towards me, so that we're almost touching, but then changes his mind and steps back.

'Without what?' I can feel tears brimming under my eyelids. I need to leave, but Manny's reluctance to let me go isn't making this very easy.

He lets out a frustrated cry and looks away over the stable yard. 'Becks, this is difficult for me to say, I've been wanting to tell you for so long...' A lock of his hair falls over his eyes and he clears his dry throat. 'I have to tell you, I...' He laughs shyly. 'This sounded a lot better in my head, I'm just going to say it... I love you.' His cheeks flush and slowly he lifts his eyes to mine trying to gauge my reaction, but before he can, a wheelbarrow full of horse dung inconveniently rattles out of the stables with Nate pushing behind.

'Good afternoon Rebekah.' The twelve-year-old nods his cap at me. 'Where do you want this lot, Manny?'

'Er, round the back,' Manny answers moving away his flushed face and trying not to catch the boy's eye. Nate, not realising he had interrupted such an intimate moment, manoeuvres away the wheelbarrow and its contents and whistles a merry tune as he leaves the stable yard.

Manny looks at me awkwardly. 'Can you forget I said anything, Becks, it was foolish of me to utter such a thing when you are about to leave... and under such circumstances.' He shakes his head in regret and walks away.

'Manny, you didn't let me answer.'

He freezes to the spot, but he doesn't turn around.

'I'd like to see your face, if I may... I don't really want to address the same sentiment to the back of your head.'

A small smile slowly emerges as he rotates his body to face mine. He closes the gap between us and takes both my hands in his. 'You need to be extra careful now,' he says softly. 'I'd like you back in one piece.' He takes my arm, enfolding it through his own and starts walking me across the yard. 'What are you going to do for work?'

'I've asked Lady Belmont to enquire after new positions for me, she has a few acquaintances in the parish.'

'Does she know of anything?'

'Only one possibility, but it's not suitable, no matter what she might say.'

'Why is it not suitable?'

'It's for a governess.'

'I'll say it again.' He stops and leans in closer with a humorous smile. 'Why is it not suitable?'

'Come on Manny, I learned to read and write six months ago.'

'And how many books have you read since? Your knowledge is better than mine because when you read you remember what you've learned... some might describe you as a genius.'

'They won't want someone like me working for them.'

He squeezes my hand gently. 'Becks, they won't know your background, if Lady Belmont is recommending you there will be no doubt of your ability, or your standing. Please...' He takes a stray strand of hair and tucks it underneath my bonnet, letting his hand slide down to gently brush my cheek. 'Consider accepting the position, if you are offered it.'

The sound of an empty wheelbarrow trundling back and the stable boy's faint whistle, causes Manny to let go of my hand and step back.

'I promise you, I'll consider it,' I whisper as his soft emerald eyes gaze directly into mine, weakening my resolve and catching me completely off guard.

Chapter Eighteen

A bell can be heard clanging loudly after I pull on the rope handle. Two large and imposing wooden doors are directly before me as I step back to face the horrors of what I might find inside.

Market Ashton poorhouse is the first place I need to search, it's where they would have come on their arrival. Pa can't work so he would have been offered accommodation and if I'm right, Henry will be here too. The fate of the others all depends on the leniency of the parish.

The ringing of the bell continues to echo behind the doors. The entire place is dreary, and a host of trees hang their leaves limply, casting a dark shadow over the lower level of the red brick building. Considering how warm July has been, I give a little shudder. So many dreadful stories about these overcrowded disease infested places have met my ears in the past, and now I'm fearful they are all true, that once you cross the threshold, you'll never see the light of day again. I'm so angry with Pa for not letting me know he couldn't pay the rent. I could have done something to help, Manny would have thought of a solution - he always does. The thought of Manny brings tears to my eyes as I stand all alone waiting for someone to answer the endless tolling of the bell.

Finally, one of the heavy oak doors creaks open and a small woman with a crisp white apron and matching bonnet greets me with a straight set mouth. She doesn't speak, so I presume it is up to me to speak first. 'I'd like to enquire about a family and if they've been to claim poor relief?'

'Name.' The woman demands, though not in the same condescending tones as Mrs Langley.

'Barnes.'

She disappears but leaves the door open. The corridor is wide and half-way down a side door opens to emit a line of children marching out in single file. A little girl turns and looks directly at me, her eyes are hollow and lifeless, and she blinks at me once before continuing her march along the corridor behind the other children. The rapid threat of tears heightens, and I flick my eyelids open and shut to steer them off course. All I want to do is hurry back to Belmont Park and wrap Lucy up in a tight embrace. This is the kind of place she would have come after her parents and sisters lost their lives in the fire; this is what she had to endure when her life was at its worst. Surely, when you hit the very depths of despair and you've nowhere else to turn, there should be a kind and re-assuring hand waiting to pull you up, not a fist that's going to knock you down deeper than where you first started.

My heart breaks – it shouldn't be like this.

'Excuse me, miss, do you want to know or not?' With a jolt I come back to reality and hear the impatient tap of the small woman's foot on the stone steps. 'John Barnes, Margaret Barnes, plus five bairns?'

'Yes, that's them.'

She reads from a large book in her arms. 'They're collecting the relief, but haven't taken up accommodation in the poor-house.'

'But my pa, he can't work.'

'I'm sorry, I know no more.'

'Have you housed them elsewhere?'

'There is no record of it.' She reads along the line. 'They collect their allotted money every Friday, that's all the book tells me.'

I thank the woman and meander slowly down the path anxious to get as far away from the place as possible. Once out on the road I consider where I should look next. Although Market Ashton is a large village, it's much smaller than the town of Belmont, so there can't be many places for my family to be hiding. Further down the lane a group of houses catch my attention and I head in their direction first, poking my head into every hidden alcove where a group of people without a home might be sheltering.

The first cottage in the cluster has a thatched roof and is neatly kept with roses bordering the front. I don't hold out much hope, but I tap on the small brass knocker anyway and wait patiently for an answer. A young girl, probably the maid, comes to the door looking worn and weary. 'Sorry to bother you, but I'm looking for a family that's moved to the area recently.'

'What's the name?' the girl asks.

'Barnes.'

The girl shakes her head, she hadn't heard of anyone by that name.

I continue knocking at all the cottages down the lane, but no one has seen or heard of any family known as Barnes.

The final rays of light from the sun disappear as I reach the end of Market Ashton and I'm engulfed in darkness. The lane I've veered onto is as isolated and lonely as I feel, and my legs become heavy as weariness washes over me. My body cannot carry me much further, I haven't eaten since breakfast and my strength is slowly ebbing away.

A flicker of light catches my eye somewhere in the pitch black. As I get closer, the shadowy shape of a farmhouse emerges and candlelight escapes through the thin cracks in its closed shutters. It's my only hope of shelter, before I curl up miserably under a hedgerow for a solitary night under the stars.

'Can I help you, miss?' A plain-looking woman answers the door.

'I beg your pardon for disturbing you at such an hour, I am a visitor to Market Ashton without a place to lay my head for the night, have you a barn I can sleep in... I don't need to be in the house?' I quickly add for fear the woman might turn me away. 'I can't afford to pay you anything, but I'll earn my keep by completing whatever chores you ask of me before I leave in the morning.'

The woman laughs. 'Is word spreading that I'm starting an inn?' Maybe I'm over tired, but the joke escapes me. 'I'm very happy to offer you the barn.' She smiles kindly. 'But you'll have to join the others, they seem fine enough, you shouldn't come to any trouble.'

'Thank you, miss, I appreciate your kindness.'

'Consider it a gift, I don't need your labour in return.'

'That is very generous.'

'If you'll follow me this way.' The woman takes a candle from the hall and steps out into the darkness, leading me across the farmyard. 'You look worn out,' she comments.

'I've travelled far today.'

'From where?'

'Belmont.'

'Well, I never...' The woman chuckles again as we reach the barn and she opens the door wide enough for me to step inside. 'These in here might be your acquaintances.'

Her comment puzzles me, but in my tired stupor I refrain from questioning her, the thought of sleep being the only thing to fill my mind. As I enter the barn there's a movement amongst a pile of hay and a figure sits up.

'You keep the light,' says the woman passing the candle into my hands.

'But you need to get back to farm-house.'

'I know that yard like the back of my hand, I'll be fine.' She leaves me as the figure amongst the hay stands up. I hold the candle up higher, trying to catch the person's face, and begin to wonder if I might have been safer in a hedgerow.

'I- I'm sorry to disturb you,' I stammer. 'The woman said I could sleep here for the night.'

'Rebekah?'

All my fears vanish when I hear the sound of this soft, scared little voice. 'Mary?'

The figure comes tumbling towards me and in the candle-light my sister's familiar face appears. 'How did you find us?'

she asks in amazement.

'I have no idea, but I thank God that I did.' I embrace her and a wave of relief floods over me. 'Is everyone here?'

'Yes, the children have been asleep for the last hour, Ma's just nodded off and Pa… I don't know, he doesn't sleep much.'

'How is Pa?'

'I've made him as comfortable as I can.' The light flickers across her pale face and she stares intensely at me, clamping down on her lower lip so the blood cannot circulate.

'Why didn't you tell me you had to move,' I ask softly, not wanting it to sound like a scolding.

'I asked Ma to write… did you not get a letter?'

'No, I received nothing.' Whether Ma neglected to write the letter or it got lost on the way is a question no one can answer, but since the journey from our old cottage to Belmont Park is merely a few miles I lean towards the former.

'How did Pa handle the journey?'

'Not well, we did the best we could, but we only had the plank and we had to keep changing carts. Danny and Tommy carried him when we couldn't hitch a lift - they were so sore when we finally arrived in Market Ashton, if it wasn't for Mrs Arthur offering us shelter in the barn, I don't know what we would have done. Poor relief is only for food and clothes, we still haven't enough for rent because we haven't been getting your wages.'

'Why didn't Pa and Henry stay in the poorhouse?'

'Pa wouldn't allow us to be split up.'

I glance around the dark barn, the smell of the dried hay reminding me of Manny. 'Where is Pa?'

'Over there.' Mary nods to the other side of the barn.

'Why is he all alone?'

'We have to keep him separate from the children; his screams wake them up.'

'Screams?'

'Yes, he has been having very vivid nightmares because of his fever.'

'He has a fever?'

'It started the day before we left Belmont, it's been two weeks and I can't get rid of it.' She looks close to tears in the flickering light, I can't image what she's been through.

'And Ma?'

'She won't speak to us.'

'Not a word?'

'No, she looks straight through us as if we're not here, at least when we were in Belmont she acknowledged our presence.'

It's in this moment I know I've made the right decision, to have left the security of Belmont Park and be with my family. 'You try and sleep, Mary.' I place a gentle hand on her shoulder. 'I'm going to see Pa.'

Carrying the candle in my hand I take my weary legs to the other side of the barn towards the dark shape huddled up on the floor. 'Pa, are you awake?'

'Rebekah?'

'Yes, it's me.' I kneel down beside him and see he's lying on top of the wooden plank he arrived on, covered over with a pile of hay. I take his hand and squeeze it tightly. 'You're cold,' I say seeing him shiver, but when I feel his forehead, he's burning hot. 'You need to see a doctor.'

'Can't afford it, Becks...argh!' He doubles up suddenly in pain, his legs remaining motionless.

'Is the pain getting worse?'

'It's not the burning sensation, it's a different pain and it's getting more and more intense - I'll not make it through another winter.'

'Don't say things like that, I'm here now, you're going to be fine.'

'I wish I had your optimism, but what good am I here? I might as well be gone.'

He's given up...

I know he gave up on Ma and their marriage a long time ago, but he's never given up on life before. After the accident, he was always adamant he would be working again and that he would recover, even when everyone told him otherwise. Pa expects the best to happen in life no matter what, it's who he is... but now this inner strength has gone and the fight is lost.

'Please don't talk like that Pa, you're alive and where there's life, there's hope.'

In the flickering candlelight I see tears are falling down his face. The sight is too much for me to bear and my body too tired to contain the emotion I feel welling up from inside. I fling myself over Pa and cry with him, clinging gently onto his tattered shirt until I fall asleep.

Chapter Nineteen

The light from the rising sun hits my face as it shines through one of the many holes in the roof of the barn. I slowly open my eyes to find my head rising and falling steadily in time with Pa – he's still alive and we have him for another day. Lifting my head from his chest, I stretch my stiff and tired body.

'Becks!' cries Tommy running across to me with his arms open wide. 'Mary said you found us - I told Maggie you'd come, didn't I Mags?'

'He did, I wasn't certain you would find us... but you did!' Maggie jumps in glee. 'You really did!'

A tap is heard on the barn doors and Mrs Arthur enters carrying two bottles of milk. The children scurry over to her and even Henry waddles across and reaches up his arms towards her.

'Drink up, you need to grow big and strong,' she says smiling at the children crowding around and lifting Henry up into her arms, giving him a little tickle on the tummy.

'Thank you, Mrs Arthur,' they all chant in unison. She puts Henry down so he can enjoy his milk and leaves the barn.

'She's done that every day since we arrived,' says Mary. 'Doesn't ask for any money, says the cows always give them surplus.'

'It's the best milk too, Becks,' says Daniel with a broad smile and a line of milk across his upper lip. I give a quiet laugh, it's been a while since I've seen happiness on the children's faces, and despite the circumstances weighing heavily upon us, I cherish the moment.

Once the bottles have been drained, I offer to take them back to the farmhouse. Mrs Arthur opens the door and takes the load from me. 'I'd like to thank you, Mrs Arthur, for looking after my family.'

'So, they do belong to you.' She frowns. 'Your father isn't well.'

'He's worsened a lot since I last saw him.'

'Would you like me to send for a doctor?'

'We can't afford it... I don't think there's much we can do for him, apart from make him comfortable.'

'Poor man.' She shakes her head in commiseration.

'Mrs Arthur?'

'Yes.' The woman's kind brown eyes wait expectantly for me to speak.

'Could you tell me if Lady Montague lives close by?'

'Her ladyship lives in Ashton Manor; it is two miles away.' As she answers the head of a little girl appears behind Mrs Arthur's plain dress.

'Oh, good day to you,' I say smiling at the child. 'What's your name?' The girl pops her head shyly back behind her mother.

'I'm sorry,' says Mrs Arthur immediately. 'My daughter can't hear you.'

I look up at the farmer's wife. 'She's deaf?'

'Yes, from birth.'

'Does she sign?'

'Sign?' Mrs Arthur furrows her forehead.

'Yes, speak using gestures.'

She laughs. 'I've never heard of such a thing.'

'What's her name?'

'This is Emma,' she says proudly. 'We normally call her Em.'

'That's a pretty name. Do you mind if I try something?'

'Not at all.'

I crouch low to the girl who's still cowering behind her mother and I wave my hand from left to right. 'Good day,' I say again loudly and make my mouth move slowly to annunciate the sounds clearly. The girl tilts her head and looks at me curiously as I take both of my forefingers and tap them together. 'E...' I pronounce slowly before lightly tapping three fingers together on my palm. '...M – that's you.' I smile and point at the girl. 'Your name...' I tap two fingers to my head and point to her again. '...is E-M.' I repeat the letters using my hands. 'You try.' I encourage the girl to copy my signs, moving her fingers into the correct positions. 'That's it,' I praise with a clap. 'Well done.' I give Emma a thumbs up and she beams with delight.

Standing up I see Mrs Arthur's eyes are glistening. 'How did you do that... does she understand?' She takes the corner of her apron and lifts it to wipe her wet eyes.

'Let's see, shall we?' I get the girls attention by tapping her on the shoulder and begin signing 'What's your name?' I wait and see what the reaction will be... it's the first time I've taught anything and I feel suddenly nervous. The little girl looks at her hands and sticks out her tongue, trying to remember which fingers to use, first she signs E and then M.

Mrs Arthur takes her daughter into an embrace and kisses the top of her head. 'We've never been able to communicate with her before. I don't know what to say...thank you – Oh, how rude of me, I don't even know your name.'

'I'm Rebekah,' I answer, the pleasure from the scene in front of me evident on my face.

'Do you know any more, what did you call them... signs?'

'Yes, though I don't know everything, but I know enough to hold a conversation.'

'Are you staying in the barn with your family? Can you teach her more?' Mrs Arthur asks eagerly.

'I'm not certain what my plans are yet, I must find work.'

'Of course.' The middle-aged woman's enthusiasm dampens, and she nods her head in understanding.

'But I'll definitely teach Emma whatever I can whilst I'm here.' Mrs Arthur is so overcome she shouts for her husband to come and witness his daughter's newly learned skill of communication. The elation within me is unexplainable. Last night my soul was so tormented with grief, for my suffering family and my dying pa, that I felt broken. But now, something good is arising and I have a passion stirring within me to help this little girl. I need to keep pushing through the hurt and remember what Manny said, from the moments of our greatest despair great blessings can grow.

As I wave goodbye and walk across the farmyard, I have a deep longing to tell Manny how I'm feeling and the happiness I experienced when that little girl communicated for the first time... but reality hits me - I'm twenty miles away from the man I love. A part of my joy diminishes and another piece of my heart shatters as I realise, I've no idea when I'll see Manny again.

It's important I find a job if I'm to get Pa out of that barn. I can't afford to wait for Lady Belmont to send me details of any positions she's heard about from her acquaintances. Therefore, I must be bold and enquire after the governess job myself – it's the only opportunity I know about. My faith lies in Manny. I hope he's telling the truth about my intellect, and that I really am naturally gifted, because if his love for me has blurred his vision, I'm about to fall flat on my face.

Ashton Manor is a red brick building larger and more imposing than Belmont Park. Without much difficulty I find the back entrance, knock and wait.

'Can I help you?' A maid with a kind face answers the door.

'I've been told your mistress is seeking a governess for her daughter, my previous employer has recommended me, is it possible to see Lady Montague?'

'I'd need to ask our housekeeper if that's possible, please come in.' The warm welcome confuses me after the greeting I had at Belmont Park and I gratefully follow the maid inside.

The atmosphere is noisy when we enter the kitchen. The room is full of staff, at least triple the number I'm used to, if not more. Kitchen maids are chopping and peeling, a group of footmen are cleaning silver spoons, housemaids are carrying large bundles of linen, a valet glides past with a handful of neatly pressed cravats, and even a messenger boy is seen weaving in and out between them all.

'Here she is, miss.' I stand when the girl who let me in comes back with an older woman following in close pursuit.

'You are here to enquire about the governess position?' confirms the housekeeper.

'Yes, miss. I'm sorry if it is an inconvenient time, but I haven't had word from my previous employer to say if the role is still available.'

'Lady Montague is currently home; I will ask if she's free to see you. Who was your previous employer?'

'Lady Belmont of Belmont Park.' The housekeeper nods and disappears.

It isn't long before she returns. 'Her ladyship will see you now, if you will follow me.' She leads me down a rabbit warren of corridors until finally she opens a door leading into the main house and guides me into a light and airy room. A footman formally announces my name and closes the door behind me.

'Good morning, Miss Barnes, it is a pleasure to make your acquaintance. Lady Belmont has spoken highly of you and she was very pleased with your services as her lady's maid.' I dip a knee before the elegant lady sitting in an armchair, her fine satin gown falling softly down to the floor.

'Thank you, ma'am. I hope I am not being too forward in coming to you today.'

'Not at all, I believe it is a good character trait.' Lady Montague speaks kindly, but I detect a hint of haughtiness which Lady Belmont did not possess. 'Are you well read?'

'Yes, ma-am.'

'Lady Belmont tells me you have read half of her library.'

'She was very kind to me and often placed Lord Belmont's books into my hands to read at my own leisure.'

'My daughter is well advanced in her studies, being fifteen-years-old, is that something you will be able to cope with?'

'I'm afraid I have no experience behind me in order to answer your question, ma'am. All I know is that I have developed a love for learning and can retain information easily.'

'When it comes to French...' begins Lady Montague. Her words produce a rising heat to fill my cheeks and I try to hide my alarm. I'm so foolish to have allowed Manny to convince me I could do such a job. I have no knowledge of foreign languages, the thought of having to teach them never crossing my mind. In the midst of my anxiety, her ladyship continues. '... the language won't be necessary; Eliza has decided she doesn't like the subject and I agree she has learned a sufficient amount to allow her to stop. We only need the basics - music, dance, literature...' Lady Montague pauses as the heat in my cheeks becomes impossible to hide. 'You look agitated, Miss Barnes.'

'I feel I have wasted your time, ma-am. I am not able to perform the duties you require.'

'Oh.' She looks affronted. 'Why is that?'

Before I can answer a girl close to my own age walks gracefully into the room. 'Mama, look at this...' She stops short upon seeing me standing before her mother and cocks her head, smiling at me with a half-puzzled, half-amused expression.

'Eliza, I am considering whether Miss Barnes might be suitable as your new governess,' announces Lady Montague to her daughter.

'*You* are going to be my governess?' The girl looks at me dubiously, until her eyes slowly widen as if a sudden realisation has dawned in her mind. 'Oh, please, Mama, this is the person I want.'

'Oh, I'm not certain if—' In a panic I try to explain how I am under qualified for the post, but Eliza cuts me off.

'Mama, please!' the girl begs pouting her lower lip and Lady Montague looks from her daughter to myself.

'Miss Barnes,' her ladyship speaks slowly, gathering her thoughts into a decision. 'Would you like to be my daughter's governess?' Any other questions about my capability to perform the task have been completely cast aside, making it clear that the will of the daughter triumphs in this house.

'I beg your pardon, ma-am, but I'm not certain if I am fully qualified. You said you require the basics… is this to include music and dance? I don't play an instrument and I have never danced a reel in my life.'

'That does not matter, if my daughter wants you, you are hired…but I will only pay ten pounds a year since you have only knowledge to offer, I suppose I can hire separate teachers for the pursuits you lack.' If she thought I'd be offended by the sum she's offered, I'm not. I haven't lost, or gained a penny, it is the exact amount Lady Belmont paid for my services as a lady's maid, and I am exceedingly grateful for her employment.

'Mama, Miss Fishwick can teach me those things, you need not worry about that.' Eliza looks eagerly at her mother waiting for a final confirmation.

Lady Montague pauses in thought pursing her lips. 'Miss Barnes.' She turns to face me. 'May I introduce your new charge, Miss Eliza Collette Montague.'

Eliza squeals in delight and it's then I suddenly realise who she is, this is the impudent girl who offered me a lift the day after I forgot the tea and Mrs Langley crushed my toe.

'What a coincidence that we should meet again… you won't tell my father will you?' Eliza leans forward in a whisper after her mother has left the room.

All the arrangements have been made and permission granted for me not to live in. Lady Montague made it clear I was to expect no increase to my wages since I wouldn't be receiving board and accommodation. The thought of trying to squeeze more money out of the Montagues never crossed my mind, I'm simply grateful to have found a position so soon.

Eliza sighs and slumps onto a beige coloured long chair which is beautifully carved with brass fittings. 'I think I'm far too old for a governess.' She sits up looking offended. 'I am fifteen after all, what else is there to learn?' She doesn't wait for an answer. 'That's why I chose you, you look around my age and you'll understand that I don't need to be at my lessons all day.' She laughs and covers her mouth. 'I assumed you were a maid that day I gave you a ride.'

'I was.'

'What a lark!' she shrieks and I ignore her obvious amusement over my standing. 'I've a maid for a governess... even better.' She lifts her eyebrows conspiratorially.

'If you think my previous position, and the fact that we are of a similar age, means you'll not have to work as hard, you might want to think again.'

'Oh, come on, Miss Barnes, you are not much older than I, you have not forgotten how to have fun... by the way, how old *are* you?'

'I have recently turned seventeen.'

'See, we could become like sisters.' She clasps her hands together clearly pleased with herself for hiring someone she thinks will easily be manipulated for her own pleasure.

'Miss Eliza...' I have to stop this now, if she thinks her work will be diminished because of my age and standing, she has assumed wrongly. 'This position is important to me, I'm paid to be your governess, not your friend, or sister. You must work, otherwise I will be let go.'

The girl puffs out her cheeks and leans back on the long chair again. It doesn't take much intellect to presume Miss Eliza Collette is used to getting her own way. However, the prospect doesn't daunt me. I am used to disciplining my own brothers and sisters and this girl is no different to them. The girl seems perfectly harmless, but she must be put in her place immediately, I cannot have her jeopardising my position because of her unwillingness to work. 'So, tell me, what have you been studying?' I ask watching her stare up at the ornately designed ceiling.

Eliza sits up, yawns and stretches out her arms. 'I'm too tired, Miss Barnes. Perhaps we could take a break?'

'We haven't started yet.'

She stands and shakes out the creases in her gown. 'But we have done a lot of talking and that makes me sleepy. You can take a look around the library whilst I lie down in my room.'

She smiles at me innocently.

'All right, since this is my first day, I will allow you to lie down - but come tomorrow we do things my way.' I make sure my eyes meet her own, keeping a firm hold to reinforce my authority. Eliza manages to keep the fixed smile on her face, but it's forced, and she sees she's met her match. 'Will you show me the way to the library, and I will find a book for us to read together after your rest?'

She makes a final study of my face before taking a cowering step towards me. 'You will not work me too hard, will you Miss Barnes?' Her sky-blue eyes turn sadly to my own - if Eliza thinks she can make me feel guilty so I neglect my responsibilities, she's wrong again.

'Do not worry Miss Eliza, you will be quite safe, I only ask that you try your best.'

'That means not having rests before work has begun, doesn't it?' she mumbles to the floor.

'That's exactly what I mean, but who's to say learning needs to be dull and tedious, you may find you don't want to rest.' Eliza catches my light-hearted tone and lifts her face to see a smile is beginning to rise slightly on both sides of my mouth – she squeals.

'Oh, Miss Barnes, we are going to have so much fun together.' She claps her hands. 'I promise I will work much better today after I rest, but from tomorrow I will follow your lead.'

This is the first time I've set foot in a library and as I enter the room my jaw drops. The room is covered from floor to ceiling with mahogany cases, the spines of the books on the shelves filling the room with colour. Tentatively, I walk inside after Eliza has left me. It feels wrong for me to be here and the slightest noise makes me jump, each creaking floorboard causing me to cautiously turn my head towards the door in case someone has come to throw me out.

I work my way slowly round the room and come to a stop when I find an interest in the section labelled *Rome*. Since Ashton Manor exudes a classical style, it can't hurt Eliza to understand the history behind the magnificent architecture of her home. I trail my fingers along the spines until I reach a dark blue book about Michelangelo and his Sistine Ceiling. Pulling it carefully off the shelf I flick through its pages, mesmerised by the beautiful engravings I find inside.

The creak of a footstep on the floor behind me awakens my ears to a newcomer into the library. Startled, I spin guiltily around as if I did not have permission to be perusing Lord Montague's bookshelves. I find a gentleman has entered. He is wearing black knee-high boots which have been shined with great care and attention, finely pressed beige breeches with not a crease to be seen, and a perfectly fitted dark green jacket. My first impulse is to utter an embarrassed apology, dip my knee and flee the room - but the words get caught in my throat, the curtsy is left unperformed and my feet are fastened to the spot as I slowly lift my eyes to his face.

Chapter Twenty

'Manny?'

He stops in the doorway and his eyes widen in recognition. One thing's for certain – he wasn't expecting to see me here. He's trying to decide how to respond and his mouth opens and closes without any audible words escaping. I'm not certain how long we both stand for, staring at each other's unexpected presence, but it feels like time has suddenly stood still.

'Miss Barnes... Miss Barnes?' I hear my name being called cheerfully down the corridor - it's Eliza and she pokes her head around the door. 'I have rested, and I am ready to learn... Oh, Manny, you are home, I had no idea you had returned.' She walks to my side. 'I see you've met my new governess... Miss Barnes, this is my brother.'

I dip a slight curtsy... but I daren't look up for fear I might give away our acquaintance.

'He is studying at Cambridge,' continues Eliza ignorant of our joint discomfort. 'You will discover he has all the brains and left me with none.' She laughs girlishly. 'Don't worry, he's not home much and won't bother us.' She makes for the door and realises I haven't followed behind. 'Come, Miss Barnes.'

I do as I'm bid and don't look up until I reach the doorway where Manny's figure is standing. Slowly, I lift my eyes until they lock with his - I pause... then follow Eliza down the corridor.

Eliza's endless chatter surrounds me as I try and make sense of what has happened. Manny is a... Montague? No, this can't be – his name is Emmanuel Smith, the groom at Belmont Park who wears baggy shirts, grubby breeches and has a lingering scent of horse manure. But this version of Manny is neatly shaven, his clothes are pressed and clean and I'm sure the aroma of rose petals met my nose.

'Is that not so, Miss Barnes?' Eliza's sky-blue eyes wait expectantly for an answer... she looks nothing like her brother,

her face is long and her figure is petite.

'I beg your pardon, Miss Eliza?'

'To be cooped up inside on such a beautiful day is rather loathsome, don't you think?'

'Yes, I do agree with you, but you have to study.' I open a book on Roman architecture, desperately trying to refocus my thoughts on the task at hand.

Eliza puffs out her cheeks. 'I am too old to study,' she says sulkily. 'I have told Mama a thousand times.'

'Yes, so you've repeatedly told me and I've only been here a few hours.'

'Sorry.' She lowers her eyelashes and I continue to mindlessly flick through the pages in the book. Suddenly one of the engravings of an Ancient Roman ruin catches my attention. 'Maybe we don't need to learn inside, Miss Eliza.'

'I've always had my lessons indoors.'

'Look at this...' I place before her examples of roman architecture. 'Books are important, but the real thing is better. Come on, I'll show you.'

We spend the next hour studying the details of Ashton Manor. Its exterior is covered with pediments, cornices and pillars, all mirror images of their ancient counterparts. We spend our time comparing what we see in the engravings to the intricate designs of the Palladian home we have full access to explore.

'This has been the most fascinating history lesson I've ever had,' declares Eliza as we enter the front door into the hall. 'You've set a high precedent, Miss Barnes. I'll expect no less from you in the future - let us dress now for luncheon.'

'Dress?' I look at my plain dress in a panic, I wasn't prepared for formal dining when I left the Arthur's farm this morning – not that I could have been any more prepared since the only dresses I own are the ones I wore in service at Belmont Park.

'Yes, you are joining us for lunch?'

'I would feel more comfortable eating downstairs in the kitchen.'

Eliza snorts. 'What a lark!' she exclaims in mirth. 'You will do no such thing, you are to dine with us, you will not be accepted downstairs.'

'Not accepted?'

She touches my arm with a look of pity. 'Poor you, do you

not know? As a governess you belong nowhere - you are in between. You are no longer cut from the same cloth as those downstairs, but I'm afraid you are also not one of us.' She lets out a short laugh as if she finds my new situation amusing. 'All my governesses have joined us for luncheon and so shall you.' She tucks her hand familiarly under my arm. 'You shall help me dress, since you are not changing.' Her nose wrinkles at my outfit as if she's noticed it for the first time. 'Miss Barnes, you really must buy a new dress, I have only this moment realised how much your current attire makes you look like a maid, and I cannot have Papa discovering the truth.'

I have never felt so awkward in my life - so much so I've almost forgotten how to eat.

'Where is Manny, Papa?' asks Eliza slurping clear onion soup from her spoon.

Lord Montague is a fierce looking gentleman whose greying side whiskers merge into his cheeks and deep bushy eyebrows almost cover his eyes, in him I can see the family resemblance, his oval face matching that of his son. 'Emmanuel is not home, Eliza,' he growls.

'He is, we saw him in the library this morning.'

Lord Montague pauses, his spoon poised in the air almost touching his lips. 'He has not presented himself to me.'

'Perhaps he needed a book for his studies and has now left.'

'Don't talk nonsense, he wouldn't come all the way from Cambridge to fetch a book. I will have words when I see the boy.' He sips the soup and fills the spoon again.

'What have you learned this morning, Eliza?' asks Lady Montague sitting next to her husband.

'The architecture of Ancient Rome, it's really rather fascinating.'

Lord Montague lifts his bushy eyebrows with interest. 'Which bit?' he growls again. His words suggest an awesome fear should be held at all times by people in his presence, and from what I deduce from our extremely short acquaintance, the oval face is the only thing he and Manny have in common - he is nothing like his son. However, Eliza seems oblivious to her father's fierce persona and continues talking airily.

'We learned about triangular pediments and friezes – oh and I like ionic pillars the best because they reflect the figures of roman ladies, the curly volutes are symbolic of their rolled-up hair. We have such capitals at the front of Ashton Manor, did you know this gives the house a distinctly feminine appearance?' She smiles as her parents shocked faces turn to her.

'Who taught you this?' demands Lord Montague with his voluminous eyebrows knitted together.

'Why, Miss Barnes of course, Father.'

The fearsome gentleman casts a glance in my direction, running his eyes up and down my face. 'You are Miss Barnes, I assume.' It's the first time he's paid any attention to me since walking into the room.

'Yes, sir.'

'Where have you come from?'

'Belmont Park.'

'There are no children at Belmont Park.'

'I was Lady Belmont's lady's maid, sir.' I swallow keeping eye contact with the man, hoping he will not dig deeper and reveal how lowly my position really is in the world.

He grunts and continues with his soup – he appears to be satisfied with my answer.

The day has ended and I have seen nothing more of Manny. I'm beginning to wonder if his sudden presence in the library was simply a trick my mind has played knowing how much I miss him. But no, it can't be my imagination - Eliza had seen him too.

Having left Ashton Manor and walked down its long winding drive, I pass the gatehouse and turn out onto the lane. A long red brick wall is built on one side marking the Montague's estate and on the other side high hedgerows shut out the fields. At some point, I am to turn left over a stile, but I can't remember how far down the lane I am to walk.

'Becks...' Manny steps out in front of me. He'd been leaning against the brick wall obviously waiting for me to leave the house. He looks at me sheepishly and without a smile.

Now the moment has come to confront him my words fail me, there are so many questions to ask that I don't know what to say first. I stand helplessly in front of him, the wind tussling Manny's curls around his head, it's like I'm staring at a stranger.

'I'm so sorry, Becks, I should have told you.' He steps towards me lifting clenched hands over his mouth, biting the knuckles on his thumb as he nervously waits for me to answer.

'Told me what exactly?' My heart is pounding, though my face remains calm. 'I'm sorry Manny, but you need to tell me exactly who you are.'

He exhales deeply and closes his eyes in regret. 'I'm Emmanuel Montague and... I live here.' He gestures towards Ashton Manor, the tip of its roof being the only thing visible from the lane.

'Who is Emmanuel Smith?'

'Also me.' He hangs his head to his chest.

'You can't be two people, Manny... which is the lie?'

'Don't say it like that, Becks.' He snaps his head back up his emerald eyes filling up with hurt.

I try to not let his vulnerability weaken my resolve to find the answers to his deception... *he's* the one who has been lying and *I* am the one who is hurt. 'Come on, Manny, which one is the lie, because you can't be born into riches and poverty at the same time.' He closes his lips together, reluctant to admit his dishonesty.

'Smith... he's the lie.'

Half of me wants to be angry, whilst the other half wants to cry – how could I have been so misled? I cross my arms and turn my face away from his.

'Please, let me explain and you might understand.'

My emotions are no longer split - anger wins. 'Don't bother explaining - I understand well enough, you've been lying to me all this time.' I need to get away from him, conflicting thoughts are racing through my mind and I don't know what to believe anymore.... *Do you trust me?* His words echo in my mind from the day Georgie disappeared. Emmanuel Smith, I trusted him with my whole heart, but Emmanuel Montague... I don't even know who he is.

My feet take me further down the lane, the stile I'm supposed to be looking out for becoming a distant thought in my mind. Manny follows behind and brings himself level with me. It's difficult, but I try to keep my focus firmly on the lane ahead. 'What about Lucy, have you lied to her too, and Hetty?'

'No one at Belmont Park knows who I really am, Becks.'

'Oh, so we've all been as gullible as each other.'

'I'm still the same person.'

My feet halt their march. 'How do you come to that conclusion?'

'I still care about the same things, about the same people… it's me, Becks.' He bends his knees and dips his head so he can look straight into my face. 'I haven't changed.' I feel the warmth of his hand slip into my own. It's familiar and comforting and I'm tempted to keep hold of it – but I can't, I don't know this version of Manny with the fancy cravat and matching waistcoat.

'Why did you do it?' I whisper letting go of his hand.

'To help others,' he says simply staring down at the hand I've left empty. 'You've no idea how frustrating it is to live the life I have.'

'I'm sure having everything handed to you on a plate is really hard work.'

'Becks, I didn't choose this life, I was born into it.'

I look away down the lane, regretting my directness. 'I'm sorry, it was wrong of me to accuse you of something you had no control over.'

'The lifestyle of the rich is blinding; you can't help others until you can truly feel sympathy with their situations. That's why I did what I did – I wanted to experience life without money so I could have a greater impact. I'm living proof of a broken heart, Becks. It wasn't easy for me to do what I've done, but I pushed the limits and held nothing back, I've given up everything and sometimes that hurts, but the rewards are worth it… I met you because of it.' He doesn't take his eyes from my face, watching in the hope I'll answer in his favour.

'Your sister said you are studying at Cambridge, is that a lie too?'

'I had to tell them something, explain why I wasn't living at Ashton Manor on a permanent basis… and you must know, Eliza is only a step-sister, we are not related by blood in any way.'

'Why didn't you tell me everything, the day *your* carriage and *your* sister brought me home, you had every opportunity to do so?'

'I should have done, I'm sorry, but I didn't want to spoil what we had. I knew you'd think differently of me and you'd never receive help from me ever again, I didn't want money to taint what we had.'

'Wait a minute, you said *again*. When have you ever flaunted money in my face?'

His cheeks turn red. 'Well, actually...'

'Manny, what did you do?'

'When Mrs Langley forbade you to have your half-day and you asked me how I changed her mind, it wasn't a swap of me for you... I gave her money.'

'You gave her money – how much?'

'The amount isn't important; it was the only way she would let you go and you needed to visit your pa.'

'So, am I to guess you are close friends with the Belmonts and that's how you secured me the position of lady's maid?'

'Becks, I swear I had nothing to do with that... yes, I know the Belmonts, but they have no idea I'm a groom in their stables, I kept a low profile purposely so I wouldn't be discovered.' It all suddenly makes sense, why Manny was so adamant to improve my future, but so reluctant to discuss his own – it's because he already has everything.

I look down the lane and see the opening in the hedgerows where a wooden stile connects the dusty track with the fields beyond. 'I need to go, I've two miles to walk before my day is over.'

'Where are you staying?'

'On the Arthur's farm.'

He chuckles. 'Trust you to seek out the Arthurs.'

'What's so funny about that?'

'Have you met Emma?'

'Yes, I have,' I reply coldly and don't say more. 'I really must go.'

It looks like he has more to say, but he reluctantly moves to the side and slides into a half-bow - he's never done that before. How can a change of outfit cause someone to act so differently? I can tell he immediately regrets his action when the tops of his cheeks glow red with embarrassment and his head is bent low towards the ground.

Chapter Twenty-One

I can hear Maggie singing to Henry as I approach the barn. It's a pleasant sound and soothes my distress after the two-mile journey thinking only of Manny and the lies he had told. The sweet song comes to an end and when I enter through the tall door, I find Maggie joyously tickling her brother under the chin, Henry is squealing in delight.

'Rebekah, Henry said his first words today!' Maggie says beaming with pride when she sees me.

'Did he?' The little boy waddles across and I lift him into my arms. 'What a clever boy you are, Henry. What was the word, Maggie?'

'He said "bye" to Mrs Arthur, it was the sweetest thing.' She comes up to me and takes the boy back. 'Come on, Henry, let's go look at the cows.' I smile after them, proud to see how Maggie is growing up and starting to help her sister with some of the workload.

'Maggie's really flourishing,' I say to Mary as she comes across to greet me.

'Mrs Arthur is a good influence on her, she's asked Maggie to start helping in the kitchen.'

'What a kind woman...' I glance through the double doors and into the yard. 'Where's Ma?'

'I've not seen her all day – she'll be back later once the sun's gone down.'

I nod, knowing Ma's routine. 'And how is Pa?'

'He's getting worse. I've tried to cool him as best I can, but his body is like a furnace.'

'I'll go to see him.' I tap Mary reassuringly on the shoulder and walk across to Pa.

He doesn't look well at all. Beads of sweat have formed on top of his forehead and his upper body is keeled over; his arms folded across his stomach.

'Are you in pain, Pa?' I ask kneeling by his side on the straw covered floor.

'You're home, Becks,' he says weakly. 'Has a day passed already? Will's going to be home soon, he might pop in for a natter.'

My brow crinkles with concern, he seems disorientated. 'Pa, you're not in Belmont anymore.'

He closes his eyes and winces, realising his mistake. I focus back on my original question, not wanting to cause him embarrassment. 'Is the pain in your back?'

'It's my stomach, I've had cramps all day.'

'Have you a damp cloth, Mary?' I call across the barn and in response she brings across a pile of washcloths and a bucket of water. 'Mrs Arthur brought these over earlier,' she explains. I thank her and take a cloth from the top of the pile, rinse it with water and begin to lightly dab Pa's forehead.

'Try and get some sleep, Pa.' I gently kiss his cheek and without an argument his eyes flicker and close.

Later on, when everyone else is finally asleep, I take my place next to Pa. He's tossing and turning his head ferociously, muttering something unintelligible in his sleep. Gently, I stroke his damp hair and try to calm his feverish jolts. After two or three attempts, he starts to respond and his body relaxes into a more natural sleep. I lie flat on my back next to him, gazing up at the rafters in the roof which have turned shadowy in the darkness. My head is heavy and I close my eyes, but I know sleep is a long way from my grasp. A picture of Manny dances before me dressed in gentleman's clothing and I hurriedly open my eyes as tears begin to form. How can he be a Montague? I wipe a tear falling down my cheek and choke back a sob, covering my mouth quickly so I don't wake Pa or the children. I close my eyes, screwing up my face tightly... I would have trusted Manny with my life.

Sleep must have caught up with me because I'm suddenly woken by a shout. I sit up, my heart racing. Everything is still and the sound of the children's heavy breathing drifts across from the other side of the barn. Rubbing the sleep away from my eyes I turn to Pa who is groaning, trapped in feverish sleep – it must have been his nightmare that woke me. I'm about to lie down again, my tired eyes already closing, when I realise Ma has not returned like Mary had said she would. It is possible she crept in without being seen, though I find this highly unlikely considering the hour I must have fallen asleep.

I groan, not wanting to leave the warmth of Pa's side, and reluctantly move myself away.

Checking the mounds in the hay I count all the children sleeping soundly, but Ma is not among them. Although not expecting to find her out here, I step into the cool night, a cloudy sky is blocking the light from the moon as an owl screeches and flies overhead. The silence is calming and I take a deep breath closing my weary eyes and leaning my head against the side of the barn's wooden door. My mind drifts to Manny and I wonder if he is awake too... I squeeze my eyes tighter and a deep pain grips me from inside, never would I have imagined that Manny would be the one to give me a broken heart...

Suddenly, the rattling of wheels down the lane interrupts the tranquil stillness and I alertly open my eyes. It's strange that someone has started their labour for the day when dawn hasn't begun to break yet. I squint through the trees blocking my view of the lane, but nothing is to be seen and the sound has stopped. I yawn and go back inside. The village and its people are unfamiliar to me, for all I know it might be a local tradesman going about his daily routine. It's not a matter I need to trouble myself with, after all, I've enough problems of my own without adding another to my plate.

This time it doesn't take me long to fall back to sleep and I wake a couple of hours later as the sun begins to rise. I roll over to see Pa's peaceful countenance and for a moment I'm relieved to see how restful he looks... almost too restful. Panic rushes through me. The way his fever was raging during the night I find it hard to believe it has suddenly disappeared.

'Pa?' I whisper not wanting to wake the others and scramble to his side - he doesn't respond. I take his limp wrist and fear spreads further within me when I can't find the pulse. I drop his hand and rush round to the other side, not that his other wrist is going to be any different, but in my panic, I don't know what else to do...

There it is. It's faint, very faint, hardly pulsing in fact, but he's alive.

'Pa?' I helplessly whisper again and this time he groans softly, tilting his head to the side.

I hold his hand tightly - there's nothing I can do.

For our second day, I've taken Eliza into the woods not far from Ashton Manor and with us we have taken a selection of books from her father's library.

'Miss Barnes, look, is this one?' A clump of leaves rustle under my feet as Eliza leaps out in front of me.

'Yes, I do believe you are correct,' I say catching up. 'It's certainly a match.' I take the book from her hands and hold the flower against the engraving.

'Isn't the pink pretty, what did you say it was called again?' She moves her nose closer to investigate. Although Eliza could have read the title of the engraving herself, I forgive her laziness, not wanting to dampen her evident enthusiasm for the subject.

'Foxglove.'

'Foxglove...' she repeats and dreamily holds out her hand to touch the trumpet shaped petal.

'Stop!' She turns in shock, her hand frozen in the air. 'It will irritate your skin, I advise you not to touch, Miss Eliza.'

Eliza pulls her hand away quickly. 'Very wise, I'm glad you are with me.' She looks at me thoughtfully. 'Who would have imagined you were once a simple maid - what a lark!' She exclaims and giggles at the notion. 'You are so knowledgeable Miss Barnes. I have had many governesses and I dare say you are the best one by far.' She pauses and eyes me shyly. 'May I ask you a favour?'

After such a compliment I can't refuse. 'Go ahead.' I shut the book and push away a fallen branch so we can retrace our steps onto the well-worn track.

'You see, the problem is I'm dreadfully keen to go into town this afternoon and Mama will not come with me.' She flutters her eyelashes. 'Would you be my escort, Miss Barnes? I'm not having lessons this afternoon anyway, and Mama will not let me leave the grounds without a suitable companion.'

Her request is not what I want to hear.

That morning I had reluctantly left the barn, only giving in because Mary had practically forced me out of the door, knowing I would instantly lose my new position if I didn't show up on my second day. She had promised to send a message via Mrs Arthur if there were any dramatic changes in Pa's condition. Having arrived to discover Eliza was not to have lessons after lunch, I optimistically hoped I would be released early from my duties so I could return home and be with Pa whose health is deteriorating at an alarming speed. However,

Eliza's pout is so pronounced I find myself agreeing to the girl's request. She squeals with pleasure and links her arm through mine as we walk through the woods and back to the house together.

'I must change for lunch,' states Eliza when we arrive in the hall and she starts to climb the stairs checking out her reflection in a mirror hanging on the pale-yellow wall. 'Oh no!' she suddenly cries, twisting her figure round to inspect the back of her gown. 'Look, Miss Barnes!'

I climb the stairs to meet her and gently lift the fabric for closer inspection. 'You must have got caught on some brambles.'

'It's ruined!' Eliza cries dramatically.

'It's not ruined, Miss Eliza,' I say softly attempting to calm her hysterics. 'It's an easy repair, I can mend it for you.'

'You can?' She lifts her tear-filled eyes.

'You go and change and I'll search for some thread downstairs, there's plenty of time to sort this before lunch.'

I make my way down to the kitchen and stop a maid hurrying through the door. 'Excuse me, I wonder if I might have a needle and thread, Miss Eliza's gown needs mending.'

'We can see to that, miss.' She smiles and starts to walk on.

'Oh, it's no problem, I used to be a lady's maid so I'm more than capable and it would save you a job.'

'That would be very kind of you, miss.'

'You can call me Rebekah, I'm staff here, like you.'

The maid looks away shyly. 'You are upstairs staff, miss, it would be improper. I'll fetch you a needle and thread if you can wait a minute.' The girl hurries away.

I'm beginning to see why Eliza spoke as she did yesterday - I no longer seem to fit anywhere.

'Rebekah...? It is you!' A familiar voice breaks into my thinking and I turn my head to look behind me.

'Kitty!' I cry in surprise. 'What are you doing here?'

'I might ask the same thing of you... I'm a kitchen maid, I've been here three months.' I think back to yesterday and don't remember seeing her, but then again, it's such a busy household she could easily have been overlooked.

'I'm pleased to see you have landed on your feet.' I smile, genuinely pleased for the girl, after the way she was sent away from Belmont Park it's good to see her looking so happy.

'Have you applied for work here?' she asks.

'I'm Miss Eliza's new governess.'

'What an achievement, do they know you were a maid of all work not even a year ago?'

'It wasn't of importance to Miss Eliza; she was eager to find someone her own age.' I'm not about to tell the girl of the family's ignorance about my roots, it's good to see her, but I still wouldn't trust her integrity.

'I thought your family were in Belmont?'

'They're claiming parish relief in Market Ashton, Lady Belmont recommended me to Lady Montague.'

'Your pa must be doing better, if he was able to make the journey.'

I knit my brows together, I don't remember telling Kitty about Pa's condition. 'Actually, he's very sick.'

'I'm sorry to hear that.'

'Kitty!' a call comes from inside the kitchen.

'That's cook, I must dash. Good to see you again, Rebekah.' She backs away and disappears into the room just as the maid returns with a reel of thread and a selection of needles.

I was correct in assuming the gown could be fixed by lunch. It had been neatly stored away with time to spare well before I took a seat next to Eliza in the dining room.

If I'd stuck to my original plan, I could be on my way home now. I can't pretend I'm not anxious about Pa. The slow, faint pulse I felt this morning scared me and I'm wondering if I should return to the barn anyway. If Eliza takes offence there will be other positions – though none that would come as easily as this one.

When Manny enters, I don't know where to look and I feel a heat rise into my cheeks as he sits on the opposite side of the table.

'How kind of you to join us Emmanuel,' mumbles Lord Montague sarcastically.

'I told you I had business in the area and was unable to attend meals yesterday.'

'You're a scholar, what business do you have? I sincerely hope you're not bothering the destitute again because you know my opinion on that subject after what they did to your mother?' The atmosphere between them is tense, and when I glance up at Lady Montague, she seems unaffected by the event referred to by her husband. Manny shifts uncomfortably in his chair and flicks his eyes fleetingly in my direction.

'I'm sorry Emmanuel, I did not hear your reply,' growls Lord Montague.

'No father, I had no business with the destitute.' Manny says crossly, a scowl spreading across his face.

'Good.' The elder gentleman bangs on the table and looks over to the door. 'Where is this food?' A footman enters at these words with a tureen in his hands. 'What has taken you so long?'

'I'm sorry, your lordship.' Bows the butler following behind the footman. 'There has been a slight delay in the kitchen.' Lord Montague mumbles something inaudible under his breath and tucks a napkin into his shirt.

'I have decided upon something,' chimes in Eliza oblivious to the conflict between her father and brother. 'We are to have a wildflower garden at Ashton Manor. Miss Barnes has introduced me to some of the most beautiful flowers I have ever seen, ones that have been right in front of me my whole life. I shall get Mr Baker to plant some for me.'

At the sound of the familiar name my ears prick up and I catch Manny watching me. Could it be the same man who I found behind Mr Allen's bakers? I dare not speak and ask more questions, not knowing my place or the rules connected to my position.

'Miss Barnes is also coming shopping with me Mama, so you need not worry about coming yourself.'

'I was not worried in the slightest, Eliza,' says Lady Montague. 'If Miss Barnes has time to spare then take her by all means, but I shall not pay for the luxury, I hired her to teach you, not take you shopping.'

'You do not need to pay her, she's coming as a friend...aren't you, Miss Barnes?' Manny almost chokes on his soup and his eyebrows lift up in surprise. Eliza glares silently at him uttering a tut under her breath. How I have managed to form such a relationship with Eliza in a matter of days is a mystery. Having it proclaimed publicly around the family table makes me feel uneasy, making friends with my employer's daughter is not something I'm trying to do.

Tactfully, I ignore the question. 'I would be happy to escort your daughter, Lady Montague and I do not expect to be paid for the pleasure. As you informed me yourself, I am not to teach Miss Eliza this afternoon, I was planning on going straight home on account of my pa being sick.'

'Your pa is sick?' It's the first thing Manny has said directly to me and he leans sympathetically across the table until he realises his overfamiliarity and sits back quickly in his chair.

'If your father is sick, I do not want you in this house, Miss Barnes,' says Lord Montague in a sudden panic.

'Father, you do not know what is wrong with the man. Miss Barnes...' Manny coughs hiding his embarrassment at using such a formal name. 'What is the matter with your father?'

'He has a fever—'

'Leave immediately.' Lord Montague drops his spoon and stands to attention, pushing his chair out from behind him.

'Father let her finish,' orders Manny before turning back to me in a calmer tone. 'Go ahead, Miss Barnes.'

I cautiously meet Lord Montague's eye. 'If you are afraid of me bringing an illness into the house, sir, that will not happen. It is a side effect of my pa's condition... he's paralysed.'

'Fever is not a symptom of paralysis.' The man's almost shouting, spit spraying out of his mouth and landing on his projecting side-whiskers.

'No, sir, but his condition is made worse because of it.'

'How ill is your father?' asks Manny ignoring Lord Montague's outburst and finding the confidence to question me further.

'I fear the end might have come before I return home.'

Manny doesn't answer. I know the news has affected him and he will be blaming himself for not having found an effective cure for Pa's condition whilst we were still at Belmont Park - not that there was anything he could have done.

'Foxgloves are my favourite,' pipes up Eliza without a thought for anyone else. 'But they irritate the skin, do you think I should not have these in my garden?'

'Eliza, you are being insensitive,' says Manny taking a sip of soup.

'No, I am not, Manny. I heard what Miss Barnes has said and I am very sorry for her, but I am trying to lighten the atmosphere.'

'Can't you see how inconsiderate you are being?' He drops his spoon to the side of the bowl.

Eliza huffs, unhappy with her brother's chastisement. 'When are you going back to Cambridge, Manny, I'd like to know because then I won't need to step around your delicate sensitivity?' She pauses. 'You may go home, Miss Barnes, we can shop tomorrow.' Although she's addressing me, Eliza looks directly at Manny. 'There, does that please you now, I am miserable because I cannot visit the haberdashers for the ribbon I desperately need for my new bonnet.'

'If I hear your father dies, Miss Barnes...' begins Lord Montague who is also completely ignoring any other conversation in the room to focus on his own concerns. '...and his illness spreads into this household you will be instantly dismissed for your falsehood.'

'Did you not listen to a word she said?' Manny bangs on the table and I can see him tightening his hand around a napkin cutting off the blood supply to his fingers. 'It has not spread to her brothers and sisters, so it cannot spread to us.'

'How do you know Miss Barnes has brothers and sisters, she has not mentioned them?' asks Lady Montague who's been listening to the dual conversations with interest.

Manny hesitates. 'I'm guessing she has a family somewhere to feed, why else would you become a governess? Do you have a family, Miss Barnes?'

'Yes, there are now eight of us, including myself.'

'Now?' cries Lord Montague. 'You mean one has died already from the illness.'

'I beg your pardon, sir, that is not the case, my second to youngest brother was taken from us and we could not locate him.'

'See, you have no need to fear, Father... you are safe in your manor.' Manny says with a touch of cynicism which doesn't go unnoticed.

'Enough!' his father shouts and more spit sprays from his mouth. 'I have had enough - you may leave, Emmanuel.' No one protests that Manny hasn't finished his lunch and he strides out of the room without looking back.

Manny is waiting for me by the brick wall as I leave the grounds by the gatehouse. Eliza had stayed true to her word and allowed me to leave after lunch, though she showed her disfavour with a protruding bottom lip.

'Let me come with you,' he says marching towards me without a greeting.

'Why, what can you do?' I don't need his charity, just because I know who he really is doesn't mean the impossible can now be achieved, money can't heal my pa.

'I can send for a doctor.'

'What good will a doctor do, he will only cover his body with leeches? Anyway, I don't want your money.'

'I'm offering you help, Becks, please take it.'

I lift my chin. 'My pa is dying and nothing can change this... he might even have passed away by the time I arrive back.' I breathe deeply, steadying my emotions by speaking words of such finality out loud. 'Besides, haven't you to get back to Belmont?'

'I gave in my notice, that is where I was yesterday when I realised you had taken the position as my sister's governess.'

'What about Lucy!' I exclaim, the poor tiny girl being my first concern.

'She'll be fine, Becks.'

'But who will protect her?'

'She has a good friendship with Hetty... right now you are more important to me.'

'You took the position so you could see life from a different perspective and now you're throwing it all away?'

'It served a purpose.'

I shake my head. 'You can leave me here, Manny,' I say realising we have walked quite a way down the lane. 'I do not need an escort.'

He reluctantly obeys and allows me to walk on without him. 'You will send for me, won't you, if there's anything I can do?'

'Manny, why won't you listen to me when I tell you there's nothing you can do.' I see the gap in the hedgerow and climb half-way over the stile. 'You might have been Lucy's miracle, but you're not mine.' I lift my dress, jump down into the field and don't look back, not wishing to see the hurt I've just inflicted on the man I used to love.

Chapter Twenty-Two

'Rebekah!' Mrs Arthur greets me at the farmhouse door. Her face looks anxious and I brace myself for the worst. 'We moved your pa into the farmhouse to make him more comfortable.'

'Thank you, Mrs Arthur. He is still…?'

'Still alive? Yes, but I don't know how long he will…' her voice trails away, neither of us being able to complete sentences which talk about such finality.

'Is Mary inside?'

'She is in the barn with the children.'

'And my ma?'

'She still hasn't returned.' No one has seen Ma since yesterday, but I can't concern myself with her whereabouts now, Pa has to be my priority. There's a chance she'll return to us a widow, and then who knows if she'll stay around for her children: judging by her current behaviour she's more likely to leave us behind to survive alone.

'Would you mind sending a message to Mary, telling her I'm home. I will see Pa now, if that's all right?' Mrs Arthur nods and shows the way up to a tiny room on the first floor.

I step cautiously inside and the floorboards creak under my feet. There he is, lying on the bed wrapped in a woollen blanket. His skin is pale, but his cheeks are crimson from the fever. There's a chair next to the bed and I sit down, stroking back a lock of hair from his clammy face.

'Rebekah?' his voice is hoarse and dry and he forces his eyes open.

'Let me get you a drink, Pa' I look around to see Mrs Arthur has left a half-full jug of water on top of a chest of drawers. I fill the glass sitting next to it and hold it up to his badly cracked lips.

'It won't be long now,' he says weakly. It's in this moment I make my decision - I'm not leaving him, even if it means losing my position - here I will be, by Pa's side until the end. I take his hand and enclose it in my own. 'I'm proud of you, Becks,' he says softly and winces as another stab of pain hits him in the stomach - I grab his hand tighter in response, relaxing my grip only when he rests his head back on the pillow.

'I don't know why you're so proud, Pa - I haven't done anything?' I whisper back in the same soft tone.

'Don't you see?' He pauses as the pain spreads all across his lower body. 'You seek out those who have been forgotten... and nothing stops you from spreading a little bit of joy into their lives...' He closes his eyes, the exertion of speaking wearing him out. 'You...my darling Rebekah... are a light... a shining bright light... and I'm so proud of you.'

Tears fall quickly down my cheeks. 'But I've lost all that, I only help the rich now.'

He opens his eyes and presses his thumb lightly on my hand. 'When you find what breaks your heart, nothing will stop you... not the rich, or the poor.'

His words pierce through me. In my quest to follow my broken heart I've lost sight of what I'm trying to achieve. The higher I go the further I seem to be from the people I want to help the most. Manny had told me when I reached the heights of governess, I would have more influence to help others, was this a lie too? I'm helping a selfish spoilt child - I was making a bigger impact as a button maker.

A faint knock sounds on the door followed by Mrs Arthur's concerned face. I wipe my tearstained cheek with the back of my hand. 'I'm sorry to bother you,' she says. 'But there's a doctor here to see your pa.'

'Oh, did you...'

'No, we didn't call for one,' she says pre-empting my question.

'Will you sit with Pa? I'll go down to see the doctor.' My lips press firmly together and I walk at a pace out of the room - I know Manny has sent him.

'Good afternoon, sir,' I say in greeting as I come to the bottom of the stairs where the doctor is waiting in the hall.

'You are Miss Barnes?' asks the doctor dressed in a plain brown jacket.

'Yes, have you come to see my pa?'

'Mr Barnes?'

I nod in reply.

'Yes, I have.'

'I'm afraid you've wasted your time; we cannot afford to pay you.'

'It has already been covered. Is the patient upstairs, I would like to see him?' He shifts his head and looks past me up the stairs. If Manny thinks he can mend our relationship with money and fancy doctors, he can think again.

'He is upstairs,' I speak in a frosty tone, but then immediately reprimand myself because none of this is the doctors' fault. 'However, I believe you might be too late.'

'Oh, has he passed on?'

'Not yet, but I think he's nearing the end.'

'I'll see what I can do.' He smiles kindly and I lead the way upstairs.

Whatever anger I feel for Manny disappears the moment I step back into the quiet room where Pa is lying in the bed looking so small and vulnerable. The doctor examines him, feeling his body in the places where Pa has been experiencing pain. With the tips of his fingers he prods his stomach and in response Pa gives a soft groan.

'I've seen cases like this before,' the doctor says turning to me. 'Your father has an infection rooted somewhere in the lower part of his body, it's typical of patients suffering from paralysis.'

'Is there anything we can do?'

'I can make suggestions, but I'm afraid the majority of cases do not survive and your pa is severely weakened. From my experiences cranberries and garlic are natural medicines you can try; they may fight the problem.' He does not sound hopeful.

After seeing the doctor out, I cross the farmyard in search of Tommy and Daniel. It doesn't take long to find them and I send them out to scavenge for cranberries in the surrounding boggy areas of woodland. After directions from Mr Arthur for the best crop, they return with a basket full which Mrs Arthur promptly squeezes into juice for Pa to sip.

I don't know if it's the cranberries or the many prayers I've offered up for a miracle, but Pa is still with us. A week has passed since the doctor's visit and his fever has finally subsided, but he remains extremely weak.

When I confronted Manny, he denied sending the doctor. He must think I'm a fool, nobody else in Market Ashton knows where we live. However, I decide to let my suspicions drop. He's taken up the daily habit of waiting for me by the red brick wall and walking me half a mile down the lane to the stile. Every day he does this, and every day I'm reminded how important he is to me... and how much I really do love him. I find we are stepping back into our natural rhythm like the way things used to be. If I discount his clothing and unfamiliar scent, concealed in every conversation and every look, is the Emmanuel Smith I used to know and love, and a little bit more of my resolve to be cross with him melts away. Surely something from our previous relationship can be salvaged? Over time I'll get over my distrust and forget the lies. Soon he'll be my old Manny again – my kind, caring and considerate Manny.

'I'm not certain this red will match now,' whines Eliza as we are walking down the small high street in the village. It's become a daily habit to walk into Market Ashton together. It hasn't taken long for me to learn it is impossible to get anything sensible out of the girl after lunch and a refreshing stroll to aid digestion is highly beneficial for all concerned. Throughout Pa's illness I haven't missed a day with Eliza, and I have Mary to thank for that. Adamant I wasn't going to leave Pa's side, Mary's insistence that saving money was more important than ever, pushed me out of the door. She's right, we must find new lodgings before the autumn arrives - we cannot spend a whole winter in a draught-ridden old barn.

'Red always matches blue, Miss Eliza, they are primary colours.'

'Yes, but such a bold colour as this ribbon, it will never match.' She pouts her lip and for a moment I think she's going to throw the ribbon onto the muddy ground.

I stifle a frustrated sigh from escaping my mouth. 'You were adamant about your choice five minutes ago when we were comparing samples in the haberdashers – you said it was perfect, what has changed your mind?'

'Miss Barnes, you will not understand such things, but if I get this wrong, I will be ridiculed for the rest of the season and I cannot allow this to happen. Mr Lovett is to be in attendance tonight and he's sure to hear the sniggers slighting my appearance if I wear this hideous ribbon.' Apparently, Market Ashton has a distinct lack of young wealthy gentlemen, and so the arrival of a Mr Lovett, who two days ago came to visit his uncle, has caused a great stir among the young ladies of the village - Eliza has been no different, and after catching a fleeting glimpse of the gentleman on horseback, already believes herself to be in love, though an acquaintanceship has yet to be formed.

'Miss Eliza, the ribbon will match and you will look beautiful in your new gown. I think you have more important things to worry about than the ribbon on your dress.'

'What do you mean?'

'You forget you need to have an introduction with the gentlemen before forming an attachment to him.'

'Oh, don't worry about that, Father will introduce us, he's acquainted with Mr Lovett's uncle.' She holds the ribbon in the air. 'No...no, it won't do. We must go back to the haberdashers.' Eliza pulls on my arm and spins us round causing me to collide with a young girl passing by my side.

'Oh, I do beg your pardon,' I say pulling Eliza back so I can apologise to the girl who is lowering a hooded cape from her head.

'Rebekah, what a surprise! I've been sent to collect some supplies for the kitchen.' Kitty reveals her face and lifts a basket out in front of her.

Eliza looks reluctant to wait and huffs behind me. I ignore her obvious impatience, believing it's a good opportunity to teach the girl that life is not always about her. I look towards Kitty. 'We are searching for ribbon to match Miss Eliza's new gown; she is attending a ball tonight.'

'I hope you find what you are looking for, miss.' says Kitty politely to Eliza, but my pupil is more interested in her fingernails than forming an acquaintance with one of her mother's kitchen maids and disregards the comment. Upon realising she's not getting a response, Kitty turns back to face me just as the sun peeks out from behind a cloud, causing her to block out the brightness with her hand. 'How is your pa?'

I smile, pleased that the girl has remembered. 'He isn't out of danger yet, but he is improving slowly, we take each day at a time.'

'That is good news.' Her reaction appears to be genuine and I can hardly believe this is the same girl whom I used to work with at Belmont Park - the change in her is remarkable. 'The society in Market Ashton must suit you Kitty, you seem so much happier than before.' Kitty blushes at the compliment.

An impatient tapping of a foot sounds behind me, causing my skin to prickle in irritation at Eliza's selfishness. 'I will let you be on your way,' says Kitty taking the hint. 'You must have a lot to get ready for the ball tonight.'

I bite my tongue as Kitty walks down the lane. If I wasn't concerned about keeping my position, I would have no concerns about informing the girl how rude she had been. I don't care if she was not interested in the conversation, she should have covered her feelings better. A young girl on the verge of womanhood needs to learn such manners or she will never survive in the society she has been born into – even I know that.

'You are quiet, Miss Barnes,' says Eliza once we reach Ashton Manor's long winding drive. What does she expect, for me to be pleased with the frivolousness I've just experienced? We had returned to the haberdasher four times after meeting Kitty, and each time she had purchased a ribbon, only to instantly regret her choice the moment we left the shop. 'You think I should have kept the red one, don't you?'

'Not at all, Miss Eliza, it was your choice, who am I to judge?' I clamp my lips firmly together so I do not speak out of place. How can the girl be so imprudent? To throw her father's money away on yards of ribbon, not caring if her discarded choices are thrown to the back of a cupboard on our arrival home. Does she not know there are starving families right on her doorstep and the money for those ribbons could have bought them bread?

'Do you think Mr Lovett likes blue?'

'I could not say.'

'I think he does—' She gasps. 'What if he likes green?'

'I don't suppose he will notice, Miss Eliza.'

She turns to me with a mouth gaping open, clearly offended by my words. 'How can you say that?'

'If my younger brothers are anything to go by, men aren't bothered about the details.'

She closes her mouth and goes on to pat my arm patronisingly, all offence forgotten. 'You don't understand such matters, Miss Barnes, you are only a maid after all.' She laughs at me, looks away, and then laughs at me for a second time.

Once again, I close my mouth, a slight pursing of the lips

forming with my disapproval. The girl has many pleasant qualities, but her total dismissal of anyone below her own position in society is discourteous, a character trait so deeply rooted that I fear she will never change. 'Miss Eliza, I might have been a maid, but I am not oblivious to the way the world works.'

Eliza snorts as more laughter escapes, but then sees my un-amused stare. 'Oh, you're serious.'

'Do you ever give charitable donations, Miss Eliza?'

'Whatever for?'

'The poor, those less fortunate than yourself.'

'Father would never allow me to do such things.'

'I think you would benefit highly from performing such an act, it would help broaden your horizons and enable you to understand how others live.'

'I don't need to understand how the poor live, I am not one of them.'

I feel myself stiffen at her words. 'You never know what mis-fortunes might befall you.'

Eliza frowns. 'What do you mean, Miss Barnes? I am rich.'

'Your father is rich,' I correct her.

'Yes, and I shall marry a wealthy gentleman...' She pulls herself closer and lowers her voice. 'It is said Mr Lovett earns eight thousand a year, just imagine that... what a lark!' She squeals and skips ahead down the drive, the thought of any charitable acts unregistered in her superficial mind.

'She's so different to you,' I say to Manny that evening after he's greeted me by the red brick wall. 'The hurting and broken are invisible to her – she's not one of them so she doesn't want to know.'

'I told you, she's my step-sister and has been spoilt rotten since the day of her birth. When I met her at the age of ten, she was already beyond rescue, having inherited the selfish ten-dencies of her mother - my father certainly hasn't helped mat-ters either. The poor will always be invisible to my family and Eliza won't change that... there's not much between her ears, so she'll never have a thought for herself.'

'Manny, you can't say that!' I cry although there's some truth in what he's said.

'It's the truth, she doesn't have a care for anyone but herself, money has no value to her, and she's used to getting her own way, like any child from a wealthy family.'

'Not unlike you then.' I grin mischievously.

'Ouch, Becks, you can't compare me to my pitiful little step-sister.'

'I would never insult you by doing such a thing, but you can't deny that *you* hate it when *you* don't get your way.' He opens his mouth to protest and I lightly touch his arm to stop him. 'No, no, please don't be offended, you're different to Eliza, you recognise the worth of other people. I'm simply making the point that you have had your way since childhood and have never known what it feels like to really be in want.' Manny takes a step back and crinkles his forehead in a slight frown. 'I'm not judging you, Manny, it's what you were born into... but your sister—'

'Step-sister,' he interposes.

'Yes...' I smile amused by his need to distance himself from Eliza. 'Your step-sister is extremely selfish, and her ignorance means she takes no consideration of how others live, at least you have tried to improve yourself.'

He looks away and chuckles softly. 'My mother would have slapped her soundly and dragged her out to see the reality of life with all its joys and sufferings.'

'You must miss her.'

'I—' He stops and observes me questioningly. 'I never told you about my mother.'

'I assumed it, on account of your father being married to a different woman.'

He sighs sadly. 'She died five years ago.'

'I'm sorry, you must miss her,' I say again.

'I do.' He takes my hand and encloses it tenderly inside his own. 'You would have liked her; you remind me of her in many ways.'

'How so? I feel we couldn't have lived more opposing lives.'

'She cared so deeply and did all she could to alleviate the misery of the broken, even if her kindness only touched one person...' His focus drifts off into the sky as if he's thinking of some far away memory. '*The best way to die is with a broken heart,*' he says softly.

'Did your ma say that?' I whisper not wanting to disturb the memory.

'Yes, the day she passed away. Her greatest joy in life was giving away what she had, but her greatest sorrow was that she could never give enough. I've tried to carry on her legacy, but my father...' He shakes his head. 'It's not difficult to see how his view on life is very different.'

I crinkle my nose. 'Erm, yes I did notice.'

'He didn't stop my mother's acts of charity, but he never encouraged them. Whilst Mother was alive, I would join her during my school holidays on her mission to save the destitute of Market Ashton and beyond, but after her death my father wouldn't allow me to continue.'

'Why ever not?'

'Fear. My mother died after contracting a fever and he claims it came from the poor she used to visit. The truth is she could have picked it up from anywhere. I'm afraid her memory is slowly being forgotten, that is why I became a groom at Belmont Park. The secrecy meant I could free myself from his bondage and criticism and begin once again to help those my mother cared so deeply about.'

'Tell me again how you managed to get the position, you said you know the Belmonts as personal friends?'

'Ah, that was Hetty's doing. After completing her studies at Braidwood's deaf school, she discovered her parents had completely abandoned her and I found her as good as dead in a ditch. Of course, I couldn't leave her there and set to finding her a position, as luck would have it, I discovered the girl was quite a cook and upon learning the Belmont's needed a new cook, it wasn't difficult to persuade Mrs Langley to take her on - that's when I learned they needed a groom.'

'Mrs Langley knew who you were and allowed you to have the position?'

He laughs, his bright green eyes shining with much amusement. 'She hasn't figured it out yet. How a change of clothes can hide your identity is quite amusing. Old Langley knew something wasn't right but could never put her finger on it. Now, I had to tread more carefully around Lady Belmont, she's a clever woman... but thankfully even a horse is tall enough to cover my lanky frame.'

We reach the stile where we part ways. Taking my hand, Manny helps me over the wooden frame, but I'm forced to look back when he keeps a tight grip of my fingers.

'Becks.' He lowers his brows in seriousness. 'We've not discussed what happened between us, you know, the day you left Belmont to search for your family.' He's right, the revelation of our love has been conveniently boxed up and left to the side, the stark reality of our differences now forcing us to bury the memory. 'We should be together. We belong... don't you think?'

'Manny, I—'

He grasps both my hands in his as I stand level with his eyes half-way over the stile. 'We could help so many people, Becks.' He waits in expectation of an answer.

'I- I'm not... not certain if we do really belong together.'

I feel his figure droop and he lowers my hands in disappointment. 'Why not?' he whispers.

I climb down from the stile so I'm standing next to him. 'It would never work, you are a gentleman and I'm... well, my family's claiming parish relief.'

'You're a governess,' he starts again in earnest. 'Anyone you come across will think you're a gentlewoman down on her luck, even my step-mother believes that. Please... don't discount me yet solely because of this...' He flaps the points of his fancy tailcoat. 'We've come so far, don't give up on us. I'm sorry I lied to you; it will never happen again.'

'Lie or no lie, you're still in line to be the next Lord Montague.'

'Becks, please...'

'I can't promise you anything, only time will give us the answer.'

'That's all I'm asking, that you give us time.' He looks relieved that I haven't pushed him away and lifts my hands to his lips before gently kissing them. 'You'll see, Becks, we will unite our broken hearts, find the joy of giving our all and then cry on each other's shoulders when our efforts aren't enough.'

Chapter Twenty-Three

The closer I get to the Arthur's farm the more I find the tension in my shoulders easing away. Why do I have a sense that things with Manny have suddenly become very complicated? He makes it all sound so simple, however I can't hide the uneasy feeling developing in the depths of my stomach. I love Manny, but I wonder if prolonging our attachment is a good idea? I'm a farm labourers' daughter, not the future Lady Montague. These two worlds should never collide… and they do, if Manny remains insistent upon us marrying. My background cannot be hidden, and if I'm honest, I can only see trouble ahead.

'Ah, there you are.' Mrs Arthur greets me at the farmhouse door wiping wet hands on her apron. 'I've someone you need to meet.' She ushers me inside and I follow curiously behind into the kitchen where Maggie is standing on a stool with her hands deep in a wooden bowl.

'Look Rebekah, I'm making bread.' She grins from ear to ear.

'All right, my girl,' Mrs Arthur says looking at the flour my sister is flicking all over the counter. 'You can't make bread if your ingredients are all over the side.'

'Sorry, Mrs Arthur.' Maggie's cheeks turn a light pink and she focuses her attention back to the bowl.

'Good work, Mags,' I whisper to the girl as I pass her by and she glows at the compliment. Mrs Arthur is being a good influence on Maggie, with our family struggling to make ends meet the girl hasn't had much individual attention and it's good seeing her so happy.

'Over here, Rebekah,' says Mrs Arthur. 'I want you to meet my cousin, Mrs Oliver.'

'It's a pleasure to meet you.' I curtsy, forgetting where I am.

'Don't bother with that nonsense here,' says the farmer's wife wafting away the polite greeting and my cheeks redden at my mistake… perhaps I'm drifting more into Manny's circle than I realise.

'Good day, Miss Barnes,' says Mrs Oliver whose nose is small and dainty like Mrs Arthurs. 'I have heard a lot about you.' The comment takes me by surprise - what is there to say about me? 'This is my boy, Thomas.' She pushes a small child in front of me. 'He's four.'

I smile warmly at the boy. 'Hello Thomas, what a good name you have, my pa and brother share it too, so I won't forget it in a hurry.'

The child doesn't respond.

'I'm sorry, he won't understand you...actually, that is why I have come. I've heard what you are doing for Emma.' I look at her blankly, the fatigue after a day with Eliza having slowed down my ability to think quickly. 'The gestures...' she tries to explain. 'What you do with your hands. I'd like you to do the same for my Thomas – I'd pay you.'

'Oh,' I say in realisation. 'Thomas is deaf.'

'Yes, since birth like our Em.'

'It's a sad fact that this condition runs in our family, Miss Barnes,' explains Mrs Arthur. 'My pa suffered the same all his life, and my poor sister when she was alive.'

'I'm not certain that I can—'

'Oh please,' begs Mrs Oliver. 'What do you charge, I will make sure you get it?' I scan the woman's clothing. She's not wearing anything better than the dress I wore before beginning in service, it's worn and looks like it hasn't been washed for many weeks. I don't suppose this woman has any money to spare.

'I do not want your money, Mrs Oliver.'

'But you will do it?' The woman's dark brown eyes swallow me up in desperation.

'I am limited to the hours I can teach Thomas; I work at Ashton Manor and much of my day is spent there with Miss Eliza.' I see the woman's disappointment. 'However, I give Emma a lesson before I leave every morning and if you can bring Thomas along too, I will teach them together.'

Mrs Oliver claps her hands in joy. 'Oh, thank you, Miss Barnes.' She comes across and plants a kiss on my cheek, the unexpected appreciation causing me to blush. 'We will be here at the crack of dawn, I promise you.'

True to her word Mrs Oliver brought Thomas the following morning and the lesson began. Emma, excited to communicate with her cousin for the first time enthusiastically helped to teach Thomas his first signs. The little boy sat quietly, shyly copying what Emma and I showed him. Emma had been a quick learner, but Thomas, whether from shyness or something else, is more reluctant and not as keen. However, I am prepared for the challenge of helping the little boy as best I can, knowing whatever knowledge I can impart will ready him for the heartless world he will eventually have to enter. I've seen what happens to those who are separated from society, and, if I have anything to do about it, I won't let this happen to Emma and Thomas.

Coming down the drive at Ashton Manor I feel rejuvenated in a way I never feel after teaching Eliza. A sense of purpose uplifts my heart and a spring in my step appears as if from nowhere, something I haven't experienced for a long time. As I lift my head to take in a deep refreshing breath of summer air, a hunched figure bending over an empty flower bed catches my attention. As I get closer, the figure looks up and waves, greeting me with a smile.

'Mr Baker!' I exclaim as the man stands up. *So, Manny did place you here as his father's gardener - I wouldn't have expected anything else.* A sudden rush of emotion spreads through me... isn't Mr Baker a reason to believe Manny's promises might have some truth behind them. Look at what he's done for this man, even under his father's nose, and if he's done it once then it's certainly possible to do it again... maybe our differences can be overcome and our efforts won't be stifled by the arrogance of the rich?

'You're a gardener now, Mr Baker?' The man looks confused as I speak. 'Flowers...' I sign, taking my thumb and index finger and touching them from cheek to check and, just to emphasise the action, I point to a rose bush next to us. Mr Baker looks in the direction of my finger and then back at me with the same confused look. 'You're a gardener now, Mr Baker,' I repeat, speaking loud and clear. 'You planted these flowers?' I point at him, then the flowers and repeat the sign. This time he understands and nods enthusiastically. 'They're beautiful.' My closed hand touches my chin and I open out my fingers as if I'm blowing a kiss to Henry.

His cheeks turn pink, pleased and embarrassed in equal measure - I know he's fully understood.

'Miss Barnes...? Miss Barnes, what are you doing?' I see Eliza coming out the front door. 'You are late.' She looks at Mr Baker curiously.

'I'm sorry, Miss Eliza. I was speaking to Mr Baker.'

'Speaking? How foolish you are Miss Barnes, he cannot hear you, you are wasting your breath with him. Come, or I will tell Mama and she will dock your wages.' Grateful that Mr Baker couldn't hear the disrespectful words she had spoken in front of him, I follow the girl into the house.

As the morning passes, a rising frustration overshadows me, stealing my fleeting lightness of heart. Eliza's selfish attitude grates upon me, every sigh and pout emphasising her ingratitude. Finally, lunch arrives and I look forward to escaping the confines of the house, even though Eliza will be accompanying me. However, the tediousness of my position is worsened when a sudden heavy shower prevents our walk into the village.

Sitting on the window seat in the living room, Eliza twists her figure towards me and allows the book in her hands to drop to her knees. 'I am dying of thirst, are you not Miss Barnes? I shall see if Mama is having tea and we shall join her.'

'I think it might be a wise idea, Miss Eliza, since you have spent more time looking at the rain on the window than reading your book.' I lift an accusing eyebrow to indicate I had noticed her preoccupation and lack of attention on the passage I had set her to read.

'I am so sorry, Miss Barnes, but I am all in a whirl... he danced with me, did I tell you?'

'Yes, you did... several times.' I say referring to Eliza's gushing report of Mr Lovett who had honoured her with the first and last dance at the previous night's ball.

'He is so graceful, so...' She pauses to think of the word. '...Distinguished.' She appears satisfied with her effort to describe the man who has currently stolen her heart and looks uncharacteristically mature. But this is all lost when she releases a sudden shrill squeal and taps her feet excitedly on the floor. 'Mrs Eliza Lovett, what a fine sounding name!' She springs to her feet. 'I shall see Mama about the tea.'

When Eliza does not reappear, I fear she has been led away by further distraction. This, under normal circumstances wouldn't be unusual, but in her current romantic state of mind, anything would appear more favourable to the girl than attending a lesson with her governess. I sigh and head out of the room to fetch her back, for certainly if she's caught, I will be the one in trouble, not the dreamy lovesick Eliza.

Voices greet my ears as I pass the drawing room and I'm relieved to hear one of the voices belongs to Eliza. I am about to walk in to reclaim my student when a second voice halts my entrance and causes me to stand frozen behind the half-open door, which conveniently conceals my presence from the occupants of the room.

'You do not need a governess anymore, Eliza. You are far too old and have all the knowledge you require to be a desirable young lady in society.'

The words spoken take me by surprise – it's Manny. Does it sound like he is trying to rid me from Ashton Manor?

'But I like Miss Barnes, she is good company for me,' Eliza answers.

'Which is going to be my next point,' continues Manny. 'Get your mother to employ Miss Barnes as your lady's companion, then you can go wherever you want whenever you want… without the headache of studying. I hear you made a new acquaintance at the ball last night and I imagine with a suitable companion by your side you would be allowed to spend more time in his company.'

'I can't deny it, I do like your argument Manny…'

'But… you seem hesitant?'

'Yes, I am.'

Manny's soft chuckle floats through the half-open door. 'What's the matter, do you fear you'll miss the joy of learning?'

Eliza feigns a laugh. 'Very funny, Manny.'

'Then what's the problem?'

'You promise you won't tell Mama.'

'My lips are sealed.'

There is a brief pause before Eliza speaks in a hushed whisper. 'Miss Barnes is…' Her voice lowers even further as if she's about to reveal a ghastly and immoral secret. '…a maid.'

Manny laughs in direct contrast to his sister's delicate handling of the revelation. 'And what's wrong with that Eliza?'

'Well,' she begins sounding slightly offended by her brother's reaction. 'If Mama found out - no, worse still, if Father found out - they would never allow Miss Barnes in our home again. Having her as my governess is one thing, but to have a maid as my lady's companion... I don't know, Manny.'

'First of all, Miss Barnes is not a maid, she's a governess, and secondly, she is a good influence on you, so it doesn't matter what her background is.'

'I think it does matter, Manny.'

'Does it?' Again, a silence fills the room and I can picture Manny tilting his head forward in an attempt to contradict his sister's selfish ideas. Suddenly, Eliza shrieks with mirth, her high-pitched note causing me to flinch and nearly bump into the half-open door.

'What a lark, to have a maid for a lady's companion!'

Manny groans. 'I do wish you would stop saying that.'

'What?' Eliza asks in ignorance.

'You are nearly a grown lady Eliza and you sound like an immature child.'

'I am not an immature child.' The sound of a stamping foot vibrates through the floorboards.

'Then don't act like one, having a lady's companion will distance you from childhood... especially if you want to keep Mr Lovett's attention.'

'Yes, of course I want to keep Mr Lovett's attention... fine, I shall do it. I will see Mama now.' The sound of light footsteps come towards the door. In panic, I look for a place to hide and in a matter of seconds a row of figures clad in suits of armour conceals my existence as I manage to duck out of sight just as Eliza skips out into the long corridor.

It is not long after this that her brother follows behind...

'Why do you want me to be Eliza's lady's companion?' I jump out in front of him, being careful not to trip over the iron foot of the armour-clad figure.

'Ah, Becks...' Manny holds a hand across his racing heart. 'You scared me... what are you doing behind there?'

'Why are you so keen to have me as a lady's companion?' I ask again narrowing my eyes, declining to comment on my eavesdropping.

'It will establish you more fully within the family.'

'I don't want to be established more fully within the family.'

'But if we are to marry...?' His half-finished sentence lingers in the air.

'Manny, we have no arrangement to marry. Why are you

trying to turn me into—' I gasp as suddenly everything makes sense. 'You've planned all this, haven't you?'

'What are you talking about?'

'At Belmont, when you were nagging me to aim higher, never wanting me to settle and pushing me to become the lady's maid—' I stop half-way through my accusation and give a short half-hearted laugh. 'Even that wasn't good enough for you, was it? You then had to convince me to claim the post of governess, not caring if it took me further away from what I wanted. It's all so obvious, why didn't I see it before... you were preparing me to become your wife, someone acceptable to your high standards.' He opens his mouth to speak. 'No, don't even try to defend your actions, Manny. None of what you did was for my benefit, it was all for you... you're just as selfish as your sister.'

'Oh Becks, that's not fair.'

'Yes, it is,' I snap back. 'You were so desperate to make me your equal that you didn't care if you changed who I was along the way. The truth is, Manny, you're ashamed of me.'

'Becks.'

His pleading eyes meet mine, but I'm so furious I won't allow his stricken expression to put me off course. I step closer to him, lowering my voice and taking a finger so it's almost jabbing him on the chest. 'Let me tell you Emmanuel Montague, it doesn't matter how high I go in society because we will never be equal. If you want us to be together, you will always be marrying below your position– that cannot be hidden – and let's not forget, as soon as your father discovers who I am it will be the end of everything.'

Manny is not flustered by my outburst. He places both hands firmly on my shoulders and lowers his head to meet my gaze. 'He will never know... and let people criticise my so-called poor judgement, I love you and I won't hide you away in shame.'

It doesn't escape my notice that Manny hasn't tried to deny the accusations, and it looks like he really has intentionally planned to elevate my position in society so we can be together. I look away at the long row of sash windows overlooking the perfectly kept formal gardens. 'I don't belong here, Manny.' My eyes close tightly and for a brief second I wish our paths had never crossed. 'Being upstairs amongst the rich is not where I belong.'

'You will get used to it.'

'What if I don't want to get used to it?'

'Then you will be denying so many people of a chance for a better life.'

'What do you mean?' I lift up my chin a little feebly and find myself looking back in his direction, feeling my resolve to fight weaken.

'I stand by what I told you, standing and wealth can give you a position to influence and help others in a way you could not imagine. Look at what *I* have been able to do because of who *I* know. I don't want to sound boastful, but Hetty would not be in the kitchens of Belmont Park if it wasn't for me and Mr Baker would not be in the grounds of Ashton Manor, and let's not forget, I could not have helped Lucy if I really were a groom, I'd be much too worried about keeping my position, but for me it wasn't about the wages, it was about how much I could give to the people I loved the most.'

'But Manny, don't you see that by taking the position of groom you were denying some poor man an honest year's wages... how is that helping the poor?'

'Don't say that Becks.' He winces, obviously convicted by this point of view.

'You want me to come up to your level, but not once have you ever considered coming down to mine.'

Manny looks away towards the suits of armour, trying to regain his composure that I have definitely unsettled. He inhales deeply and shakes his head. 'How can you say that Becks? I've dedicated two years of my life to working amongst the staff at Belmont Park, I became one of you.'

'No, you could come and go as you pleased. What you're asking me to do is permanent, your position was temporary and you were playing a game that you could end whenever things got too uncomfortable.'

'That's not true.'

'Are you telling me, that in the two years you worked at Belmont, you never once went home and enjoyed the luxury of a rose infused soak in the tub or a feast prepared by your father's servants?'

He looks uncomfortable and shuffles his feet.

'Oh, there you are Miss Barnes.' Eliza appears before he can answer and she looks strangely at her brother. 'Who's ruffled your feathers, Manny?' She laughs her merry laugh and turns to me. 'Mama wishes to see you in the parlour.'

Eliza walks away, but looks over her shoulder, seeing I am not following behind. 'Come on, Miss Barnes, Mama says we can join her for tea.'

I take a step forward, so does Manny. 'Accept the position,' he whispers loosely taking hold of my wrist. 'You won't get another offer like it again.'

'Miss Barnes?' Eliza is waiting for me at the end of the row of armour. 'Are you coming?'

'Yes, Eliza, I am.'

Eliza disappears round the corner and I release my hand from Manny's gentle hold. We stare at each other, our mouths set hard in a straight line and I walk silently away.

Chapter Twenty-Four

Sipping my tea, I wait for the offer to be made. My mind is a whirl of possibilities, trying to assess my options from all angles. If I decline the offer to be Eliza's lady's companion, then I have lost my job. Although I'm sure Mrs Arthur would let me work on the farm, it would bring in little money. The barn has to be a temporary measure, we can't live with the Arthur's forever, and I'm doubtful if securing alternative accommodation is possible, even on my current salary. But if I agree...

'Mama has something to ask you, Miss Barnes,' says Eliza slipping excitedly to the edge of her chair and intruding into my thoughts.

I put my cup down to my lap and wait for the inevitable to be offered.

'My daughter no longer needs a governess, Miss Barnes,' begins Lady Montague tapping the side of her tea-cup with a spoon. 'However, we are pleased with what you have done in so little time and we would like you to be Eliza's companion instead... please note your wages will not increase.' She adds this on the end, as if I've been waiting for an opportune moment to squeeze more money from her purse.

'Thank you for the offer, ma'am. How long do I have to think it over?'

Eliza's mouth drops. 'You are not saying yes?'

'I am not saying yes or no, but I would like time to think over my options.'

'What other options do you have Miss Barnes?' asks Lady Montague with a mixture of interest and haughtiness, as if I have slighted her offer by having the audacity to have alternative plans for my life other than serving her daughter.

'Miss Barnes!' exclaims Eliza. 'You cannot turn down such an opportunity.'

The two ladies cast uniformly shocked eyes at me and I shuffle uncomfortably in my chair. I will sound like an utter fool if I tell them I actually have no other options. It appears

I must make my decision now and my eyelashes blink several times quicker than usual as I try to retain my composure. The thought of continuing to suffer alongside this girl does not fill me with much joy ... there will be other positions in the village, surely?

The footsteps of a passing footman in the hall echo into the room. I need to make my decision and stop this excruciating silence. I open my mouth, only to close it again. My answer will directly affect my family. I will get another position to pay for accommodation, I do not have to stay attached to Ashton Manor. But how long will it be before I'm earning again and what will happen to Pa if we have to endure a winter in that barn? We cannot trespass on the Arthur's goodwill forever and, unless we pay them rent, the tiny box shaped room cannot be Pa's for much longer... What am I to do?

I blink again. It's a simple yes or no, but the consequences are great and I can't get this wrong. My mouth opens and shuts again... what about Manny? Accepting the post as lady's companion really means I'm accepting Manny. If I decline, will it mean I lose him forever?

I swallow... 'All right, I accept. Thank you for the opportunity Lady Montague.'

Eliza leans back in her chair looking relieved. 'Oh, you had me worried, Miss Barnes - I simply cannot do without you. What a la—' she stops herself, most likely remembering her brother's recent reprimand about using that certain phrase. She giggles self-consciously and changes her exclamation. 'Isn't it wonderful... no more studying!' She stands and twirls round the room. 'Oh, I could burst with happiness. It's almost like you're one of the family now, Miss Barnes.'

I smile weakly and let out a pitiful splutter - Eliza's words speak more truth than she knows.

A few weeks later the rain is pouring down from the heavens.

'I say we run for it,' suggests Tommy peeking through the tiny slit in the tall barn door.

'Me too,' agrees Daniel. 'I wouldn't want Mrs Arthur's effort to go to waste.'

'We can't eat burnt bacon,' adds Tommy. The mere mention of bacon causes Daniel's mouth to salivate and Maggie tightens her bonnet in readiness to follow her brothers across the yard. When we first arrived at the Arthurs, the kindly farmer's wife and her husband had promised us the use of their barn for shelter, somehow this offer of accommodation only, has slowly grown to include housekeeping. Every-day Mrs Arthur not only provides the children with fresh milk, but she cooks breakfast, lunch and dinner for our hungry brood. Of course, we pay her for the trouble, using the money we receive from the parish.

'What do you think Rebekah?' asks Maggie watching the rain continue to pelt down from the darkened sky.

'I say…' The boys look eagerly at my face, uncertain if I'm going to spoil their breakfast. 'We go for it!'

Tommy shouts 'Hooray!'

Danny hisses out a joyous 'Oh, yes!'

Henry claps his hands and I pick him up.

'Ready?' I say and we all take up a pose, preparing ourselves to run with all our might – because we're about to get very wet. 'One…two…three!'

We all scurry across the yard which is hidden by a carpet of puddles. Half-way towards the farmhouse I look over to see Maggie screaming in delight, Daniel laughing and holding onto his cap, and Tommy trying to blow dripping wet hair out of his eyes. We arrive in the small hall giggling with great exhilaration, I don't think we've ever been so happy before.

'Oh, you poor things, look how wet you are!' exclaims Mrs Arthur coming to greet us.

'It's all worth it for your bacon, Mrs Arthur,' says Daniel charmingly.

'My bacon won't rescue you if you catch a cold,' answers the farmer's wife.

'I beg to differ.' Mrs Arthur smiles back at the boy and we all trudge through to take our seats.

'Sit by the fire, Rebekah and get yourself dry.' She takes my shawl, shakes off the water drops and hangs it over a fire screen to dry.

'I wouldn't worry about that, Mrs Arthur. I've to walk to the manor in an hour and it doesn't look as if this rain will let up by then.'

'I dare say it won't, but you can at least start warm and dry.' She ushers me to a new seat closer to the fire.

'What delights are coming with the bacon today, Mrs Arthur?' asks Tommy tipping back on two chair legs and straining his neck to look onto the range.

'Eggs any good for you?' comes the reply from Mrs Arthur who promptly presents our plates on the table.

'Perfect.' Tommy grins and lifts his fork, hardly letting the plate touch the table before attacking the fried egg before him.

Half-way through our meal Mr Arthur comes in, shaking a spray of rain from his coat and stomping his boots. Mrs Arthur immediately comes across and takes the wet coat, hanging it next to my shawl in front of the fire. She leads her husband to the table and places a plateful of breakfast in front of him too.

'There's a parcel for you in the corridor, Rebekah,' says the farmer.

'A parcel?' I frown. Who would be sending me a parcel?

'Well, I assume it's for you... matches the other two you have.' I don't catch his meaning and I leave my breakfast to head into the narrow hall where a girl is standing, dripping onto the tiled floor.

'Good morning,' I say looking behind me to see if Mr Arthur has followed to give a further explanation, but he hasn't. 'Can I help?'

The girl sniffs but doesn't answer.

'Would you like a warm drink you look wet through?' Again, I get no response and I'm beginning to understand Mr Arthur's cryptic comment.

I lead her into the kitchen. 'Mrs Arthur, do you know this girl?'

'Ah, good day Beatrice.' Mrs Arthur wipes her hands on her apron and shuffles towards the timid looking girl, automatically turning her towards the fire. 'This is Mrs Dibden's maid, she suffers the same as our Emma.'

The girl holds out a note and Mrs Arthur takes it in exchange for a cup of tea. She gratefully takes the cup and sits at the table with the others.

'It's for you, Rebekah,' says Mrs Arthur scanning the contents.

With great curiosity I take the folded paper. 'She wants Beatrice to learn with Emma and Thomas.' I explain as my eyes scan the note. 'Mrs Dibden says Beatrice is only to learn simple gestures for important things like *washing, dusting* and...' I squint not quite able to make out the untidy scrawl. '...*Making tea*. Well, I'm afraid I would be teaching more than that...and Mrs Dibden will need to learn the signs herself otherwise how is she to communicate?'

'Mrs Dibden is a funny old thing, you won't get her coming for lessons,' says Mrs Arthur. 'But if you teach Beatrice and she can use them in her work, she'll soon teach her mistress.'

'Are there any others I need to know about?' I say with a laugh, slightly overwhelmed by the obvious need within the community.

'Bessie's boy is deaf, isn't he Mr Arthur?'

The farmer nods and swallows a mouthful of eggs. 'And Cassandra, the tenant farmer's daughter.'

'Oh yes, I forgot about her.'

'Why are there so many residing in Market Ashton?' I ask smiling at the girl who is standing next to me waiting for an answer.

'You often find little communities growing, there's safety in numbers.'

I nod. It's true, Mr Baker was all alone in Belmont and he became a victim to the town's brutish gang, preying on anyone who they thought was different and they didn't understand.

'You're getting a good little school running, aren't you?' Mrs Arthur pats me on the shoulder as she passes with a freshly filled teapot and reaches over her husband to pour him another cup. She looks up and smiles at me. 'You should consider charging; you could make your fortune.'

'From three pupils, unlikely.'

'No, but it's a start.' Before she dashes back to the kitchen, she holds my gaze and I'm sure I see her eyes fill with tears as if... as if she's proud of my achievements. I wonder if Ma would be proud of me... wherever she is? We haven't discovered her whereabouts, though to be honest we haven't tried hard, she'll find us when she's ready and we'll welcome her back, as we'll always do.

The latch on the front door is heard clicking open and Mrs Oliver barges into the room, muttering loudly over the state of the weather. Thomas enters behind his mother and stands holding his hands out in front of the fire.

'How are you, Thomas?' I sign making sure the boy sees my face.

He lifts both hands up in a claw like posture and spreads his fingers wide before drawing them in together. I laugh with pleasure and the little boy smiles shyly.

'Yes, you are wet,' I say before turning my attention to his mother. 'Do you mind if I take my pa his breakfast before we start the lesson, Mrs Oliver?'

'Not at all, Rebekah. You're doing such a marvellous job with Thomas; I can't thank you enough.' She smiles lovingly at her son as Mrs Arthur passes a tray into my hands.

The portion of food I'm carrying up to Pa is small compared to the hearty portions Mrs Arthur is dishing up downstairs. 'Good morning, Pa,' I say cheerily as I enter the little bedroom.

Scanning his face, I place the tray on a side table as I help him to sit up in bed. His skin is still pale and dark red circles hang under his eyes. The infection has left him weak and I know half the food before him will go untouched.

'How are you feeling?' I move the tray to his lap.

'I want to say I feel better, Becks.' He sighs and looks straight out the window. 'Some mornings I wake up wishing the infection had taken me.' He's been talking like this a lot lately and you'd think I'd get used to it and learn to let the words drift straight out of my memory – but I can't do this, and each time he utters a desire to be gone from this world, I feel a stab in my heart.

'I'm so sorry, Pa,' I whisper taking his hand.

'Don't be.' He smiles sadly and closes his eyes. 'That's enough about my pitiful existence, tell me about you, Becks.'

'What about?'

'Anything.'

'I told you I'm to be Miss Eliza's lady's companion.'

'Yes, I remember you told me...' He opens his eyes. 'Did I say how proud I am of you?' His hand tightens around mine and I have to look away. 'What's the matter?'

'It's... it's nothing, really.'

'Talk to me.' Pa stares straight into my eyes desperate to be of some use, so sick of always being the invalid. 'You're not happy?'

'No...' I say slowly. 'Have you ever felt frustrated because the one thing you want to do, is the one thing that's out of your reach?'

He chuckles. 'Look who you're taking too.'

'Oh, yes,' I glance down to his legs. 'Sorry Pa, that was insensitive of me.'

'No offence taken, Becks.' He shuffles trying to get comfy and I lean over to plump his pillow. 'Listen, if you're not happy then leave, you'll find something else... I'll still be proud of you.'

'I know that Pa, but it's not that simple.'

'Life is short, Becks, you should do what makes you happy.'

I don't answer. The truth is my discontent has been building for weeks and I know I'm not happy. Every day I spend with Eliza makes me feel like I'm taking a step away from where I really want to be, and it's... it's hurtful. I'm trying to mask it, but my heart aches because I've lost my purpose. The lonely, the outcasts and the destitute are right on my doorstep and I'm doing nothing to help them.

The closest I get to contentment is sitting in a room with Emma and Thomas, teaching them all I have to offer... but how much is this really helping? For my efforts to have a significant impact on their future I need to be teaching them all day, every day, educating them as well as teaching them signs. This will not happen in the limited time I can offer them and so another piece of my heart shatters. I feel broken and utterly helpless with no sign of the blessings on the horizon.

After spending a few more minutes with Pa, I leave to begin my lesson, including Beatrice who watches me with great interest. There's quite a sense of purpose now there are three of them and I can see in their faces how excited they are to be communicating with each other, especially now Thomas' initial shyness has vanished. I could spend my whole day with these children, their smiling faces fill me with so much hope I feel I could do this forever... if only the world ran on happiness and not money, I would be secure for life.

My feet trudge heavily over the fields towards Ashton Manor and a sadness descends over me. If my overall goal is to be with Manny, then he was right to persuade his sister to make me her lady's companion. I now share the family's intimate space, wherever they go, I go. It feels like I'm pretending to be a gentleman's daughter, practising for the time I become Manny's wife. When the weather is cold or wet, we all sit together inside, reading, sewing, listening to Eliza play the pianoforte and sing, when the weather is fine, we stroll around the gardens, or take a walk into the village. Life is not strenuous, in fact, it's dull and repetitive, sitting idly and wallowing in luxury. My days start off with such a purpose, giving the gift of speech to three children who were born without the ability to hear, a gift everyone else takes for granted. But then I arrive at Ashton Manor, and my purpose immediately fades and wastes away, sitting for hours amidst nothingness.

November has finally arrived along with bitter winter winds; the long days of summer are a distant memory. Standing on the corner in front of the haberdashers I wriggle my feet to regain some warmth and slip my hands further into the muff Eliza has kindly lent to me. My cheeks blow out with impatience and a white puff of cold air escapes my mouth as I do so. Eliza has her back turned to me, purposely cutting me out of the conversation. She stands away from me, laughing and squealing girlishly with a friend we hadn't expected to see on our trip into Market Ashton.

My eyes wander up and down the street. It's not a busy centre, with only a handful of shops to support the local community, but today there are pockets of people walking up and down, pressing their noses against windows and purchasing essentials to take home. I take another look at a group of women talking quietly together and complaining about the price of the bread they've bought. That's when I see a hunched figure crouching by the side of the bakers, wearing a tattered shawl pulled closely over her shoulders. My eyes are drawn down to a basket placed in front of the woman when suddenly a leg kicks out and I see a tiny baby lying inside, most likely a new-born, faintly crying and flaying itself around trying to remove the blanket tucked around it.

I cross the road, unseen by Eliza who still has her back turned to me.

'Can you spare a penny, miss?' The girl looks up hopefully.

'I'm sorry, I have no money.' It's true, half my wages go to Mrs Arthur, the other half is safely hidden away steadily building funds to move my family into new accommodation - I never carry a money purse fastened onto my dress because I've nothing to put inside it.

The girl tuts. 'You're all same - I suppose the fairies brought you that fine muff.'

I glance across to Eliza. 'Actually, I've borrowed it.' I pull the item from my hands and hold it out. 'Here, you take it.'

The girl wrinkles her nose. 'I'd rather have the penny,' she says sticking out a hand and hoping I've been lying to her and that I really do have a money bag hidden away somewhere under my dress.

'I'm sorry, I really have no money.' I push the muff closer to her. 'Please, at least take it for the baby, it will be a cushion for her head.'

'It's a boy.'

'I- I'm sorry...' The woman tuts again as I stumble over what to say, picks up her basket and walks away leaving me holding the outstretched muff in my hands.

'Miss Barnes!' It's Eliza calling across the road. 'What are you doing over there?'

I watch the girl and her basket disappearing behind the bakers - what just happened? I catch my reflection in the shop window and suddenly see myself through the girl's eyes... she declined my help because I've been transformed into one of them. My hand softly touches the dress I'm wearing, passed down to me from Eliza because it was no longer fashionable, it's far from plain, the light-yellow cotton being printed with pretty little roses. My eyes stare back at my reflection, sadly moving my hand onto my straw bonnet, another finely made unwanted accessory handed down to me... in shock I realise I no longer look like a pauper and I'm unrecognisable even to my peers.

'Come, Miss Barnes, or we will be late.' Eliza waves frantically at me from the other side of the road. I blink and shake my head, trying to pull myself out of my daze. 'I have to change before the guests arrive this afternoon, even if you don't want to... Mr Lovett cannot see me improperly dressed.'

I do give the girl credit; I hadn't expected the charm of Mr Lovett to continue several months after her infatuation started. The bad side to this is the infinite number of social gatherings now held at Ashton Manor. Her mother never misses an opportunity to organise a dinner so that this young gentleman, amongst other noble families, can be invited. Such an event has been planned for tonights entertainment and so the evaluation of my appearance in the shop window must give way to Eliza's need to prepare her toilette.

Eliza's anxiety about being too late to change was pointless.

Nearly an hour has passed since we entered the living room to wait for the expected guests and not one has arrived.

'Miss Barnes...? Miss Barnes! What is the matter with you?' Eliza clicks her fingers in my face. 'I have asked you the same question twice and both times you have ignored me. 'Are you well?'

'Oh, I am sorry. I... yes, I've a little headache.' I say coming out of my reverie.

'Good, you are not allowed be ill. I have high hopes for to-night and I need you by my side so I can remain respectable at all times... Of course, if I am successful with Mr Lovett, I shall no longer need you.' She lets out a single exclamation and my lips partly open, but don't have a chance of forming a single syllable. 'Oh, don't worry, Miss Barnes, I've high hopes for you as well!' She lifts her eyebrow cunningly and Manny, who is sitting opposite our own sofa, looks up with interest.

'And what, may I ask, are these high hopes you have for your companion, Eliza?'

'I believe Mr Lovett is bringing an acquaintance with him this evening.' She leans forward towards her brother and whispers. 'He is supposed to be a clergyman.' She sits back again looking pleased with herself. 'What good fortune, Miss Barnes, if you were to catch him, such a security and good fortune for you. Don't look so concerned...' This time she leans closer to me instead of Manny. 'I won't tell him about the position you once had.' She taps the side of her nose. 'Our little secret.' She finishes her discretion with a wink and looks across to the other side of the room to check her mother isn't listening.

'I don't think Miss Barnes is looking for a husband,' says Manny looking amused.

'How would you know, Manny?' asks Eliza. 'She must marry at some point.'

'Agreed, but perhaps Miss Barnes already has someone in mind.' He raises his eyebrows intriguingly.

I purse my lips and scowl lightly - What does he think he's doing?

'Oh no!' exclaims Eliza jumping up in her chair and turning to face me. 'Please, say this is not true, Miss Barnes...' She lowers her voice upon noticing her mother has looked up from her book. 'Don't tell me you have a beau from Belmont, not some footman or groom – you could do so much better.' I feel my cheeks burn and try to hide my discomfort, making a concerted effort not to look directly at Manny. Eliza squeals. 'There is someone!'

'Not so loud, Eliza.' calls Lady Montague from the other side of the room. 'We are expecting the Jensons to arrive at any time and I do not want them entering to your girlish screams.'

'Sorry, mother,' calls back Eliza and immediately speaks with more discretion. 'What is his name... no, is he handsome... who is his family?' She perches herself on the edge of her seat and, if it's possible, my cheeks burn even brighter.

Manny leans back on the sofa, lifting one foot to rest across his knee and placing one arm along the top of the upholstered seat, looking perfectly at ease. 'Yes, who is this man because if he is not up to standard my sister will gladly find you someone more suitable?' He wiggles his eyebrows mischievously. What is his problem, does he enjoy watching me suffer?

The door swings open and a footman announces the arrival of the Jensons. Eliza, distracted by the guests entering the room, stands to her feet. I take the opportunity to glare at Manny who is trying to suppress his laugher. He shrugs his shoulders with a smirk, as if to suggest he couldn't help himself. Personally, I do not see any cause for amusement.

'Mr and Mrs Jenson, ma'am,' announces the footman.

'Oh, I am so sorry, Jane.' Mrs Jenson bursts into the room as the rest of us stand to our feet 'Our nursery maid is sick and the boy would not stay with anyone else without screaming the whole house down - I don't know what the matter is with him.' At this point a small boy scurries out from behind his mother and Lady Montague looks down her nose at him, clearly appalled by his presence.

'He cannot stay here,' the hostess says frostily. 'I will send him down to the kitchen, he can be the housekeeper's problem.' She signals to the footman who is still waiting at the door, holding it open for Mr Jenson who enters the room and stands next to his wife. 'Take this boy down to the kitchen, he is to be kept downstairs until Mr and Mrs Jenson leave tonight.'

The footman nods and comes straight across to collect the boy, turning him round so his face spins directly into my view.

'Georgie?' I whisper the name under my breath at first and no one hears me but Manny, whose mirth vanishes and he looks at me strangely. 'Georgie?' I say a little louder and with a greater confidence so that this time Eliza turns her head to face me too.

It's him...

'Georgie!' I stand to my feet and as I do the boy turns his eyes to meet mine.

Chapter Twenty-Five

He's taller now a year has gone by, his face is longer and his cheeks have filled out, but it's him. I know it is.

'Becks?' Manny stands and coughs suddenly as he realises he's used a shortened version of my name. 'Miss Barnes?' he says to cover his blunder.

'Manny, it's Georgie.' My eyes open wide and I don't care if I've just used his familiar name.

The boy stares back at me.

Mrs Jenson furrows her forehead. 'No, this is John.'

'I'm sorry you are mistaken; this is my brother. He was taken from us about a year ago - Georgie, it's Rebekah.' I look at the boy and I'm certain he recognises me, but he obviously appears very confused.

Mrs Jenson laughs and looks at her hostess. 'Who is this woman?'

'This is Eliza's companion, Miss Barnes,' replies Lady Montague.

Mr Jenson steps in. 'I'm sorry young lady. This is our son; you must be mistaken.'

'No, I'm not,' I speak calmly and move towards Georgie. Mrs Jenson shields him away from me with her arm.

'Miss Barnes,' says Lady Montague sternly. 'What is the matter with you?'

'I'm sorry, ma'am, but this is my brother.'

'You are wrong and I must ask you to stop accusing Mrs Jenson of kidnapping.'

'Perhaps you have adopted the boy without knowing where he came from?' I say, it's a plausible suggestion, but one that is immediately rejected.

'I beg your pardon, Miss Barnes, but the boy is ours,' says Mr Jenson raising his voice in agitation.

'I can prove it's my brother.' Silence descends upon the room, no one speaks and so I continue. 'He has a crescent shaped mark on the back of his right leg, it's been there since birth. I know it well, the number of times I changed him.'

Mrs Jenson noticeably pales when I say the words, but still, nobody rushes to check the truth of my words.

'Are you certain about this?' asks Manny searching my face.

'Yes.' I hold his eyes imploring him to fight on my behalf.

He nods lightly, before walking slowly to the boy. He crouches down on the floor to face him. 'Good day, young man.' He smiles warmly. 'I know this sounds strange, but I need to see underneath your stocking, is that all right with you?'

The boy looks at Manny, then lifts his head to stare straight at me. His lower lip momentarily wobbles before he nods his consent.

'Emmanuel!' Lord Montague, who has so far watched the events unfold quietly, cries out, standing looking horrified next to his wife. 'Enough, do not embarrass our guests by doing such a thing.'

'There is clearly some confusion, Father. This is the only way to resolve the dispute.'

Lord Montague mumbles something inaudible but doesn't stop proceedings as Manny unbuttons the stocking and peers behind the boy's leg. After inspecting the area, he stands and lifts his eyes to meet my own. My heart beats quickly and all of a sudden, I'm afraid that I am wrong, but this child looks so much like Georgie... it's not possible for me to be mistaken, is it?

'The scar is there.'

'Impossible!' Mr Jenson marches straight across, pushes Manny out of the way, and inspects the child's leg for himself.

'Beck-beck,' whispers the boy whose eyes are suddenly filling with unshed tears. I take a step towards the poor boy, but Manny stops me with an arm... turning his body away to mask our closeness to each other.

'This can't be...' says Mr Jenson aghast. 'Mrs Jenson how does this girl know about the mark, has she been in our employment in my absence?'

'No, sir,' answers his wife looking at the floor. 'I have never seen the girl before.'

'Then explain how this child is her brother.'

Mrs Jenson looks around at the faces all staring at her. 'It c-can't be her b-brother,' she speaks hesitantly touching her brow. 'The child I took was a beggar's boy, dirty and wearing rags... not a relation to a lady's companion.'

'The child you took?' repeats her husband through his teeth.

Mrs Jenson cries out in hysterics. 'Please, don't be cross with me, my dear. You desperately wanted a son which I couldn't give you, and then you went to sea.' She steps closer to her husband, bending her shoulders over in a posture of repentance. 'I didn't know if you'd ever return so I took the risk and made up my pregnancy to make you happy. But then a year ago, when you told me you were returning, I needed a child, so I went out to look for one.'

'You stole someone else's child?' shouts Mr Jenson.

'Yes, but I chose this one because I didn't think anyone would care that he was missing, looking so deprived as he was.'

'You have no right to take anyone's child, Mrs Jenson,' says Manny trying to calm the situation. 'No matter how deprived they might look.'

'I- I'm sorry,' sobs Mrs Jenson. 'I thought he was an orphan; he was all alone.'

'My sister left him for a matter of minutes outside our cottage – he was not alone.'

'I'm sorry.' She falls on her knees, her shoulders shaking.

Manny releases my arm and I slowly walk towards Georgie, kneeling before him and wiping away the tears that have rolled down his cheeks. 'You do remember me, Georgie?' I whisper.

He nods. 'Where's Mary?' he asks in such a grown-up little voice that I am quite overwhelmed.

'At home... our new home.' I smile with tears filling my own eyes.

'I don't understand,' says Lady Montague. 'How is this beggar boy your brother?'

Eliza's pleading eyes dart to where I'm kneeling with Georgie, begging me not to reveal who I really am, but I'm not going to hide the truth. 'It's quite simple Lady Montague, this boy is my brother because, according to your description, I am a beggar's daughter.' Eliza sinks into the chair behind her and Manny looks troubled, his lips parted in consternation.

Lady Montague is not impressed. 'Explain yourself immediately Miss Barnes, I was led to believe you were a lady's maid for Lady Belmont when you approached us to be Eliza's governess.'

'Yes, I was, but before that I was a maid of all work and before that I made buttons.'

Lady Montague almost faints with the shock and Eliza cries to the footman to bring her mother's smelling salts.

'You lying deceitful girl – you are one of *them*.' Lord Montague takes over, pointing an accusing finger towards me. 'I will not have you here in my house spreading all your diseases.'

'Father!' cries Manny. 'Look at her, does she look like a beggar to you?'

'Where does your family live?' Lord Montague continues ignoring his son. 'Where do you go every evening?'

My eyes automatically dart to Manny, knowing my response could ruin everything for us.

'She goes home to her family,' answers Manny hiding his distress well. 'Father, you cannot—'

'Where?' interrupts his lordship.

'In the property they—'

'Not you!' roars Lord Montague at his son. 'Her.' He jabs a finger at me again. 'I want to hear it from her.'

'We are currently residing with the Arthurs.' I answer tactfully, purposely ignoring the small detail that we are in fact living in the barn and not the farmhouse. 'As you know we have recently moved to Market Ashton and we have yet to find suitable accommodation.'

'Why haven't you? You have had ample time; the village is not that big.'

'We have limited funds.' It's the truth and he can take from it what he wants, he can call us beggars if he desires.

'What does your father do?' He must have forgotten he already knows the answer.

'Stop interrogating her,' shouts Manny crossly. 'She is from a good family.'

'How would you know?' snarls Lord Montague.

Manny opens his mouth and for a second doesn't speak. 'Can't you tell?' he finally says. 'Her character is honourable and her standing in society is favourable. Miss Barnes deserves acknowledgement, it is not every day a servant girl reaches the heights of a lady's companion, she is to be respected and admired for such an achievement.' It's the kind of speech I expect he's rehearsed a thousand times in his head, waiting for an opportunity to praise my good qualities as his perspective bride.

Lord Montague looks unmoved, staring straight past his son. 'What does your father do, Miss Barnes?'

'He is unable to work, sir, owing to an accident which left him unable to walk.'

'And what was he before this accident?' His eyes narrow fiercely, piercing into mine - I cannot answer the question. I'm a farm labourers' daughter - it would end everything.

'If you please, your lordship, I would like to attend to my brother and take him back home to my family,' I say finding all the courage I can muster to ignore his lordship's demand for further information.

'Please, Father,' chimes in Eliza before he has chance to deny my request. 'The Lovetts will be arriving soon, everything will be ruined if that child remains.' For the first time, Eliza's selfishness has saved me.

Lord Montague glances around the room, first at Mrs Jenson still sobbing on the floor, next at his wife spread out on the sofa, a maid now wafting smelling salts under her nose, and then at the boy whose tears have brought on a sniffling nose. Reluctantly, he realises the family's honour is in jeopardy and the scene before him needs clearing up as quickly as possible before the remaining guests arrive, among them a prospective suitor for his daughter.

I take his silence as permission to leave and scooping my arm around Georgie I usher the boy out the room.

Mary is overcome when she sees me walking into the barn with Georgie by my side. It even brings a smile to Pa's face. 'You've grown taller, my boy,' he says proudly as we all crowd around his bed in the farmhouse. He takes Mary's hand and squeezes it tight when he sees a tear trickling down her face. 'Welcome home, son.'

The almost four-year-old Georgie is quieter than the little boy who used to toddle around our little cottage gnawing everything in sight to sooth his growing molars. It's going to take some time for him to settle in, after all, he has had the upbringing of a future gentleman during one of the most formative years of his life, and if I'm right, he's most likely been hidden away in a nursery, his only source of love coming from a maid.

As we huddle around Pa, smiles on everybody's faces, the door opens and Emma comes in. She signs my name and holds both hands flat to her tummy, one in front of the other, swinging the top one out and in as if it's on a hinge.

'The door...for me?' I ask repeating the sign and pointing at myself. The girl nods.

'Must be another pupil for you, Becks.' Laughs Pa. 'Who else would seek you out?' Emma grabs my hand and leads me away down the farmhouse stairs before I have chance to respond.

No one is standing in the hall and I assume Mrs Arthur has invited my guest into the kitchen... Emma tugs on my arm. I hadn't realised I'd frozen to the spot upon hearing the sound of the voice inside. The girl tugs at my sleeve again, practically pulling me through the doorway.

'Manny?' As I enter he stands from the table where he had been sipping tea and smooths down his double-breasted navy-blue jacket.

'I'm afraid I can't offer you sugar, Mr Montague,' says Mrs Arthur apologetically topping up his cup with boiling water from the kettle.

'None needed, thank you, Mrs Arthur.'

'Well,' Mrs Arthur looks at me with interest. 'I'll give you some privacy.' She performs a respectful bob before Manny and dashes out the room. She purposely leaves the door wide open, whether this is to protect my honour, or so that she can listen in curiously, I don't know - I believe it is perhaps a bit of both.

'What are you doing here?' I half-whisper casting cautious eyes to the door as we both sit at the table.

Manny chuckles. 'You caused quite a sensation this afternoon.'

'What do you expect? They had my brother! Stop looking so amused.'

'You could have waited and told me after dinner.'

'And see him go home with the Jensons?'

'We could have got him back.'

'I'm sorry, I wasn't prepared to let him out of my sight...are you here to tell me I no longer have a position at the manor?'

'I'm here to tell you to be careful.' He leans forward and

lowers his voice. 'My father is watching you closely, one mistake and it will be all over.'

'Maybe that's not a bad thing.'

'Becks, you can't mean—'

'Manny, I'm not comfortable in my position and don't think I ever will be.'

'You haven't given it enough time, it's a way of life you're not used to.'

'I have no purpose at the manor, I've lost all understanding of who I am.' I'm not going to skirt around my feelings, Manny needs to know.

He shakes his head. 'That's foolish talk.'

'Manny, a woman in town almost spat at me today. I wanted to help her, but she turned me away because I looked like one of you.'

'It happens, not everyone appreciates help from the wealthy, they think we're looking down on them and flaunting our riches in their faces.'

'Well, I don't like it.'

'Not everyone you meet will be like that.'

I try not to look into his face and focus on the floor. 'I feel trapped.'

'As my wife you will have great influence and you will be able to change so many lives for the better.'

'Please tell me how, because I'm struggling to see the answer?'

He takes a hand and gently raises my chin. 'Do you trust me?' On the day of Georgie's disappearance, the answer was obvious... but now after all that's happened? It's not that I don't trust Manny. I know he'll protect me forever and love me implicitly. It's not his character I don't trust, it's the life he's offering me - I don't trust it will make me happy.

My continued silence in answer to his question doesn't seem to affect him and the next minute he's pulling something out of his pocket causing tears to fill my eyes. 'Where did you get my –?' I falter because I can't take my eyes of the tiny hand-stitched doll sitting in his hand.

'It's not yours, Becks.' He slips a hand into his opposite pocket and pulls out an identical perfectly stitched doll. I take one and as I blink, a teardrop falls onto the soft cotton dress.

'Becks,' he whispers. 'You think it's not possible to love

others and make a lasting impact if you choose to become a Montague, but I'm here to tell you that you're wrong.'

'Why do you have these?' I sniff and glance at the doll in my hand running my fingers through the strands of golden hair.

'My mother made them.'

I take in a breath... 'This is what changed everything for me.' My voice wobbles and I press my lips together trying to prevent an outburst of free-flowing tears pouring down my face.

'I know.' He cups my cheek in his hand and strokes it with his thumb. 'You could do the same for others, it's not impossible.'

I move his hand away and hold onto it tightly. 'Would you ever contemplate leaving your family to marry me? We've always talked about how I could fit in with your life, but you could just as easily fit in with mine, you've done it once before, you could do it again.'

The question takes him by surprise.

'Becks, I couldn't, my father would disinherit me in an instant. I can't marry—' he stops in mid-sentence and hangs his head in shame.

'It's all right, you can say it - you can't marry someone like me.'

'I don't mean it like that, you know I don't. But you must understand I would lose everything, and we can't help those we want to without the necessary funds.'

'Can't we?'

'Of course not, we want to change lives not give a momentary respite before the hunger returns.'

'Are you saying you won't marry me if I leave Ashton Manor?'

'It's not that I won't marry you, Becks, I love you, it's just that I can't.'

'So what if you lose all your money, Manny, you have a good family name, you can earn it all back.'

'It's not that easy.'

'Why not?' I slip my hand out from his and narrow my eyes - I already know the answer.

'Oh, come on, Becks, you know if I marry you, I'll be marrying below my station.'

'Are you ashamed to tell your family you're in love with a farm labourer's daughter?'

'Fine, do you want me to say it – yes, I'm ashamed. I'll be embarrassed in front of everyone I know and my good judgement will be in tatters - there are certain barriers that one cannot cross.'

'It didn't appear to bother Emmanuel Smith.' This shuts Manny up - he knows I'm right.

'T-that was different,' he stutters.

'How?'

'It was hidden and I didn't have to reveal who I was, it didn't hurt anybody.'

'Marrying me is going to hurt you?'

'My family will disown me – cut me off.'

I sit back in my chair with folded arms. 'And that's a problem because...?'

He runs a hand through his curly dark brown hair and exhales loudly in frustration. 'All I'm saying is you'll be foolish to give up your position, especially since you've worked so hard to achieve it – you couldn't even read when I first met you. You've performed the impossible, from maid of all work to a lady's companion, it's an amazingly rare triumph.'

'Will I be foolish because if I give it up, I'll also be giving you up?' I had to say it, Manny wasn't going to, but it had to be spoken so we know where we stand.

'Becks,' he says softly. 'You can't give up on me.'

'Neither can you give up on me, Manny. You would make the sacrifice if you really loved me.'

'Don't try to make me feel guilty, you know I can't.'

'Can't or won't?' He's already told me the answer, but I don't believe him. 'You told me to find out what really breaks my heart, and I don't believe it's here. You told me to hold nothing back and to give all I have but, I'm sorry, Manny, I don't think I can do that as your wife.'

'Trust me, you can.'

'Can you promise me that?'

He leans toward me, lifts up my hands and presses them to his lips, keeping them close to his face. 'I need you by my side, please, don't leave me.' His emerald eyes search my own in desperation. 'Please...'

'I don't know, Manny.' Tears begin forming again as I see the panic in his face.

'But you're not saying no?'

I bite my lip, now the time has come I can't do it... I can't let him go. 'No,' I say. 'I'm not saying no.'

He lets out a relieved breath. 'We'll work this out, Becks, together, I promise.' Leaning back in his chair he glances around the kitchen. 'First thing we need to do is remove your family from the farm.'

I sit up, alert. 'Manny, please don't, we're happy here.'

'Your pa can't sleep on a barn floor.'

'He's not, Mrs Arthur won't let him.'

'But you are.' He lifts his eyebrows accusingly. 'You can't sleep on a barn floor, Becks, neither can your brothers and sisters.'

'Don't you think I know that Manny,' I say with a sharp edge to my voice. 'I'm saving my wages so we can rent a cottage.'

'Save your money, I'll pay now and get you out of here tomorrow. I'll even pay Mr Greaves rent for your old place in Belmont and get you all home... I'll match the poor relief contribution.'

'Manny, I don't want your money.'

'You'll be my wife soon, that money will soon be ours.'

'That's not the point... listen, I know you won't understand this, but we are happy here and I'm not moving us back to Belmont where there are no prospects for us. The boys are working on the farm with Mr Arthur, gaining skills they can't learn from Pa, and Maggie's blossoming under Mrs Arthur's guidance in the kitchen, she's building a confidence Ma was never able to give her. If we go back to Belmont now everything will fall on Mary's shoulders again, so please, go against all of your instincts to fix everything and leave us alone.'

'I can't allow you to stay here, Becks, my conscience won't let me. Your father needs to be at home... even Georgie needs to be in a familiar environment, the poor lad must be so confused.'

'Promise me you'll leave us alone, Manny… and I mean promise, not like when the doctor showed up on our doorstep.'

'I told you, that wasn't me.'

I find it hard to believe him and clamp my lips firmly shut. Lying isn't beyond him, it wasn't too long ago that I was fooled into thinking he was a groom. My thoughts take me by surprise, can I really marry a man I don't completely trust not to lie to my face?

Do you trust me? Unknown to Manny, his question lingers in the air as he stands to leave. 'I promise,' he says. 'Your family stays here; I won't do a thing.'

Chapter Twenty-Six

I receive a frosty reception the following day when I arrive at Ashton Manor. Even Eliza is not her usual self and retires to her room with a headache. Not long after this I am summoned into his lordship's study.

'Miss Barnes,' he begins with fierce eyes piercing straight through me, causing me fear far beyond anything I felt in the presence of Mrs Langley. 'I have been considerably unsettled by the incident which we shall not refer to.' I don't speak, summoning all my might to stand on my trembling legs. 'It is not the boy I am worried about,' he continues. 'If Mrs Jenson is foolish enough to procure a child by stealing, it is her own fault. But what I *cannot abide...*' he emphasises the words loudly and I flinch. '...is that someone living amongst my family has such dangerous connections. Last night we were interrupted, and I'd like to finish our conversation, you do understand, I cannot risk any illness being brought into my home?'

'Yes, your lordship,' I mutter with my chin lowered towards the floor and wonder if anyone has ever told him how hysterical he sounds... probably not, I for one wouldn't dare criticise his character to his face.

Lord Montague sits imposingly behind his desk, his hands locked together in front of him. 'Perhaps now you can tell me who your father is?'

'Thomas Barnes, sir.'

'I understand from what you told me he is an invalid.'

'Yes, sir.'

'What did he do before?'

I'm not going to lie - this is who I am and if he does not like it then I will deal with the consequences. 'He was a farm labourer.'

The heavy sound of his breathing fills the silence, waiting for him to dismiss me... for some reason he delays responding and I find myself getting more and more agitated.

Please, just let me go...

Then I realise, it's what I want. If his lordship dismisses me then the decision is taken out of my hands, I can say goodbye to Manny knowing I could do nothing more to secure my position amongst his family.

He grunts and rubs the whiskers of his beard. 'It's unfortunate Eliza has taken quite a liking to you. When I told her that I was considering your dismissal this morning she became extremely agitated. Therefore, I do not wish to take you away from her, especially since I am hoping a marriage contract will be signed between herself and Mr Lovett in a matter of months, it seems pointless to find a suitable companion as your replacement for such a short amount of time. So, I have a proposal for you, Miss Barnes. You are to come and live here at Ashton Manor with no further connection to your family.'

It's not really a proposal, it's a demand.

'You are cutting me off from my family, sir?'

'Yes, is that going to be a problem?'

Actually, yes it will be... But I cannot utter this before him.

'What is your answer, Miss Barnes?'

'No, sir, it won't be a problem. Shall I collect my things?'

'Yes, do so immediately. I will have the housekeeper make you up a room.' He dismisses me from the study and I stand momentarily dazed outside the door - I am doing this for Manny.

'Back so soon?' comments Mrs Arthur as I open the kitchen door in the farmhouse.

I've just come from the barn after saying goodbye to Mary, she encouraged me to go, despite my reluctance. 'We are doing so well with the Arthurs,' she told me with a rosy glow coming to her cheeks, the nutritious food from the kitchen having taken away her unhealthy complexion. 'I might be able to work soon myself: Mrs Arthur has promised to watch Henry for a few hours a day so I can add to your wages.' I shouldn't be anxious about leaving them, and I know they are being well looked after, but... not being able to see them with my own eyes, is heart breaking.

I hover by the kitchen door. 'I've come to take my leave, Mrs Arthur.'

'Where are you going?' The farmer's wife pulls a pie from the oven, the fruit sizzling underneath the golden pastry.

'I've been asked to take up residence at Ashton Manor.'

Mrs Arthur lifts her bent posture and puts the dish on the side. 'We shall miss you around here...' She takes one look at me anxiously gnawing my bottom lip. 'What is troubling you?'

'Will you take care of Pa, make sure he's comfortable?'

'Of course,' she smiles sadly. 'I'll look after them all. Will you be able to continue your work with Emma?'

The question is another reminder of what I'm leaving behind and my heart feels a stab of pain. 'I don't think that is possible, Mrs Arthur...I'm sorry.'

'No matter,' she says with complete understanding. 'I thank you for what you have done for my girl, truly I do.' The appreciation is hard to take, there's so much I still need to teach the girl, my work is not even half-way to completion. As if they've heard our conversation, two laughing children run into the kitchen. Emma tugs at my dress and wags a finger at me from left to right, taps her thumb twice to her chin, and finally curls one of her thumbs and an index finger into a 'C' shape, rotating it round in a circle.

'What's my favourite colour?' I sign back. Emma nods her head.

'Mm,' I put a finger on my chin to exaggerate my thinking. 'Yellow, I think.' I lift an open hand and shake it near my ear.

Thomas points both of his index fingers and taps them together in front of himself.

'You like yellow too?' I point to him and repeat the sign for yellow. He nods and grins. Emma pokes me and repeats Thomas' sign, tapping both of her fingers together and adding another gesture where she lifts her hand to the side of her head and signs the word for sun.

'Yes, the sun is yellow too.' I sigh, looking at these two truly incredible children, overcoming all the odds and discovering the ability to speak. Scooping them both up in my arms, I kiss them on the head before releasing them to run out of the room, the sound of laughter trailing behind them. Agreeing to live with the Montagues means more than cutting myself off from my own family, I will have to sacrifice all the things that fill me with joy, and that will be the most difficult thing of all.

December comes rolling along and snow covers the grounds of Ashton Manor.

'Isn't it beautiful,' says Eliza gazing out of the window at the untouched white blanket of snow all the way down the long drive. 'It's almost going to be a shame when the Lovett's carriage comes trundling along.'

'Almost?' Manny lifts a mischievous eyebrow.

'My Mr Lovett can spoil whatever he wants, turn the snow to slush for all I care, as long as he can get here, I don't mind'

'He's not *your* Mr Lovett yet, Miss Eliza,' I remind the girl.

'No.' She sighs. 'What's taking him so long?'

'You have only just turned sixteen,' reminds Manny.

'All the more reason for him to propose before anyone else does,' she says haughtily. 'I won't be around for long when the word spreads that I am out.'

Manny snorts and shakes his head, focusing his attention back on the book in his hands. The scene has been a familiar one of late, the three of us resting in each other's company, the cold weather dissuading Eliza from venturing out and Manny secretly soaking up every minute he can spend in my presence within the safety of his step-sister's company.

'Don't you have studying to do?' Eliza asks coldly.

'Nothing until next term.'

'Then haven't you got other, more 'manly' pursuits to follow.'

'Perhaps.' He grins. 'Why, are you not enjoying my company?'

'There is something called too much of a good thing,' she says drily.

'What about you, Miss Barnes, is my presence becoming irksome to you too?' Manny turns to me, a twinkle in his eye.

Irksome wouldn't be the word I'd use... constricting, perhaps... or suffocating. I can't deny the growing knot in my stomach whenever I watch him lounging so comfortably in Ashton Manor's finely furnished rooms. It's the life I will be leading too, and every secretive smile and glance from Manny fills me with a sense of unease, knowing he's imagining our future together.

'Leave Miss Barnes alone. She is too polite to answer truthfully,' says Eliza fighting on my behalf.

'Indeed.' He folds his arms and leans back on the sofa, lifting his eyebrows humorously.

'You should leave us alone, Manny, otherwise people will start to get ideas.'

'What ideas would those be, Eliza?'

'That you are forming an attachment to her, it isn't so far-fetched, I've never seen you so much in my life... now, I know Miss Barnes has gone up in Father's estimation, but still, how preposterous would that be!' My cheeks redden at Eliza's indiscreet put down, talking as if I weren't in the room.

'Father has praised Miss Barnes?' says Manny in surprise. 'When did this happen, I must have missed it?'

'Yes, the other day when you were out riding and we were enjoying time *without* your presence, Father commended Miss Barnes for protecting our family at the cost of losing her own, he seemed rather impressed and promised her a superior reference when Mr Lovett finally does take me away as his bride.'

Manny turns and smiles at me with pride, his look of affection twisting my stomach even tighter, gaining Lord Montague's acceptance has taken me deeper into the family and has made our marriage an even greater possibility. The thought fills me with dread as I consider a future of idleness and self-indulgence, but these things are nothing compared with the hypocrisy I will have to display on a daily basis, our acts of compassion will take us to the poor, we will feed and clothe them, but when the job is complete, we will retreat back to our luxurious surroundings and live a life totally unconcerned about the people living on our doorstep.

'Congratulations, Miss Barnes,' says Manny. 'You really must have made an impression.' He stands and straightens the creases in his tails. 'Since my sister has made it so clear that I am unwanted, I shall leave you. I bid you adieu.' He bows smartly before me and leaves the room.

'Don't mind him,' says Eliza wafting her hand towards the closing door. 'He shall not bother you for much longer, Father will send him back to Cambridge soon, he is not normally at the manor for such a long period of time.'

I smile as best I can, trying to convince Eliza I'm not in the least bothered by Manny's presence, but a niggling thought flashes into my mind, and it disturbs me so much that I find my fingers gripping onto the embroidery hoop I'm holding in my hands.

'Are you well, Miss Barnes?' asks Eliza looking up at me.

'Erm, no, I don't think I am.' I swallow and put the hoop down by the side of the chair. 'If you will excuse me, Miss

Eliza, I think I need some fresh air.'

My sudden insight has unnerved me... and I don't think I'm mistaken. I search the recesses of my mind trying to find an example, but I can't - not once have I seen Manny go out of his way to help someone less fortunate since I arrived at Ashton Manor. In Belmont, he couldn't stop himself from performing good deeds - the steps for Lucy, signing with Hetty, rescuing Mr Baker, even teaching me to read. But here, in his own home, I've seen him do nothing. I know his father places restrictions on him, but the Manny I know wouldn't let this stand in his way - not once have I seen him communicating with the servants or sneaking a loaf of bread to a starving family. I've only seen him partake of the luxury around him, completely segregating himself from the people he says he wants to help so much... maybe I'm wrong, but I don't see a broken heart. Within a moment I've realised what feels so wrong, it's not only the luxurious surroundings and the manners of the rich which I don't want in my future, but it's Manny. I fell in love with Emmanuel Smith. Emmanuel Montague is still a stranger to me.

'Rebekah!' I've made my way round to the side of the manor, where the footmen have shovelled a pathway through the snow. I spin round to see Kitty chasing after me.

'Is everything all right, Kitty? She looks agitated, her hair swirling out from underneath her lace cap.

'I've some terrible news.'

'Oh dear,' I naturally touch her left elbow to console her. 'Whatever has happened, is it your family?'

'No, it's yours.'

I feel the blood drain out of my face and I clutch onto Kitty. I have not heard anything from the farm since I left - no news is good news, that's what I assumed, and since Mrs Arthur is the only one who can write on my family's behalf, I hadn't expected frequent communication. I pray silently that Georgie is safe, hoping that the Jenson's haven't come to take him back.

'I've just returned from the village and I saw Mary... she's your sister, isn't she?'

'Yes, she is.' I feel my hands begin to shake and Kitty steadies them in her own.

'I am so sorry to tell you this, but they've just buried your Pa.' Her words float around me in the air and it feels like the ground is spinning. 'I'm so sorry, Rebekah.'

'What… What…?' I can't get the sentence out. 'I need to sit down,' I say feeling suddenly faint. Kitty guides me to a bench that isn't far from us and after we've sat down, I try to steady my breath. 'What happened?' I say in a choked voice that I hardly recognise as my own.

'Mary said the fever returned, another infection.'

'But they never told me.'

'It all happened so quickly, I didn't think there was time.'

'Pa…' I whisper and rest my head in my hands.

Kitty wraps an arm around my shoulders as I begin to sob. Now I know there is nothing left to shatter. My heart is completely broken. Pa is dead and I haven't said goodbye.

Chapter Twenty-Seven

I don't know how I've ended up here…

When Eliza found out about the death of my pa, she sent me away. 'Take the morning off, Miss Barnes, I can see it's upset you.' Her patronising attitude was infuriating… of course it's upset me, anyone who's had a devoted pa like mine would be upset. I walked over the fields, oblivious to my surroundings, not caring I was knee deep in snow and frozen to the bone.

Now I am here, standing outside the farmhouse and gazing up at the window where my pa spent his final days. It hadn't been my intention to walk in this direction, since I am forbidden to associate with my family, but my feet naturally took over, my heart desperately seeking out comfort and somewhere to grieve.

I tap on the farmhouse door and Mrs Arthur's face greets me; her own eyes full of sorrow. 'Rebekah,' she looks surprised to see me. 'We weren't expecting you.'

'I've come to say goodbye.'

'You're too late,' she says sadly.

'I know. Is Mary here, I'd like to see her?'

Mrs Arthur wrings her hands together in worry. 'But Rebekah, they've gone.'

'Who's gone?'

'All of them – Mary, Mags, the boys—'

'Where have they gone?' I feel my panic rising - I cannot lose everyone in a single day. I suppose they can no longer claim Pa's poor relief, but for the parish to end payments so soon after his death is heartless and cruel.

'I told them they could stay, but the man with the cart wouldn't listen.' Her hands start to tremble and I take them both in my own, trying to calm my own fears as much as hers.

'What man?' I ask.

'I don't know, a man came with a cart and said he had orders to take them back home to Belmont.'

'They've nowhere to live in Belmont.'

'That's what Mary said, she told him they no longer had permission to live in the labourer's cottages, but then the man said it was no longer an issue, that Mr Greaves had been paid six months of rent in advance so they could move back immediately.'

'But they were happy here, did Mary not consider staying... or asking the man to wait until they had spoken to me?'

'Of course she did, but the man was adamant it was an offer that would not be repeated, he said if they chose not to return with him, they could not return at all.'

'And so, they just went?' My voice wobbles as I speak, taking a firmer hold onto Mrs Arthur's hands.

'They decided it would be for the best of all concerned, that old barn is no good for them over winter, it leaks and it's damp, if any one of them gets a sniffle it could easily turn into something nasty.'

'How long ago did they leave?'

'Oh, not quite an hour ago - you shan't catch them, Rebekah, not without a horse. I shall miss your little Mags,' she says quietly to herself. 'Will you stay on at the manor?'

I give an unconvincing nod.

Mrs Arthur wipes the corner of her wet eye with her apron. 'Well, at least we still have you close by.'

My heart is heavy when I finally leave the farm. Everyone I love has left me. This is how I'll feel when I finally become a Montague. I'll be lost to my family, for surely, they'll not be welcome in our home. Emmanuel Smith would have loved and accepted them, but as for Emmanuel Montague, his shame will create a barrier between us and them. I stand on the crest of the hill looking back at the farmhouse, watching a billow of smoke escape from the chimney. 'Goodbye, Pa,' I whisper into the icy wind knowing it's time I leave and not look back... but I can't do it. I can't turn my back on the farmhouse and I sink down to my knees as parts of my final conversation with my pa float into my memory... *When you find what breaks your heart, nothing will stop you.* Did he really say that... nothing? My eyes fill with tears, my nose prickling as I allow them to build up under my eyelids. *Life is short, Becks. You should do what makes you happy.* Pa knew this only too well. He laboured all his life, but what for? I didn't know his hopes and dreams, he never shared them with me. But I could take a guess at one of the things his heart would have longed for, from the moment we all came into the world, all he wanted was to see his children happy.

'All right, Pa.' I say aloud into the empty field, the tears now rolling uncontrollably down my face. 'I'm going to be happy.' I stand and turn with determination away from the farm. My heart is broken and I'm going to receive the promise of the blessing that should follow - nothing is going to stop me.

The first logical step is for me to hand in my notice. Ashton Manor has nothing for me, in fact it's doing me more harm than good. Lady Montague takes the news well and seems relieved that I'm going without leaving a stain on the family's reputation. Eliza is not so easy to console.

'I demand you stay, Miss Barnes,' she insists when every other form of bribery and cajoling has failed.

'I'm sorry, Miss Eliza. My future isn't here.'

'But *my* future is!'

'Yes, I understand, but I'm sure you will easily find a new companion to be by your side.'

'No one like you,' she replies sulkily and pouts her lower lip.

'I have told your mother I will stay on for two weeks so you can find a replacement.'

She coldly looks me over. 'You can leave now; I don't want you for two more weeks if I know you're leaving.'

'But, Miss Eliza, you shall not be able to spend time in company without an escort, what about Mr Lovett?'

'I'll manage.' She turns her back slightly on the chair she is sitting on and folds her arms.

'Really, I am happy to remain for the time set.'

'If you stay for the two weeks you have suggested, is there a possibility you will change your mind and continue being my companion until my marriage?'

'No, I'm sorry.'

'Then go now.' There is no point arguing with her in this mood. I wish her well and leave the girl to wallow in her own self-pity before going to pack my belongings.

There is now only one more person I need to find. Emmanuel Smith would be in the stables, but as for Emmanuel Montague, I've no idea. I begin searching the house, but feel uncomfortable doing so, knowing I would be questioned if someone found me. I must leave the grounds and think of a way to contact him. Under no circumstances can I go home without seeing him.

A wave of guilt floods over me as I walk down the drive. I'm not running away – I will talk to him. I look up to see a gentleman striding towards me wearing a dark green coat and sparkling emerald eyes to match. My insides tense with a strange mixture of relief to be seeing Manny and apprehension about the news I am about to give him.

He spies the wooden box under my arm. 'Where are you going?'

'Home.' My eyes dart to the ground.

'And by home you mean?'

A sudden rush of irritation springs up and I lift my eyes to meet his. 'Don't look so innocent, Manny, I know it was you.' He looks blankly at me. 'You know exactly what I mean by home, you paid the rent on the cottage in Belmont and sent a man with a cart to collect them.'

'Becks, really, I don't know what you are talking about.'

'I told you to leave us alone.'

'I did… your pa shouldn't be travelling in his condition; has he really been taken back to Belmont in a cart?'

He doesn't know…

'Manny, my…' I stare at him, hoping he won't make me say the words.

His face drops. 'What's happened?'

'My… my pa is—' My hand covers my lips. 'He's dead.'

Manny's eyes widen as he takes in the news and watches fresh tears trickle down my face. 'Oh Becks.' I can see he wants to comfort me, but he glances warily up at the windows behind us and holds himself back.

My shoulders shudder as I try to hold in my grief. 'I must go, Manny.' I attempt to side-step around him, but he stands in my way.

'Wait, you can't go, Becks… what about us?' He sounds hurt and I turn back to face him.

'I can't do it, Manny.' I wipe my wet cheek. 'I tried, but I don't belong here.'

This time he steps straight up to me and grasps me lightly by the shoulders. 'You *do* belong.'

'Please, let go of me, anyone could see us from the windows.' He does what I ask.

'I can't believe this.' He runs a hand through his curly hair. 'Please, what can I do to make you stay.'

I gaze at him. 'Leave with me.'

'That is the one thing I can't do,' he says in agony. 'Please don't go, allow yourself time to grieve for your pa, you'll feel differently with time.'

'I'm not leaving because my pa is no longer with us, it's not a reaction to his death.'

'Then why are you going? My father is starting to think highly of you, he's beginning to see what I see. Becks, we're nearly there. We can marry soon with the approval of my family and then we can begin a life together, working for the good of others.'

'I don't—' I pause and take a steadying breath knowing how much hurt I'm about to cause him. 'I don't love you Manny.' The words almost knock him over. 'I love Emmanuel Smith, not Emmanuel Montague.'

'But Becks, it's the same person, they're both me.'

'No, I'm afraid they're not.' We stand, allowing the wind to gently blow around our faces, tousling locks of Manny's curls and fluttering the ribbons on my bonnet.

'What can I do to make you change your mind?' he asks, looking as if he's also about to shed a tear.

'You once told me a broken heart means giving until it hurts, holding nothing back and pouring yourself out for those you love the most. If you want to keep me, then you need to lose everything.'

He looks away and presses his lips together. 'I'm sorry,' he croaks. 'I can't do that.'

'Then I need to say goodbye.' I slowly turn around and begin to walk away.

He doesn't stop me.

I keep walking, my eyes firmly planted on the gates in the distance. I don't look back because I know I will not be able to endure the pain in his eyes and I'll break down right here on the drive, because the grief of losing Pa and Manny on the same day will blur together in one great outpouring. All I hear is the rhythmic crunching of the ground underneath my feet and it takes all my strength to place one foot in front of another. With a great effort, I focus on my breathing...

Breathe in... Breathe out...

I stifle a sob but keep moving forward. Each step I make taking me further away from him.

Breathe in... Breathe out...

I turn the corner at the gates - we will never meet again.

Chapter Twenty-Eight

It was a long journey on the stagecoach. Despite the smooth-ness of the turnpike road, the carriage was overcrowded and stuffy and I found myself pressed up against several passengers who clearly hadn't washed in weeks, maybe even months.

The coach finally sets me down in the high street. Every-thing inside of me fights the urge to head straight to our little cottage, but it's vital I earn an income as soon as possible so we can survive by our own independence. Now we're all back, Mary will have Henry and Georgie to mother, since Ma has abandoned us to our fate and even though Daniel, Thomas and Maggie can all work, their contribution will be a pittance. It's all down to me to provide enough money for food and shel-ter, Manny certainly won't be paying for us any longer and Mr Greaves will throw us out once the six months are over if we still can't pay our rent.

It's a strain, walking the four miles from the high street to Belmont Park after the long journey and emotional battering I have taken today. Night is beginning to fall when I reach the back entrance and the familiar earthy odour meets my nose from the damp moss that is still trailing down the brickwork. I tap on the door and after a few moments it creaks open to reveal two little eyes staring out at me, I smile. I know who those eyes belong to.

'Rebekah?' The eyes widen, the door flings open and Lucy runs out, flinging her arms round me. 'What are you doing here?' Her excitement is contagious and momentarily I forget the aching in my heart. Taking my hand, she doesn't wait for an answer and drags me into the kitchen.

Hetty doesn't hear us enter and Lucy taps her on the shoul-der. When the cook turns her face she beams with joy and she clasps me in a tight embrace, the glimmer of a tear forming in the corner of her eye. Once she releases me, her eyes look dir-ectly to the door and with palms flat and facing up, she moves them round in small circles. 'Ma-nn-y?'

She assumes he's with me and my heart dips.

'We thought Manny was with you, since he went so soon after you left Belmont,' explains Lucy looking at me anxiously. 'He wrote and told me how he had found you and that your pa had been ill.'

'He wrote to you?' I didn't know he'd been in contact, I thought he'd abandoned them.

'Yes, he didn't want to leave me alone even though he couldn't be physically present.' That sounds so much like Manny – and I thought Emmanuel Montague didn't care like his counterpart did.

'I'm sorry,' I say quickly before I dwell for too long on what I've lost. 'He's not with me.' I shake my head so Hetty understands what I've said.

Lucy looks disappointed, but brightens up when she says, 'Lady Belmont will be so pleased to know you're back. She's been asking after you.'

'She has?'

'I've been telling her your news when Manny sends me a letter. Did the doctor find you?' My eyebrows knit together and Lucy sees my confused face. 'She sent a doctor when Manny told us your pa had been ill, it was a great relief to find out he had overcome the infection.'

I feel my mouth hang half-open. Manny didn't send for the doctor... am I also to assume I wrongly accused him of paying the rent on the cottage and sending a driver to pick up my family? Maybe he had listened to me when I told him to leave us alone. I'd supposed Emmanuel Montague hadn't developed the same sensitivity, now I'm wondering if I was wrong? But, even if I'd known Manny wasn't involved, things would have turned out the same and I still would have left.

'How is your pa? Lucy's question cuts into my thoughts.

'My pa...?' My focus is all over the place, my mind a muddle of blurry thoughts.

'Rebekah, are you well?' The tiny maid places a hand on my arm.

'Erm, yes – I...' I lift my eyes to the girl's face. 'Actually, I could do with sitting down.' Lucy guides me to the table and pulls out a chair for me to sit on. Hetty places a cup of hot milk in front of me and for a moment, if I close my eyes, it feels like I'm back at the Arthurs, being looked after by the kindly farmer's wife. The tears begin to build again as the events of the day threaten to overwhelm me.

'Whatever is the matter, Rebekah?' Lucy crouches at my side and takes my hand.

'My pa is dead,' I whisper and my eyes stare straight ahead. Lucy gasps and wraps her arms around me. Hetty, not knowing the cause of my suffering, but fully understanding my grief, grips me tightly around the shoulders and with my two friends by my side I release the pain and sorrow and cry uncontrollably until I have nothing left to give.

Lucy sneaks me up to her room so I can sleep. I had intended to seek out Mrs Langley tonight, but there's no way I can see her in my state with eyes that are bloodshot and cheeks that are blotchy.

In the early hours of the morning I rise with Lucy. It feels good to be up before the sun again and helping Hetty in the kitchen, despite an aching head after a disturbed night's sleep. I help set the table for the servant's breakfast and have just laid out the cutlery when a familiar voice shrills out behind me. 'What's the meaning of this?'

My stomach tenses and I twist my figure to face the housekeeper, the very person whom I had come to see. 'Good morning, Mrs Langley.' I try to smile, but I don't think it forms on my face.

'Why are you back?' she snaps, the familiar triangular nose looking down at me as if I'm the last person she wants to see.

'I have come to enquire after work.'

'We have a new lady's maid and we require no governesses as you know.' She purses her lips tightly.

'I do not want to be restored to the position of lady's maid, Mrs Langley, I am enquiring if I can reclaim my position as maid of all work.'

The housekeeper's lips purse even tighter, so much so it almost deforms her face. 'All right, I will take you on as maid of all work.'

'Thank—'

'But know this, there will be no progression, if a position opens up you will not claim it, there will be no personal gains because you used to have the ear of her ladyship. You stay at the bottom because that's where you belong. Do I make myself clear?'

A weight lifts slightly off my shoulders, which is strange considering what Mrs Langley has just proclaimed. But this *is* where I should be. Right at the bottom with the poor and hopeless, however this time, I've come back with a purpose. Manny was wrong, this is where I belong... it's where we both belong and I wish he was standing by my side. 'I understand, Mrs Langley.'

'Good. You start immediately.'

'I need to check on my brothers and sisters, I have not been home since I arrived.'

'You start now or never.'

'I'm sorry, but my pa has recently passed away, I must see my family are coping without him.'

She gives a sly smile. 'You start now or never, Barnes.'

I lift my chin. 'Very well, I will start immediately – but you need to know I will be taking my half-days off like I am entitled to do. If there's a problem with that I will request it from Lady Belmont.'

'Don't expect any special favours, Barnes, like I said you no longer have her ladyship's ear, there's a new lady's maid now.' She smiles smugly as if she's claimed a victory over me.

'Who is that?' I ask with interest.

'My daughter.'

Life falls back into its old routine and my body aches all over again after the months of luxury I've experienced at Ashton Manor. Up with the dawn, cleaning and lighting the fires, scrubbing the floors, peeling the vegetables, taking out the slops, suffering through the most demeaning and inhumane jobs Mrs Langley can throw at me. I do it all with as much grace as I can find. I take the insults that the housekeeper hurls at me, the kicks to the shins when I get something wrong. I suffer it all for the sake of my family who are relying on my wages. I send them faithfully, though I am yet to see them or hear word that all is well.

However, I'd be lying if I said it was all hardship. It's good to be back with Lucy, knowing I can protect her once again. She's back as a scullery maid after her fleeting role as a kitchen maid, Mrs Langley demoted her as soon as she was able, not wanting a single bit of my influence to touch the corridors of Belmont Park. One day, as Lucy's hands are elbow deep in the scullery sink, I notice she's hunched over, her body a little too tall for the job she's doing. When I look down, I see the problem – she's still standing on Manny's handmade wooden step though the year has seen her grow too tall to use it.

'You know you don't have to use that anymore,' I say watching her.

Lucy glances self-consciously down to her feet. 'Oh, I know.' Her cheeks redden as she looks at me, her eyes filled with sadness - she misses him too.

Hetty loses no time in filling my mind with more signs and gestures. I soak them all up, gleaning as much knowledge as I can, but I know I can't have her by my side forever. If I'm to ever break free of this place I must find a new way to increase my understanding. This much is certain, I won't allow myself to stay here, I will follow the pieces of my shattered heart and receive the joy which I know is waiting for me.

Every day I need to fight the urge to give up. I must keep moving forward, even when the new and unfamiliar faces at Belmont Park cause me to stumble and suffer a mixture of emotions. Each time a meal comes round I have to mentally prepare myself to watch the new groom come and eat his fill. He's a perfectly nice boy from the other side of town and he smells like straw and horses – but it's not the same. No matter how long I allow my thoughts to drift into the past, the fireplace remains empty and Manny isn't coming to warm his hands on the flames. Then there is the other face that unsettles me greatly. Mrs Parsons, though much nicer than her mother, beams and smiles at me all day. Her words are sweet and flattering, but I haven't missed her eyes following me round, not letting me out of her sight when I'm in her presence. If I hadn't already met her, I'd think she was eying me up and assessing if I had come back to steal back my old position. But it's not with distrust that she's watching me, her eyes express something different and with caution I go about my days, anxiously waiting for the time I can see my family again and assure myself that all is well.

It is with great surprise a few weeks later that I'm granted my request for a half-day off without having to appeal to Lady Belmont. Upon reaching the top of the hill, the sight of our cottage fills me with little joy when I remember how happy we had been with the Arthurs. The children had been thriving there, would they be flourishing to the same extent now? I see the ivy is still overgrown, the windows dirty and the door beginning to peel paint. I give a great sigh, walk down the hill and open the front door.

Mary is scrubbing the floor when I enter and she lifts up her head, moving the hair out of her face with an arm. 'Rebekah, what are you doing home?'

'I've come to make sure you're all well.'

'Yes, we are well.' She stands from her knees. 'Though we've been concerned about you.'

'You have?'

'Yes, your wages have reduced.' Lines of worry crease across the girl's forehead. 'We feared you were in trouble, but we never heard from you.'

'I've returned to Belmont Park as maid of all work.'

'That is such a drop in position.'

'It's all right, I chose to come home to be with you.' Mary presses her lips together and attempts a smile. 'Where is everyone?' Looking around for the first time I realise the room is empty.

'Daniel and Tommy are working with Mr Greaves.'

'I'm glad they've found something, it will help... and Maggie?' Mary bites down on her lips even more, draining all the colour away. 'Is she working too?' I ask trying to read her expression. Mary shakes her head. 'She's with Georgie and Henry then?' My sister nods, but her chin trembles. 'What's the matter, Mary?' I take her hand and notice that her red rimmed eyes have returned and her face is drawn.

'It's Ma, she...' Mary looks away, not able to meet my eye. 'She's got the children.'

For a moment I don't understand. 'How could Ma have the children, she abandoned us back in Market Ashton... where is she now?'

'Next door,' Mary whispers her face still turned away from mine.

My forehead furrows deeply. 'Next door?'

'Yes, with Uncle Will.'

'They are married?'

This time Mary looks at me in confusion as she darts her eyes to my face. 'That is against the law, Rebekah, even Ma wouldn't do something as foolish as that.'

'But Pa—' A movement from the shadowy corner causes me

to jolt with shock - I must be going mad, something on the bed moved... no, *someone* on the bed moved.

'Rebekah... is that you?' The voice I thought I'd never hear again floats into my ears.

'Pa?' I almost choke on a sob and find myself stumbling across the room and into him arms.

'Hey, hey, what's the matter, Becks?' I hear his calm but concerned voice and feel his hand stroking the top of my head. 'Everything's alright, Becks, everything's alright.'

I lie there in the safety of his arms for what feels like hours. Finally, I lift my head once I've gained the ability to speak coherently again. 'I thought you were dead,' I say wiping my eyes with a corner of Pa's tattered blanket.

'Who told you that?' he says softly cradling my hand in his.

'Kitty.'

'Who's Kitty?' asks Mary who has come to sit next to me on the bed and is maternally holding my other hand. I stare out in front of me, trying to figure out how the information had been miscommunicated, but it hadn't. Kitty had given me such facts and details that could only mean one thing – she was lying.

'Becks?' Pa tightens his grip on my hand, bringing me out of my head and back into the room.

'It doesn't matter,' I say with a sniff. 'That's not important right now... tell me what's happened with Ma... you said she's with—' I crinkle my nose trying to remember what Mary had told me.

'With Uncle Will.'

'You mean she's left Pa and brazenly living in sin next door?'

'That's correct, it was a shock to see her here when we arrived home from Market Ashton.'

I turn to Pa in outrage. 'Pa, you can't let her do this.'

'What am I to do, Becks, fight Will to claim back my wife, I'm hardly going to win?' He stares down at his useless legs.

'Why has she taken the children?'

'We don't know,' says Mary with a hint of bitterness to her tone. 'She doesn't even care for them.' I'm startled by her response, but I can't blame her, not with what the poor girl has had to shoulder in the last year. 'She wanted me to go with her too, but I wasn't going to leave Pa behind, who would look after him?'

I frown and shake my head at a loss for words. How could she leave her husband alone and take all his children from him? Does she not understand the shame and disgrace she's brought upon his family name? Even someone with an ounce of compassion for mankind wouldn't do what she's done.

I stand abruptly.

'Where are you going, Rebekah?' asks Mary looking up anxiously.

'Pa can't fight for us, but I can.' Clenching my fists, I march straight out of the cottage to the identical one next door. I bang with all my might on the door, repeatedly, until it opens.

'Stop hammering the door down, will you – oh, Rebekah!' Will's fair eyebrows rise in surprise. 'I thought you were in Market Ashton?'

'I was. I need to speak to Ma; I believe she is with you.' I glare piercingly at our neighbour leaving him in no doubt that I'm far from impressed by his actions.

'Beck-Beck!' Henry toddles up behind Will almost pushing him out of the way to get to me. 'Beck-Beck play?' My anger disappears momentarily as my youngest brother takes me by the hand and tries to drag me further into the cottage.

'Not right now Henry, I need to see Ma.' I plant my feet firmly in the doorway.

'Ma-ma?' He looks up at me with round innocent eyes and a stab of guilt hits my chest. None of this is my fault, but to think this blameless boy is unknowingly caught up in such shameful circumstances. I shouldn't have let Ma disappear. I swept the issue under the carpet, believing she would come back to us, but it was obvious Ma wasn't handling the situation well, she wouldn't speak to anyone, she kept herself isolated, something was wrong and I didn't help her... but I didn't think she'd do this... not with Uncle Will.

'How could you do such a thing?' I say to Will in a hushed voice turning my mouth away from Henry.

'We haven't done anything,' Will says defensively and then looks away.

'You've taken a married woman under your roof and you're

telling me you haven't done anything wrong – tongues wag Will.'

'Things might have been different if your pa had provided for her.'

'He can't walk!'

'What about before the accident?'

'You couldn't get a more hard-working labourer than Pa, you know that, you've laboured with him since you were young.'

'I'm not referring to his hard work in the fields.' I ignore the comment, if he has an argument with Pa than he needs to sort it out himself.

'Do you even care for her?'

'Of course I do, otherwise I wouldn't have told her to get the bairns, she was going to leave them with your pa.' Will glances behind him into the cottage and I follow the trail of his eyes, squinting into the darkened room for the first time and seeing Ma working quietly at a table chopping carrots.

'Don't blame me, Rebekah,' Ma suddenly says defensively without looking up.

'You left Pa behind.'

'No, I did not.'

'I'm sorry, but next door are *your* husband and *your* daughter – alone. Look up at me!' I don't think I've ever yelled at Ma before. 'Look up at me!'

She slowly lifts her face, her chin held high and lips held tightly together.

'Explain, Ma!'

'I couldn't cope anymore.'

'Not a good enough excuse,' I snap back. 'We were safe with the Arthurs and provided for, you didn't have to do anything.'

'I gave Mary the option of coming with me,' she says as if this makes a difference.

'What about Pa?'

'Well, he couldn't come - I've left him for another man.' Unblinking, Ma looks me straight in the eye.

'So, you hoped Pa would die alone leaving you free to re-marry?' This causes her to remove her gaze and she shuffles un-comfortably as I hit on the truth. 'Why did you come back for the children?'

'They are mine and Will said I shouldn't leave them because one day they'd bring home an income. Besides, Will has re-cently come into an inheritance and is about to become a ten-ant farmer. I will employ a maid of all work to look after the little ones, the others can go out to work.'

'That's all you care about, isn't it... money? All my life you've complained about not having enough, always looking at what you don't have, rather than what you do have. I agree that life hasn't been easy this last year, but we've had a roof over our heads, friends to help us along the way and we've had each other, isn't that good enough for you?'

'Rebekah you don't understand.'

'There's nothing to understand, apart from the fact you're a heartless and selfish woman.'

'When you've travelled the road I have you'll understand why I am like I am - I can never forgive your pa for where he's brought us to.'

'I don't care what Pa may or may not have done. Ma, you can-not live unmarried with another man...especially when your husband lives next door.'

'Your father is paralysed!' she screams with her mouth so wide I can see down her throat.

I don't let her outburst throw me off track me. 'Does para-lysed mean dead now...are you widowed?'

'Will is good to me, he provides an income, one that is about to increase.'

'You're a fool, Ma and you've brought disgrace upon us. I didn't think you were capable of such things.'

'How dare you call me a fool.'

'It's what you are, Ma,' I say sadly shaking my head. 'Instead of letting your family help, you pushed yourself further away from us, you made yourself vulnerable and now everyone has to deal with the consequences. Was it Will that night, picking you up in a cart under the cover of darkness?'

She doesn't answer.

'I think you'd better leave, Rebekah,' says Will shuffling towards me.

'Fine, but I'm taking the children with me – you don't deserve them.' I bend down and take Henry's hand and follow this up by scooping up Maggie and Georgie, who had been in a darkened corner mutely watching events unfold.

I pause at the door and glare at Ma. 'You can decide if you come with us or not.' She holds my eyes for a few seconds, before dropping her glance to the table. She picks up the knife and continues to chop the carrots.

'What's going on?' asks a bewildered Mary when I storm back into our own cottage with the children in front of me.

'She's not taking Pa's children away from him.'

'What about Ma, is she coming home?'

'She seems to be content with her situation.' I drag out a chair from under the table and bang it on the floor before sitting down. 'Send a message to Daniel and Tommy, tell them to come home to Pa tonight.' My head falls into my hands and I close my eyes.

'Are you all right, Rebekah?' Mary puts a cautious hand on my shoulder.

I take a deep inhale and lift my head – that's when I see the figure lurking over Pa's bed. 'Who's that?'

'Oh, she's been so kind to us since moving home... Lady Belmont has sent her,' explains Mary.

I frown, squinting into the darkness in time to see our guest turn around.

'Rebekah, so good to see you.' The cheeriness in the voice is fake, but it's instantly familiar. Distress washes over me as a line of sunlight breaks through the ivy-covered window and lights up the face of Mrs Parsons walking towards me from out of the shadows.

Chapter Twenty-Nine

'If you've come home to look after your pa your help isn't needed, I'm afraid you've wasted your half-day off,' says Mrs Parsons with a look of triumph.

I can't believe this woman is in my house. She's been waiting for her chance for months and now she's finally made her way inside. A wave of nausea hits me... what does she even want?

'Mrs Parsons was waiting to greet us on our arrival home, Rebekah,' explains Mary behind me. 'She's been ever so kind.'

'Lady Belmont sent me with a basket of essentials to help you all settle in.' Mrs Parsons adds and travels across to the sink, pulling out a few unwashed pots and pans as if she owned the place.

'If you only came to drop off a gift basket then why have you returned?' I narrow my eyes suspiciously.

'I had to make sure my Thomas was recovering after the trip from Market Ashton.'

My Thomas...

I watch her cross the room again, this time to plump up Pa's pillow.

'I am quite comfortable, Clara,' Pa says irritably, trying to flap the woman away. 'Now you must go, I do not want further shame upon my name, Margaret has already caused enough trouble.'

'Such a selfish woman, she never cared about you.'

'Clara.' His sharp tone has a sense of warning, but the intruder seems to ignore this.

'You deserve someone better, Thomas – let me sit you up.'

'No, thank you, I'm perfectly fine.'

'You should be sitting up, it's nearly midday.'

'My daughters can help me when I'm ready.' She sees his brow crinkle into a frown and looks hurt. 'Thomas, I'm only trying to help you.'

'Thank you, Clara.' He softens his tone and takes her hand, patting it lightly. 'But no help is needed.' Mrs Parsons appears to be appeased and smiles slyly over in my direction, not removing her hand when Pa lets loose his grip.

'You heard my pa,' I say warningly. 'There is nothing we need, so you can be on your way.'

A short huff escapes Mrs Parson's lips. 'Your pa needs a woman to nurse him.'

'He has me, I have the necessary skills to look after a man I've been nursing for more than a year now.' She huffs again. 'Good day, Mrs Parsons.' I open the door, it's time for her to leave. 'I will see you back at Belmont Park.'

Taking the hint, she strides across the room with her chin jutting out, I bang the door closed behind her and slide the bolt across.

'Is there a problem Rebekah?' asks Mary in confusion.

'I don't trust that woman. She's been following me around for months - she's up to something.'

'Clara Parsons is an old fussy acquaintance,' says Pa from across the room. 'She's bringing us food, don't stop her, we need the help.'

'But you just said...'

'I don't need someone fussing over *me*, but someone fussing over my children makes a change, the loss of Mrs Arthur will be felt less keenly... especially now we're all back under one roof.' He looks at the three children who have returned with me and smiles sadly.

'She's an unmarried woman, Pa.'

'Mary's always here.'

'Mary's a child... it's what it looks like.'

'You've spent too much time with the gentry, Becks.'

'Pa, you shouldn't be letting her into your home unless you're planning on...' The nausea returns seeing an expression of guilt spreading across Pa's face.

'Unless Pa's planning what?' asks Mary.

I walk slowly towards Pa in his bed. 'You can't afford a divorce, Pa, only those with money and influence can afford such a thing, you'll need an Act of Parliament.' I whisper. 'We can barely feed ourselves... not to mention the scandal.'

'Clara will provide me with the money I need, she's already promised that, and with regard to the scandal, not one person of our class will care, we can't sink much lower.'

'Where's she getting the money from, her ma's only a house-keeper?'

'I don't know, Becks.'

'You haven't asked her!'

'I don't need to, she's a friend.'

'She could have got it from anywhere.'

'Listen Becks, this year has been difficult enough, if we don't do something we'll be back on parish relief once our six months is up.'

My face pales. 'Pa, you can't.'

'She's a good woman and will look after us.'

'No, Pa... please.' I've no strength left to build an argument, *please* will have to be enough.

'I've known Clara since childhood, there's not a bad bone in her. I don't understand what you have against her?'

I can't answer him, because I don't know myself. There's simply an uneasy feeling deep down inside of me... but what kind of an argument is that as it's not going to persuade him any differently?

I head towards the door without a word.

'You're going so soon?' Pa calls after me sounding a little anxious.

'I've some errands to run for Mrs Langley,' I lie, but the tiny room of the cottage suddenly feels like it's closing in on me and I have to leave.

'We'll see you in four weeks then?' It comes out of Pa's mouth like a question, as if he's uncertain I'll return.

Without meeting his eye, I barely give a nod before shutting the door behind me.

I could have taken a short cut back to Belmont, bypassing the high street, it's market day and it will be busy, slowing my journey down considerably - but there's something I need to do. So, I head with determination into the centre of the town, pushing aside my anxieties about Pa and what the future might hold for us.

You often find little communities growing, there's safety in numbers. It's what Mrs Arthur had said and the observation hasn't left me. Although I know Mr Baker *was* alone, that little girl was not, the one hiding in the bushes all those months ago at Belmont Park, she must have had a family, she was too young to look after herself.

I find a bench opposite the stallholders selling their wares as swarms of customers crowd around to purchase their required goods. If you're poor and hungry this is the perfect opportunity to come out begging, you never know what might be handed to you, a loaf of bread, a piece of fruit, maybe even a penny. I sit, scanning the faces of the crowd, looking for a familiar face, but I cannot see one. My eyes then trail the legs, where stockings and gowns are blurring together, trying to see any tiny forms weaving in and out unseen. I shuffle nervously on the seat, my time is running out and my half-day is nearly over, soon I'll have to return to Belmont Park.

The crowds merge into the background as a wave of loneliness floods over me. I'm so sure this is what I want and I'm determined to push through no matter what, but... what if I can't do this alone? If I'd remained at Ashton Manor there would have been restrictions, however, Manny would have made sure I found fulfilment. He would have known how to make my plans into reality, known the right people and had enough money to achieve it all. I've thrown it all away, I should have stayed. Instead, here I am, sitting on a bench in the hope I might see a homeless child, who may or may not take me towards my goal. Without Manny here, I feel helpless and life just feels... empty. He's left an unbridgeable gap in my heart and I'm not sure if it can ever be filled again.

'Hey!' Footsteps sound in my ears and I'm alerted to a mucky faced boy, who causes me to jolt as he sits next to me on the bench and pokes me out of my sorrow. 'Where've you been?'

I blink twice and my eye is drawn towards the crescent-shaped white scar running directly underneath his eye to the bridge of his nose.

'You've grown,' I say a smile forming on my lips as I recognise the boy I've been looking for.

The boy laughs. 'My jacket doesn't fit now, look!' He shows me his half-mast sleeves with obvious pride. 'Have you been somewhere?'

'Yes, Market Ashton.'

'That's why I couldn't find you.'

'Have you been looking for me?'

'Yes, not for more food,' he adds quickly. 'I remembered you said you couldn't help us anymore. I was only looking out for you because you were so kind to us – we don't see many friendly faces.' He looks down to his hands and cleans a dirty fingernail.

'I never asked your name.'

'It's Billy.'

'I wonder if I can ask a favour, Billy? Do you know a girl—'

'I know many girls.' He interrupts with a grin. 'Depends which one you want to know?'

'This is quite a specific one... she can't hear.'

'How old?'

'About four or five... wait a minute, you asked me how old, does that mean you know more than one?'

'There's two sisters, down the lane over there.' He gestures through the crowds. 'Neither can hear... and there's a boy about a mile from here as well.'

'Do you know them; can you take me there?'

'Sure, but they all work during the day, they won't be back home until nightfall.'

'Can you meet me later on and take me then?'

'Of course, I'll meet you here on this bench and we'll walk down the lane together.'

I watch Billy disappear into the crowd and feel a satisfaction growing inside, trying to overcome all my frustration and pain. If I can only use my broken heart to push me into what I desire to do and allow it to propel me into my future, perhaps I will accomplish something with my life after all. I stand and brush down my dress. It's not what Manny had hoped for me – for us, but I'm not giving up, I'll allow nothing to weigh me down. *Someone with a broken heart holds nothing back.* That's what he told me and now I'm living it. Poverty won't stop me, Pa's physical infirmity won't stop me, Ma's foolishness and even the threat of Mrs Parsons won't stop me. I'm doing this – I'm holding nothing back.

'Hey...Hey, stop that boy!' Mr Allen's shout summons my attention and I turn my head to see him rushing down the high street. A stout boy with little legs pumping quickly pushes passed me. 'Miss Barnes, stop him!' shouts the baker again in pursuit. Without thinking, I hold out my hand and grab the boy by the shoulder.

'Get off me.' The boy tries to wriggle out of my grasp as the baker breathlessly catches up and clips the child round the ear.

He swipes a loaf of bread from his hands. 'If I see you again, there will be trouble, you hear me... I'll call the militia.'

'Militia won't care about a loaf of bread.' The boy gets another smack around the ear and Mr Allen stomps back to his bakery muttering under his breath.

'Why'd you grab me, I could have got away?' the boy says accusingly, rubbing his smarting head. 'Oh, it's you.' He says looking up to see who had apprehended him - he doesn't seem too pleased to see me.

The tiny little pointed nose leaves me in no doubt this is

Gus Langley and I let him go. 'Doesn't your ma teach you steeling's wrong,' I ask with a frown – I'm fed up with the Langley's today and I can't believe another one has landed in my path.

He ignores my comment. 'You shouldn't have grabbed me, especially after what Nan's done to help you, and your stupid pa too.'

'Excuse me.' I'm aghast at his speech, what has Mrs Langley ever done for me?

'Do I have to spell it out?' he says mocking my look of confusion. 'Nan gave you the position at Belmont Park when there wasn't one.'

'I'd been away in Market Ashton; she was probably forced to do it as a favour for Lady Belmont.'

'No, I mean the first time. Belmont Park's never had a maid of all work, they've enough money to take on maids for every room in the house if they wanted to, why would they need a maid of all work?' He does make a fair point, one that I've not considered before, maids of all work are normally lone maids in smaller households and not seen in the larger country estates.

He snorts and nods his head as if I'm an idiot. 'I don't understand the fascination with your family.'

'What do you mean?'

'Belmont Park was fully staffed after your pa's accident, they didn't need more maids, however, Auntie Clara sought you out specially - they think I don't know these things, but I listen...' It all makes sense now, that's why Lady Belmont didn't know I existed when she found me scrubbing the floor. I assumed she was simply ignorant of the household she was running, but her ladyship really didn't have an idea she had hired a maid of all work, because she hadn't, Mrs Langley had done it in secret... but why? My forehead creases in thought, trying to put the pieces together as Gus continues to ramble on by my side. '...and now you go and grab me by the shoulder - you owe me a loaf of bread, I have a long list of people who owe me, Nan being one of them after what I did at the farm.'

At the farm?

'I beg your pardon; did you say at the farm?'

'Yeah, I did.' He laughs jeeringly and my eyes narrow suspiciously – he knows something about Pa.

'What did you do?'

'Now that would be telling.' He grins mischievously and taps the side of his nose. 'You'd better ask Nan; I've told you too much all ready.' He leaves me and struts across the high street, lifting his head high and whistling as if he holds all the answers in the world.

Upon returning to Belmont Park I immediately seek out Mrs Langley in her quarters - there are questions I need answers to.

'Can I help you, Barnes?' she asks without emotion looking up from her desk.

'Yes, you can,' I say staring her straight in the eye. 'I've recently had an interesting conversation with your grandson.'

'Which one?' she asks seemingly ignoring the fact I've barged into her room without knocking, it's almost as if she's expected it – it's not like her to miss an opportunity to reprimand me.

'The one that likes to steal.'

She gives a low chuckle full of pride. 'That will be Gus, he's a little terror.'

'He seemed to imply you had business on Mr Greaves' farm. Now, can you tell me, why do you, a mere housekeeper, have concerns with farming?'

'He has a wild imagination.' She looks down to the papers on her desk and starts organising them into piles.

'You're telling me you know nothing about what Gus is saying?'

'Not a thing.' She doesn't look up.

'I have another question.'

'Haven't you work to do, Barnes?' she drones as if bored by my presence.

'Actually, I've an hour before my half-day is officially over, so no, I don't have work to do.' Mrs Langley purses her lips and surveys me. 'Why did you create a position for me at Belmont Park?'

'I'd dishonour her ladyship if I denied you work after you'd held the position of lady's maid.'

'No, that's not what I'm talking about – the first time. Gus said you created a position for me... why?'

'Is that what he said?'

'Yes.' The housekeeper looks down and speaks to the desk mumbling something incoherently under her breath.

'If you know something about the accident, I'd like to hear it. It's not been an easy year for my pa and further complications whilst living in Market Ashton were nearly fatal.'

'Oh yes, I heard you nearly lost him.' She says slyly, her lips curling up in a half-smile – the same reaction she gave on the day of my interview when I told her Pa was paralysed. 'You'll be pleased to know he's not dead.'

'I don't believe loss of life is very amusing, Mrs Langley. My pa suffered from an infection due to a condition that has left him crippled since the accident, a condition he will never re- cover from - it is no laughing matter. If you desire to keep your knowledge to yourself, then fine, I'll find out another way.' I march towards the door, not wishing to remain in the pres- ence of this vile woman any longer than necessary.

Mrs Langley gives a sharp laugh. 'You still think it was an accident.'

I swivel round slowly, taking my hand away from the door handle and see the housekeeper shaking her head, chuckling in disbelief of my supposed foolishness. 'What did you say?'

'You heard me, and since my careless grandson - who will get a clip around the ear when I next see him - has told you so much, I suppose I have no reason to conceal the truth from you now.' She stands up and comes round the side of her desk. 'Thomas Barnes was supposed to be engaged to my daughter,' she says calmly, though not without the hint of anger bub- bling underneath. 'He deserves everything that happened to him.'

'You mean this all happened because he broke an engagement to Mrs Parsons?'

'Oh, don't worry, your mother made sure an engagement was never made. She came barging into the neighbourhood and took all our hopes and dreams away – Thomas Barnes was going to improve our position in society. Clara was going to cross the class boundary; it was a sure thing.'

I crinkle my forehead and wrinkle my nose – perhaps she's thinking of a different Thomas Barnes. 'I don't think my pa could have brought your family riches or a higher standing – he's a farm labourer, always has been.'

'Only because of his own doing, Mr Curtis, the land agent, was watching and I'd heard rumours of him one day becoming a tenant farmer in his own right. He's a clever man is your pa; the farm would have prospered and who knows what would have come next.'

'I'm sorry, but I've never heard of such a story.'

'That's because your beloved pa is a disappointment and he didn't want you knowing the truth.'

'My pa is not a disappointment.'

'Oh, is that so... is he a tenant farmer?' I open my mouth to answer, but her leering eyes cause my words to dry up. 'That's what I thought.' She narrows her eyes and paces slowly up and down the room in front of me. 'Had my daughter been his wife the predictions about your pa's future would have come to pass. My family might be in service, but we are not poor, we could have provided extra income for investment and not squandered away his chances like your stupid fool of a mother did.'

'Excuse me, but if my ma didn't break an engagement, I don't understand why you are laying the blame upon her, especially when the events you describe have nothing to do with you and your family.'

'Don't defend her.'

'I will – she's my ma.'

'She broke my daughter's heart.'

'Don't you mean my pa did, he's the one who didn't offer her marriage.'

'No, it was your ma. They would have married if it weren't for her, she blinded your pa and stole him away. Anyway, you won't defend her for much longer, not when you find out what she's done.' A smug smile forms on her face.

'I already know what she's done.' This momentarily wipes away her superior glow, not being the one to deliver the shameful blow.

'Ah, then you know your pa will be free soon. This is our chance... not that there's much to be revived, but for some reason my daughter still loves him and believes there is something to be gained. Your pa will soon divorce that woman and you'll have to call me Nan.'

'He can't afford a divorce.'

'Clara can, her late husband was very generous to her in his will, he was a lawyer, don't tell me a little bit of trickery won't get you places, I play quite a good gentlewoman, the poor man died in ignorance of our true roots, probably because Gus wasn't involved, the little blabbermouth... but that's a story for another day.'

I ignore this new revelation, it has nothing to do with me, even though it does explain why Mrs Parsons always looks so finely dressed compared to her mother. 'Even so, what use is Pa to you now, he cannot work.'

'Yes, that is a shame because it was only meant to be a couple of broken bones, a broken leg at worst.'

My mouth gapes open – what did she say?

'Don't look so shocked, Barnes, revenge happens. I paid my grandson to push him from the top of the barn, it was unfortunate that he fell awkwardly.'

The blood drains out of my face and I hold onto the wall to steady myself. 'I'm sorry, Mrs Langley. I don't feel well.' The housekeeper silently pulls out a chair so I can sit down and lower my faint head between my knees.

'Thought it might be a bit of a shock,' she says enjoying my discomfort.

I lift my head slowly, ignoring the pounding that has started above my eye. 'You said unfortunate – he nearly died.' I lower my head back between my knees, trying to regain my balance.

She chortles as if it is all a joke. 'Yes, he did.'

I don't care if I faint, I need to confront the woman who plotted my fathers so called 'accident' face to face. Standing on wobbly legs, I take a firm grip on the back of the chair for support. 'He's lying in bed completely helpless, with no sense of worth - he's a broken man and now his best friend has taken his wife and heaped shame upon us.'

'Ah yes, it didn't take much for William to be convinced of his new love for Margaret Barnes.'

'You bribed him?'

'Yes, I did. You see, Thomas Barnes was supposed to be injured for a short while only, thus rendering him useless only for a season, but causing his wife to give up on him sooner. I do hand it to your ma, she's made of tougher stuff than I originally thought. I paid for William to collect your ma from Market Ashton, good thing little Lucy seemed to know your whereabouts.'

'My pa cannot work; he cannot raise your position in society.'

'No, he cannot, but Clara loves him, always has done – even when she was married to the late Mr Parsons. I told you, her heart was broken, her love will always belong to him. I tried to persuade her to leave it alone, but she wouldn't listen. I like to make my children happy, Barnes, I do what I need to do in order to make that happen. It wasn't difficult. First, we had to provide you with a position so we could keep an eye on your pa's condition and assess how bad he really was. The next thing was to lure your ma away, then after that...'

'Nan, you won't want to hear this, but Gus has told that girl everything, oh—' Kitty has barged into the room and stops short upon seeing me.

'Ah, Kitty, such perfect timing. I was about to explain your part in our tale to Barnes.' The girl's cheeks redden and I get the impression there's remorse in her eyes.

'You told me my pa was dead,' I say trying to remain calm and speaking through clenched teeth in order to do so. Kitty looks aghast at Mrs Langley, her mouth half-open.

'Tell her, Kitty.'

Kitty doesn't speak.

'I beg forgiveness for my grand-daughter, she seems to have lost her tongue.' The housekeeper narrows her eyes with a look of disgust. 'Kitty was sent to watch you, Barnes.'

'You weren't really a kitchen maid in Ashton Manor, were you?'

'No,' Kitty says quietly, looking at the ground. 'I have a friend who works in the kitchens, that's how I got in.'

'You told me you didn't know Mrs Parsons and Gus was only a neighbour.'

'I lied.'

'And you,' I turn to face Mrs Langley. 'You dismissed your own granddaughter?'

'It had to be done, she ruined our plan and let her own personal desires come before her family loyalties. Lady Belmont should have found you on that day, not our former groom.' She glares piercingly at Kitty once again. 'She took away my chance to gain real influence in the house, she was supposed to be lady's maid, not you.'

'Lady Belmont didn't want her.'

The housekeeper's nostril twitches. 'So it seems... we sent her to Market Ashton as a punishment.'

I turn back to Kitty. 'Why tell me my pa was dead? I can't think of anything that's crueller and more hurtful.'

The girl is almost crying, full of remorse unlike her grandmother. 'I'm so sorry, Rebekah, but I had to do it.'

'That's enough, Kitty, let's not get emotional about this.' Mrs Langley holds up a hand and the girl sniffles, obediently closing her mouth. 'We needed you out of the way, Barnes, your presence was not needed in Belmont until my daughter had formed her attachment - we knew you would cause problems.'

'Divorce takes years to achieve, the parliamentary divorce is a particularly long and drawn-out process, it's a right reserved for the upper classes, what you're planning on doing is impossible.'

'We'll work it out.'

'And surely I would have returned at some point during this time while you were "working it out", I wasn't going to leave my brothers and sisters alone.'

'Kitty would have seen to it, without your pa at home it was unlikely you'd give up such a position as you held and return home simply to visit your brothers and sisters. Unfortunately, my granddaughter failed again and let you slip through her fingers.' Kitty's cheeks burn again, this time turning the tips of her ears red.

'But...' I shake my head. 'I still don't understand. Even if you perform some miracle and get the divorce, my pa cannot support your daughter.'

'My daughter is resourceful; she can support him now she is lady's maid for Lady Belmont. After all, she managed to convince her ladyship to give your family security for six months.'

I close my eyes and take a breath – it wasn't Manny. Our final conversation was me accusing him of something he didn't do. I look up, trying to continue the conversation before my own remorse sets in. 'What about his children, can she support them too?'

'I believe your mother has taken the children... all but one, who is now free to work. There will not be many mouths to feed.'

My lip curls slightly at the corner – she doesn't know. 'You might not be aware I brought them all home.'

Her conceited smile slips from her face and she mutters something under her breath.

'You predicted I'd cause problems, Mrs Langley, and I will – your daughter will not marry my pa.'

The housekeeper quickly regains her composure. 'We'll work around it; Clara always wanted a big family.' We stand glaring at each other, both with narrowed eyes whilst Kitty shuffles awkwardly beside us.

'Well,' I say coldly. 'I hope you're pleased with what you have done.'

Mrs Langley lifts her chin at an angle that compliments her nose. 'It will make my daughter happy, so yes, I am pleased.'

'At the expense of my family?'

'Unfortunately, there will always be some casualties when life is not played fair.'

My time here is up, I cannot abide this woman's lack of remorse any longer. 'I thank you for restoring me to the position of maid of all work, Mrs Langley, but I am now declining it.' I spin on my heel, relieved my faintness from the initial shock has disappeared. She only wants me at Belmont Park to keep an eye on me, it has nothing to do with honouring Lady Belmont. 'I do not need your help to make my way in the world, you have done quite enough already.'

Chapter Thirty

This is my chance. I'm not certain if it will even work, but it needs to, now I don't have a source of income for my family.

Billy meets me as planned and under cover of darkness we make our way down the lane he had pointed to earlier. It's lined with cottages that look smaller than ours, if that's even possible.

'It's this one.' Billy stops at the last cottage and nods towards a red-painted door. He leaves me now his job is done and scurries back down the lane.

I step forward to knock, my stomach full of nerves. A pretty middle-aged woman with olive skin and hard brown eyes greets me when the door opens. 'Yes?'

'I'm sorry to bother you, Mrs...' I hesitate, realising I don't even know the woman's name. I cough with embarrassment to cover my error. 'My name is Rebekah Barnes.'

Her eyes soften. 'Oh yes, I've heard of your family. I was sorry to hear about your pa, my husband tells me he's no longer able to work in the fields.'

'Thank you, I'm afraid his condition is irreversible.'

'Is there something I can help you with?' She leans against the wooden doorframe looking weary.

'Erm, yes, actually there is... this is going to sound strange, but I need to talk to you about your daughters.' Her head jolts and she looks wearily behind her into the candlelit room. 'It's all right,' I reassure her quickly. 'I met your daughter, the youngest one, she came to Belmont Park for food when I was a maid there.'

The woman smiles. 'I'm sorry about that, she's full of courage is that one.'

'No, it wasn't a problem, Mrs... I'm sorry, I don't know your name.'

'Reid, Mrs Reid.'

'Mrs Reid,' I smile and then take a deep breath. 'I got the impression your daughter doesn't sign.'

'What do you mean?'

'I mean, use hand gestures to communicate.'

'I've not heard of such a thing.'

'If I could take a bit of your time I'd like to help, if I can.'

After spending an encouraging time with the Reid's I leave feeling confident my plan could work, that's as long as the one person I've still to speak to agrees to my proposal.

Slowly I make my way home to break the news to Mary that I no longer have a job. At the top of the hill I gaze down on the row of cottages standing side by side and my eye gravitates to Uncle Will's home. My heart feels heavy, I can't leave things as they are...

I find myself knocking on our neighbour's door again, though this time I'm calmer and the knock is slow and light. 'Where's Ma?' I ask when he answers it.

He rolls his eyes at me. 'What do you want Rebekah? You made your opinion of our situation perfectly clear when you were here earlier.'

'I need to speak to Ma,' I say coldly looking past his shoulder.

Will grunts and shouts behind him. 'Margaret, your daughter wishes to speak with you.' He walks away not taking his scowling eye off me as Ma comes to take his place at the door.

'What do you want?' She huffs with a wrinkled nose.

'It's all a sham, Ma.' I say in a hushed tone so Will can't hear. 'Uncle Will has been paid to lure you away.'

'You're talking nonsense.'

'Pa was meant for someone else and this is your reward for stealing him away - the accident was planned.'

'Who's been whispering stories in your ears, I didn't steal your father from anyone.'

'I'm afraid Mrs Langley thinks differently.'

Ma's face drains of all its colour before turning bright red. 'Clara,' she says through clenched teeth.

'Yes, you know her?'

'She thought your pa was *her* property until I came to the village. She's still bitter that she didn't get him – ha!' Ma lets out a short sharp exclamation. 'What's this you say about your pa's accident being planned?'

'The Langley's did it, so you would give up on Pa and Clara could have him instead.' Ma's lips set straight upon hearing this, almost as if she can't quite decide if her old enemy has gained the victory after all.

Will comes up behind her and places a hand softly on her back. 'Is everything all right, Margaret?'

I step in before she has chance to answer. 'How much did they pay you?' I ask calmly turning on Will. 'You should be ashamed; Pa is your friend.'

'I needed the money, you can't blame me, Rebekah'

I shake my head. 'I understand the wages of a farm labourer doesn't bring in a lot of income, but you're unmarried with no children or relations to look after, you should be able to live comfortably on what you earn.'

He jabs a finger into my face. 'Don't judge me, Rebekah, nor your ma either, not when you don't have all the facts.'

'How can I know all the facts if she doesn't talk to me. Ma,' I soften my voice. 'I know you've struggled, but we can't help you unless you talk to us.'

She looks up at me, her face tired and worn. 'Motherhood in these conditions was never going to work for me.'

'These conditions... what conditions would have worked for you, Ma?'

'My father was a man of class. I grew up with an estate to play in and maids to feed me.'

I tilt my head in sympathy, if this is true, it's no wonder she's struggled. 'You never told me this.'

'I was ashamed.'

'What happened Ma?'

'My father lost it all. He owned a shipping company on the coast, but several bad winters saw him lose many of his ships and eventually he went bankrupt. We came to Belmont to hide; the shame was too great for us to bear. I could have been a better mother if I'd had a nursery maid by my side, I would have enjoyed your company when I called for you and been able to send you away when my nerves became troubled by your helpless cries, just like my own mother. We would have been all right then, I think.'

'You used to sing to me,' I say recalling the distant memory.

She smiled – I don't think I've seen Ma smile before. 'I used to love singing and I'd perform for all our guests as a child. I remember singing over you, Rebekah, I tried to be a good mother, I really did, but I...' She trails away and closes her eyes. 'Your pa was my only chance of regaining it all. My father set it all up, Tom was to become a tenant farmer and if that went well who knows where it would have led him. My father still had contacts in high places, those who hadn't shunned us, it was still possible to lift us from the depths we'd sunk too.'

'I don't remember Pa ever being a tenant farmer.'

'He never got the opportunity, your pa lost everything too, because of a foolish investment he made.'

'Come on, Margaret,' interrupts Will who's been listening by her side. 'Tom made the transaction, but you know he didn't want to make the investment, did he?'

'It was a sure thing, Will, he needed a push in the right direction.' She turns to me to explain. 'There was a new shipping company my father had heard about, he knew the business, it was a good investment. If your pa increased his wealth, I knew we could procure a larger tenancy, it would see us well-established and quicken our rise in wealth, my father deserved to regain his place in society after the blow he'd suffered. I convinced your pa to invest, which he did, but the ship was lost on its maiden voyage and the company was ruined before it even started – Tom lost everything, all of his savings and the recent inheritance he'd received from an distant relative... we had no money left to rent the farm.'

'You can't blame Pa for what happened, Ma, not when it was really you who pushed him into investing.'

'Your pa could have made his way again, he's a clever man,' she says her voice full of bitterness. 'But he was content to settle and remain a farm labourer.'

'Margaret,' says Will accusingly. 'Tom couldn't afford to pay rent on a farm tenancy, a farm labourers' income would never allow this, once that inheritance was gone there was no going back.'

'And I've been tied to poverty ever since,' she cries in frustration.

'I understand your disappointments Ma, but you can't change any of it. Please, come home, otherwise Pa will be lost to you forever.'

'Good.' She folds her arms obstinately.

'Ma, Uncle Will does not love you, he's been bribed to take you. Let's say you stay here, what will happen next?' Ma shrugs. 'More babies and as far as I can see Uncle Will has the same prospects as Pa, apart from the fact he's able bodied. Your life will be no different.'

'I'm using the money to rent a farm, Rebekah,' says Will. 'I'm going up in the world.' He gives a shy grin.

'I'm not a foolish, child,' scolds Ma looking at me. 'We've discussed this, Will's promised me a nursery maid to help with any children, I've told you that already.'

'Ma, you don't understand, a farmer's wife isn't a life of luxury. You saw Mrs Arthur, didn't you? She's a tenant farmer's wife, did she have a maid to help with Emma?' Ma stands there, her lips parted, reality slowly dawning on her. 'In fact, life will be harder because your livelihood will depend upon you looking after everything, the animals, the crops, selling your goods at the right price, collecting in the harvests. It's a tough life... and even if you could afford a nursery maid, it's not as simple as spending half an hour with your children after tea and then sending them away, you won't be a member of the gentry, far from it. I'm afraid the life you had as a child is gone and you won't be happy again unless you accept this and move on, counting the blessings which you do have.'

Ma doesn't speak...

Neither does Will...

It's their choice now, whether Ma ever comes back to us again.

The following day I rise early, before even Pa is awake. As I scramble in the dark down the lanes and over fields my mind flits discontentedly between the loss of Manny, Ma's disillusionment, the planned accident, the threat of Mrs Parsons, and to... the Belmonts - it's a relief when I finally arrive.

'Psst, Lucy.'

Lucy is half-way across the yard carrying a basket full of coal, she looks around in confusion.

'Lucy,' I whisper as loudly as I dare and wave a hand from my hiding place. She sees me and hurries over to the row of hedges behind the stables.

'Rebekah?'

'Lucy, I need your help.'

'What are you doing in the hedges, I thought you'd left Belmont Park yesterday?'

'I did. Listen, I need to see Lady Belmont, but I'd rather not run into Mrs Langley... or Mrs Parsons.'

'Oh.' The little girl glances wearily back towards the kitchen.

'I don't want to get you into trouble, but maybe you could pass a message on, via a footman, to her ladyship.'

'Have you got a note?' she asks before nervously chewing her lip. I hand her a piece of paper already inscribed with a pre-written message.

'I'll stay here. I need an answer.' The girl nods and stuffs the paper into her apron before scurrying across the yard and through the back entrance. I wait, with a twig sticking uncomfortably into my back, until Lucy reappears.

'The answer is yes,' she says.

I smile as an excited nervousness fills my stomach. 'Thank you, Lucy.'

'What is "yes"?' Lucy asks.

'It doesn't matter.'

'Are you in trouble?'

'I hope not.' I smile again and tap the girl on the arm before running round to the front of the house.

A footman is there to greet me – he's new, I don't recognise him. 'Miss Barnes?' He bows and invites me to follow him inside leading me into the breakfast room.

'Rebekah,' calls Lady Belmont from the end of the long-polished table. 'Now this is a surprise, and so early.' She makes a point of staring at her unfinished breakfast.

'I'm sorry, your ladyship.' I curtsy. 'I have a matter to discuss with you.'

'So I gather from your note. Come and sit.' She gestures to the chair on her left and I obediently do as I'm told.

After a long discussion, by which time the table had been cleared, Lady Belmont asks me yet another question. 'And what about your father?'

The question startles me. 'Pa?'

'Yes, surely he can be involved in your new venture.'

'Of course, I'd like him to be, but I don't see how.'

'Leave that to me.' She tilts her chin causing me to knit my eyebrows together, wondering what on earth she could do to change Pa's hopeless existence... if it's even possible. 'So, remind me again, where will this school be situated?'

'Mrs Reid has suggested we use her cottage, it is unoccupied during the day.'

'And you will be the only teacher?'

'Yes, for now.'

'Are you sure you only want my patronage and financial support?'

'Yes, until I can find pupils who can afford to pay.'

'Well, I must say it's a very ambitious plan, Rebekah, but if anyone can succeed, I believe you can.'

'Thank you, ma'am.'

When I first told Lady Belmont I wanted to start a school for deaf children she was initially unconvinced, but the more I spoke the greater my passion became for the subject. I told her I'd already found my first two pupils and hoped, if I was successful, more children would be drawn to the area, under the simple premise that deaf communities live together for support and encouragement. I had then gone on to explain how an investment was needed so I could provide the children with at least one nourishing meal a day during teaching hours. She questioned me on my own source of income, since my pupils were not offering to pay fees, and when I admitted I didn't have one, she agreed to support me financially for a twelve-month period, as long as I committed to making it into a viable business and sought out children who could pay for their lessons, in addition to those she could fund herself. In the end, my desire to teach the deaf children of Belmont how to communicate with the world was greeted with much approval and I really couldn't have left feeling much happier than I do now.

It is signs of the first fruits - I can feel it.

On the other side of heart break great blessings wait... Manny was right. A pang of sadness breaks into my joy, the blessings are coming and Manny is not here to share them with me.

Chapter Thirty-One

'Ouch… where have all these chairs come from?'

I've returned to the cottage after visiting Lady Belmont and I find I'm greeted by a room full of new furniture, bashing my shin into a chair standing right in front of the door.

'It's all from Mrs Parsons,' says Tommy picking up the chair and taking it to the table where the rest of the children are eating bread and butter. 'We all have one each now.' He grins.

It's a kind gesture, but I don't like it. 'We don't need so many chairs,' I grumble.

'The children need somewhere to sit and eat.' Mrs Parsons rounds the table, spreading another slice of bread for Henry.

'Shouldn't you be working?'

'It's my half-day off.'

'If that's so then why were you here yesterday?'

'Rebekah don't be ungrateful,' calls Pa from his bed, he's sitting up and eating his own plateful of bread and butter.

'Where'd the bread come from?' I ask cautiously watching our guest pouring milk into a cup for Georgie.

'Mrs Parsons,' says Daniel with a broad grin, bread-crumbs stuck to his face with butter.

It's happening… she's taking over. Everything looks more organised and everyone looks more cared for than they have for months. She's making herself indispensable. The next thing will be cutting the… ivy. I look up to the window and a bright shaft of light is bursting through onto Pa's bed, the shadows not so defined anymore now several pointed leaves have been cut away.

'Come and have some bread, Rebekah,' says Mary.

'I'm not hungry,' I mumble just as Mrs Parsons swoops down

on Georgie who is about to spill his milk - of course, she catches the cup in time. A fresh wave of nausea surfaces as I see the woman so in control of the children, there's no yelling or screaming, no tension or underlying bitterness. She's more than capable of filling Ma's role, even more so... all that remains is for Pa to be looking at her with... love in his eyes.

I focus on Pa, which is easy to do now the ivy's been cut away and the darkness has lifted. He's watching her every move and he's... smiling.

This has got to stop.

Pa needs to know who he's letting into his home to look after his children.

'Does Pa know?' I blurt out across the children munching their food.

Mrs Parsons looks up with a face of innocence and sees me glaring straight at her, my eyes fiery and unblinking. 'Oh, I'm sorry, were you talking to me?'

'Yes, I was talking to you. Does Pa know?'

'Rebekah.' Pa's voice has a warning tone to it, but I don't heed it and continue anyway.

'I found out your secret.'

Mrs Parsons gives a merry little laugh and finds a cloth to wipe down the table. 'I have no secrets, Rebekah.'

'Oh, I must be mistaken then.'

She looks up at me before removing some crumbs from underneath Tommy's elbow. 'Yes, you must.'

'Your niece, Kitty, sends you her greetings by the way.'

'Rebekah, leave it,' demands Pa becoming agitated, he can tell I'm not letting this go. But the pleasant smile that had been planted on Mrs Parsons face has disappeared. Pa needs to hear this; he's not going to stop me.

'Kitty?' mutters Mary quietly under her breath, scrunching up her face. 'Wasn't she the girl who told you Pa was dead?'

The room falls quiet.

'When was Pa dead?' asks Daniel looking at me for an answer.

'That's a good question, Mrs Parsons would you care to answer that one, since it was you who sent Kitty to lie to my face?'

'I have no responsibility over the actions of my niece.'

'Oh, so you didn't try to separate me from my family so you could marry Pa before I returned to stop you?'

'Rebekah, enough,' bellows Pa. 'I don't know what your history is with Clara but making things up isn't going to help anyone.'

'Pa, I'm not making this up, you don't know what she's done.'

'Either you stay and be civilised or you leave, you choose.'

Well, I'm doing neither, and if Pa is going to side with his future bride then I need to speak up now before I'm expelled from the cottage forever. 'She's the reason for your accident... if that's what you can call it.' Mrs Parsons face grows pale. 'Yes, I thought you might tremble at those words. Her nephew pushed you Pa, as a chain of events that would lead to Ma leaving you and Clara gaining you.'

'No, Becks, no one was to blame.'

'Pa, you've got to listen to me.' I walk over to the bed and kneel on the floor in front of him. 'I am telling you the truth, when have I ever lied to you?' He rubs his bristly beard with his hand in thought because, he clearly realises that lying to him is something I have never done.

'Clara?' He looks at his old childhood acquaintance waiting for an answer, but she remains silent.

'Tell him,' I say seeing panic rise in her face. 'Or I will.'

'You can't blame me, Tom.' She falls towards Pa and drops on the floor, pushing me out of the way and leaning over the bed. 'I loved you too much to leave you with that woman.'

Pa's eyes become wide and his eyebrows lift. 'You did this to me?'

'It wasn't supposed to be a permanent injury,' she sobs.

'I was pushed from the first floor of a barn, Clara, what did you expect to happen?'

'I'll nurse you Tom, not like that horrid woman next door, I'll take care of you and your children... speak to me, Tom...' She hysterically grabs his shirt sleeve and jolts him from side to side, tears streaming down her face. 'I married Mr Parsons for you... for us, so that I would one day have enough funds to claim you back as my husband and have some sort of standing in society to provide us with an Act of Parliament for our divorce. I planned it all Tom. We are meant to be together; I can't live without you.' She begins to weep uncontrollably.

'Leave,' Pa says calmly, his face as hard as stone.

'No, Tom, please,' she begs frantically, clawing at his arm. 'I'm sorry, I will make it right, I will.'

'Are you going to heal my legs, Clara?'

'No, but—'

'Leave.'

'Tom—'

'You heard him,' I say breaking into her tearful attempts to change his mind. 'Leave and don't ever come back.' At first, she doesn't move, and looks at Pa with her mouth fully open, waiting for him to show mercy to her. 'Do you want me to come over there and throw you out!' I take one step towards her and it's enough to frighten her into leaving. She lifts a hand over her mouth and runs out of the cottage sobbing.

'Come here, Becks.' In the silence after her exit Pa holds out his hand, my whole body is trembling after the encounter and his warm touch calms me down considerably as I slip my hand in his. He gently pulls me down so he can kiss my forehead. 'Thank you.'

Winter finally draws to a close and the warm spring winds start to blow, a pleasant change from the icy cold chills we've had to suffer. Every day I make my way to the Reid's home to teach their daughters, Alice and Martha, and it isn't long before Billy seeks out Joseph, who becomes my third pupil. With my wages and rent paid by Lady Belmont and the boys bringing in an income from Mr Greaves, we somehow scrape enough money together for food. We never eat enough and our stomachs are constantly rumbling, but we're alive and happy.

Ma never came home to us, and I don't suppose she will now. They moved away when a tenancy became available for Uncle Will, and I'm grateful that the permanent reminder of our shame is no longer living next door. It makes me wonder if Will really did love her, remaining loyal to his promises even after the truth had been revealed – perhaps Ma will be happy someday, she deserves to be.

One day in early spring the sound of wheels clatters outside of our cottage and the children run out in great excitement, it's not often carriages or carts trundle down our little lane.

'Go find out what that is, Becks,' says Pa sitting up in bed and straining his neck. 'I can't quite see through the window.'

When I arrive outside a large cart has pulled up with the strangest contraption I've ever seen. The driver jumps down and nods his cap in greeting. 'Miss Barnes?' he asks.

'Yes, that's me.' The children have gathered around and we watch with great curiosity as he opens the back of the cart and unties the rope which has been holding the object in place. 'What is this?'

'I believe it's a bath chair, miss.' The driver rolls before me a comfortable looking chair attached to two large wheels at the back, and one smaller wheel at the front.

After my initial surprise, concern raises its head. 'I can't pay you anything, sir.'

'All taken care of, miss. I wish you a good day.' He doffs his cap to me and climbs into the cart, leaving me open mouthed as he clicks his horse to move on, pull the cart away and back up the lane. The children gather round the object in awe and the next thing I know a fully suited footman comes strolling down the hill.

'Good day, Miss Barnes.' I instantly recognise him from Belmont Park.

'Matthew, it's good to see you,' I say still feeling a little bewildered.

'That's quite a contraption.' He nods at the object.

'Indeed… Tommy, get down.' I say quickly, spying the boy climbing up into the chair.

'What is it, Rebekah?' asks Maggie with great interest.

'It's a bath chair,' explains Matthew just as the driver of the cart had said. 'I used to work for an earl who owned one of these. Whoever is in the seat can steer it here…' he says wriggling a handle attached to a long pole and connected to the front wheel. '… And whoever is pushing does so from the back.' He indicates a handle fastened to the chair. 'Oh, this is from Lady Belmont.' He hands me a note.

'Thank you, Matthew.' He nods and leaves us to inspect the surprising gift.

'This is scarcely to be believed,' I say as tears form in my eyes and I forget the note in my hand.

Daniel hops into the chair. 'Can I try it first?'

'No, I want to,' shouts Tommy trying to pull his brother off the seat.

'Actually, I think it's only fair we let Pa take the first spin, don't you think?' I say with the widest smile I've ever experienced in my life.

The children are running up and down, taking it in turns to push Pa, Henry sits on his knee laughing and squealing, clapping his chubby little hands.

'My turn, my turn,' says Tommy jumping up and down.

'Let Georgie have a go.' I push the quiet boy closer to the wheelchair.

'All right, but I'm next,' says Tommy running cheerfully alongside.

I've never seen everyone so happy… Pa is a different man. His hair is flowing back with the wind as Georgie pushes him round in a large circle, his eyes are full of hope and he's laughing… it's been a long time since his face has presented such a beautiful sight. I laugh along from a distance until a moment of sadness sneaks into my heart - why didn't Manny think of this, it would have fixed everything? Pa doesn't need his legs to be working in order to be happy, this is all he needed to have a new start. It's a... miracle.

I watch on, missing Manny so much it hurts. I hug my arms around my waist, reminding myself that this suffering will eventually pass and my sorrow at losing him will weaken - I'll begin to live again, pouring my wounded heart into the new purpose I've discovered that brings me such great joy.

'Hey Becks!' Pa waves at me, and Tommy, who's managed to weasel his way into steering the chair, pushes him across to me. 'Daniel said you received a letter from Lady Belmont, what did it say?'

'Oh, I completely forgot.' I pull the letter out from my long sleeve and turn it over to see the burgundy Belmont seal and break it open... *Dear Mr Barnes,*' I begin. 'It's for you, Pa... *May I first congratulate you on your daughters daring venture of starting a school for deaf children, her selfless love for others is a great reflection upon yourself. As you are aware, I have agreed to finance your daughter's ambitions for a twelve-month period in the hope it will be successful and eventually become financially independent. However, I fear that Rebekah cannot achieve this alone, she is young and has a heart to teach, not a heart to gain profit. Therefore, I would like to extend my financial support to yourself, if you will agree, to become the school's overseer, giving guidance and advice to your daughter, in addition to making the establishment a viable business in its own right. I hereby commit to providing you with a weekly income, also for a twelve-month period, under the same terms and conditions I have given your daughter...*' I lift glistening eyes to Pa, who mirrors my emotion.

'What else does she say?' asks Daniel.

'That's it, she signs off.' I laugh a mixture of joy and tears.

'The chair must be from Lady Belmont,' suggests Mary. 'Pa would need transport to get him to the Reid's and the message arrived at the same time as the cart.'

'I'll clean your boots, Pa,' says Maggie enthusiastically running back to the cottage. 'You can't go to work in bare feet!'

'When will you start Pa?' asks Daniel leaning on the chair and hopping up and down on the spot.

'As soon as possible, I suppose,' he says smiling, but looking slightly overwhelmed.

'I'll boil some water, you can't leave the cottage looking like that,' says Mary sounding motherly. 'You can go with Rebekah in the morning. Daniel and Tommy, come help me fetch the water.' The boys follow Mary, whilst Georgie and Maggie push Pa back into the cottage with Henry still sitting on his lap.

I inhale a breath of satisfaction, my hands placed lightly on my hips. I take a long look around me, the sun shining in my eyes so brightly I have to shield them from the glare. As my gaze rests on the hillside, a figure stands at the top, outlined against the sunlight, and I watch him working his way down the lane towards me.

'I don't know why I didn't think of it before.'

'What—' I can't get the words out; he's taken my breath away. I look at him from head to feet, his smart tail jacket and clean pressed breeches have gone and in replacement he's wearing his old ragged shirt and mud-stained breeches. This is not Emmanuel Montague standing before me, it's Emmanuel Smith.

'The perfect solution, I think.' He grins looking at the cottage over my shoulder.

'You sent the chair?'

'I hope that was alright?' he asks a little uncertainly.

'Of course, I've not seen Pa that happy in a long time... Manny—'

'You were right, by the way,' he interrupts before I can finish.

'About what?'

'About Emmanuel Montague. I'd grown so frustrated over my father's attitude that I stopped trying, it was easier that way.'

'It's understandable.'

'It's unacceptable. Here's me asking you to give up everything, when I wouldn't do the same thing myself. My heart is broken because I've lost you, I can't live without you, Becks.' He takes my hands and presses them to his lips, holding them so closely I can feel his warm breath on my skin. 'Be my wife,' he whispers, lifting his soft emerald eyes to look directly into my own.

'Who's asking?' I whisper back.

He looks down and smiles, a blush of pink touching the top of his cheeks. 'Emmanuel Smith.'

It's the answer I've been looking for all along. 'What about your father, aren't you worried about what he'll do?'

'He's cut me off – I'm no longer a Montague.'

'You've already told him?'

'I love you, whether or not you say yes to me, it's a fact and I'm not hiding it.'

'You've given up everything?'

He laughs and holds his arms out wide. 'This is all you get, Becks... do you still want me?'

My heart is pounding in my chest and I gaze up into his face before breaking out into a smile. 'Yes!' I cry. 'I'll have you, Mr Smith.' Catching his tall figure off guard I fling my arms around him and he swings me round as we laugh together in pure joy.

'You do realise you can't legally be Mrs Smith, don't you?' he says coming to a standstill and resting his head lightly against mine.

'We'll be Smith at heart.'

'Forever and always.' He leans closer and kisses me softly on the lips.

Pa is the happiest man on the face of the earth. Gaining a wheelchair and prospective son-in-law on the same day – though, in his tattered shirt and grubby breeches it took a bit of convincing to persuade Pa that Manny really was the son of a lord. It's the first time Manny has met Pa, but they instantly form a bond. When I tell him Manny was responsible for the bath chair, Pa takes the former groom's hand in a strong, firm handshake, with so many tears forming his eyes that he can hardly utter his thanks.

'Would it be possible to steal your daughter, Mr Barnes?' asks Manny after a while.

'Aren't you already doing so?' says Pa lifting up his eyebrows humorously.

Manny smiles. 'I mean, for the rest of the day. I'll have her back before nightfall, I promise.'

Pa agrees and Manny takes me by the hand. 'Where are we going?' I ask catching the scent of a strange mixture of rose petal and horse manure.

'You'll see.' He has a gleam in his eye that tells me he's up to something and I excitedly allow him to lead me away over the hill to where a tilbury is waiting, with a horse standing patiently tied up to a tree.

'I thought you'd given up everything?' I lift an eyebrow in humorous accusation.

'I have, but this is mine - a gift from my grandfather when I turned eighteen. May I...' I hold out his hand and he helps me climb into the seat.

'Where are you taking me?' I ask again, holding onto my bonnet as the wind blows gently into my face.

'You'll see,' he says with a smile.

'Have you ever been this way before?' he asks after we've been travelling a while.

'Never, the furthest I've been is Market Ashton.'

'Then you wouldn't know what lies an hour to the east.' A seagull calls in the air over our heads and draws my eyes to the top of a grassy mound where a strip of blue, coloured differently to the sky, comes into view.

'The sea...' I whisper in awe at the sight before me.

'You like it?'

'It's beautiful,' I say breathlessly. 'Why didn't I know we were so close to the sea?' Ma had said my grandfather's business was in shipping, she hadn't come far when they came to Belmont in hiding. I take in the view as the horse continues to lead us along the clifftop until Manny finally tugs the reins and pulls us to a stop.

'We're here.' He grins stepping out of the tilbury and skipping round to help me down. He keeps hold of my hand until I've regained my steadiness, the trip in the unfamiliar transportation having thrown me off balance. 'Are you ready?' he asks and twist me by the shoulders to face a large double fronted cottage, set back from the lane leading down to the sea.

'It's lovely, but why are we here?'

'Do you want it?'

'Manny, we can't afford this...you haven't any money now, remember.'

'Well...' He screws up his face. 'That's not quite true.'

I tilt my head. 'What do you mean?'

'Last month I received my grandfather's inheritance, my father can't touch it, it's in my name.'

'So, you don't exactly come with nothing.' I nudge him in the ribs at his deception.

'Will you allow me to tell you what I propose to do with his money?' The wind ruffles my hair and the smell of the sea swirls into my nose for the first time in my life.

'I'm listening, Mr Smith.'

Manny rubs his hands together in excitement. 'First, we buy this house—' I open my mouth to protest. He doesn't know what I've been doing in Belmont without him - what about Pa, the children, my new school - I can't leave it all so soon. He places a hand over my lips before I can utter a single concern. 'Hear me out before you tell me off for fixing everything, I promise you, this is good... alright?' I nod and he slips his warm hand into mine. 'So,' he continues. 'This house will be ours, purchased in full, then with the remaining money I propose we continue what you started at the Arthurs.' My mouth falls open again, but this time in shock rather than to list any rising reservations. 'Emma and Thomas have already agreed to be our first pupils, I spoke to Mrs Arthur and Mrs Oliver, they are both fully in agreement. The house is big enough to accommodate them and more, which there will be, when the word spreads... what are you laughing at?'

'I love you, Manny.'

'And that's funny, is it?'

'It is when you realise what I've been doing since I left Market Ashton. I think I might have three more pupils to add... and an overseer.... oh, and a patroness.'

'You have been busy.'

'Is there enough space for Mary and the children?' I ask because although this is perfect, I couldn't leave anyone behind.

'Absolutely.'

'Eventually we'll have used up all of your grandfather's inheritance.'

'Yes, eventually, but we'll be established by then... so tell me, what do you think?'

My laughter has been replaced by a rush of overwhelming emotion. Never could I have imagined this would be possible, and I am so thankful to Manny for making it happen. 'It's perfect.'

Manny wipes a tear from the corner of my eye. 'Still want to marry me?' he says softly.

'I do, that's as long as you want a girl with a broken heart.'

He takes my hand lightly in his and kisses it softly. 'I've heard the greatest blessings come from broken hearts.'

Acknowledgements

I'd like to thank Craig Groeschel, pastor at Life. Church in Oklahoma, for preaching the sermon *Dangerous Prayers: Break My Heart* which inspired me to write Rebekah's story... the biggest blessings come from the biggest breakings.

Thank you to my editors, Paul Dalheim and Alan Crosse, for all your meticulous hard work and for finding all the 21st century terminology that had crept into my 19th Century world!

Thank you to my amazing family for all your support, I couldn't have done it without you!

To all my readers, thank you for buying...

The Girl Who Wanted a Broken Heart

If you enjoyed reading this book,
why not consider writing
a review on Amazon
so others can discover it too.

Check out Erika's website at...
www.erikacrosse.co.uk
where you can read Erika's latest blog
and sign up for her email updates

You can also follow Erika on
Facebook and Instagram.

Or send her an email to...
erikacrosseinfo@gmail.com

Printed in Great Britain
by Amazon